WHEN A ROOK TAKES THE QUEEN

A NOVEL

By
EDWARD IZZI

WHEN A ROOK TAKES THE QUEEN

Copyright © 2021 by Cassino Publishing, Inc.

All rights reserved. No part of this book may be reproduced or transmitted in any form or by any means without written permission from the author.

ISBN 978-1-63760-145-7

AUTHOR'S DISCLAIMER

This book, "When A Rook Takes the Queen," is a complete work of fiction. All names, characters, businesses, places, events, references, and incidents are either the products of the author's imagination or are used in a fictitious manner to tell the story.

Any references to real-life characters or events are used purely to recite a narrative for enjoyment purposes.

Some actual events inspired this fictional story. The names, dates, places, events, circumstances, and real characters in this story have been changed or altered for entertainment purposes.

For Nello Marrocco

An amazing man with a handlebar mustache, who worked hard, overcame setbacks and loved his family and friends.
But most of all, he loved to laugh.
When he wasn't laughing with you, he was laughing at you...

An avid reader, he's hopefully enjoying these books in heaven.

ABOUT THE AUTHOR

Edward Izzi is a native of Detroit, Michigan, and is a Certified Public Accountant with a successful accounting firm in suburban Chicago, Illinois.

He is the father of four grown children and a sassy teenage granddaughter, Brianna.

He currently lives in Chicago, where he often loses while playing chess.

Chicago Gambit

A gambit starts when war is declared,
The game may now begin.
A bishop moves, beyond its space,
The white pawn moves within.

As blood now drips on a checkered board,
Checkmate is now foreseen.
When the bishop kills a formidable knight,
...a black rook takes the queen.

CHAPTER ONE
THE SUNDAY GARDEN - JULY 19TH

The sun was beating down hard on that summer Sunday afternoon, as an African American woman was cultivating the weeds from her backyard garden. She had planted tomatoes, beans, eggplants, and green peppers after Mother's Day that spring, and her expansive vegetable garden was starting to grow.

It had been a very wet spring, and the summer sun on that July afternoon was now providing the light and heat to make the plants in her vegetable garden flourish.

The older, politically connected woman found solace in her gardening. Her backyard vegetable, 'mini-farm,' felt like miles away from the reality of her all-too-important position within the City of Chicago and City Hall. She habitually put on her gardening gloves, took out her garden tools, and shut off her cell phone every evening after work.

The woman had very few activities that she truly enjoyed, and gardening in her backyard was practically her only passion. Her bodyguards and police detail stood outside in front of her red-brick bungalow house in Logan Square. With the recent racial riots, 'Black Lives Matter' marches, and now the rampant looting that has been going on in the Chicago Loop, the former assistant prosecutor felt like her life and her administration was constantly being threatened.

At the age of fifty-five, Mayor Janice Kollar had been elected as the Mayor of Chicago almost three years ago. To say that her mayoral term as the city's new boss has been going anything but smoothly was an understatement.

There was in-fighting in the City Council, making it almost impossible to pass a favorable city budget. She was at odds with the Chicago School Board and the Chicago Teacher's Union over teachers' demands for pay raises and strike threats.

But most of all, the city's murder rates are at their highest that they have been in the last thirty years, despite her platform of cracking down on gang fighting and intercity violence. The dubious title of 'Murder City USA' had been famously passed onto the Windy City. The mayor was under a tremendous amount of pressure from as high up as the President of the United States to do something about it.

From all the observers from every direction nationwide, the City of Chicago's crime rate was spiraling out of control. Young children were being shot and killed for merely walking home from school or playing on the street. Arsons, building defamation, and destruction were on the rise. Drive-by shootings were becoming a daily routine in the dangerous south and west side neighborhoods and on the expressways.

Vehicles were getting car-jacked with young children still inside. Home burglaries and car thefts were rising in every Chicago neighborhood. Drunk driving incidents within the city were becoming commonplace. Violent rapes and brutal, inter-racial beatings were going on everywhere. Illegal drug use and sales were rampant and out of control.

The black and Latino gangs were now taking over the streets, especially on the South and West Sides. The city's civil unrest was getting worse by the day, with every summer weekend highlighting higher murder and crime incidents than the weekend before.

The Chicago Police Department was fighting a losing battle. They were all ordered by the mayor's office not to retaliate against mobs of rioters and looters destroying the city, using a 'Black Lives Matter' mantra.

Alderman Jose Sandoval from the West Loop neighborhood has now called for Mayor Kollar's resignation. He was verbally making the same observation that most of the other aldermen within the City of Chicago have privately and publicly concluded:

The mayor has lost control of the city.

According to the Chicago Tribune's current headlines on that Sunday, the City of Chicago was out of control. It was clear to everyone that the current mayor could not maintain law and order within the Second City.

Despite the increased crime rates and the interracial riots occurring daily within the City, Mayor Kollar was in her garden on that Sunday afternoon, trying to put all of that out of her mind. Her gardening was the only activity that seemed to calm her down, as even her doctors had warned her of the increased stress levels that her job was putting on her physically.

As an African American, openly gay mayor, Kollar was expected to do great things in the city. She was elected on an anti-crime platform. The young white and openly gay millennials and the African American community hoped to implement positive liberal change and control the city's rising crime rates.

Kollar grasped her hand trowel and gardening tools and got down on her knees, getting her new blue jeans extremely dirty. She was fervently pulling weeds, turning over the dirt, and pruning the growing tomato plants that were now showing newly sprouted vegetation. Her garden was indeed her place of refuge. With every turn of her hand trowel, with every weed she pulled from the ground, her magnanimous problems running the city seemed further and further away.

As Mayor Kollar stood up, two loud sniper shots were suddenly coming from the house's direction next door.

It was 4:26 pm.

The mayor's domestic partner, Sheila Peacock, was inside preparing Sunday dinner that afternoon when she heard the loud shots. When she looked out the window towards the backyard garden, she screamed at the top of her lungs.

Mayor Janice Kollar was sprawled on the ground, blood seeping from the back of her head onto her meticulously groomed vegetable garden.

Peacock ran outside to get the police detail in charge of protecting the mayor, and the emergency 911 number was immediately called. Within five minutes, several EMS trucks from the Chicago Fire Department arrived in front of the mayor's home. The paramedics rushed to the mayor's sprawled body and began giving her CPR and trying to revive the fallen city leader.

The mayor's domestic partner watched in horror as the paramedics worked on Kollar, hoping beyond hope that she could be revived. She had suffered two bullet wounds in the back of her head, and it was apparent that a high-powered rifle was used. She was gravely and mortally wounded before her body hit the ground.

The EMS paramedics from Chicago Fire Engine No. Twelve quickly loaded the gravely wounded mayor onto a stretcher and rushed her to Northwestern Hospital's Emergency Room.

It was 4:35 pm.

When she arrived there, several doctors immediately brought her into surgery to repair and remove the bullets that were still lodged in her head. Her heart had stopped pumping twice, and she had to be paddled back to life while the Emergency Room physicians continued to work on her.

But unfortunately, her heart monitor flat-lined for the third time, as all the doctors looked up at the clock.

The City of Chicago's Mayor Janice Kollar was now dead, horrifically killed from two bullets fired by an unknown sniper.

It was now 4:53 pm.

Within thirty minutes, the horrifying assassination of Chicago's first openly gay, black woman mayor had been accomplished. The first time a Chicago mayor had been killed in office since Mayor Anton Cermak had been killed in Miami by a lone assassin with connections to the Chicago underworld in 1933.

By five o'clock, all of the television news channels interrupted their regular Sunday afternoon broadcasts to make the emergency announcement.

The Reverend Fr. Colin J. Fitzgerald, or 'Father Fitz' as he was affectionately called, had been relaxing in the living room of his rectory at St. Simeon Catholic Parish on East 79th Street in Chicago.

The Catholic priest was an older pastor in his mid-sixties, around six feet tall with salt and pepper hair and horn-rimmed glasses. Fitzgerald had become very popular within the Chicago media for his very vocal, well-publicized news conferences, which he always held on his church's front steps.

Fr. Fitz was well known for denouncing the rising violent crimes and moral injustices against humanity within the city. His very vocal opinions and principled stands have now made him the moral conscious of Chicago. He had also led a well-publicized anti-abortion rally last year in front of Chicago-Western Medical Center when the Illinois legislature passed the Reproductive Health Act (RHA), repealing the state's Partial-Birth Abortion Ban Act and the Illinois Abortion Act of 1975.

Fr. Fitz has always been very outspoken in the news media to the Archdiocese of Chicago's chagrin. He had become a prominent activist against the city's violence over the last twenty years.

He had been perusing the Sunday edition of the Chicago Tribune and was trying to rest after saying three, long, uncomfortable masses that day.

His old, one-hundred-ten-year-old church was without air conditioning that Sunday, which made saying morning masses under such warm conditions even more unpleasant. He had put out a public request at all the holy masses for someone to donate their services in either repairing or replacing the parish air-conditioning units.

His large, Gothically designed church was located in a predominately poor, black neighborhood, and donations for repairs to the old church's antiquated air conditioning units were desperately needed.

A fan was blowing from the corner of his living room as Fr. Fitz sat there in a white tee-shirt and shorts, trying to stay cool with the July temperatures exceeding 98 degrees.

He was watching a televised baseball game between the Chicago White Sox and the Detroit Tigers at that moment when a special news broadcast comes on the television:

"WMRQ Eyewitness News has just learned that the Mayor of Chicago, Janice Kollar, has been assassinated in her home in Logan Square approximately thirty minutes ago. She was rushed to Northwestern University Hospital's emergency room and underwent surgery when the doctors there pronounced her dead at 4:53 pm."

Fr. Fitz went into shock. He immediately buried his head in his hands, then grasped the gold crucifix that he always wore before saying a quick prayer out loud. Next to the couch where he was sitting was the Sunday edition of the Chicago Tribune, displaying the headlines from their veteran reporter, Lawrence McKay.

He looked at the Sunday edition with tears in eyes, now agreeing with the reporter's captions and assessment of the city's current state of affairs:

The City of Chicago Now Up for Grabs

CHAPTER TWO
CHICAGO TRIBUNE – A TRAGIC DAY

I was in the newsroom earlier that morning, finishing a story on the gangland violence that had been going on that July weekend. As a veteran reporter for the Chicago Tribune, I always felt like I lived my life from deadline to deadline. With the hot July weather outside, I would have rather been doing anything else except working in that hot newsroom that weekend. The most prevailing thought on my mind at that moment was where I could find a cool, refreshing swimming pool, complete with poolside drinks.

Although I was divorced and lived alone in Sauganash, I had promised my mother that I would stop by her house in Norridge for Sunday dinner with her. She was cooking my favorite Italian dish, Pappardelle con Sugo di Manzo, and she had expected me to be there by 4:00 pm. Being from intense Italian and Scottish roots, my love and appreciation for homemade pasta were beyond reproach.

It was already 4:45 pm on that Sunday afternoon, and needless to say, I was late. I was still sitting at my desk, trying to finish that news story, which was supposed to be turned in by six o'clock. At that moment, my desk phone rang, and I immediately knew who it was.

"Lawrence McKay." I was expecting it to be my mother.

"Larry? Where are you at? I tried calling your cell phone, but there was no answer."

It was my Assistant Editor, Tom Olsen. I looked at my cell phone sitting on my desk. I had the ringer on silent, figuring my mother would be blowing up my phone when I wasn't behind her door at four o'clock.

"I'm sitting at my desk, trying to finish this gangbanger story you've asked me to finish. I'm supposed to be at my Mom's for dinner when…"

He then rudely interrupted me.

"Larry, the Mayor has been shot!"

"What?"

"It just came over the wire…where are you?

I was shocked at first and holding the phone tightly to my ear, trying to make sure that I didn't hear things. I had trouble hearing things lately, and I wondered if I should be thinking about getting some help for my gradual hearing loss in my right ear.

"You heard me. Mayor Kollar has been shot at her home in Logan Square. About fifteen minutes ago. They just brought her into Northwestern Memorial Hospital. It doesn't look good."

I was listening intently, trying to get my head around this shocking news—a few long seconds of silence.

"At her home? She has a security detail. She has so many cops protecting her around her house. How the hell did she get shot?"

"A sniper of some kind. They wheeled her into Northwestern while she was still wearing her gardening clothes. Her domestic partner said she was working in her garden in the backyard when she heard two loud shots fired."

I ran my hands through my graying, practically almost white hair, still shaking my head.

"I can't fucking believe this. Not even the mayor is safe at her home."

"No shit," my editor commented. "You're still at the newsroom?"

"Yeah, you just caught me. I'm late for my mother's house for…"

"I need you to cover this story, buddy boy, and you're the closest reporter I have to the hospital," he exclaimed. I could hear the panic in his voice. "You need to get over there ASAP."

My emergency reflexes kicked in, and I knew that I had to drop everything and run over there as soon as I could.

"Okay, I'll call you back."

So much for a nice, quiet Sunday dinner with my mother.

I grabbed my backpack with my laptop and cell phone. There was no time to wait for the elevator, I thought to myself. I ran down seven floors of stairs, and I was in front of the Chicago Tribune Building to catch a taxicab.

Although this was an emergency, the only thing that I was thinking about at that immediate moment was how my mother was going to react to my blowing off Sunday dinner.

"Larry, you're late," she answered as I was calling my mother to let her know I would not be home to eat her specially prepared meal for me.

"Mom, I can't make it home right now. There is an emergency, and I have to run to Northwestern Hospital."

"Larry? Are you okay?"

"No, Mom, the mayor has been shot. I am running over there now to cover the story."

I could feel myself swerving in the backseat of that taxicab as he was trying to avoid all of the traffic on Lower Wacker Drive.

"What about dinner? I made your favorite." She was almost eighty years old, so she wasn't always as sensible as she used to be. My mother was starting to get a little senile at her old age. And as usual, there was never any emergency that ever took precedence over Sunday dinners at my mother's house.

"Mom, I've gotta work. I can't make it right now. Keep it warm. I'll call you when I'm done," as I abruptly hung up my cell phone.

My mother, Francesca, a first-generation Tuscan-Italian, had been a widow since the passing of my father, Gerald, from Parkinson's Disease last year. She lived alone with her yellow Labrador, Ruby, in Norridge. I had thought about selling my townhouse in Sauganash and moving in with her. But I knew that I was a little too old at the ripe old age of 58-years-old to be living at home. Still, I found myself driving over there at least three times a week to check on her.

And canceling an all too important Sunday dinner at my mother's house was always a cardinal sin. It never mattered what else was going on in this violent world that I was journalistically covering. As a bachelor and divorcee, I figured that I had saved myself from the usual lecture. She always interrogated me about 'when I was going it settle down and find a nice girl.'

"I did find a nice girl, Ma. She took me to the cleaners," referring to my twelve-year marriage to my ex-wife, Mary Jo. She was a seasoned court reporter in Cook County who had more than her share of attorney connections and legal, late-night rendezvous.

"That 'puttana' was not a nice girl. I told you she would cheat on you before you even married her," she always says, continually reminding me how many times she had warned me about marrying my ex-wife.

I told the cab driver to 'step on it' and get me to Northwestern Memorial Hospital as soon as he could. I counted three traffic lights that he had blown off to get me there, so I knew I had to give the cabbie a generous tip. I was in front of the hospital in no time, and the front entrance was already starting to look like a zoo.

As I stepped out of the taxicab, I had already spotted the Channel 8 News Truck parked along the emergency room entrance. My buddy was already there, getting ready to do a news feed. This son-of-a-bitch never missed a beat.

Charles "Chaz" Rizzo is a news journalist and investigative reporter from WDRV-8 Eyewitness News. He's a short, stocky guy who successfully intimidates everyone into giving him the information he's looking for, especially the Chicago coppers. He must have gotten the police blogger over the radio before my assistant editor did, and he had already beaten me to the punch.

Chaz was a well-dressed, arrogant bastard who pushed himself around on everyone with his press badge as though he were an over-sized linebacker for the Chicago Bears. Rizzo reported mostly on "syndicate crime" investigations, as he was their so-called "Mafia reporter." Since the boys from the mob have been behaving themselves lately in Chicago, he had been putting his nose into my City Hall beat.

"You never miss a trick, do you?" I annoyingly said to him as he was ready to do his news feed.

"Hey Larry, Happy Sunday," smiling that cheshire cat grin of his.

"Fancy seeing you here."

"Yeah, right. Figures you would get here first."

"The early bird gets the worm, amigo," he said, still smiling. "Better get in there. They're about to announce Mayor Kollar's death."

I was shocked. "Kollar's dead?"

"Yeah, my sources tell me she died ten minutes ago. Two bullet wounds to the head. She flatlined three times."

"How the hell did a killer manage to shoot her in the head with all of her goddamn neighborhood security?"

"It was a sniper, Larry. The police are tearing through the neighborhood as we speak. They think it might be from the house next door."

I paused to pull out my notepad and started writing down some notes while Chaz gave me some of the '411' on the Mayor's assassination. Rizzo, despite his being an arrogant bastard, was an excellent news journalist. He always managed to get one up on the other news channels, social media, the coppers, and fat, slow newspapermen like me.

"Okay, Larry. Now get lost. I have to do this newsfeed," he smiled and shook my hand.

His cameraman motioned him that he was about to go live on the air in less than thirty seconds.

I walked into the emergency room entrance and tried to fight through a crowd of anxious reporters. A podium had been set up not far from the front door, and other reporters and news channels were already getting ready to do the live feed from the hospital news conference.

After fifteen minutes or so, a short, overweight doctor finally appeared in front of the podium. He was still wearing his surgery gown, and a nurse was following close behind him. When he realized he was going to be live on the air, the doctor quickly took off his surgery gown and fixed his hair with both of his hands, hoping that he looked presentable:

"My name is Dr. Alex Reynolds, and I'm the Head of Emergency Surgery here at Northwestern Memorial Hospital. At approximately 4:40 pm, Mayor Janice Kollar was rushed into our emergency room with two bullet wounds to the back of her head. When she arrived here, she had already lost a significant amount of blood. We immediately rushed her into surgery and were able to remove two Winchester sniper-style bullets in the back of her head. She had flat-lined three times during surgery, and we were not able to revive her. Her time of death was 4:53 pm."

Several reporters were already asking the doctor intense questions regarding the place, time, and shooting method. The emergency surgeon had little information. He tried to answer what few questions he could regarding her surgery and medical condition. Dr. Reynolds then passed the microphone over to the Chicago Police Superintendent Walter Byron, who answered several more questions. Byron didn't know much, other than that the coppers were scouring the areas around the Mayor's house in Logan Square and had little to no leads as to who the assassin was.

It was so uncanny. I had already written an article for the Sunday edition regarding all of the out-of-control riot acts, vandalism, and that the murders in the City of Chicago were at their highest levels since the Prohibition days of Al Capone and his gang of murderers.

My top weekend headline was 'City of Chicago Up for Grabs', and I couldn't have been more spot-on. With the whole city going out of control by all of the gang bangers, hoodlums, and drug lords in this town, it seemed as though the entire civilized population was getting overrun by violence. And now, with the mayor killed in her back yard, things in Chicago couldn't have looked more desperate.

"Chief, Mayor Kollar is dead," I promptly announced to my assistant editor as I was walking outside of the emergency room to use my cell phone.

"Yeah, I heard. What else do you know?"

"All that we could confirm was that it was from two sniper's bullets from a nearby location. Possibly next to her house."

The Chief was unusually silent for about five seconds.

"How quick can you bang out this story?"

"If I run back to the newsroom, I can bang out a thousand words before late tonight."

"Okay, Larry. Keep it short and sweet. It's already headline news at CNN."

"Great, I'm not surprised. Who's the reporter?"

"Some broad I've never heard of before. Her name is Talia Bowerman."

The reporter's name didn't sound familiar. I looked around, and I saw the CNN news truck parked on the other side of East Huron Street, with a female news reporter finishing up her live newsfeed in front of the hospital. As I walked past her looking for a taxicab, she made eye contact with me and smiled.

CNN's Talia Bowerman was a blue-eyed brunette and shapely news reporter who looked more like a Cosmopolitan cover girl than a journalist. She acutely resembled Courtney Cox from 'Friends' and looked mesmerizing.

I smiled back at her as I was able to get the attention of a taxicab. Climbing in, I started scribbling some notes as the cabby was rushing me back to the Chicago Tribune newsroom on North Michigan Avenue.

As I was trying to write the news article, I was in total disbelief about what was happening in the City of Chicago. The crime rate was out of control, no thanks to Kollar's sympathetic administration to the so-called victims of police violence and brutality.

She had instructed the Chicago Police Department to treat the violent criminals, looters, and gang bangers with kid gloves. She seemed to be more worried about the violent criminals being unfairly roughed up and unjustly beaten up by the police than she was concerned about the gun violence in this city.

But who wanted Mayor Kollar dead? Was there a political motive for killing the very unpopular mayor? How would the African American community now react? Would this be another excuse to riot and vandalize the city as they have done in the very recent past? There would be civil unrest in this town for sure. But God-forbid if the actual sniper turns out to be a white Caucasian. Then there would be inter-city riots, going out of control as this city has never seen.

I was still at the newsroom at 8:30 pm when I finally finished writing my news article. I left a message for the most formidable ward alderman in Chicago's City Council, Edward Barrett of the Fourteenth Ward. I tried to get his immediate response to the mayor's death and include his hopefully, congenial comments in my news article.

I then called my mother, letting her know that I would be coming over to her house to have a late dinner and spend the night. I was now famished, as I hadn't had time most of the day to eat anything at all since breakfast.

Indeed, this city was up for grabs. As I shut off my laptop, I said a quick prayer to myself.

The future of the City of Chicago was now in God's hands.

CHAPTER THREE
THE SUPERINTENDENT OF POLICE

The modest greystone building on 3559 West Shakespeare Avenue was surrounded by several Chicago squad cars as the Police Superintendent Walter Byron arrived at the scene that Sunday afternoon. The EMS trucks had left the mayor's residence earlier, and the police had blocked off the area surrounding the mayor's street and the neighboring Central Park Avenue.

The African American Superintendent of Chicago's Finest had just gotten the dispatch from his home in Lincoln Park. He didn't waste any time changing from his casual clothing to his police uniform, rushing over to Northwestern Hospital. When he had heard that Mayor Kollar had been shot, Chief Byron automatically assumed the worst.

The City of Chicago had been besieged with violence that sweltering summer, and Superintendent Byron was under an enormous amount of pressure from Mayor Kollar and the City Council to do something about the violence that was ruthlessly taking over the city.

He had been very vocal with the Mayor about how and what methods he could use in curtailing the violence that was going on in the South and West Side neighborhoods. His police patrols were ordered not to retaliate when gang members threw objects such as bottle rockets and stone objects at police. The Police Superintendent publicly spoke of clearing the city corners of drug dealers and announced 1,200 more officers would be on the streets for that past Fourth of July weekend, which was typically the most violent time of year in Chicago. But he was also limited to the number of additional officers he could utilize, down from the 1,500 officers deployed a year ago. Byron said in the media that he wanted to curtail overtime to give his officers a break.

But as far as Superintendent Byron was concerned, Kollar was sending him into a 'gunfight with a green, plastic squirt gun.' The city's violence was becoming out of control, and Kollar wasn't allowing his police force to deal with the city violence using the same methods that the Chicago P.D. had used in the past.

Long gone were the days of the 'shoot to kill' orders used by Mayor Richard J. Daley to deal with the Democratic Riots of 1968. Long past was the brutality driven police districts in dealing with the dangerous drug lords and street gangs responsible for all of the ruthless violence.

Mayor Kollar wanted to clean up the city of its violence and its all-time murder rates. But she had grand illusions of all of the dangerous criminals peacefully protesting arm-in-arm, singing 'Kumbaya' down Roosevelt Road. Those days of peaceful protests and the civil rights marches of Martin Luther King were long gone. As far as Superintendent Byron was concerned, the mayor didn't know how to deal with the city's turbulence.

"It's not enough for a mayor or a police superintendent or city government," the mayor would say in addressing Chicago's violence and trying to reach those responsible for it.

"Each of us has to ask ourselves, what more can we do every single day in our lives to wrap our arms around these children. And I don't mean just the victims; I mean the shooters as well. What do we need to do to reach them, to give them hope and love and have them recognize the sanctity of human life?"

As far as Superintendent Byron was concerned, Mayor Kollar was living in 'La-La Land.' He was an African American veteran patrol officer who began his career in 1988. He was initially appointed as the Commander of the Sixth Chicago Police District in 2012 before being named by the previous Mayor Ron Liebowitz as the new Superintendent of the Chicago Police Department in March 2016, succeeding Superintendent Robert O'Conner.

With over thirty-two years of police experience, he knew that treating Chicago's hardened gang criminals and street corner drug dealers with kid's gloves weren't going to work.

Byron now leads a department of over 13,400 officers, the second-largest police department in the United States. He has defended the use of force training, more community policing, and a court monitor to oversee department-wide reforms, including the Department of Justice and the Chicago Police Accountability Task Force. The task force was initiated by Mayor Ronald M. Leibowitz to internally investigate the shooting death of Lorenzo Addams in October 2016 and was once headed by the present mayor. Kollar was appointed head council in 2017 by Mayor Ron Leibowitz to restore the public's trust after Mayor Leibowitz delayed releasing the video of James Von Stueben's s fatal shooting of Lorenzo Addams for over a year.

Byron said that the Lorenzo Addams incident in October 2016 changed Chicago's trust in the city's police department and that officer morale fell due to the lack of faith.

Chicago's homicide rate stood at a 20-year high of 792 in 2016 when Byron was appointed superintendent and dropped to 561 by the end of 2018.

Byron credited the use of intensive data analytics to decrease homicides, violence, and shootings. He approved the Department of Justice's investigation into Chicago P.D. shootings that found pervasive, excessive use of physical force, and prolific racial profiling and discrimination by the Chicago Police Department. This has resulted in a consent decree, a federally-enforced agreement that oversees the current Chicago P.D. reforms.

As a result of the consent decree, Byron had validated the Chicago P.D.'s community policing efforts, making very substantial improvements in officer training, which eventually led to decreased officer-related shootings.

But for the current Mayor of Chicago, these reforms were not enough. As a result, the Chicago P.D. was forced to significantly 'ease off' of the city's criminals taking over the city.

As Police Superintendent Byron pulled his squad car in front of the fallen Mayor's residence in Logan Square, he realized that the city's violence had now gotten entirely out of control.

Enough was enough, he said to himself.

His tensions between himself and Mayor Kollar were no secret to anyone in the City of Chicago. She had immediately chastised the city's 'Top Cop' for treating suspects too harshly. Chief Byron was well known for his 'hit now, question later' attitude towards its prevalent criminal violators and intense law enforcement. Byron was a hardliner, very familiar with the gangs and the street criminals taking over the city. Byron was accused of 'looking the other way' when his police officers roughed up several gang members during the previous summer for attacking and raping a nine-year-old little girl in Englewood.

'Getting tough on criminals' was Byron's only solution to the city's intense violence, and Mayor Kollar wanted no part of it. The tensions were becoming so extreme that the Mayor had recently excluded the Chief of Police from a recent news conference regarding some prior robberies and protests occurring earlier that year.

"Anybody talk to ballistics? Where's the crime lab?" the Superintendent jumped out of his squad car swinging, demanding to know answers right away.

"We're not sure, Chief. But we think that the bullets came from the upper story window next door."

"Who lives there? Has anyone gotten in there to investigate yet?"

"The house has been vacant for a few months, sir. There looks to be some forced entry on the back door."

Three Chicago patrolmen led the Superintendent towards the back door of the three-story bungalow house next door.

"Has this door been dusted for prints?" he demanded to know, as someone handed Chief

Byron a pair of rubber gloves so that he could inspect the perceived shooter's next to where the assassin fired off the two shots that killed the mayor. The back door looks like it had been jimmied with a simple screwdriver as they all entered the vacant house and walked upstairs to the house's upper story.

There in the attic, across the other side of the room, was an open window with a dark, small fabric used as some makeshift drapes. It looks like the shooter had time to open and close the window behind the curtain, and two shell casings were lying several feet away from the window.

Chief Byron looked around the empty, vacant room and took a long, deep breath.

"Bring these shell casings to the crime lab. And make sure we get some dustings on this window," as he looked at one of the patrolmen.

"The shooter had time to even open and shut the window after he fired off the shots," he commented.

"He must have fired off the rifle and escaped out the back door. Somebody had to have seen this son-of-a-bitch."

At that moment, Detective Tommy Morton from the Sixteenth District had just arrived at the crime scene. He entered the vacant house next door and walked upstairs with several other patrolmen.

Detective Tommy Morton was a twenty-year veteran who had recently transferred to the Sixteenth District. He was an old school copper who graduated at the top of the police academy after a four-year stint in the Marines. Morton was honorably discharged after three tours in Iraq, was an explosives specialist and a skilled long-range marksman.

"Hey Chief Byron," the detective acknowledged Chicago's Superintendent.

"Who's going to be working this case?" Byron immediately demanded to know.

"I don't know, sir. I just arrived here after I heard the radio dispatch, and I wasn't too far away. I was investigating a car theft several blocks away."

"Where's your buddy, Dorian? Aren't you guys supposed to be 'Batman and Robin?'"

"More like 'Starsky and Hutch,'" commented one of the other patrolmen, as Detective Morton now gave him a dirty look.

Byron managed to crack a smile.

"I haven't seen him today, sir. I'm sure he's at the Sixteenth."

The Superintendent referred to the 'Pedophile Priest' killings that the two of them worked on two summers ago and cracked the case wide open. They had now developed an excellent reputation for investigating and solving vicious criminal and homicide cases within the department.

"Put a team of detectives together, Morton. Let's not waste any time solving this homicide. We are now talking about collaring the assassins who murdered Mayor Kollar," Byron directed.

"We need to jump on this!" as he was looking at the other patrolmen standing around the attic, looking as though the answers to this horrific assassination were going to jump off of the walls and this crime would just solve itself.

Superintendent Byron hated to see his patrolmen standing around instead of jumping to solve a crime, especially the high-profile murder of the Mayor of Chicago.

Everyone filed out of the vacant house as the crime lab technicians entered the building. They were going to spend the next several hours dusting for prints and reconstructing the crime scene, putting together the prospective rifle scope range, and matching the shell casings to the rifle used for the assassination.

Detective Morton had just exited the vacant building when he spotted an old friend when they were working together as patrolmen at the Eighteenth District.

"Wow, this must be a copper reunion today?" he thundered as he enthusiastically hugged Tommy Morton.

"Where's your partner Dorian?"

"He will be here shortly. He was tied up in another homicide investigation today that he was finishing some paperwork on."

Detective Dennis Romanowski was with District Eighteen on North Larrabee Street on the Near North Side. He was a twenty-five-year veteran with the Chicago P.D. and had an excellent reputation for being incredibly tenacious and extremely detailed within the department.

"So, who's going to be working this case?" Romanowski asked Detective Morton.

Tommy lit up a Marlboro Light cigarette while offering up one to Romanowski.

"No thanks, I quit."

"Smart man," Tommy commented.

Tommy Morton was a walking, talking chimney. He never went anywhere without his pack of Marlboro Lights in his coat pocket, smoking close to three packs of cigarettes a day. Morton spoke with a raspy voice, which resulted from many years of sticking a cigarette in his mouth since the age of twelve. It was a bad habit that he learned growing up in the Cragin neighborhood near Belmont Avenue, and he had struggled all his life to quit smoking.

"Byron asked me to put together a team of detectives to investigate this murder," as he took out his silver, butane lighter and torched the end of his cigarette.

"You've got nothing to do right now, right?" he asked Romanowski.

"What makes you think that? I only came here to snoop around. I heard the radio dispatch, and I thought I'd run over here to see if you guys needed any help."

Tommy Morton smiled.

"They don't call you at the Eighteenth 'Mrs. Kravitz' for nothing," as he took a long drag from his cigarette, blowing out several smoke circles, a talent at which he was quite proficient.

"Help us out, Denny. It will be like old times."

"And work with that fucking cranky partner of yours? Are you kidding me? It would be like working with Detective Sipowicz from NYPD Blue. He's a moody son-of-a-bitch," Denny commented.

"I don't know how you do it."

"Relax," Detective Morton smiled.

"I'll keep a leash on him. Besides, we could use your help. We need a detailed, anal detective like you on this case."

Denny Romanowski thought about it for several moments while Tommy continued to blow cigarette smoke in his face.

"Okay, but I ain't makin' no press statements. Public relations isn't one of my strong suits."

"Don't worry. We've got Dorian for that job. Chaz Rizzo has got his tongue in his ear most of the time, so you won't have to worry. Besides, I've got a feeling that Byron is going to want to handle most of the press on this case."

Romanowski smiled.

"Okay. Just make sure Dorian keeps his fingers out of my Dunkin' Donuts box."

Tommy finished his cigarette and stomped it on the ground, making sure that his cigarette butt was extinguished and buried deep on top of the street pavement.

"God forbid somebody steel one of those stale fucking bagels!" Morton chuckled.

They both shook hands as if to make a pact. With the three of them investigating this high-profile homicide, there were over seventy-five years of investigative police experience between the three of them. They had all solved enough homicide cases to know their way around, and they knew that they had an excellent chance of solving this case.

Morton, Dorian, and Romanowski. It sounds like one of those high-powered, ambulance-chasing legal firms that advertise on late-night TV. They're working together would be like the Justice League of the Chicago Police Department.

Detective Morton walked back to his squad car, smiling. He knew that if the three of them couldn't crack this case, nobody could.

Before he climbed inside, he figured he would start the investigation by coordinating the other police officers at the crime scene to do some door-knocking around the neighborhood and determine if anyone had seen anything.

Then he thought for a moment.

Would the assassin have been running through the Logan Square neighborhood with a rifle in his hands?

Fat chance of that, he thought. Nobody with the balls to shoot the mayor in her own home would be stupid enough to blatantly go running around the quiet neighborhood, exposing a high-powered rifle in her back yard. It had to be an assembled weapon—a cheap, collapsible rifle, perhaps.

Nobody heard any shots, so a silencer was probably attached to the rifle as well.

The killer had to have enough time to exit the vacant house and quickly disassemble the portable long-range weapon. He must have been carrying some gun bag or weapon case while escaping from the home.

Was it a lone gunman? Was it someone who acted alone in assassinating the mayor? Was it someone whose only plan was to take out Mayor Kollar, without any other scheme or political motive?

Mayor Kollar managed to accumulate an awful lot of enemies in the short time she was in office. There could be a long list of potential suspects, a detailed catalog of adversaries who would have wanted nothing more than to see Mayor Janice Kollar dead.

Detective Tommy Morton had no idea how extensive that list was.

Chapter Four
The Black Cobras-That Same Day

Lorenzo 'Big Dog' Philips was sitting on the couch on that Sunday afternoon with a few of his gang member friends. Two of his other buddies, James 'Two-Bit' Harding and David 'Downtown' Coolidge, were sitting there with him on that day, hanging out in his living room on the South Side of Chicago. They had the White Sox baseball game blaring full blast, as Big Dog had to talk over the volume of the TV set loudly.

"Go grab me a beer in 'da fridge," he shouted to Downtown, as he was sitting on the opposite chair doing a line of cocaine or 'blow' on the coffee table with a rolled-up dollar bill up his nose.

"You don't see I'm busy, man."

"Yeah, motha-fucka, all you is doin' is wasting 'dat shit on the floor, man," Big Dog responded.

He was half-heartedly trying to read the White Sox baseball game's score against the Detroit Tigers that afternoon but could only figure out that they were still in the third inning. His other gang member friend was half asleep on the other couch, trying to keep his eyes open after doing a line of 'blow' earlier that morning.

"Never mind, Nigga. I'll get it myself," as he disgruntledly got up from the coach to go over to the refrigerator in the kitchen, which was always well stocked with beer.

The house on 6522 S. Union Street had been owned by thirty-nine-year-old 'Big Dog' Philips for several years and was the main

Southside hangout for his notorious street gang, the Black Cobras. They were the most influential African American street gang in the Southside, with their headquarters mainly located at Big Dog's house in Englewood. They boasted of having over five hundred members throughout the south and west sides of Chicago, and Big Dog was considered one of their leaders.

The Black Cobras have a long, sorted history in the City of Chicago. They were first organized in 1958 when a group of young teenagers from Hyde Park, Englewood, and Kenwood came together as friends to create an alliance to combat their enemies. By the beginning of 1961, David Drysdale, also known as "King David," took sole leadership of the Black Cobras and appointed different members to oversee other areas of neighborhoods.

Drysdale's goal was to claim small gangs around the area and turn them into factions of the Cobras. Throughout the 1960s until the 1990s, the Black Cobras had grown from a small street gang from the South Side of Chicago to one of the city's largest, strongest gangs. Despite all of the various bloodshed with other rival gangs and its gang members, King David became the formidable gang leader until 1999, when King David was killed in an argument with another gang member. This caused a backlash of violence amongst its street gang members, with several of its members being killed from 1999 until 2004. The rivalry came to an end with the stepping in of Lorenzo 'King Big Dog' Philips. His leadership came to pass after another unfortunate incident.

Robert "Cookie" Sanders joined the Black Cobras in 2004 at the age of 11 years old. He was the little brother of another prominent gang member and was inducted into the Black Cobras at a very tender age, despite various other gang members' protests. He was given a 9MM semiautomatic pistol by his gang chief and was sent out to kill some adversary gang members. While aiming at one of his rivals, a stray bullet from Cookie's gun hit and killed 14-year-old pedestrian Sherell Devon.

This incident brought much-unwanted attention to the Black Cobras from local and national news. One of the gang leaders sent out two brothers, Darryl and Anthony Hardy, to get rid of Cookie. They were worried that the eleven-year-old child turned gang member might be convinced to become an informant for the Chicago P.D. The two brothers lured Cookie into an underpass and shot him in the back of his head twice. They were later captured and convicted of first-degree murder, both receiving life prison sentences. This incident brought more attention to the Black Cobras despite their efforts to cover it up.

The Black Cobras now have over 200 sets of 'subsidiary gangs' scattered about different neighborhoods in the South and West Sides of Chicago, with around 20 to 25 members in each group. The highest-ranking leadership role is "King," a position that King Big Dog has held for fifteen years. Permanent leadership ranks also include the Minister, Assistant Co-Minister, and the Demetrius. The lowest ranking positions are the soldiers and representatives. Their activities include, but are not limited to, drugs and arms trafficking, illegal gambling, kidnapping, money laundering, racketeering, and local prostitution.

Big Dog was watching Downtown snort up the white powder up his nose when there was a sudden newsflash on the television, interrupting the baseball game:

"WMRQ Eyewitness News has just learned that the Mayor of Chicago, Janice Kollar, has been assassinated in her home in Logan Square approximately thirty minutes ago. She was rushed to Northwestern University Hospital's emergency room and underwent surgery when the doctors there pronounced her dead at 4:53 pm."

Big Dog was momentarily speechless, as Downtown and Two-Bit vocally exclaimed their disbelief.

"Now what motha-fucka would take out our sista-mayor? I don't believe this fuckin' shit, man," exclaimed Two-Bit, as he pounded his hand on the armrest of the easy chair he was sitting in.

Downtown looked up at the television and said the phrase 'what da' fuck' several times out loud, momentarily interrupting his personal 'getting high' session.

"Some white-dude motha-fucka, Dog, I'm tellin' ya. This is a fuckin' hit, man."

Big Dog only sat there on the couch, studying the TV set. It was as if the head and king of the Black Cobras had gone into mild shock, as he was utterly speechless. For several long minutes, Big Dog had no words. He wondered how this new tragedy was now going to affect the current activities of his street gang. He and his gang members were involved in much of the rioting and looting during that previous Memorial Day weekend in downtown Chicago and the Loop. There had been large protests caused by the unnecessary choking death of Anthony Perkins in Minneapolis several weeks ago.

The Anthony Perkins protests in Minneapolis–Saint Paul were an ongoing series of civil unrest riots that began on that previous Memorial Day Weekend.

The Minneapolis riots began as a response to the killing of Anthony Perkins, a 46-year-old African-American man who died on May 25 during an arrest after David Chambers, a Minneapolis Police Department officer, knelt on Perkins's neck for nearly eight minutes as three other officers looked on. Unrest spilled over into Saint Paul, other locations in the Twin Cities metropolitan region, and then throughout the country. Perkin's death and local unrest inspired a global protest movement against police brutality and racial inequality.

The protests in Chicago that weekend became a series of civil disturbances in which the Black Cobras were actively involved. The demonstrations were in support of Anthony Perkins and against the violent use of police brutality. Protesters had gathered on in Millennium Park and marched through the Loop chanting Perkins's name.

His gang members joined many of the demonstrators, who had shut down several downtown streets and blocked traffic on the Eisenhower Expressway. Near the intersection of State and

Harrison streets, several of his gang members were seen throwing bottles and climbing onto cars. During those protests, one person died, and six others were shot. The Chicago Police reported multiple arrests and damaged property. About a dozen officers were injured, and Mayor Kollar called on protesters to remain peaceful, stating that the president was inciting the violence.

As the King of the Black Cobras, Big Dog Philips knew that mayor Kollar's assassination would now incite more rioting, more looting, and more vandalism than what was previously provoked with the police murder of Anthony Perkins.

Deep down inside, 39-year-old Big Dog was scared to death.

Big Dog was older than most of his gang members, and he had become tired and weary of the violent, day-to-day activities that he had been involved with as the Black Cobra King. He was the father of four children, all conceived with different 'baby-mommas,' and practically had no relationship with any of them. He knew that as an active gang member in one of the most violent gangs in Chicago, he had already surpassed a gang member's average life expectancy.

Truth be told, Big Dog was exhausted. He was not ready for another round of violent protests that his gang member admirals and warlords would insist on pursuing. He knew that the peaceful demonstrations of the 'Black Lives Matter' activists and the Antifa protestors would be leading the charge in violent city protest movements that were about to occur.

The Antifa movement consisted of individuals with anti-authoritarian, anti-capitalist, and anti-fascist political views. Their political beliefs subscribed to left-wing ideologies of communism, Marxism, social democracy, and socialism. Many of these Antifa members had infiltrated his Black Cobra gang and were now throwing more gasoline into the fire.

There would now be more protests, as his black brothers and various other gang members would take to the streets again, and more rioting and looting would occur. But only this time, with the pacifist black women mayor now dead, he wasn't so sure that these riots would not come without more violence and potential killings. How long would the police stand by and watch the rioters and looters have their way with the open vandalism and theft that had previously occurred that Memorial holiday weekend before?

Any black gang member or political activist knew that Mayor Kollar was the only person holding back the Chicago Police from violently responding to many violent protesters. He had recalled the lessons he had learned in school regarding the Chicago Riots of 1968 at the Democratic Convention and how then-Mayor Richard J. Daley had instructed his riot, police patrols, and detail to 'shoot to kill.' He knew that many of the city's political powers had been fed up with all of the unnecessary riots occurring that summer. Many large retailers and business owners were closing up their stores for good and abandoning their lavish retail spaces in the Chicago Loop and Michigan Avenue to find safer ground. As the head of the Black Cobras, he would have to approve of the civil unrest, rioting, and looting that was now about to occur again. He would be forced by his gang member brothers to act, to take violent refuge against the white establishment forces that incited the violent, tragic death of Mayor Kollar.

Black Dog glared at the TV set.

"I don't believe this shit," he said out loud.

Downtown and Two-Bit, who now are both pretty high, were starting to get themselves worked up. They were both high ranking gang members in their middle twenties, who thrived on the violent gang activities that rendered the large sums of cash that they were all habitually earning. They both knew there would be a massive demand for more black-market guns, ammunition, and especially, AK-47 rifles that the Black Cobras were well known for selling at a profit at street market prices.

But the gang leader was apprehensive.

Big Dog had just been arrested that past January on federal gun and drug offenses and was out on a $1,000,000 bond. There had been a years-long investigation along with twenty-three other suspects in their drug and gun marketing activities by FBI agents who were able to infiltrate and acquire information from his street gang. They had been busted to actively distribute black market and stolen guns to various gang members needing unregistered weapons and firearms in the city's South Side.

The authorities recovered twenty-four firearms and fifteen kilograms of cocaine, several bags of fentanyl-laced heroin, crack cocaine, ecstasy, and nearly $62,600 in cash from their Englewood neighborhood. Although he posted a cash bond and was awaiting trial this upcoming November, several of his fellow gang members were still locked up in Cook County Jail.

As he finished his bottled beer, he only gazed at the baseball game that had now continued to be broadcast on the television. He wasn't paying any more attention to the White Sox and was now more concerned about the upcoming future events that were now about to occur and overrun this city.

Big Dog Philips, King of the Black Cobras, the largest street gang in Chicago, was tired. There will now be more calls to supply more illegal guns and ammunition to more gang members. Everyone will be getting 'ammoed up' for the increased city violence in the next several days. There would be more violence, more police shootings, and indeed, more death. As he glared at the television, that Sunday's newspaper was sitting on top of the couch next to Two-Bit, displaying that current Chicago Tribune headline.

Indeed, this city will be up for grabs.

CHAPTER FIVE
THE OLD GUARD-JULY 20TH

The sweltering heat didn't stop the veteran alderman of the Fourteenth Ward from going to his law office on that Monday morning. He usually arrived at his law firm on North LaSalle Street at seven o'clock every morning to catch up on oncoming events, emails, voicemails, messages from colleagues, and review the schedule with his office staff.

On that Monday morning, the veteran alderman had a copy of the Chicago Tribune's morning edition in his hand. He placed it on top of the coffee table in his office while putting his Starbucks Americano coffee on the drink coaster next to his desktop computer. Despite the morning headlines on that day, the alderman was in an exceptionally good mood.

He sat down at his desk, and while taking the first sip of his overpriced coffee and smiled while reading the morning headlines:

Mayor Kollar Assassinated at Her Home

He opened the paper and perused the details of the tragic news that he had already heard on all of the evening Chicago broadcasts the night before.

The alderman could not have been more pleased.

Alderman Edward J. Barrett was a senior member of the Chicago City Council and currently represents the city's Southwest Side. As a long-time member of the Democratic Party, he was first elected to the Chicago City Council in 1967 and now represents its

Southwest Side. He is currently the powerful Chairman of the Council's Committee on Finance.

Barrett has been called one of Chicago's 'most formidable alderman' by the Chicago Tribune. He was also named one of the '100 Most Powerful Chicagoans' by Chicago Magazine, describing him as 'one of the last of the old-school Chicago machine politicians.'

Barrett has been the longest-serving alderman in Chicago history. He was a leader of the "Vulakovich 29" during the first term of Mayor Harold Washington and the 'Council Wars' era. Barrett and his staff were the subjects of many federal and local investigations, and members of his team were the targets of indictments and convictions involving payroll and contracting irregularities.

Barrett is the lead partner with Kefauver & Barrett, a law firm specializing in property tax appeals on North LaSalle Street. His firm has served clients who do business with the city and has provided services to many influential clients, including Donald Trump.

Since Mayor Janice Kollar's election in April 2019, he had been besieged with federal and state investigations. The newly elected Mayor was a former state prosecutor, and it didn't take a Harvard genius to figure where all of the political heat was coming. She had campaigned on a platform of decreased city crime and political corruption, and she wasted no time pointing her finger at his aldermanic office.

Barrett's office at Chicago City Hall and his aldermanic ward office had been seized by federal agents, who ejected staff and papered over the doors and windows. In June 2019, Barrett was charged with attempted extortion for allegedly using his political office to drive business for his law firm.

Since this new mayor's election, Barrett's political power and city-wide influence have significantly dwindled, and the 76-year old alderman was not happy. Barrett and his political 'old-school machine' have been severely crippled since this new mayor's election. He has been spending a significant amount of time defending his political actions and ward decisions over the last few decades from prying federal agents.

To say that Mayor Janice Kollar has made Eddie Barrett's personal and political life completely miserable was an understatement.

To now read about the mayor's assassination the day before at her home has only given him a reason to celebrate on that muggy, summer morning.

It had been a well-known fact around Chicago's political circles that nothing in the City Council ever got approved without Eddie Barrett's blessing. As the chairman of the city council's Committee on Finance, all relevant city business passed across Barrett's desk.

That chairmanship has been described as 'the No. 2 spot in city government'. The Finance Committee must recommend almost all expenditures, tax matters, and many city contracts before the full Council can consider them.

As Chairman of the Committee on Finance, Barrett controls a 63-member staff and $2.2-million annual budget, dwarfing other council committees' resources. In the city's self-managed workman's compensation program, the Finance Committee determines and approves payment amounts in disability claims. As Chairman of the Committee on Finance, Barrett controls a $1.3M per year taxpayer-funded payroll account available to council members with no scrutiny.

Barrett is also a member of the city council's Aviation committees; Budget and Government Operation; Energy, Environmental Protection and Public Utilities; and Zoning. Additionally, Barrett is a member of the Chicago Planning Commission and Economic Development Commission. He controls three well-funded political action committees, the "Friends of Edward Barrett," the "14th Ward Regular Democratic Organization," and "The Burnham Committee."

Barrett's campaign funds totaled almost four million dollars, higher than any other alderman and one of the largest in Illinois. Illinois judges are elected in partisan elections. A significant aspect of Barrett's influence derives from his role as the longtime chairman of the Cook County Democratic Party's judicial slating subcommittee.

To that end, except for the Mayor herself, Barrett was the most powerful politician in Chicago. And with the current mayor now dead, Eddie Barrett had more than enough reasons to celebrate.

"Good morning, boss."

The attractive, middle-aged legal assistant entered his office, making sure that Eddie Barrett had his morning coffee on his desk. Sandra Pawlowski had been his administrative assistant and paralegal for over twenty-five years, and the alderman trusted her completely. She assisted him in all of his city and legal office transactions on a day-to-day basis. It would be safe to say that Sandra instinctively knows where all of the skeletons are.

"Good morning, Sandra. How was your weekend?" he cheerfully asked his associate.

"Wonderful," she only said, not wanting to sound too triumphant over the fallen mayor's death.

She smiled as he continued to read the morning paper while sipping on his Starbucks.

"Can we all assume that we will be having fewer federal guests in our office after yesterday's events?" she curiously asked.

"One can only presume, Sandra. With the mayor's killer now on the loose and the city violence continuing to escalate, I would think that the Feds have bigger fish to fry right now."

They both smiled, assuming that his law office and alderman's ward office on Archer Avenue would see less activity from the Federal Bureau of Investigation.

"What are my appointments today?" he asked his associate.

"You have an appointment at the ward office with several aldermen who wish to speak with you regarding the Mayor's death and appointing her successor. You need to be at the ward office by one o'clock." Sandra mentioned while looking at her notes.

"Yes, we need to meet in light of yesterday's events."

Despite Barrett's enthusiasm over Kollar's death, he needed to participate and plan for the newly appointed mayor to resume

Kollar's mayoral office's remaining term. It was imperative that a smooth transition was made and that there would not be another disruption of his political power with the newly appointed mayor.

"Also, the Judge wishes to see you at ten-thirty," she also mentioned.

'The Judge' she was referring to was Judge Augustino Chiaramonte. He was a federal judge within Chicago's Northern District of Illinois Seventh Circuit Court. He had been on the circuit court for almost thirty years and had a very close, personal relationship with the alderman. Because of Chiaramonte's federal judiciary position, his relationship with the city's most powerful alderman would be frowned upon by any outside parties or the news media who knew of their close association.

One might say that the judge was another of those few individuals whose name is on the list titled, *'Knows Where All the Dead Bodies Are Buried.'*

Barrett spent the next few hours reading the paper, answering a few e-mails, and taking a few business calls that morning. Almost all were about the mayor's sudden death the day before. With her unexpected death, everyone in the City of Chicago was looking to Barrett to make all of the significant decisions in running the city's business.

At ten o'clock, the alderman could hear the judge's voice walking past Sandra's desk, inviting himself into his office.

"Good morning, Eddie."

The two hugged one another as if they were related blood brothers. They had known each other for over forty years and had a very close, very discrete personal friendship. So discrete that the two of them were very careful never to be seen together in public.

"It's a good morning indeed, Judge," Barrett smiled as they both sat down on the black leather couch in the alderman's posh and well-decorated office.

Sandra brought in a cup of espresso for Judge Chiaramonte, with a small shot of Sambuca, just the way he liked it.

"Thanks, Sandra," as he motioned her to close his office door behind her when she left.

As the two sat down, the judge immediately quizzed the alderman.

"So, Eddie, what are your thoughts? Who do you think did this?"

"Could have been anybody. Kollar managed to make a lot of enemies in the short time that she was in office," Barrett replied.

The judge shook his head while taking his first sip.

"Could have been someone from one of the city gangs, perhaps. It could have been an organized crime hit by one of the families. She was fighting with them too," Eddie said.

"Which family?"

"I'm not sure. The last time I heard from them, all of the family capos were not too happy with her and her crackdown on them over trying to eliminate the Columbus Day holiday."

The judge paused for a moment.

"Really?"

"And don't even get me started on those Christopher Columbus statues in the city," Barrett grumbled.

Judge Chiaramonte took another sip of his Sambuca flavored espresso.

"Don't forget, the white supremacists were angry with her as well," Chiaramonte interjected. "Those Nazi bastards have had it out for her since her election."

Eddie Barrett shook his head, sipping the last drop of his now cold Starbucks coffee. He then smiled and made that famous smirk of his that the judge only knew too well.

"How much do you know?" the judge asked. He was now suspicious, believing that possibly, his aldermanic best friend could conceivably have had a hand in this.

"Just enough to keep you stupid," Eddie smiled.

With that comment, the judge wondered if the order to kill Mayor Kollar came directly from the Fourteenth Ward alderman himself.

If it had, it would not have been the first time. Eddie Barrett was very well connected to everyone who played on both sides of the street. He had powerful political friends in Washington. He was connected to all of the crime families of Chicago's 'Outfit.' He knew of all the street gangs' leaders on both the South and West Sides of Chicago.

Barrett knew all of the good guys. He knew all the bad guys. The Fourteenth Ward alderman was very well connected indeed. He certainly wasn't afraid to use his political powers to exert and exercise whatever needed to be done to dispose of a political opponent. The alderman was a dangerous man to have as an enemy.

Eddie Barrett had something on everybody. Years ago, a Chicago Tribune

reporter made the mistake of accusing him of being the 'Edgar J. Hoover' of City Hall.
That reporter is no longer around.
"You're right. I don't want to know. I have enough problems being your friend, let alone hearing any confidential information about the mayor's death. Especially from your office."
They both smiled as Barrett raised his empty Starbucks coffee cup to the judge as if to make a toast.
"Here's to Mayor Janice Kollar. May she rest in peace."
Chiaramonte smiled with his close friend, nodding his head. They both gleefully acknowledged the fortunate circumstance of the Chicago mayor's sudden death and their wishes for her peaceful afterlife.
"So now what, Eddie?"
"We have a meeting at my ward office at one o'clock today. Twelve of the alderman are going to be meeting me there to discuss the appointment of the new mayor and arrangements for Kollar's funeral."
"Has the press gotten a hold of you yet?"
"Larry McKay from the Tribune already left a message."
"Will you talk to him before the meeting?"
"Our ward office only stated condolences to Kollar's family, and that was all I mentioned to McKay. He's a good reporter, and I don't think he'll try to throw anyone under the bus."
The two sat there and discussed other Chicago politics when the judge inquired about Kollar's successor.
"What are your thoughts?"

"I think it's gotta be someone we can control. Someone who isn't going to get into City Hall and start shooting off their mouth like a loose cannon the way Kollar did. We need someone who is going to 'honor his colleagues'," he emphasized.

"We need someone who isn't going to rock the boat and who will take orders."

The judge sat there for a moment.

"Are you thinking of another African-American?"

"No. They are too sympathetic to the city minorities. These black and Hispanic gangs have control of the city right now. We need someone who can display some balls but can also be controlled."

They sat there for a few moments, taking inventory of all of the aldermen in the city council who would possibly be considered the right candidate. They both knew that they were in a precarious position. They had to find an aldermanic candidate who would appease the minorities in the city but still appeal to the white population.

The judge mentioned a few names that didn't seem to initially appeal to Barrett until he suggested the alderman from the Fifteenth Ward.

"How about Ray Sanchez? He's a Puerto Rican who's been on the city council for a while, and he appeals to the white, the black, and the Latino consensus."

Barrett thought about it silently for several minutes.

"You know, that may be a good compromise. The only problem with Sanchez is that he doesn't know how to keep his mouth shut. He's always talking to the reporters."

Barrett went to grasp his Starbucks cup before realizing it was empty.

"And he loves his Twitter account."

"Yeah, but he's likable. The media reporters love him, and he has a great relationship with the African Americans, the whites, and the Hispanics. He's relatively young, and he's well respected within the community," Chiaramonte stated.

"Yes, but can he be controlled?"

"I think if you have a 'Come-to-Jesus' meeting with him, you will have to let him know that he takes orders from the city bosses."

Barrett thought for a moment.

"He might be a good compromise candidate. I will run his name past the other aldermen at the meeting at 1:00 pm."

The judge finished his espresso and then directly looked at the alderman.

"I think he's our boy, Eddie."

They both smiled, knowing that they may have just hand-picked the next Mayor of Chicago. They shook hands and gave each other a brief hug before the judge departed Barrett's law office.

"Call me after the meeting," the judge requested from the alderman.

"Read it in the papers!" Barrett laughed as he waved off his best friend.

By 1:15 pm, all twelve of the most potent and most outspoken alderman with the City of Chicago were assembled at the Fourteenth Ward office of Edward J. Barrett on West 51st Street. They were all seated in the ward conference room, including three African Americans, three Latinos, and six white Caucasians (two Italian, two Irish, one who was Jewish, one who was of Polish descent) council members. All the gentlemen seated there have worked together before making decisions on behalf of the City of Chicago.

The twelve aldermen, who usually worked together and amicably got along, created a voting block that was able to sway the other aldermen in the council to vote with 'Barrett's Dirty Dozen,' as the media have often called them.

After five hours of hashing, loud arguments, and discussion, and with several large pizzas delivered by Mamma Maria's Pizzeria down the street, they had all agreed. Alderman Barrett had gotten his way with his city councilmen, his 'dirty dozen.'

The veteran councilman from South Ashland Avenue, Fifteenth Ward Alderman Raymond J. Sanchez, would be the next Mayor of Chicago.

Eddie Barrett crossed his fingers as they all shook hands and smiled at their agreed-upon choice for their new candidate. The alderman assumed that Raymond Sanchez would be a mayor who could be trusted, manipulated, and controlled.

He would soon find out otherwise.

CHAPTER SIX
FUNERAL WAKE IN BRIDGEPORT -JULY 24TH

The last few days of July were relatively mild ones in Chicago, as the blistering hot temperatures of that summer were taking a break on everyone who was having to depend on their air conditioners and cooling centers to stay comfortable.

Thankfully, it was barely seventy degrees on that day, as the cool winds off of Lake Michigan were giving everyone in the Windy City a much-needed break from the scorching summer temperatures.

Crowds of mourners were assembling in front of A.J. Coletti Funeral Home on 33rd Street in Bridgeport on that Friday afternoon. The funeral chapel was an old, brownstone building that had been in the old Irish-Italian neighborhood of Bridgeport for over eighty years. The third generation of the Coletti Family was now in charge of servicing the older families still associated with that neighborhood. The area around Bridgeport has seen many changes over the years with the urban renewal of recent times, and the funeral home has seen more than its share of inner-city change.

The Coletti Family had endured the rough times of the past and now prospered with the traditional old-time Italian, Irish, and Polish families coming back to Bridgeport for their loved ones' funeral service.

On that day, a ninety-four-year-old mother of a very influential, very infamous businessman was being waked from that funeral chapel that Friday, with her funeral services to begin the next Saturday morning at nine o'clock.

In fact, so influential that there were two cars filled with FBI agents sitting across the street from the funeral home, taking down license plate numbers and snapping pictures of everyone entering the building.

As crowds began to assemble inside, the deceased woman's 65-year-old son stood next to the casket with his immediate family. His daughter Gianna, his son-in-law, and several nephews all stood by his side as they greeted all those entering the funeral home to pay their respects. His sister and brother in law, Antonio and Costanza Fazio were also sitting on the long couch facing the casket.

Carmela DiMatteo had passed away Monday evening from long term complications of Alzheimer's Disease, with her entire family at her side. She lived a long, fruitful life as the DiMatteo Family matriarch, whose husband Vito started the DiMatteo Tomato Distribution Company back in 1953 on Lake Street near the Fulton Market. Her only son had now developed and expanded the business into the billion-dollar national business that it has now flourished into today.

With over a billion dollars in sales and assets, the tomato distribution company has expanded to Georgia, Nevada, and New York locations.

All of this expansion and successful business investing can only be credited to Carmela's only son, the very person everyone was paying their respects to.

'Sorry for your loss" or 'my condolences' in Italian were the common phrases used by everyone going through the single-file line of people that day. All of them were patiently waiting to pay their respects by kneeling in front of the casket and saying a quick prayer for the old woman's eternal repose.

"Le mie sentite condoglianze per la perdita di tua madre", expressed Onorio Roselli to the old woman's son, conveying his heartfelt condolences. He was the head of the Roselli crime family on the West Side of Chicago on Grand Avenue and had come, like everyone else, to pay his respects.

"If you need anything, please let me know," said Joseph Lucatelli, the 'capo' of the Lucatelli Family from the Hegewisch neighborhood on the very South Side of Chicago.

"Mi dispiace, le mie condoglianze," said Frank Mercurio, expressing his condolences. He was now the new 'capo' of the North Side's Marchese Family since losing their family crime boss, Carlo Marchese, back in December 2018. He then kissed him on both of his cheeks as a sign of respect.

Anthony 'Little Tony' DiMatteo was flattered that all of the other crime bosses from their respective Chicago crime families had come to Bridgeport to pay their respects to him and his family on losing his beloved mother. Little Tony was very close to his mother Carmela, especially after his father's loss some thirty years ago. He had always looked after his mother, making sure that he and his wife would stop there at the Villa Madonna Nursing Home in the old neighborhood on Sunday afternoons to visit and attend to her needs.

Antonio DiMatteo was born in a small town called Cervaro, about 89 miles south of

Rome. As a child, he had immigrated with his family when he was only three years old. He then grew up in the Bridgeport neighborhood in Chicago, several blocks away from where Mayor Daley and his family lived.

Both he and his older sister, Costanza, went to Nativity of Our Lord Catholic School. He was basically a good kid until he started getting involved with some local street gangs, which eventually got him into trouble.

By the time he was thirteen years old, he was a juvenile delinquent and had a 'rap sheet' the length of his forearm. Despite his family being upper middle class and financially comfortable in the Bridgeport neighborhood, he chose to continuously get into trouble and hang around the wrong crowd.

He was involved in several local robberies and was implicated in some local gang beatings and auto thefts. In the tenth grade, Tony was kicked out of Richards High School for beating up and critically injuring one of his Math instructors. He then spent several years in the juvenile court system and spent four years in Statesville for armed robbery and attempted murder.

But it wasn't until he joined the family business that "Little Tony" gained his callous, ruthless reputation. His father, Vito DiMatteo, had started a food distribution entity, handling the sales and shipment of produce to grocery stores all over the country from their giant warehouse on South Ashland Avenue.

The DiMatteo's were also infamous for their other family businesses: The largest bookmaking and loan sharking operation in the city. They supplied a majority of the video poker games and slot machines throughout Chicagoland.

Little Tony was well known and recognized by 'mob watchers' and the FBI as being "The Capo" of all the Chicago crime organizations.

DiMatteo ran a very successful operation from both sides of the law. He had a vast array of 'drivers,' or enforcers, who installed machines, made collections, accounted and administrated "accounts receivables." During the day, his drivers were Teamsters making food and other produce deliveries to various grocery stores throughout the city. After hours, he had a select group of enforcers of fifty or more men, who effectively did "whatever was necessary" to collect on all his receivables, both on and off the books.

He had vast business interests, including investments in two Chicago area casinos, several restaurants, and various real estate developments throughout the city and suburbs. Chicago Crain's had recently estimated his net worth to be in the billions.

At 65 years old, Little Tony was still fit and trim at five feet, five inches tall. Although his black raven hair had turned entirely white over the years, he was still relatively healthy for his age. He maintained a rigorous fitness schedule that included weightlifting and cardio five times a week. Little Tony arrived at his warehouse at four-thirty every morning and worked out in his gym in excess of two hours every day.

Since the 'disappearance' of Little Tony's personal close friend and family priest, Monsignor Joseph Kilbane, both he and his family no longer had a personal connection to the Catholic Church. Monsignor Kilbane had grown up with Little Tony in the Bridgeport neighborhood, and they had been very close friends until two years ago. When Little Tony assisted Monsignor Kilbane in 'disappearing' from Chicago, he had no interest in forging another relationship with another church pastor or priest.

This put the DiMatteo Family in a precarious position now with the death of his mother. Carmela DiMatteo was a devout Catholic and expected to be given last rites and be buried according to the church's canon laws. As 'Mama Carmela' was dying at the nursing home where she was residing, Little Tony was nervous about asking another priest to come and give his mother her last rites and reconciliation.

His daughter Gianna had a close friend who knew Fr. Colin Fitzgerald very well from St. Simeon Church on 79th Street in the Auburn-Gresham neighborhood. When Gianna called Fr. Fitz to come and give the last rights to her grandmother Carmela, Fr. Fitz was more than happy to do so.

As seven o'clock had approached, several hundred people had come to the Coletti Funeral Home to pay their respects to Little Tony's mother. Fr. Fitz had just arrived to say the rosary at eight o'clock and to prepare for the funeral mass for Carmela DiMatteo.

"Pop, this is Fr. Fitz, the priest who came to give Nonna her last rights last week," Gianna said, as Little Tony shook the hands of the popular priest from St. Simeon's Church.

"Pleased to meet you, Father."

"Likewise, Tony. I've heard a lot about you."

"Well, if you heard it from the FBI, none of it is true," Tony joked, as they both laughed.

"I was wondering if perhaps you and I could talk, and you could give me some ideas about what your mother was like and the kind of Catholic Christian that she was. This would help me in preparing for my homily at her funeral mass tomorrow morning."

Although Tony was listening, he wasn't interested in talking to Fr. Fitz. Since Monsignor Kilbane had left town, he wasn't interested in talking to another priest about anything, least of all his mother.

"I would love to, Father. But I'm pretty tied up here right now. I'm sure you and my daughter can talk, and she could give you some ideas about what my mother was like."

Fr. Fitz felt as though he had been immediately blown off as Gianna gave her father a very dirty look. At that moment, she took charge of the situation and brought Fr. Fitz to the back of the chapel and sat down with him on two of the folding chairs.

"You'll have to excuse my father, Fr. Fitz. Ever since Fr. Joe disappeared two years ago, my father hasn't had any interest whatsoever in speaking to another priest."

"You mean Monsignor Kilbane?"

"Yes. My dad was very close to him, and he hasn't taken his disappearance very well. They grew up together in the Bridgeport neighborhood."

Knowing about the situation of Kilbane and his involvement with the 'Pedophile Priest Murders' two years ago, the pastor had heard some rumblings in the news media regarding his disappearance.

"I understand."

They sat there in silence for several long seconds.

"What can you tell me about your grandmother?"

"Well, for Nonna, her family was everything. She was a wonderful cook, a supportive wife to my Nonno before he died, and was always there for her children. She was a role model for all of us and took an active interest in all of our lives."

"I see," Fr. Fitz replied.

"What did she like to do?"

"Cooking, sewing, she loved to knit and enjoyed her expansive garden in her backyard in Bridgeport. She also loved opera music and listened to Luciano Pavarotti and Andrea Botticelli all the time," Gianna replied.

"Was she a good Catholic?"

"Yes, she never missed a Sunday. She would sometimes go to mass two or three times a week at Our Lady of the Nativity in the old neighborhood."

"Hmmm, sounds like a wonderful lady. How did she interact with your father? What things did she enjoy doing for him?"

"Well," Gianna replied, "she would cook for him every chance that she had, especially on Sundays after church."

Gianna went silent for a moment as Fr. Fitz was still intently listening.

"I remember as a little girl, we would all go over to my Nonna's house on Sundays, and we would have such a wonderful dinner there with my cousins who came to visit as well and me," she reminisced.

"Then, after dinner, my Nonna and my father would go into the living room and play cards, or sometimes, chess."

"Your grandmother played chess with your father?"

"Well, yes. My dad got bored with playing cards with my grandmother all the time, so he taught her how to play chess," she explained.

"Nonna loved it. It got to the point that my Nonna only wanted to play chess and nothing else. She would play chess with my father, my uncle, my cousins, and even with me. She became very good at it."

Fr. Fitz started to smile, amused at the thought of this little old Italian lady taking an interest in playing chess.

"So, she was a chess master of sorts."

"Oh, indeed, Father. She was good! She continued to play chess until she got Alzheimer's and couldn't remember how to play the game anymore."

They both laughed together as Fr. Fitz was making mental notes about Gianna's grandmother's cute characteristics.

Perhaps it was a coincidence that Fr. Fitz was also a very active, very gifted chess player as well. He was the president of his chess club and was a state grandmaster in high school. He played chess with anyone interested in playing with him while he was in the Mundelein Seminary.

Fr. Fitz found it very relaxing when he sat down to play chess with any of his close friends, parishioners, or family members. He would go to the park near North Street Beach on Saturday afternoons, where the local chess clubs usually gathered. The pastor hosted a chess tournament at his church once a year and started a parish chess club. He would often do a pick-up chess game with anyone available to play.

He found it very interesting that Little Tony would play chess with his aging mother on Sundays. He never figured him to be a chess player.

A good chess player had to have an enormous passion for the game. A good chess player needed to remember patterns, game openings, endgames, strategic tactics, and make careful and calculated moves under pressure. It also took a considerable amount of intelligence and patience. One needed the ability to focus and concentrate on the game for long periods.

These are all traits of very productive, very successful people. It is no wonder that many influential leaders and businesspeople around the world were also outstanding chess players.

Thus, judging by Little Tony's success throughout his life, it would also make sense that he was probably a very effective chess player as well.

He had also heard of Little Tony's ruthlessness, his brutality, and his callous ability to do whatever he needed to do to get the job done.

Fr. Fitz wasn't naïve. He had heard and read all about Little Tony's dangerous temper and some of the evil crimes he allegedly responsible for. As the 'Capo dei Capi,' Fr. Fitz was well aware of the consequences of having such a dangerous liaison to someone who was

the head of all of the Chicago crime families in Chicago.
DiMatteo was always under investigation and scrutiny by the Department of Justice. The Federal Bureau of Investigation was continually harassing him. His acronym for the FBI was 'Forever Bothering Italians.' His tax returns were consistently audited every three years. And he was always being pulled over and questioned by the Chicago P.D.
Anthony DiMatteo was a powerful, wealthy man indeed. And his far-reaching, evil control usually came from the loaded barrel of his Beretta 92 MM pistol.
Fitz knew that DiMatteo did whatever he had to do to accomplish whatever task he needed to be done. And he didn't tolerate anyone who got in his way.
Ever.
Little Tony always won and always came out on top, at any cost. Even if it demanded his making an adversary or a personal enemy disappear. Fr. Fitz knew that this man danced with the devil on a regular basis.
Without exaggeration, the pastor knew that this was a man without any conscience or scruples.
But Fr. Fitz also looked at Little Tony as a challenge, as if he were a 'lost soul who had forgotten his humble connection with the Lord.'
Most religious men of the cloth would have immediately written off such callous, hardened criminals of Little Tony's character as a complete and total waste of time.
He didn't need 'Billy Graham' or 'Jimmy Swaggart' to softly whisper in his ear and warn him. He didn't need any bible busting

evangelist to officially proclaim DiMatteo as a dangerous, cryptic demon beyond salvation.

Fr. Fitz looked at the 'capo dei capi' quite differently and was well aware of who he was about to deal with. He saw him as an opportunity to not only 'save his soul,' but to, perhaps, acquire a very powerful friend and political connection that he could always count on for a favor or assistance down the road.

With his poor church on West 79th Street struggling to pay its bills from week to week, Fr. Fitz thought of DiMatteo as possibly, an excellent friend to have. He didn't care how many of the Lord's ten commandments Little Tony may have regularly broken. The Catholic priest figured that if he could win over Little Tony's trust and friendship, he could count on him to assist him with whatever tasks he needed, especially around the parish.

If one was prudently vigilant, even Satan could be a resourceful friend, the famous, outspoken pastor often thought.

"Take away his matches, and you can checkmate even the devil," Fr. Fitz would often say to his chess-playing friends.

Fr. Fitz said the rosary at the funeral chapel that evening, reciting the appropriate 'Our Father's, 'Hail Mary's and three of the sacred mysteries. Within an hour, the rosary was completed, and all the attendees paid their final respects to Little Tony and his family.

"Thank you for coming, Father," Gianna approached Fr. Fitz, expressing her gratitude for his being able to assist her family in their time of need.

"It was my pleasure, Gianna."

He looked over to where Little Tony was standing, still greeting guests, and accepting condolences from friends and family in the reception line. Little Tony barely even acknowledged Fr. Fitz.

"Please tell your father that I look forward to saying the funeral mass for your grandmother tomorrow morning."

"I'm sure he will be pleased to see you, Father." They both shook hands, and Fr. Fitz proceeded to leave the funeral home.

As he got into his car, Fr. Fitz thought of an incredible idea. He smiled to himself, knowing that it would be a long shot.

An idea that for all involved, might very well assist everyone. It was a notion that would possibly help his impoverished Catholic parish. It was an incredible suggestion that could potentially benefit Little Tony and his family.

But most of all, it was an idea that could save the city that Fr. Fitz so dearly loved from all of the vicious, senseless violence that the city was currently suffering.

And it only involved a simple chess game.

Chapter Seven
A Mother's Funeral-The Following Morning

The large rain puddles were amassing and accumulating in front of Our Lady of the Nativity Church in Bridgeport on that rainy morning as the funeral procession arrived. They were turning into large lakes in the parking lot.

Fr. Colin Fitzgerald stood in front of the church dressed in his vestments, accompanied by two altar boys. One of them held a large umbrella in the downpouring rain as the popular Catholic priest waited for the black hearse to come to a full stop in front of the church.

"Let us pray for God's servant, Carmela DiMatteo, as we come together for the celebration of her life," he started the funeral ceremony as he blessed the black and silver-lined casket outside in front of the church.

The six pallbearers dutifully carried the casket up the old, greystone church steps through the vestibule, as the cantor sang 'How Great Thou Art' in an operatic, majestic tenor voice.

Little Tony DiMatteo and his wife Angelina, accompanied by their daughter Gianna and her husband, followed the casket closely as it proceeded to the church's front entrance. Three hundred or more mourners followed the immediate family into the church, most of them paying their respects to the family out of obligation.

The heads of the five Chicago crime families were all there at the church that morning, along with their associates and respective underboss es. They all knew that the capo dei capi was taking attendance, mentally making sure that everyone was there to pay their respects in burying his 92-year-old mother.

"She lived a good, long life," Frank Mercurio loudly said to one of his associates as they were all entering the church.

"Should we all be so lucky? Sign us up," as several other attendees smiled at the Marchese family capo's loud comment.

Fr. Fitz proceeded to celebrate the funeral mass as all of the pews within the gothic designed Bridgeport church were filled. He said a very poignant eulogy, equating Mama Carmela's life as the queen chess piece on a board game, watching, overseeing, and taking care of her immediate family of token pawns. He mentioned her love of cooking, family, and her love of the strategic game of moving chess pieces on a checkered board.

Little Tony DiMatteo was quietly moved to tears at the celebrant's homily, as he acknowledged his mother's lifelong devotion to her family and her children. He knew that his mother's dedication to their family legacy was always without question, including their business activities' darker side. Little Tony's mother still turned a blind eye, and even sometimes, a quiet nod, to the DiMatteo Family's violent crime activities in and around Chicago.

Crime watchers often equated Little Tony's old mother to The Godfather movie's Connie Corleone. She would often suggest that her son send his adversaries a box of cannoli as the first step to anyone who would dare stand in the family's way.

As Little Tony was often overheard complaining to his consigliere, Sal Marrocco, about his adversaries in front of his mother, Mama Carmela would always softly suggest,
"Invia loro una scatola di cannoli."

Whenever someone suddenly received a box of cannoli, compliments of the DiMatteo Family, they immediately got the message:

Get in line with the family program, or get ready for the dirt nap.

As the funeral mass was concluding, the loud tenor voice from the choir loft of the old church reverberated the 'Ave Maria' song for all to hear. Her casket was solemnly loaded into the back of the black Coletti Funeral Home hearse and taken for internment to Resurrection Cemetery on 95th Street. Her funeral and burial were concluded by 1:00 pm that afternoon.

Later that day, over one hundred guests gathered at a funeral luncheon at the Casabianca Ristorante on Taylor Street. Fr. Fitz was invited to attend and dutifully said grace before the meal. As the funeral guests were standing near the bar after finishing their elaborate luncheon, Gianna approached the popular priest and thanked him for his services that day, giving him an envelope filled with cash.

"Thank you so much for helping us out today, Father Fitz," as she graciously hugged the pastor. Fr. Fitz put the envelope into his black suitcoat pocket. Based on the envelope's thickness, he knew that there were at least five thousand dollars in cash stuffed inside.

"It was my pleasure, Gianna."

She continued to compliment Fr. Fitz on his funeral eulogy to her grandmother, thanking him for graciously mentioning her love of family and the game of chess. She then looked over to her father, standing at the bar holding a drink and socializing with the other funeral guests. As they made eye contact, Little Tony knew that he had to approach Fr. Fitz and dutifully thank him for his celebration of his mother's funeral mass.

"Thank you, Father, for coming today," he said to the priest, with his daughter standing next to her father, making sure that he was genuinely gracious and polite.

"I was touched by your kind words regarding my mother."

"She sounded like a wonderful, dedicated mother and grandmother to her family," Fr. Fitz observed.

The three of them continued to make small talk, as Little Tony's eyes were wandering elsewhere, looking utterly disinterested in standing in front of the pastor's presence that afternoon. As his daughter was suddenly pulled away by another luncheon guest, Fr. Fitz saw the opportunity to speak to Little Tony alone.

"Do you mind if I call you Tony?"

"Of course not, Father."

"I understand that Monsignor Kilbane was quite a close friend of yours."

"Yes, we were childhood friends. We went to grade school together."

"Perhaps you felt much closer to God with the intense friendship with your close priest friend…would that be correct?" Fr. Fitz casually observed.

"Perhaps," DiMatteo replied, not knowing where that conversation was going.

"God is always here to help you make new friendships. Our Lord looks for reasons and ways to bring you closer to his passionate way of life," the priest mentioned.

Little Tony smirked and then looked at the priest suspiciously.

"Look, Father, if you're looking for a way to get me into your confessional at your church, forget about it."

"Why, Tony?"

"Are you kidding? The rafters of your church will begin to crack and crumble the minute I enter the front church doors."

Fr. Fitz gleefully smiled.

"I'm not asking you to come in through the front doors."

Little Tony only stood there politely, waiting for the priest to ask him for a large donation.

There was a moment of silence.

"I usually invite a friend over for dinner at our rectory every Wednesday evening. I was hoping I could persuade you to come over for dinner this Wednesday."

Now the Capo dei Capi started to sound impatient.

"Look, Father. If you're looking to save my soul, stop wasting your time. All the devils have a special reservation for me in hell," he smiled, trying to make light of his eventual fate.

"I'm not looking to save your soul, Tony." Fr. Fitz starkly replied.

"I'm looking to kick your ass in a chess game."

Little Tony looked at Fr. Fitz.

"Huh?"

"A chess game. Wednesday night is chess night at our rectory. I usually invite a friend over for Mrs. Valenti's wonderful Italian 'cenettas' and an intense game of chess afterward."

Little Tony looked amused as he answered the Catholic priest's invitation.

"I'm sorry, Father. I'm far too busy to come over to your rectory for dinner and chess. We have a lot going on right now, and it would be very difficult to..."

Fr. Fitz interrupted him.

"Wouldn't it be a wonderful way to honor your mother and to have a friendly chess game with a servant of the Lord," he suggested.

Little Tony stared at the pastor, now wondering if he was serious.

"We both know how refreshing a good game of chess can be for the mind, Tony. They say that chess players live well into their senior years, using their brains to stay active. It's no doubt that your mother stayed as sharp as she was, thanks to her love of the mental game of chess," Fr. Fitz pointed out.

Little Tony smiled.

"I'll think about it, Father," as he blankly dismissed the pastor's invitation.

Little Tony was extremely busy these days, especially with the city unrest that was currently going on at the time. His several restaurant holdings and customers were having difficulty during all of this political and social unrest. As he began to walk away, Fr. Fitz called out the Mafioso.

"I guess it would be intimidating for you to be embarrassed by an old priest like myself in a game of chess."

Little Tony glared back at Fr. Fitz, the total expression on his face completely changing.

"I don't get embarrassed by anyone, Father."

Fr. Fitz smiled, "The world of chess is a kingdom where many of its greatest leaders have been thoroughly humbled."

A moment of silence as the two of them studied each other. It had been a very long time since the Capo dei Capi had been challenged or threatened to be intimidated. Least of all, by a Catholic priest in a friendly game of chess.

Little Tony looked at Fr. Fitz, smiling at first, then taking a long sip of his Jack Daniels on the Rocks.

Then Fr. Fitz upped the ante.

"I'll tell you what, Tony. Come over for dinner this Wednesday, and we'll both enjoy an amazing Italian dinner from Mrs. Valenti. Then we'll have that game of chess. If you win, I'll give this envelope back to you," he said, pulling out the white envelope stuffed with large bills from his coat pocket.

"But if you lose, you'll make another donation, to the tune of whatever is in this envelope."

Little Tony laughed to himself.

This fucking priest has got a lot of balls, challenging him to anything, he thought to himself.

Tony took another swallow from his drink tumbler and walked closer to the Catholic priest, extending his hand.

"You do realize who you're challenging? You do know this, right?"

A moment of silence.

"You do know who you're fucking dealing with...right, Father?"

Fr. Fitz smiled, shaking Little Tony's hand in silence.

"You know, Father, I don't like to lose. In fact, I take losing at anything very personally," the Capo dei Capi emphasized.

"Well, hopefully, you're up for the challenge, Tony. Maybe your mother's spirit will guide you along the way."

Little Tony shook his head.

"Yeah, Father, just maybe."

He then looked at the Catholic priest, making another affirmation statement before returning to his funeral luncheon guests.

"I will be there, Father. Don't get too attached to that envelope."

"I won't, Tony. We'll see you at six-thirty this Wednesday. Mrs. Valenti doesn't like our dinner guests to be late."

Tony grinned at the priest, shaking his head.

"I like you, Father. You've got a lot of balls. I'll see you on Wednesday."

They both shook hands again, and Little Tony walked back to the bar, greeting more luncheon guests and ordering another drink.

Father Fitz placed his drink glass on one of the tables near the door and waived to Gianna, who wasn't standing too far away.

As he walked out of that restaurant on Taylor Street, he knew that he had set the table. He immediately realized that even though Little Tony was a very dangerous man who could never be trusted, there was some usefulness in befriending Little Tony DiMatteo.

The flock of his poverty-stricken worshippers was in financial trouble, and they needed some serious help from his church. He could no longer afford to stock the weekly food pantries for which St. Simeon Parish was responsible. There were people in his church that were being turned away because there wasn't enough food to go around.

There were severe, expensive repairs that St. Simeon direly needed, and there was no financial assistance available to him or his church from the Archdiocese of Chicago. The Archdiocese had financial problems, and he couldn't ask them for help.

But more importantly, the City of Chicago was in a violent, horrific state. With the recent assassination of Mayor Kollar and the new installation of this new mayor, Fr. Fitz knew that the city, with its dreadful state of affairs, was in great need of assistance.

Fr. Fitz needed to appeal for the help of the city's organized crime network. And the only way that was going to happen was if he could befriend them, convincing them to trust him as more than just a Man of God.

Fr. Fitz needed them to confide in him as their ally, as their confidant in fighting and regaining the city from the ugly depths of its current violence.

He needed the city's expansive crime family network to help take control of the town that he so greatly loved, bring it back from the violent gangs and ruthless looters whom the city's police force was powerless in combatting against.

He needed the dark guns of Chicago's organized crime families to correctly point their aim at the Windy City's real enemies.

What better way to do this than a white chess piece on a checkered board to declare checkmate on the city's black king?

Chapter Eight
A New Mayor's Appointment -July 27th

The grueling hot days of summer continued thorough out the last week of July, as the stage was being set for the political fireworks that were about to be displayed in the Chicago City Council.

The power struggle to replace the late Mayor Janice Kollar after she was violently assassinated in her backyard on that muggy summer day would be a brutal one indeed. The display witnessed by all those present on that following Tuesday night and Wednesday morning on the Chicago City Council floor would become an intense, war-room battle. It was an all-night event, with council members jockeying for position to have some say in who the next Mayor of Chicago would be.

The big difference was that the divvying up of power after Kollar's death was done in the traditional Chicago manner...behind closed doors and out of the public eye. When the deal finally was cut in the aldermanic offices of Alderman Edward Barrett, the participants made sure that everything was secure before it was brought to the city's council. The 'Barrett Dirty Dozen' had a deal to push Fifteenth Ward Aldermen Raymond Sanchez's appointment. He was a compromise candidate amongst the various other names bounced around and entertained in Barrett's closed-door meeting.

But when the City Council finally met on that Tuesday at 7:30 pm, it seemed as though all bets were off. The twelve aldermen who had initially met at Barrett's office during the prior week were starting to vacillate, as other influences from their constituents were having second thoughts about Ray Sanchez and his loyalties to Edward Barrett.

"Sanchez is two-faced," several aldermen from the West Side of Chicago stated when hearing about Barrett's choice for the next mayor.

"Sanchez is a snake that can't be trusted," said several other African American aldermen from Chicago's South Side.

"Sanchez is a crook and a drug addict," said many other business colleagues associated with the Fifteenth Ward politician.

Before the gavel hit the podium by the mayor pro-tempore, the circus was in full swing. All of the wheeling-dealing over the next twenty-four hours was out in the open, with council members meeting in clusters on the council floor and in the rear antechamber. Some of them were meeting "privately" behind the clear glass door of the council's committee meeting room, with cigars in hand, clearly visible to whoever wanted to look in. The power factions in the late mayor's death and the aftermath also bore startling resemblances to the initial meetings held in Barrett's Fourteenth Ward office, with many of the same principals pushing for the same result.

Hours after Kollar died from her gunshot wounds at Northwestern Hospital, Alderman Waylon Smith of the Thirty-Fourth Ward, the president pro tempore of the City Council, announced that he was the new mayor, an announcement urged by a group of several other African American leaders led by various city leaders. Riding roughshod and leading the charge was no less than the Reverend Jacob Jennings of the Operation Impulse faction, which rallied a large number of the city's African American voter block. Barrett loyalists, commanded by the Fourteenth Ward alderman himself, tried to refute that claim and initially locked the mayor's office doors so that Smith could not make a symbolic takeover of Kollar's desk.

The old guard aldermen, or 'Barrett's Dirty Dozen,' were not excited about letting any of their city-wide power slip away. They met in secret at the ward offices of Eddie Barrett while Mayor Janice Kollar's body was in full view, lying in state for two days in the Logan Square Baptist Church on Lawndale and Belden Avenues.

On the day before Kollar's funeral, the deal was officially cut, and Barrett's old guard conceded some large sacrificial compromises. Alderman Waylon Smith would be given the powerful Finance Committee's chairmanship in exchange for not running for the acting-mayor post. This assignment pleased the Reverend Jake Jennings's political block of black voters, believing that they now had a powerful man looking out for their interests.

Finally, as was the original plan of the 'Dirty Dozen,' with all of the political overtures and wheeling and dealing behind closed doors, Eddie Barrett had gotten his way. Raymond J. Sanchez, the Fifteenth Ward alderman, would be given the acting mayor's job, presuming that he would play ball with Barrett and his good old boys. There would be no need for a special election to be held in six months. As long as Sanchez played nice with all the various factions of Chicago's City Council, an upcoming election in six months would only be a rubber stamp to his eminent succession of Mayor Kollar.

Appeasing the Polish block on the council, the new post of vice mayor was created and given to Alderman Andrej Kalinowski of the Thirty-Fifth Ward.

By the time the City Council meeting was over, everyone was placated, and Sanchez was elected as the new mayor in a final brief session by a vote of 47-0, with no opponents and dissenting votes cast.

At that moment, Eddie Barrett was exhausted but pleased. He initially underestimated the City Council, believing that the twelve aldermen he usually had in his pocket would easily sway the rest of the council. He figured everyone would blindly go along with Barrett's recommendations, along with his high-powered cronies. Although the 'Barrett Dirty Dozen' finally did get their way, it came with a much higher price. Large liters of blood were surrendered in the form of the

City Council's all-powerful Finance Committee. The loss of control of the influential Finance Committee's chairmanship was a position that Barrett held for decades, and he wasn't pleased about relinquishing that post.

As the political carnage from the council meetings was finally being collected and resolved, the new mayor, Raymond Sanchez, was now in charge of Chicago. Within the next few weeks during that following August, everyone within the city's most potent rafters of political influence and authority, along with State of Illinois politicians, paid homage to the new mayor.

"Thank you for your support," Mayor-elect Sanchez stated to his newly convened City Council.

"I will be the kind of mayor that all of you can be proud of," he stated to his constituents.

But in reality, Mayor Sanchez was a wolf in sheep's clothing. He had controlled and practically hidden his political viewpoints and his pending agenda from view to all those who had a distinctive say in his behind closed doors election.

Truth be told, he was neither a conservative, a liberal, nor even a conformist. Mayor Raymond Sanchez was an opportunist, and he would peddle his mayoral influences to anyone willing to compensate him for his outstanding efforts. The South and West Side council members had already realized what a two-faced liar Sanchez was. He would champion the side that lucratively made the most monetary sense for him, and he was not about to be anyone's puppet.

Least of all, Eddie Barrett's. It didn't take very long for the Fourteenth Ward Alderman to realize that pushing for Ray Sanchez as the city's successor mayor was a huge political mistake. Whenever Barrett and his cronies made a directive to the new mayor, he would only nod his head and smile. He would later close the door and do whatever he pleased, to assist whoever his new best friends with the fattest checkbooks were on that particular period.

Ray Sanchez was now the new mayor. The other Latino aldermen gave him a new nickname, 'El Rey,' or The King. Everyone in the Chicago City Council now realized that their new mayor was always for sale, and he was willing to make any deal behind cigar-smoked rooms and locked doors whenever there was a large stipend for him.

One summer morning, Judge Chiaramonte had stopped by Eddie Barrett's law office on North LaSalle Street to visit his close friend. Of course, Sandra's double espressos with a generous shot of sambuca was also an added perk.

"How's our new mayor treating you?" the judge happened to ask.

"Fuck you." Barrett begrudgingly chimed.

"What?"

"You heard me. Fuck you. That's what the new mayor tells my boys and me whenever we have a political favor or a directive that we need from him," Barrett angrily stated. The alderman always referred to his 'Dirty Dozen' as 'his boys.'

"We tell him what we need done. He smiles, nods his head, and says 'fuck you' under his breath. Then the rotten bastard does whatever he wants."

"That's not good," the judge exclaimed. "Does he realize who he's fucking with?"

Eddie Barrett went into his cigar humidor at that moment and withdrew a Cohiba cigar, shipped directly from Havana. He usually didn't invade his humidor until late afternoons, but at that moment, his Cuban cigar was the only available alternative to his smoking something stronger. Lighting it up with his silver-plated lighter, he went on to explain himself to the judge.

"This son-of-a-bitch forgot who put him there. This fucking bastard thinks he can now do whatever the fuck he wants without any ramifications from any of us."

"Really?"

The two of them sat there in his office while Chiaramonte slowly sipped his Italian espresso while Barrett tried to calm himself down while blowing cigar smoke.

"Did you try talking to him?"

"Oh, yes, several times over the phone."

"And what did he say?" the judge inquired.

The alderman took a few more puffs of his cigar, making perfect smoke circles in the air. It was as though he didn't want to respond to the judge's inquiry. There were only several more minutes of silence.

"Well? What did Sanchez say?"

At that moment, Barrett put his cigar into his extra-large, travertine marble ashtray.

"That son-of-a-bitch says, 'I know what you know, Eddie. And if I were you, I would play nice in the sandbox. I have sources that tell me that there is a connection between in Kollar's assassination and your Fourteenth Ward office."

The judge only sat there on that black leather couch without saying a word. He was speechless.

"This fucking bastard thinks he has me by the balls."

The judge sat there on the couch, listening to Barrett openly complain about the new mayor and his cold attitude towards Eddie Barrett and his political machine. He had openly feared that he and his political pals were going to have trouble with Ray Sanchez. He had a bad reputation with several of the other aldermen, and they tried to warn him. Many had openly complained about Sanchez being very two-faced and morally corrupt and that he didn't like to share the spoils of his political office with his district cronies.

Truth be told, it wasn't just the new mayor's dishonesty that Eddie Barrett feared. It was his personal, greedy corruption and blatant bribery that scared the living shit out of him. He was practically putting his mayoral office up 'for sale' to the highest bidder for whatever political or unethical favors needed to be done. And, of course, Sanchez regularly took his dividends in large, brown paper shopping bags.

"This is your fault," the alderman blatantly accused the judge. "I should have never listened to your fucking suggestion. I knew Sanchez would double-cross us," glaring at the judge with the dirtiest of looks. The judge calmly finished his premium octane double espresso and looked at the alderman.

"Eddie, what happens when you have rats in the cheese factory?"

The alderman blatantly ignored the judge.

"What do you think happens when a mouse gets cornered up against the wall by a large rat?"

Barrett looked at Chiaramonte, so upset with him and himself that he didn't even bother to acknowledge his question.

"What do you think the mouse does?" again asking his riddle.

Eddie Barrett just looked at the judge and waved him off, openly ignoring him.

"The mouse calls the cats," he pauses.

"And then, when the cats can't control the rats, the cats call in the dogs," he answered with a smile.

The alderman gave him another dirty look.

"So, what are we doing now? Watching Tom and Fucking Jerry cartoons?"

The judge smiled. "Don't you have some friends in Washington?"

A long moment of silence.

"Some very powerful friends?" Judge Chiaramonte reiterated.

Barrett picked up his half-smoked cigar from the ashtray and relit it up with his silver butane lighter. After taking several long puffs, the judge could now tell that the aldermen were very deep in thought.

"So, you're thinking FBI?"

"Maybe, or the IRS, perhaps," the judge suggested.

"Get them to wire up an informant and catch him receiving and accepting one of his brown paper bags."

Eddie Barrett took another long toke on his cigar and then `slowly began to smile.

Chiaramonte then grabbed his coat and began to leave Barrett's office.

"When you have rats, you call in the cats," the judge said with a smile on his face.

"When you can't control the cats, you call in the dogs," Judge Chiaramonte concluded.

Taking another long puff, Eddie Barrett smiled at his judicial friend.

"And when the dogs scare the cats, and the cats go away..." Eddie said, then taking another puff of his Havana cigar, blowing several smoke circles in the air.

"Then the mouse eats the cheese."

CHAPTER NINE
MAYOR KOLLAR'S FUNERAL JULY 31ST

It was the last day of July on what turned out to be one of the summer's hottest days. The temperature started at ninety-six degrees and continued to swelter to almost one hundred five. Being in an air-conditioned room or a refreshing body of water, complete with poolside drinks, was definitely the order of the day. But unfortunately, I had neither as I pulled up to Logan Square Baptist Church on Lawndale and Belden Avenues for Mayor Kollar's funeral.

On that day, I realized that I probably needed to put more freon into the air conditioning unit of my BMW X5. The cold air in my car seemed to barely feel lukewarm as I drove several blocks to find a parking space. The funeral service didn't start until ten o'clock but being an hour early didn't help me that morning. There were lines of people waiting to get inside to view the body of Chicago's first black female mayor, who was tragically assassinated more than a week ago. She had been lying in state for two days, as the crowds of people wishing to view her body seemed to never stop.

Wearing short sleeves and a tie, I held my light blue sport coat very closely, hoping that when I put it on in the church, it would cover up some of the sweat that was already protruding on my crisp white shirt. I had a press pass, so I figured I would at least be standing or sitting somewhere inside. I could only hope that they had working air conditioning as I passed the long line of people extending several blocks. I noticed a few familiar people in line waiting to pay their respects, including several Chicago alderman and a couple of state representatives.

I greeted everyone that I immediately knew in line, as it was too hot to be standing outside, waiting to go into the Baptist church to view the body. I cut through the crowds using my press badge until I was able to enter.

It was almost forty-five minutes before I was close enough to get to the casket and view the body of the late Chicago Mayor. Mayor Janice Kollar's black with silver-handled casket was ornately placed in front of the church, with several Chicago Police Officers standing guard on each side.

She was dressed in her usual gray business suit jacket with a white shirt and corsage on her lapel, sprinkled with small white carnations and red roses. I smiled to myself, knowing how prideful these undertakers usually are with every detail, successfully making their subjects look as though they were only taking a long, peaceful nap. There were flower arrangements everywhere, most of them adorning the front of the church's altar, as people were solemnly filing past her body.

As I started walking towards the back of the church to find a place to sit down, I saw a familiar face and immediately made eye contact. He motioned me to sit next to him, as he was able to make room in an already crowded church pew.

"What's up, Larry?"

"Hey Chaz, thanks for saving me a seat."

"I was going to offer it to someone a little prettier, but I noticed that she went to sit somewhere else."

Leave it to Chaz Rizzo to continually be on the hunt, pursuing his usual 'pussy-posse', even at a funeral service.

Chaz Rizzo was a flashy, well-dressed news reporter who never left his house without looking like he was modeling for a fashion show. It didn't take a genius to figure out that he did most of his wardrobe shopping at every men's clothing store on Michigan Avenue. He probably dropped a 'G-note' every month just on his multi-colored, designer underwear. Rizzo flashed around his Italian suits and chic, high-end clothing like some upscale, Las Vegas casino boss.

Chaz Rizzo was also single, like me. He had been married and divorced so many times, I couldn't keep track of all his ex-wives in my head. Whenever I saw him at any social event, he was always with a different woman. They were always pretty blondes, with well-endowed, 'deli-style' breasts and typically, not very bright.

On that morning, Chaz looked like he had jumped out of a page from the popular Gentlemen's Quarterly magazine. He was wearing a dark Canali, pinstriped suit, a crisp white shirt, and one of his well matching Valentino striped ties. Because I was sitting near next to him, I could smell his men's cologne, which had the fragrance of being anything but cheap.

While I was struggling to stay cool and sit calmly in that church pew without overheating, Rizzo looked extremely comfortable. The hot

Baptist church felt overly stuffy, which probably had over three hundred people sitting inside. The heat index in that church had to be in the triple digits, which didn't seem to bother Chaz Rizzo.

"Why aren't you sweating?" I point blankly asked him.

"I doused myself in Johnson's baby powder. You should try it sometime," he proudly smiled, trying to keep his voice to a very low whisper.

Another minute passed, and I was bored, so I made light of the moment.

"What cologne are you wearing, Rizzo? You're starting to turn me on."

"What are you doing now, hitting on me in church?"

"You're dressed and smelling so nice today; I'm thinking of putting your picture on my fridge."

Rizzo starting laughing to himself, amused at the direction of our bromance conversation.

"Not in front of all these fucking politicians, McKay."

I had known Chaz Rizzo for several years, ever since we both started working together as journalists in this town. While he had worked in the television newsroom at Channel Eight, I started at the bottom of the food chain as a junior reporter for the Chicago Tribune. We ran into each other almost every other week trying to cover the same story that our respective employers had assigned us to, and we became fast friends.

Rizzo eventually became Channel Eight's star reporter, usually working on mobbed-up crime stories or, more recently, the pedophile priest murders that were coming out of the Archdiocese of Chicago.

He had a great relationship with the Chicago Police, especially some of the homicide detectives in the Sixteenth, Eighteenth Districts, and the Intelligence Unit over in the Twenty-First. Even though some of his newsroom tips were borderline gossip, he was an excellent connection to have when trying to break a story.

"So, Chaz, help me out here; which marriage are you on?" I decided to give him a hard time.

"Just divorced number five, not that it's any of your fucking business, McKay."

"You didn't learn after the first four?"

"Who are you now, my fucking therapist?"

"I'd rather be your suit tailor. He's the one getting most of your money."

"Eat shit, McKay."

We continued our pleasant conversation while people-watching, observing some of Chicago's more notable dignitaries and politicians file past the mayor's casket. As the crowds were starting to die down, and the church service was about to begin, I decided to pick Rizzo's brain.

"So, who do you think did this?"

"Seriously, I can't make up my mind. But if I were a betting man, I would start snooping around in the Fourteenth Ward," Chaz suggested.

"If anybody had a hard-on for Kollar, it was him."

I looked at him, trying to look surprised. "Barrett?"

"Shhhh! Not so loud."

"Seriously?"

Rizzo looked at me.

"Come on, McKay. Think about it. The FBI went into his ward office a few months ago and come out with a semi-truck full of boxes and computers."

Rizzo paused for a moment.

"He's had the 'Federales' crawling in and out of his ass since Kollar took office."

"Yeah, that was a few months ago, Chaz. But they haven't filed any charges yet, and Barrett never seems to look worried about it."

Rizzo looked at me, intently.

"Believe me, McKay. He's worried."

I shook my head and tried to look interested in the funeral service that was starting to begin. The pastor immediately started with some obscure gospel passage, and a large choir of over two dozen African American gospel vocalists started singing loudly on queue.

But I wasn't even paying attention, and I tuned out everyone and everything around me. My mind was only thinking about the city's most powerful politician. I had plenty of news beat experience, covering City Hall and Chicago politics for more than two decades. I was very familiar enough with Eddie Barrett and his 'Dirty Dozen.'

These guys were shrewd and very slick. Barrett and his boys always met behind closed doors at either his ward office or in some other obscure location, and they were very discrete. I always got the impression that it would take a federal phone tap or a wired-up political rat to take down Barrett and his cronies.

But Eddie Barrett was always one step ahead of the game. He was meticulous and very selective as to whom he let into his inner circle. He was way too smart and too cautious to leave a paper trail or computer files for federal agents to find anything on him.

When the FBI raided Barrett's office several months ago, I was immediately convinced that the federal agents would come up empty-handed. These federal agents were going to meticulously go through that truckload of fourteenth ward boxes, documents, and computer files with a fine-tooth comb, and I already knew that these agents weren't going to find a fucking thing.

I looked over to Rizzo sitting next to me, hoping that he could hear me talking to him over the loud, handclapping, gospel funeral.

"Chaz, maybe it was a mob hit?" I suggested.

Mayor Kollar had come down very hard on the Chicago Outfit during her days as a Cook County Prosecutor. It wasn't any surprise that she extended her vengeance against Chicago's crime families after being elected mayor.

"Are you kidding, McKay? The boys are a lot smarter than that. Do you think they would send out a sniper on a Sunday afternoon to take out the mayor? Those guys don't need the heat right now. The Chicago Families are all fighting for survival. They're all too smart and too busy to be associating themselves with any high-end sniper murders or political assassinations."

Rizzo looked at me for a few silent moments, not saying another word. By that moment, we were all standing in our church pews while the gospel choir was clapping and loudly singing 'Praise Jesus' songs. The funeral attendees were now dancing in their seats, singing and clapping to the music. By then, the solemn funeral service for the fallen mayor had turned into a bible busting, southern evangelical revival. This Baptist, African American funeral was a far cry from any Catholic funerals I usually attended.

"Like I said," Chaz continued to make his point, his voice carrying over the loud music.

"My money is on Barrett."

I looked at Rizzo, remembering what an encyclopedia of information he has always been, especially when it came to City Hall politics and Chicago's 'Outfit.' He was a treasure trove of material, street data, and juicy gossip that most of the time was useful to any reporter like me stumped for leads in a news story.

We both sat there and suffered through the remainder of that funeral service for over an hour. By the time that 'bible-busting tent revival' was over with, it was almost eleven-thirty in the morning. My white shirt was drenched, knowing that whatever cheap antiperspirant I was using that morning was not working. I couldn't wait to get out of there.

I said good-bye to Rizzo and starting walking outside amidst all of the crowds of people trying to exit the warm, stuffy church.

As I was walking on the sidewalk towards my car, I noticed several Chicago Police squad cars parked adjacent to the church. Several patrolmen and plainclothes detectives were outside congregating. One of them was having a cigarette, and I knew who he was.

"Good Morning, Tommy. Were you singing and clapping your hands in church this morning?"

"Please, I couldn't wait to run out of there!"

Tommy Morton was a detective with the Sixteenth District in Jefferson Park. He was one of the more experienced veteran police detectives whom the Chicago Police Department used to crack their significant cases. Although I was a reporter, we had mutual respect for one another, although sometimes I got the impression that he didn't always like me. We shook hands, and he introduced me to a few other detectives whose names I didn't recognize.

"So, what's up, McKay? Why aren't you retired yet?"

"Sitting around on the couch and watching my grass grow isn't my thing, Detective. How's your pallie, Phil Dorian?"

I knew about his detective partner Philip Dorian from the Sixteenth District ever since they solved those "Pedophile Priest Murders" that was going around two summers ago.

"Cranky as ever."

He stood there for a moment with his detective friends and lit up another cigarette.

"Where were you sitting?" he asked.

"Right next to your buddy, Chaz Rizzo."

I knew about Tommy Morton and Rizzo's contentious relationship from the several run-ins I heard the two of them had with one another over the years.

He just smiled.

"Yeah, he waved to me as he was going inside."

It was getting sweltering standing outside, and even with my sport coat off, I was starting to sweat.

"Tommy, what's your take on all of this," I boldly asked, not expecting an honest answer.

"Take on what?"

Morton was trying to play stupid in front of his detective friends.

"What's the latest and greatest on this murder, Detective? I'm sure you and your buddies here are working this homicide, especially the assassination of the mayor."

He looked at me, surprised that I dared to ask such a question in front of a church where the funeral was still going on.

"Do you ever stop being a reporter, McKay?" he retorted, trying to act tough in front of his detective friends.

"Nope."

"Guess you'll have to figure it out on your own, McKay. We were all ordered to keep our mouths shut in front of the media," Morton smirked, tossing his cigarette butt onto the middle of the street.

Since Tommy Morton was playing a tough guy in front of his Chicago P.D. buddies, I decided to volley one back at him before walking away.

"Then I guess I'll be seeing you guys around in the Fourteenth Ward."

Morton then looked at me.

"Fourteenth Ward? What are you talking about, McKay?"

I smiled back at them, knowing that I was doing a number on their heads.

"You're late to the party, as usual, Tommy. You and Dorian always seem to be the last ones in the conga line," I replied.

"You guys, take care."

As always, the newsroom media and newspaper reporters always seemed to be a step ahead of the Chicago coppers in this town. I had four Chicago P.D. detectives giving me these contorted, dirty looks as I walked away from them and towards my car parked on the next block.

As I unlocked my BMW SUV and turned on my lukewarm air conditioning, I sat there for a moment, trying to process all of the information that Rizzo had divulged at the mayor's funeral.

Could Alderman Eddie Barrett, the most powerful politician in Chicago, be responsible for Mayor Janice Kollar's death? Everyone in town knew about the FBI investigation into the Fourteenth Ward and all of the shady, backroom political deals that Barrett and his boys conducted.

But presuming that he was responsible for her death, how would Barrett have had anything to gain with taking out the mayor? He was already under investigation. If the federal agents had found anything relevant, they would have indicted him by now.

Kollar's sudden death would not hasten or delay any potential indictment or the investigation at large. So, what would Barrett have to gain by taking out the mayor? And if it wasn't the alderman, who could have planned and executed this assassination?

It had already been a week since the mayor's assassination, and so far, no arrests had been made. And to no surprise, the Chicago P.D. was tight-lipped as to who and where their investigation was going.

There was only one dead mayor with no suspects, no information, no arrests, and nobody in this damn town was talking.

I then realized that the road to solving Mayor Kollar's tragic murder would indeed be a precarious one.

CHAPTER TEN
MAYOR RAYMOND SANCHEZ - AUGUST 4TH

The urban sunbeams of that early Chicago morning were casting large shadows on the mayor's desk, as he entered his executive suite on the fourth floor of City Hall.

Mayor Raymond Sanchez had arrived early on that Tuesday morning in August, as was his usual arrival time of 7:00 am. His entourage of plainclothes detectives and security detail came over to pick him up from his Fifteenth Ward home early at 6:15 every morning.

The black Lincoln Navigator always successfully negotiated the early morning traffic on Western Avenue from his two-story greystone residence on South Aberdeen to City Hall at 121 North LaSalle Street. There was still time to spare for the Starbucks drive-thru every morning, as Sanchez enjoyed his usual venti cappuccino with an extra shot of espresso.

As his security detail always took control of the bustling Chicago traffic, the Mayor's Chief of Staff, Pedro Alvarez, usually rode into work with him, debriefing him of any newsworthy headlines and outstanding issues that would more than likely occupy his day.

As Mayor Sanchez walked into his mayoral office, he couldn't help but smile to himself. He was now the occupant of the most powerful political office in Illinois and the mayor of perhaps one of the country's most formidable cities. He was now the new king, once occupied by such politico heavyweights as William 'Big Bill' Thompson, Democratic Party boss Richard J. Daley, his son, Richard M. (Richie) Daley, and recently, Rahm Emanuel.

Now crowned as the city's new king, Sanchez would oversee his palatial urban kingdom with his golden scepter. He was now the new monarch of the Windy City, from the vast foray of upscale, overpriced properties of the Gold Coast districts to the gritty, gang-infested neighborhoods of the South Side. Sanchez knew that his urban political power was now all-encompassing. He knew that all of the city's power brokers would now need his stamp of approval and even, perhaps, contribute various tokens of appreciation to reassure that their new king would look the other way.

Raymond Sanchez had more than a good reason to smile and be pleased with himself as the newly appointed Mayor of Chicago.

Mayor Raymond Sanchez had come a long, long way.

As the oldest child from a poor, Puerto Rican family, his mother would often hide welfare checks from his reckless, abusive father on Chicago's West Side.

His father, Chello, was a part-time janitor at one of Chicago's public schools and a full-time alcoholic. He would often abandon his mother and family to sit at some gin mill for days at a time. His desperate mother, Anna, cleaned houses and did laundry for upscale families in Lincoln Park, while young Raymond would often have to miss school to babysit his four younger siblings. Very often, there was no food or money in the house, while his mother would take three buses back and forth to her various part-time jobs in Chicago's Loop.

Determined to get an education, young Raymond enrolled at night school classes to finish his college courses while waiting tables at an Italian restaurant on Taylor Street. He eventually graduated from the University of Illinois Circle Campus with a business degree in finance.

The ambitious young graduate then acquired a job working as a personal banker at Northern Trust Bank on LaSalle Street. It was there that a banking customer asked him to work on an aldermanic election campaign, assisting some of the other political activists in his Fourteenth Ward.

Sanchez soon took an active interest in politics, realizing that the road to financial success was about who you know, not what you know. It was all about being at the right place, at the right time.

"You need to learn how to kiss the right asses," his ward bosses used to advise him.

All of the political action, all the right players, and all of the untapped golden opportunities were located in Chicago's Fourteenth Ward. He would often collect cash envelopes for his ward bosses from prospective business owners looking for liquor licenses or business permits in their districts. Sanchez worked hard, showing his loyalty, and rose through the ranks before eventually being elected as the Fourteenth Ward alderman.

Although he was appointed as the new mayor by various power brokers like Eddie Barrett's Dirty Dozen, he had acquired enough dirt on all of them to dismiss their corrupt, political demands and enjoy the monetary spoils of Chicago politics all for himself.

Ray Sanchez was now on top of the city's food chain, and he wasn't about to take any political prisoners. The new mayor put everyone on notice that Chicago's City Hall was discretely up for sale, and no city business would be done without paying the price of admission. He was going to rake it all in for himself, and he wasn't going to let anyone get in his way.

Least of all, Eddie Barrett.

Well aware of the alderman's political power, Sanchez knew that Barrett could very easily be controlled with a significant amount of paid covert information and blackmail. Recently informing him of his knowledge and direct connection to Mayor Kollar's assassination, the new mayor now had the corrupt, veteran alderman on a proverbial leash. Nothing was going to get done without mayor Sanchez's approval, and the menu price list of daily specials had been passed out to everyone.

Everyone was going to have to 'pay to play,' including Barrett. Although the new mayor preached reforms and tax cuts to the city's community's various factions, it didn't take a financial genius to figure out that the new mayor was all out for himself.

Sanchez made himself comfortable at his executive, oak wooden, antique desk that he had just purchased from Sotheby's for a mere $74,000. Careful not to spill any coffee on his wooden desktop, he perused his emails and scanned the local papers before reviewing his schedule.

Several council members had made an appointment to meet with him and a South Loop development group, headed by a developer, John Patrico. It regarded the rezoning of some vacant land and properties on South Michigan Avenue. There had been some environmental issues regarding the vacant land's rezoning, and they needed the mayor's office's assistance to facilitate its development.

Mayor Sanchez smiled to himself. That transaction should easily net over one hundred thousand dollars in 'real estate commissions' through a real estate limited liability corporation indirectly tied into Sanchez.

At about nine-thirty, his secretary Stephanie had paged him on his desk phone.

"Mr. Mayor, there is an alderman here to see you."

"Who is it, Stephanie? I don't have any time for any unscheduled meetings this morning."

"He insists on coming to see you, Mr. Mayor."

"Who is it?" he asked again.

No sooner did the mayor ask that question when the dark walnut, double doors of his office were abruptly opened up, and the alderman barged into his office.

"We need to have a little talk, Sanchez."

It was Alderman Edward Barrett.

The mayor smiled to himself as he placed his right hand on the top drawer of his desk.

Inside was a loaded Beretta 9MM handgun.

Barrett sat on one of two of the black, leather chairs placed neatly in front of his antique oak desk.

"Eddie! What a pleasure it is to see you. Can I get you anything?" he pleasantly asked with his hand still on the handle of his desk drawer.

"Let's cut the bullshit, Sanchez. I don't appreciate being hustled and pushed around the city council while you check off your lucrative, paper bag agenda. I've got several developments that need your blessing in getting through the building department, and you're completely blowing us off," Barrett angrily replied.

"Are we talking about that new development on South Archer Avenue? I told you, Eddie. There are some environmental issues there. You guys are going to have to clean that land up before you can even think about submitting any plans to the building department."

"Bullshit, Sanchez! Those defective, environmental Phase Two reports can easily be rectified with your help. Those plans have been stalled in the building department, no help from your office."

Barrett gazed directly at the new mayor.

"You're fucking stonewalling me."

The mayor smiled. "I told you, Eddie. All new development proposals need to pay the building department assessments that are charged by the..."

"Fuck you, Ray. That's just another way of your getting your hands on some cash and *extort* my clients in this development."

Mayor Sanchez smiled and chuckled to himself. He had never seen Eddie Barrett so angry before, and he didn't trust his temper. Sanchez knew that the veteran ward alderman had an uncontrollable temperament and was capable of anything. He continued to keep his one hand on the desk drawer, just in case.

"Eddie, you know we don't use that word around here. Besides, that 'E-word' is something you and your cronies have very much perfected in the City Council."

Eddie Barrett rose from his chair and placed both of his hands on top of Mayor Sanchez's desk. He was standing less than twelve inches away from the mayor's face.

"We need to get this deal done, and my guys are not going to pay you 'a hundred-G' to make this happen."

Now feeling threatened, Sanchez opened his desk drawer, pulled out the loaded Beretta, and then calmly placed it on top of his desk.

"I'm the new mayor now, Eddie. And as I told you before, I will not be your puppet. And I will not be anyone else's fucking puppet while I'm in this office. And as far as demanding any 'paper bag money' is concerned, you and your cronies invented that method. You guys have been shaking down and cutting up your stash since Mayor Daley was around."

Eddie Barrett looked at the gun on top of the mayor's desk and then immediately sat down on his chair. Although he was carrying a Magnum revolver on his hip behind his coat pocket, he figured he better cool it. He now realized that Ray Sanchez was as fucking crazy as he was corrupt.

"So, there's a new crook in town, is that what you're saying, Sanchez?"

The new mayor glared at the alderman.

That morning was not the day to have a gunfight in the mayor's office. The two men gazed at each other silently for what seemed like several long minutes until Barrett broke the silence.

"I put you in here, Sanchez. And I will do whatever I have to do to get you out. You forgot where you came from, and you're going to be fucking going back there in a hurry," the angry alderman said, gritting his teeth with his venom foaming at the mouth.

The first-generation mayor of Puerto Rican descent only smiled at Alderman Barrett, his hand still securely covering his pistol sitting on his desk.

"Eddie, all I have to do is dial one, single telephone number, and the Chicago FBI agents can be here at City Hall in less than five minutes. They will be more than happy to receive the documents, emails, and tape recordings that I have pointing directly at you as the one who planned Kollar's murder."

"Fuck you, Sanchez. You've got shit," the alderman sneered.

Now the new mayor laughed.

"Do you think I would bluff about something like that, Eddie? I wouldn't call my poker hand if I were you."

The alderman glared at the mayor.

"Fold your cards, Eddie. Let's all play nice at the poker table. Have your client send over that paper bag we discussed, and he'll get his permits."

The alderman was now silent, looking intently at the mayor. He now knew that Sanchez had him exactly where he wanted him, and he only wanted to curse himself for going against his better judgment.

Raymond Sanchez was a greedy, dirty, double-crossing scumbag, and he should have never listened to the judge. This mayor bastard has gotten himself foolishly inebriated on his own power, and he was looking to play hardball with anyone who would challenge his authority.

"This game isn't over, Sanchez. You fucking forgot who put you here."

A moment of silence.

"May I remind you that I have been an alderman in this town ever since you were pulling your schlong and reading Playboys in the third grade, you ungrateful fuck,"

Barrett was now seething with venom and anger as he looked as though he was willing to leap over the mayor's desk and grab him by his fucking throat.

Mayor Sanchez only laughed even louder at the alderman as Barrett turned and walked out of the mayor's office.

"I would think twice if I were you, Eddie," he called out as Barrett was leaving his office.

"Have a nice day," Mayor Sanchez called out, as Alderman Eddie Barrett bitterly slammed the door behind him.

The mayor smiled to himself and placed the revolver back in his top desk drawer. Sanchez then went into his wooden cigar humidor sitting on the credenza behind his desk. He pulled out one of his Arturo Fuentes cigars, cut the end, and lit it up with a silver lighter that he had sitting on the corner of his desk.

Puffing cigar smoke circles toward his office window, he glared out at the view of the city and the blue, distinctive waters of Lake Michigan. He was delighted with himself, knowing that he had justifiably put the city's most formidable politician and powerbroker in his place.

Eddie Barrett was a bully, he thought to himself. He had no right to make any demands on him, now that he was the new city boss. Sanchez was going to do whatever he saw fit to do. He would run the City of Chicago his way, without any intimidation or political demands from 'the old guard' or any of Barrett's 'Dirty Dozen.'

He stared out of his fourth-floor office window. Mayor Raymond Sanchez took note of the blue waters of Chicago's Great Lake, looking so remarkably calm on that bright, summer morning.

The mayor abruptly put out his cigar. Sanchez then took out his keys and unlocked the bottom drawer of his desk. Rolling up a crisp, one dollar bill, he pulled out an eight-ounce bag or an 'Eight-Ball' of cocaine. While using a small teaspoon, he gently deposited a small line of coke on his desktop and snorted it up immediately. The mayor had now taken his morning fix.

Looking out his fourth story window, he couldn't help but notice how enticing Lake Michigan looked on that August summer morning.

Mayor Raymond Sanchez had no idea how many dead bodies Eddie Barrett was responsible for putting into that lake.

CHAPTER ELEVEN
REPORTER INVESTIGATIONS-THAT SAME DAY

It was just after eight o'clock in the morning as I settled in my office with my usual Starbucks coffee. It was Friday, and I was anxious to start my weekend plans early. I figured I would put in a full day in the newsroom and try to cut out at four o'clock or so to enjoy one of the last few weekends of the summer.

It had been a little over two weeks since Mayor Janice Kollar's assassination and funeral. I had just finished writing the final biographical feature story that week in the Chicago Tribune regarding the late mayor's career and how her death would significantly impact the city and its' aftermath.

By all accounts, I had gone pretty easy on her. It was a unique news story on the life and death of the 'well-respected' mayor, who had desperately tried to collectively bring all the warring factions of a fractured city together. Several of my newsroom colleagues thought it was a very classy and respectful piece.

The words 'well-respected' was used quite loosely in my news article.

The editorial piece that I had written as a tribute and farewell to Chicago's mayor was anything but the truth. I couldn't remember the last time a mayor of our city was so unpopular.

The headline for the top news story for the paper on that day after her death was titled "Passing of a City Hall Peacemaker," and I received complimentary emails on the story, including one from her significant other, Sheila Peacock.

Maybe in death, I had felt a lot of sympathy for the embattled head of our city. The 'Wolves of LaSalle Street' didn't give her a fighting chance, and the complex affairs and violent street crimes spiraled out of control.

Although it was a complimentary news story, realistically, I was still stumped. So far, the question hadn't been answered:

Who killed Mayor Kollar?

I had been turning over all of the mayor's possible enemies and trying to figure out who the actual assassin could have been. I was mulling over her long list of rivals and adversaries over and over in my mind, and I couldn't get it out of my head.

It amazed me how many possible enemies this first black, female, lesbian mayor had managed to accumulate in the short period that she was in office.

She was at odds with the Chicago City Council, and especially its power brokers. Alderman Eddie Barrett and his 'Dirty Dozen' made no secret of how difficult she was to work with. She had animosity towards the Chicago Police Department and its Chief Superintendent, Walter Byron. Kollar was extremely disliked by the police and firemen's fraternal organizations and their unions. The city's clergy and mostly, the Archdiocese of Chicago was extremely resentful of Mayor Kollar for her hard lines and criticisms of their handling of the 'Pedophile Priest Murders' that had occurred two summers ago.

But most of all, she was extremely unpopular with the city's street gangs and Chicago's underworld.

My Chicago Tribune article was a flattering, respectful, courteous tribute to a woman who ran for mayor with very good intentions but was wholly intimidated and blown away by the realities of the city's old school politics.

The City of Chicago was still a corrupt, 'making-deals-in-smoke-filled-rooms' kind of city, and Mayor Kollar was utterly unprepared. She was a former Cook County Prosecutor who thought running a complex city like Chicago would be no more difficult than enforcing a plea deal with the judge.

Electing Janice Kollar for Mayor of Chicago was like sending a kindergarten teacher into a college fraternity party to enforce a ten o'clock curfew on a Thursday night. The political wolves in this town ate her alive, and she didn't stand a chance.

As I was sitting at my desk settling in, I had no more than taken the first sip of my Starbucks coffee when my desk phone rang.

"Lawrence McKay."

"Your lips must be pretty fucking sore, buddy boy."

It was my assistant editor, Tom Olsen.

"Why?"

"From all of the sucking up that you did on those complimentary mayoral editorials you wrote last week," he boldly exclaimed.

It didn't matter how many accolades I received from my newsroom colleagues; my assistant editor was a hard man to please.

From the sound of his voice, I could tell that he was probably only half-joking.

John Thomas Olsen had been my assistant editor for the last five years, coming over from the Chicago Herald, where he had been a veteran City Hall beat reporter. He was an intense, hard-nosed, gritty editor who flaunted his penchant for scotch whisky, unfiltered cigarettes, junk food, and ugly one-night stands. Olsen was a bitter divorcee' who had just had his ass handed to him by his wife's attorney after a turbulent, twenty-year marriage.

Judging by how he talked to the other female reporters in the newsroom, it didn't take a Rhodes Scholar to figure out that Olsen had little respect for the opposite sex. Despite all of the complaints and reprimands to the Tribune's management, Tom Olsen managed to always talk his way out of any human resource criticisms, grievances, and sexual harassment complaints that were verbally communicated with our paper's senior editors.

Tom Olsen was a bald, shorter man in his middle fifties, probably no more than five feet, six inches tall. He tried to suck in his protruding stomach whenever he was walking around the newsroom with several glazed Dunkin' Donuts in his hand.

Olsen loved his Jack Daniels on the Rocks and never met a pizza that he didn't like. His top desk drawer was filled with Domino's, Lou Malnati's, Rosati's, and Jet's Pizza coupons. I can't put a number on how many times I watched that man devour a large pepperoni pizza by himself during lunch.

He came across extremely demeaning, calling his reporters either 'little missy,' 'buddy boy,' or referring to all of us in the newsroom as 'lab rats.'

Wherever you went into his office, you had to bring along your 'A-game.'

But despite his many personal flaws, Olsen was a hard-working assistant editor and a very gifted newsroom journalist. He arrived at his office every day at six in the morning and was always the last person to leave the newsroom. He knew how to handle his job exceptionally well. Olsen seemed always to find the right fit of reporting assignments to the right personalities of every Chicago Tribune reporter working under him.

Olsen grew up in Chicago, coming from an upscale, affluent Northshore family in Winnetka. He went to Loyola Academy and graduated from Northwestern University's prestigious Medill School of Journalism back in 1985. He was a hard-nosed, 'take-no-prisoners' kind of Chicago Herald reporter before abandoning them and jumping over to the Chicago Tribune five years ago as an assistant editor.

I originally had a tough time working for my new assistant editor. Having celebrated my fifty-third birthday at the time and employed by the Chicago Tribune for almost three decades, I was somewhat bitter when I was passed over for the assistant editor position. I regretfully had to watch an outsider like Tom Olsen get hired from a rival newspaper and get the job.

I considered leaving the Tribune and began circulating my resume around other newspapers in the Midwest, East Coast, and particularly Boston and New York.

Here was a veteran Chicago Herald reporter who was now an assistant editor of our newspaper, demanding an elite set of journalistic values to an already arrogant assembly of English Literature elitists.

A majority of us reporters at the Chicago Tribune are admittedly very arrogant. Working for a Chicago Herald reporter who was now a Chicago Tribune assistant editor was well beneath our journalistic aspirations.

Most of us Tribune reporters wouldn't be caught dead wrapping our daily catch with that other Chicago newspaper. The standard joke at the Tribune was that every daily subscription of the Chicago Herald came with a complimentary Disney coloring book and Crayola box of crayons.

Their journalistic reporting was usually substandard and very unsophisticated, using very plain English and colloquial phraseology that blue-collar workers, union tradespeople, and truck drivers could easily understand.

But in time, Tom Olsen did eventually earn our professional admiration and respect. He demanded perfection from all of his news staff and never accepted anything less. His critiques and disapprovals to first draft news articles were never kind, and he wasn't afraid to ream out any reporter who didn't measure up to his lofty journalistic standards. Olsen was very quality conscious and expected nothing less than one hundred percent from his newsroom reporters.

"Come into my office if you have a minute, buddy boy," he loudly requested in his usually low graveling voice. This was probably from the long-term effects of drinking Jack Daniels' for years, smoking unfiltered Lucky Strikes, and engaging in his ultra-high cholesterol diets.

As I walked into his office holding my Starbucks coffee, I was usually afraid to set it down on his desk without his handing me one of his wooden drink cup coasters. His dark, mahogany wooden desk looked like it had been stolen or borrowed from the Chicago Historical Society's attic. Nothing in his office was out of place, from his expensive Mountbatten fountain pen desk set to his expansive collection of crystal paperweights from around the world, strategically placed on a glass display case in the corner of his office.

Every time I walked into his office, I thought I was sitting in my grandmother's living room.

"What's up, boss man?"

"What's going on with the Kollar investigation? Have you figured out who killed her yet?"

"I've been rather busy, Tom."

"Of course, you have. You've been so busy throwing rose petals on Mayor Kollar's grave that you haven't had any time to figure out who put her there," pausing for a moment.

Olsen always likes to start his one on one conversations by trying to put me on edge.

"So, where the fuck are we at with this murder investigation?"

At that moment, my caffeine immediately kicked in.

"You know, Tom, I don't get you. First, you tell me to write up some favorable memorial pieces on our martyred, gunned-down mayor.

Then you bust my balls for not making any progress on her murder investigation."

Olsen started glaring at me before putting an unlit Lucky Strike cigarette in his mouth.

"Really? I said write a good news article, not some flowery prose out of some fucking Lord Byron poetry book."

"You ran with it, boss man."

He liked it when I called him that. It probably made him feel like some Mississippi plantation-slave owner.

"Against my better judgment. You're lucky that you've been around here for so long, McKay. Otherwise, you'd be composing your wordy, flowery poetry for the paper's obituary section."

I laughed in his face. "Maybe I have a future writing Hallmark greeting cards."

"Keep it up," he growled.

"You're just jealous that I got a nice phone call from Mayor Kollar's lesbian wife, and you didn't," I retorted.

"Spare me the bullshit, McKay."

He then started twirling that unlit cigarette in his mouth while looking as though he were deep in thought.

"So, who ordered the hit on Mayor Kollar? What have you found out so far?" Olsen asked, now addressing my presence at a professional, respectable level.

"I don't know, boss. She had so many fucking enemies in this town. I can't make up my mind where to start."

He looked at me, still trying to keep up with our bantering back and forth.

"Maybe you can help me set up a large wheel in my office, with the names of all the possible suspects that hated her guts, just like the 'Wheel of Fortune.'"

"Oh, great, McKay. And I supposed you're going to be Vanna White?"

"I don't have her legs, boss."

Maybe I was modest. At five feet, ten inches tall, my Rob Lowe good looks well accompanied my almost slim and trim figure, minus the sexy legs.

At that moment, Olsen started getting impatient.

"Stop fucking with me, buddy boy. What have you got?"

"Not much, boss man."

"What? You were at her funeral, McKay. Did you find out anything? What rumblings did you hear?"

"Not much. Everyone at the funeral was too busy whispering 'good riddance' under their breath. No one was wondering who her actual assassin was. The only ones who were mourning her at her funeral service were all of the African Americans and the gay community from Boys Town."

"What's the latest and greatest from Superintendent Byron? Where are they at in this investigation?"

"Only that he has his best police detectives working on this case," I replied.

"And which ones would that be?"

I then pulled out my cell phone, where I sometimes write down notes when I don't have a pen or paper to write on.

"According to my buddy from Channel Eight," I eagerly read, "Detectives Philip Dorian, Tommy Morton, and Dennis Romanowski."

Olsen looked at me, almost ready to swallow his unlit cigarette.

"Your buddy from Channel Eight? Please don't tell me you're talking to fucking Chaz Rizzo?"

"Well yeah, boss. We sat together at the mayor's funeral."

Olsen rolled his eyes up in the air.

"And he told you that? How the fuck does he know?"

"Said he got it from CPD," I replied.

"I wouldn't believe anything that came out of that fucking guy's mouth," Olsen growled.

"Not even for directions to the men's shithouse."

"I only believe him because he's tight with Dorian over at the Sixteenth District. The detective mentioned to him that he was working this case with his partner and Romanowski from the Eighteenth," I retorted, still wishing he would light up his cigarette already.

"Can you get in front of Dorian?"

"Not likely. That's why I was talking to Rizzo. He seems to be the only one who can get any information out of him."

There was a moment of silence as we were both turning ideas over in our heads.

"Try talking to Dennis Romanowski over at the Eighteenth. He seems to be a little more approachable than Dorian or Morton. You probably have a better shot at getting any information out of him."

"I'll try, boss," I said with a smile, taking another long sip of my semi-warm cup of Starbucks Americano coffee.

Olsen then started to shake his head.

"I wonder how Eddie Barrett is connected to all this?"

"Barrett? Really?"

"He's been rumored to have displaced several of his closest enemies into the bottom of Lake Michigan in years past," my assistant editor rationalized.

I only shook my head.

"Barrett isn't that stupid. Besides, who would be his likely gunmen?"

"Really, McKay? Think about it. Barrett has every Chicago mob boss and gang-banging warlord on his cellular speed dial. He could single-handedly order a hit on almost any politician he needed to get out of his way," Olsen rationalized, now chewing his unlit cigarette to the point of no return.

"I would agree, boss. Except that Mayor Kollar was the one who had the federal agents over at the FBI investigating him in his Fourteenth Ward office," I responded.

"Besides, Barrett is too smart to set himself up to be a prime suspect in a political hit and an assassination of a Chicago mayor."

"Don't be so sure, McKay. Eddie Barrett has been known to do a lot of bold, ballsy things in this town."

"I'm not sure, Tom. If Barrett were involved, I'm sure he would have insulated himself enough so that none of his City Hall cronies or street connections could ever rat him out," I replied, now swallowing the last drop of my coffee.

I then handed my empty styrofoam cup to my very anal assistant editor for its proper disposal.

"Start with Romanowski over at the Eighteenth. Maybe he can give you some investigative leads," Olsen suggested.

I got up from his wooden mahogany museum chair and began to make my way towards his office exit. As I was leaving, Olsen barked out another directive.

"And do me a favor, McKay? Keep your distance from Chaz Rizzo. We're not interested in doing any National Enquirer stories."

I looked at him and smiled.

"You know, boss, that isn't a bad idea. If I can get him to sit down at a gin mill and buy him drinks, maybe I pump out some serious leads out of him."

"Please, McKay. Whatever you get 'outta him, I don't want to know about it," Olsen answered.

"Now get 'outta here."

I gladly closed his office door behind me and took the closest path back to my office cubicle. I pulled out my paper pad and started scribbling down some notes and a few leads that I had discussed with Olsen.

I then went on the internet and looked up Detective Romanowski's District address, figuring that I had a better shot at dropping in on him than trying to make an appointment with his desk sergeant.

I had no idea where all the twists and turns of this investigative journey were about to take me.

CHAPTER TWELVE
THE PARKING GARAGE - AUGUST 4TH

A late-model, dark blue Ford Escape pulled into the multi-story parking lot on South Wabash near East Eighth Street on that hot summer evening. It was past midnight, and there were very few cars parked in the multi-layered parking facility on that Tuesday night. Because it was so close to Columbia College nearby, the parking lot was popular with those college students commuting to the business school for night classes.

As he pulled into the garage, he made sure that the parking garage's fourth floor was void of any cars.

The floor was empty.

The driver of the Ford Escape found a parking spot and waited. He was a taller man with a dark complexion and was casually well dressed, wearing light khaki Chino pants and a black Polo shirt. He usually conducted his covert meetings in that particular parking for its lack of lighting and location far away from the Chicago Loop. Since the parking lot lights went dim after eleven o'clock, it was the perfect site for any clandestine meeting.

At about 12:15, a black Chevrolet pickup truck pulled into the parking lot and the parking space next to the Ford Escape. The truck shut off its engine and sat there silently for several minutes. The pickup truck's glass windows were dark and blackened, as the driver of the Ford Escape couldn't see who was behind the wheel. His superiors only instructed him to meet at that specific location at that particular time, as a very important drop off was about to be made.

At approximately 12:30, an African American male, roughly in his late thirties, wearing a black tee-shirt and baggy pants, got out of the truck and approached the Ford Escape from the passenger side.

"Are you Javier?" the black man asked the driver of the dark blue Ford.

"Open up your truck doors, and show me that you're alone," the well-dressed man immediately demanded.

The black man opened both truck doors, disclosing that he had indeed arrived alone. He then went back to the car, where Javier opened the passenger door for the black man to get inside.

"You must be Terrell."

"I am," the black man responded. Both men were aware that they were using fake names as their aliases and contacted each other using burner phones that could not be used again or traced.

Javier reached over to his car's back seat and pulled out an old, worn brown briefcase. He then placed it on his lap in his car's front seat and opened it up, disclosing its contents.

There were fifteen stacks of neatly bundled one-hundred-dollar bills, in denominations of one thousand dollars tightly wrapped in each bundle, totaling one hundred and fifty thousand dollars.

Terrell looked at the contents of the briefcase and smiled. He knew that his boss would be happy to finally receive the payoff they had patiently waited for the assassination hit they had performed on Mayor Kollar two weeks before.

Terrell was a tall, African American, thirty-six-year-old ex-convict with quite a checkered past. He had been convicted several times and had served his time at the Menard Correctional Facility downstate. He had spent so much time at Menard that he knew most of the jail guards on a first name basis, having been there several times since he was eighteen years old.

To say that he was a life-long career criminal was an understatement. His last stint in prison was for attempted murder in a bank robbery gone wrong, where he had severally wounded a security guard back in 2002. He had just been released on good behavior six months ago and was now back on the streets doing what he did best.

Both men kept their real names and identities secret from one another, and both made it extra clear that after this transaction was completed, neither one would ever have the pleasure of seeing the other person again.

But what was more impressive was the anonymity of the parties for whom they worked. Javier had no idea who Terrell was or who employed them, and vice versa. The only thing that they were aware of was that Javier was in charge of meeting Terrell at the parking garage to make the cash handoff for a political hit on a very influential and very powerful person in City Hall.

Nobody asked any questions. Nobody asked for any details. It was a simple transaction, where a dilapidated brown briefcase filled with one hundred and fifty thousand dollars in unmarked bills was quietly passed off from one party to another.

This was not their first go around.

Javier worked for a very influential faction, whose wealth and influence in Chicago's City was without question. He had been familiar with making brown bag transactions for his boss many times before, and he found it very discreet and safe to do so in that particular parking garage.

Terrell was also familiar with doing business covertly for his superiors. Having done several drugs and other covert deals in the past for his boss, he knew how to stay under the radar to ensure that these large monetary transactions were done without any knowledge of anyone else from the outside world.

He received a three percent cut of whatever he delivered to his bosses, and he knew not to ask any questions. He was there to receive that dilapidated brown briefcase and do nothing else.

Take the briefcase and bring it from Point A to Point B, he was instructed.

Stay stupid and keep your mouth shut, he was told.

This was a task that Terrell was very good at doing. Having just been released from the joint six months prior, he could use the money and was not about to ask any real questions.

Forty-five hundred dollars was a nice score, he thought to himself.

"It's all there," Javier said to Terrell.

He quickly closed the briefcase and handed it to Terrell.

Smiling, he offered to shake Javier's hand, but Javier refused. He only looked at his open hand and instructed him to leave.

"You need to get the fuck out of here," he only said.

Javier was with a very prominent, very influential organization indeed. They were quite used to paying for professional hits on people who needed to be taken out and pushed out of the way. With Mayor Kollar's assassination, many influential people believed that their lives would be much better off without the former prosecutor-turned-mayor around.

Mayor Kollar was an idealistic do-gooder. She was a civic leader who became a politician with minimal administrative experience in the government sector, other than her stint as a Cook County prosecutor. Kollar saw herself as a 'super-hero' of sorts, who would chase away all of the bad guys out of City Hall and clean up her embattled city. She was obviously very naïve politically, thinking that as the 'new sheriff in town,' she could clean up decades of corruption in City Hall.

She had absolutely no fucking idea what she was up against.

With her assassination, the city's various political and criminal sectors could now go back to business as usual. As always, it was who you knew and how you were connected that greased the wheels of the local democracy of the Second City. Building permits without city council approval could now be issued for a fee, and governmental jobs for political favors could now be granted without the supervision of any legal watchdogs or the State's Attorney's office.

For the price of one hundred and fifty thousand dollars and two bullets, the City of Chicago was now back in business.

Terrell grabbed the briefcase and opened the passenger door.

"You have a nice life," was all that he said to Javier as he quickly got out of the vehicle and into his black pickup truck.

He turned on the ignition. He then rapidly pulled out of his parking space and out of the parking garage within seconds.

Javier sat in his car for a few long minutes, waiting for the black pickup truck to get far enough away from that location for him to leave safely. He looked around the parking garage and then suddenly noticed something very unusual.

Approximately three hundred yards away was a black Ford Crown Victoria parked in another parking space. Observing upon closer inspection, he could tell that another person was sitting inside of that vehicle.

Javier sat still, waiting for someone to come out of that car. The stranger had observed the handoff between Terrell and himself.

How did he not notice that vehicle before? Was it parked there the whole time?

At that moment, Javier became very apprehensive. Someone must have been tipped off to this transaction, and someone was there to witness the handoff. At that moment, Javier went into his glove box and pulled out his Beretta 92MM handgun. He quickly inserted the gun clip and shoved the gun inside his belt, under his black Polo shirt.

He then exited his Ford Escape and began to walk towards the dark, unmarked Crown Victoria. As he walked closer, he noticed a man sitting in his car, making eye contact with him.

Javier had never seen him before. The stranger had dark salt and pepper hair and was wearing sunglasses in a dark parking garage.

As Javier approached the vehicle, he was within fifty feet of the car. The Crown Victoria suddenly started up and began to drive at high speed towards him.

Javier pulled out his handgun and got a shot off at the vehicle, completely missing the moving target. As the car got closer to Javier, it quickly veered out of the way and exited the parking garage at high speed. Javier fell to the ground as the car narrowly missed running him over. Within seconds, the unmarked vehicle was gone.

Who was it behind the wheel? Javier didn't recognize him, and he must have observed the entire transaction. He got up and dusted himself off, putting his gun back into his pants behind his belt buckle. Javier then quickly rushed to the edge of the parking lot facing South Wabash. He noticed the car going northbound, towards the city and the Eisenhower Expressway. But it was too late for him to go after the car. He didn't get a license plate number. Javier didn't recognize the driver. He only saw the dark Crown Victoria going northbound, peeling its tires as it exited the parking garage.

Someone else knew about their secret, clandestine meeting and transaction, but he had no idea who. This whole operation was conducted very discretely, and only his boss knew about this 'hired hit.'

Javier got extraordinarily nervous and began to sweat profusely. He knew that if he told his boss that someone else had seen them making the handoff in the parking lot, he would be blamed for not being careful.

A mistake like that could very well cost him his life.

This professional hit was to be done under total secrecy for very obvious reasons, and Javier had made sure that no one else was on that parking lot floor when he pulled his car in earlier. The vehicle must have pulled into the parking lot from the other side of the garage without his noticing.

Javier quickly got back into his Ford Escape and started the ignition. Stepping on the accelerator, he pulled out of the parking lot as soon as he could. Javier knew that he had to run out of there before someone else had discovered him there.

Was that person some kind of informant? Javier knew that undercover cops usually drove unmarked Crown Victoria vehicles. Was it an undercover detective from the Chicago P.D.? Was it someone from one of Chicago's organized crime families who had become privy to this secret hit? Was it someone from City Hall? Was it someone that his boss had hired to ensure that the whole cash payoff occurred without a hitch?

As he was going southbound on Wabash Avenue, his burner phone started ringing.

It was his boss.

"No problems?" a familiar voice over the burner phone said.

There was a hesitation of about five seconds.
"No problems, boss. No problems at all."
"Good."
There was a long silence over the line until he heard a click from the other end. Javier then hit the end button of his cellular phone.

As he drove southbound on Wabash, he kept turning the face of that driver over and over in his head. The strange driver was an older man, dark-haired with salt and pepper hair, dark complexion, wearing very dark sunglasses as he exited the unlit parking garage. He never saw the man before, and he was unfamiliar.

Who in the hell could he be?

Javier said a prayer to himself. He realized that he couldn't tell anyone that another vehicle was in that parking garage, probably watching them make the handoff. He would have to deny ever seeing anyone else.

He had no idea that there were other parties very interested in this transaction.

Chapter Thirteen
The Chess Game-August 5th

The aroma of the tomato sauce had run rampant throughout the church rectory, as Fr. Colin Fitzgerald had changed into his casual attire for dinner on that Wednesday evening. Wearing a blue, button-down Oxford shirt and his favorite pair of Levi jeans, the pastor was excited to receive his special dinner guest for that evening.

Most of Fr. Fitz's parishioners and close friends were well aware of his Wednesday night chess matches after dinner in the old but elaborate living room of his church rectory on West 79th Street. The typical plan included a vast, ornate Italian meal specially prepared by his seventy-two-year-old house cook, Mrs. Madeline Valenti, where the pastor would usually enjoy with a few of his guests. After an hour or so of enjoying their exquisite dinner, they would retreat to his living room, where the priest would have his chess set arranged and ready to play.

But that evening was a special one indeed. A few days ago, Fr. Fitz had specifically requested Anthony 'Little Tony' DiMatteo the honor of his presence, enjoying a quiet dinner together and relaxing afterward for a friendly game of chess.

At precisely six-thirty, the front doorbell rang. Fr. Fitz eagerly glanced out the front window to see a new, shiny black Maserati parked in front of St. Simeon's rectory on West 79th Street. His heart started to beat a little faster, anticipating that this evening would turn out to be the way he had hoped.

He pulled the brass knob of the old, walnut entrance door and greeted his guest.

"Hello, Tony. So glad you could make it."

"The traffic getting down here was brutal, Father. I don't know how you manage to get anywhere around here," Little Tony gripped, describing the severe traffic problems that have plagued the very busy, one lane boulevard for several years.

They both shook hands as the Capo dei Capi entered the rectory. He was immediately assaulted by the tomato sauce's aroma smell from the kitchen as he followed the older pastor into the dining room of that old parish residence.

He seemed to tower over the short but stocky Mafioso at over six feet tall as they both sat down at the dinner table. The long, mahogany dining room table was surrounded by twelve chairs and could have doubled for an elaborate conference table with its oak-laden chairs and red velvet cushion seats. Mrs. Valenti had set the table for two, with Fr. Fitz's chair at the end of the dining room table and Tony's table setting immediately to his left. The gold-plated, white porcelain dinnerware and gold-plated forks and knives looked like they had been put out for service from Buckingham Palace instead of the parish rectory of St. Simeon.

"Gee, Father. You better make sure that you frisk me before I leave tonight," Little Tony joked as they both sat down at the table.

"I may be stealing some of these gold platted utensils before I leave."

"Don't be fooled by the expensive dinnerware, Tony. They were a gift from the Archdiocese over fifty years ago to our parish and are only used on rare occasions," the pastor explained.

"Well, I guess if the church needs the money, you can always hock the silverware," Tony chuckled.

At that moment, Mrs. Valenti brought out an elaborate antipasto tray with some slices of prosciutto-wrapped in cantaloupe, black pitted olives, several pieces of mortadella lunchmeat, several portions of cheese and freshly toasted bruschetta bread with olive oil and freshly diced tomatoes. The older lady, dressed in a long, white apron, was introduced to the infamous crime family member, as the two of them exchanged pleasantries with several Italian phrases.

"How would you like to come and work for me?" Tony joked as he began to sample the antipasto food goodies that were intricately placed on the large serving plate.

"Grazie, Signore DiMatteo. But the pastor is very good to me," she smiled, responding with a very slight Italian accent.

Fr. Fitz and Little Tony began to talk and engage in an amicable, intellectual conversation about politics and religion. Mrs. Valenti brought over the main pasta dish of farfalle with vodka sauce, entrees of veal parmigiana con fungi, insalata con pesce, and some other elaborate Italian delights. The two of them enjoyed the extravagant Italian meal for almost two hours, as they engaged in a convoluted discussion of each other's political beliefs and viewpoints.

Although Fr. Fitz was a staunch Democrat, he was not in favor of the current political unrest that was going on throughout the city. He felt very strongly that the radical minorities should find other, more peaceful means of instigating the social change and racial inequities they were trying to address. Being a lifelong Republican, Little Tony felt no need for the radical left demonstrations even to be occurring, let alone exhibiting protests and violence on Chicago's streets.

After Italian espressos and tiramisu' desserts were served, the two of them walked over to the rectory living room. Dark, cherry wood adorned the formal living room's four walls with matching crown molding intricately placed along with the ceiling. Two antique lamps were lit on each side of the room, with a glass-topped coffee table set in the middle of the chamber. On top was a costly, ivory chess set, with each chess piece placed in their appropriate starting position on an old, wooden checkered board. On each side of the coffee table was a high backed, dark velvet chair set appropriately for each player, waiting for the two of them to engage in the intricate board game.

"Shall we?" the pastor invited Little Tony to sit down, immediately choosing the black chess pieces as his weapons of choice.

"I'll take black, Father, since I'm the one with the criminal record," Tony joked, as the smiling priest sat behind the board game, getting himself ready to make the first move. He started by moving his white pawn two spaces forward, which was his typical opening move:

White – g4.
Tony immediately responded by moving his black pawn to its appropriate beginning move:
Black – d4.
Fr. Fitz made the next move:
White – f4.
Tony sat there and pondered the pastor's second chess move, and then moved his pawn:
Black – f3.
Then the Fr. Fitz made his next move:
White – h4.
Little Tony immediately saw the opportunity to take his queen chess piece and attack his king, putting the pastor in check. But he instead moved his bishop:
Black – Bd3.
Fr. Fitz then moved his rook:
White –Rh3.
Little Tony then saw the opportunity to put the pastor in check:
Black – Qxh5, overtaking his white pawn.
"Check" Little Tony exclaimed.
Fr. Fitz looked at Little Tony, immediately realizing that the Mafioso had put his queen chess piece in immediate jeopardy by placing it in front of the rook, where it would instantly be taken:
White – Rxh4.
"Rook takes Queen," Fr. Fitz announced.
"Oh fuck, I lost my queen," Little Tony observed. At that moment, the pastor realized that Little Tony was probably very rusty in exposing his queen to be immediately overtaken by his white rook.
But then Tony cleverly moved his bishop.
Black – Bg3.

"Checkmate," Little Tony announced.

The Capo dei Capi had beaten the pastor in just five moves.

Fr. Fitz smiled at the Mafioso. He then tipped over his king, now acknowledging his loss to the Chicago Capo.
"Well, that was a short game," the pastor stated.
Fr. Fitz then got up from his chair and walked over to his bureau drawer near the lamp, where he had kept a white envelope stuffed with five thousand dollars in new, crisp, one-hundred-dollar bills. He then surrendered the envelope to the Mafia don.
"Well, that was the easiest five thousand bucks I ever made," Little Tony smiled, looking very pleased with himself.
At that moment, Fr. Fitz seized the opportunity.
"Tony, have you ever thought about getting involved in helping control some of the violence that is going on right now in our city?"
The Capo dei Capi looked at the church pastor.
"Getting involved? How the hell can I get involved?"
"You know, Tony, the last time there was any real tranquility in Chicago when the organized crime outfits were controlling Chicago," the pastor opened.
"The politicians were on the take, and 'The Outfit' were keeping peace with the warring factions that were trying to overtake this city," Fr. Fitz informed him.

"Yeah, back during the Fifties and Sixties, when Mayor Daley was running this fucking town," Tony replied.

"There was never any doubt that the organized crime families like the Giancana's and the Accardo's were the ones keeping the peace in Chicago," the pastor observed.

Little Tony slowly smiled.

"Yeah, those were the days."

"So, what happened, Tony? Why can't those days of 'The Outfit' come back to where the politicians were put in their places, and the street gangs were kept in control?"

He was cautious not to use the word 'Mafia.'

Little Tony looked at the pastor, almost as though he had suddenly become ignorant.

"Father, are you fucking kidding me? We now have the FBI with their fucking RICO laws tailing and busting our asses for the last forty years. We can't even fart sideways anymore without their goddamn wiretaps and family informants flipping on us and sticking it up our asses at every turn," Tony replied.

"We've all had to keep a low profile just to survive, Father."

He paused for a moment, then bluntly summarized,

"Those days are fucking long gone."

"But they don't have to be, especially now, Tony," the pastor responded.

Little Tony glared at the pastor, trying to figure out what his angle was in all of this.

"With all of the looting and violence going on, the established businesses in the city are now desperate and looking for ways to escape all of the violence. They need protection from all of the looters and gangs that are hiding behind these 'Black Lives Matter' protests, Tony."

There was a moment of silence between the two of them as Fr. Fitz began to make his point.

"The only ones who can legitimately provide that protection are the organized crime families in this city."

"Protection, huh?"

"Well yeah, Tony. What if the organized crime families in Chicago starting working together to provide protection? What if 'The Outfit' began offering security, if you will, to all of these businesses getting looted with all of this inner-city violence that is going on between these warring street gangs?"

"Security how, Father?"

Fr. Fitz looked directly into Little Tony's eyes.

"The coppers can't shoot to kill anymore, so why can't the security companies?" the pastor asked.

"What's stopping a security guard from shooting and killing a looter carrying a violent weapon of some kind as he is breaking down windows and stealing merchandise?" Fr. Fitz posed as a question to the Chicago Mafioso.

"What's stopping these criminals from being shot to death by some security guard who felt that his life was being threatened as his store was being looted and vandalized?"

Little Tony looked at the pastor.

"None of all of this inner-city violence is my problem, Father."

Tony then smiled at the priest.

"Since when is a Catholic priest promoting violence and murder as a form of advocating peace in the city?"

"Do you see any other options, Tony?" the pastor asked.

"The police can't do anything anymore. If the cops even so much as touch an offender, especially an African American one, protests of violence and looting immediately begin in this city. Not even Michigan Avenue is safe anymore."

Little Tony looked intently at the pastor.

"We're in the food distribution business, Father. We don't go around 'acing' and 'whacking' people anymore. That shit stopped a long time ago, and there's too much heat in that now. Those days are long gone. We can't even go after the rats who owe us money like we used to. The Feds got us by the balls!" Little Tony protested.

"And by the way, Father...what's your angle in all of this? Why do you care who's controlling the city and all the violence that's going on?"

Fr. Fitz then looked even more intently at Little Tony.

"My parishioners are afraid, Tony. They're afraid to walk the streets. I have hungry families that won't even leave their houses anymore because they're too afraid they'll be shot. With no parishioners, Tony, we have no contributions and now, very little money."

There was a moment of silence between the two of the most significant heavyweights within Chicago's city limits. One was a well-known political activist who has successfully hidden behind his parish church's large, intricate doors. The other was the most formidable syndicate crime boss in the Windy City.

"Come on, Tony. Let's cut the crap. You're the head of one of the strongest, most dangerous crime families in the City of Chicago right now. If anybody can bring peace into this city with the butt of a gun, it would be you, Tony."

"We're legitimate businessmen, Father. We don't do that shit."

Fr. Fitz laughed out loud.

"And I believe that for all of about three seconds. When your interests and business assets are being threatened, you always do whatever you have to do to take control of the situation," the priest rightfully observed.

Little Tony looked down on the chessboard and shook his head, smiling.

"You threw this fucking chess game, didn't you?" Little Tony observed.

"You threw this chess match so that you could corner me into hearing your lecture and preach to me about how 'The Outfit' should retake control of this city."

The pastor smiled.

"No, Tony. You beat me, fair and square."

"In five moves, Father? Who the fuck are you bullshitting?"

Fr. Fitz smiled broadly at Little Tony.

"Come back next Wednesday and give me the chance to win my money back."

While still holding the envelope filled with cash, Little Tony placed it back in the middle of the chessboard, knocking down a few chess pieces in the process.

"You can have this money back, Father. You don't have to entice and bribe me into coming back here and gambling with you over a game of chess."

He then rose from his chair and started to walk towards the front door of the rectory.

The parish pastor walked after him as if he was trying to stop him from going to the door.

'Tony, come back here next Wednesday. We'll have dinner and play another game of chess. Besides, my ego is hurting right now. I can't remember the last time I was beaten and checkmated in five easy moves."

The Mafioso shook his head.

"You threw that game, Father, admit it! I wasn't born fucking yesterday. A seasoned chess master like yourself? Come on, Fr. Fitz, cut the bullshit!"

Fr. Fitz smiled.

"You beat me fair and square, Tony. Besides, I enjoyed our very entertaining sociology discussion tonight."

He paused for a moment.

"You know, Tony, you're a very smart man. It takes a considerable amount of intelligence and tenacity to get to the position where you are now in your life. You're not the ruthless criminal that you portray yourself out to others. You're a brilliant, decent man."

Little Tony smiled at the pastor. He knew that he was being sucked up to and flattered, but he liked it all the same.

He then extended his hand out to Fr. Fitz.

"Don't tell anybody," Tony grinned.

"Come back here next Wednesday, Tony. I would love to have you back. I truly enjoyed your company tonight."

The two of them shook hands as Tony grasped the doorknob, then exiting the front entrance.

"See you next week, Father."

Fr. Fitz then closed the front door behind him as he walked down the front stairs and into his waiting black Maserati.

The St. Simeon pastor *did indeed* throw that chess match. He didn't want to scare and intimidate Little Tony immediately with his seasoned, sophisticated chess skills. Father Fitzgerald had been playing chess since he was at St. Barnabas Grade School in Chicago's Beverly neighborhood. He knew how to successfully 'throw' a chess match.

Fr. Fitz also knew that, deep in his heart, that Little Tony would never accept and keep that cash envelope. He felt that by letting DiMatteo win at chess and hold his money, Tony DiMatteo would become his captive audience.

Little Tony was forced that evening to listen to his sociology lecture. The crime boss was coerced into hearing the pastor preach to him about how Chicago's intricate crime families could quickly and forcefully fix the city's urban problems.

As he turned on the outdoor porch light and watched Little Tony pull away, Fr. Colin Fitzgerald smiled to himself.

He knew that he had successfully planted the seed.

CHAPTER FOURTEEN
NORTH KEELER AVENUE-AUGUST 6TH

It was a comfortable summer evening in Chicago, as several Black Cobras cruised southbound on South Halsted Street. It was just past eleven o'clock, and James 'Two-Bit' Harding, David 'Downtown' Coolidge, and a few other Cobra brothers were cruising their territory on that evening. They had just made a score on a sale of some 'white powder' that night, and two of them were doing an 'eight-ball' in the back seat while Downtown was maneuvering their black, late model Rolls Royce Phantom. He was snorting on his silver flask filled with Jim Beam Whiskey while making sure he was keeping his eye on the road.

It had been a good night so far. They had collected three thousand dollars in cash from a drug sale, plus another fifty 'Benjamin's' from a crack house on 115th in the Putnam neighborhood. They were sitting on quite a bit of cash in the car, but Two-Bit wasn't worried. They had a shopping bag filled with money from that evening stuffed under the front seat of their car. Two-Bit wanted to get back to their house on South Union Street so that he could cut up the money with Big-Dog Phillips and the others.

But that wasn't all of it. Two-Bit had another stash in the trunk of the car that he had in a locked briefcase that he had picked up from Terrell for a handoff he had received in the parking garage early that morning. That briefcase was the proceeds from the 'contract fees' that they would be cutting up and passing out to the brother Black Cobras who had handled that little 'hit' that was done in Logan Square last July 19th.

One-hundred-fifty thousand was initially in that briefcase. Three percent or $4,500 went to Terrell the Collector, who had received Javier's handoff at the parking garage on South Wabash the night before. With the $145,500 leftover, Downtown and Two-Bit took their cut of twenty percent or $29,100 to split between themselves. That was their fee for finding the shooter who was willing to go into that second floor of that vacant house next door to Mayor Kollar's home and fire off two rounds from a collapsible rifle in the middle of a Sunday afternoon.

When Downtown and Two-Bit were given the contract, Javier told them that the money was coming from someone 'big' in the city, and they needed that contract done before the end of July. They made the mistake of not telling Big-Dog Phillips about it because they both knew that he would never do such a contract hit. Plus, because of Big-Dog being out on bail, they both knew that he or the Black Cobras couldn't 'officially' get involved in such a high profile murder.

At first, the two gang-members had trouble finding anyone within their gang of Black Cobras who could successfully perform the contract with a high-power rifle from over one hundred yards away. Nobody in their gang was that good of a marksman, so the two went elsewhere to find a sharp-shooter.

Two-Bit had a tight connection with the Satan's Disciples, a small street gang on the west side of Chicago. He had a very close relationship with his first cousin, Giovante 'Lil' Bro' Johnson, whom he had known all of his life. He had tried to recruit his cousin away from the small west side gang. But Lil' Bro felt an allegiance to the head of their little club, a dangerous man by the name of Amatore 'Three Chin' Stewart.

Three Chin Stewart was amply named for his five-foot, six-inch, two-hundred-and-eighty-pound frame. He wore three large 18-karat Italian chains around his neck and had two gold teeth in his mouth. Two-Bit only got along with him because of his cousin, but deep down, he was warned by others not to trust him.

He happened to ask his cousin if they knew or had anyone with a collapsible rifle who could hit a target from one hundred yards away. His first cousin knew of a sharpshooting marksman in their gang who could successfully pull off this contract. Because they wanted to stay anonymous and didn't want to know his identity, they sent one of their other Cobra gang members to observe this Satan's Disciple sharpshooter during target practice in a vacant lot last Memorial Day Weekend.

According to their connection, Satan's Disciples indeed had a capable sharpshooter who could carry out the hit. Two-Bit fronted a deposit of five-thousand dollars to Satan's Disciple gang leader, and they would be responsible for getting the shooting done. When the political assassination was accomplished, Downtown and Two-Bit would pay the remainder of the contract amount, minus their deposits and collection fees.

Two-Bit and Downtown didn't know who the actual assassin was. And they didn't want to know. Their first concern was that they receive the cash from the parking garage handoff between Terrell and Javier. Afterward, their problem was getting the rest of the money to his cousin and the Satan's Disciples and taking their cut without Big Dog's knowledge.

There was one last stop that evening, and it wasn't going to happen until after midnight. Two-Bit and Downtown, along with their Cobra bodyguards, were to hook-up in an alley on the west side of Chicago in a vacant residential garage, which they agreed to meet up and make the hand-off. The alley was located off Grand Avenue and North Keeler Avenue, and Two-Bit had the exact address.

At 12:55, the black Rolls Royce pulled up in front of the house on 1406 North Keeler Avenue, turned off its lights, and the four of them sat in their car in silence. Two-Bit immediately noticed a 'For Sale' sign sitting in front of the house on the lawn. There were no lights on anywhere in the house, and it looked noticeably vacant.

"This house is fuckin' empty, brothas," Downtown observed.

This area was not within their street gang territory, and Two-Bit knew that there was a risk going into that neighborhood without any other outside protection. They all took out their 'Glocks' and made sure their gun clips were attached and fully loaded.

"You sure dis' tha' place we meetin'?" one of the Cobras asked Two-Bit.

"Yeah, bitch. I hope they ain't no otha' muthafuckaz 'round ta' lite our asses the fuck up." Two-Bit responded.

The four of them realized that they were out of their element in making a very large cash handoff to some other gang members that were not a part of their group.

They waited in front of the house until Two-Bit got the text from his cousin, 'Lil Bro.' They then pulled into the alley slowly until locating the garage where the meeting was going to occur. One of Satan's Disciples was standing outside to direct the Rolls Royce inside.

The car pulled inside the well-lit garage, and they shut off the car. The four of them got out of the vehicle, and Two-Bit man-hugged his cousin.

"Was' up, brotha? Ya' lookin' good muthafucka. Glad we was able to pull this shit out, man."

"Yeah, dude. We got every fuckin' city pig chasin' our fuckin' asses, man. There's a lotta goddamn heat comin' down, muthafucka," Lil' Bro replied.

There were three other Satan's Disciples standing around, all carrying their handguns displayed over their tee shirts.

"You got da' presidents, man?"

"Yeah, they's all in da' briefcase in the back trunk."

At that moment, Downtown opened the trunk of the Rolls Royce and pulled out the old, brown briefcase. He took out the key from his pocket and opened the case.

There was a little over one hundred and forty-five thousand dollars in cash.

"It's all fuckin' there."

"Yeah, but Terrell the Collector took $4500 for his collection fee. Now you owe me five thousand dollars from the deposit I gave you upfront plus our twenty percent."

Two-Bit and Downtown had agreed to cut up the rest of the money in the garage when they arrived.

Downtown put the dark, old briefcase on top of the wooden table next to a silver toolbox and opened it up. Two-Bit and Downtown began to count up the money in the suitcase out loud in front of Little Bro and three other Satan's Disciples.

"It's all there, brotha. One-hundred and forty-five large," Two-Bit said.

At that moment, Two-Bit began to count out their twenty percent commission fee of $29,000, plus the upfront deposit of $5000, or $34,000. As they were counting up the cash, another one of the Satan's Disciples pulled out an AK-47 that he had hidden behind the garage door and pointed it at the four Black Cobras.

At that moment, Three-Chin loudly spoke up, not taking kindly to the Black Cobras taking their cut of the money.

"Put that fuckin' money back, muthafucka. You guys ain't taken shit."

"Wait a fuckin' minute, man. We made a fuckin' deal, Nigga. We's takin' our twenty percent off the top plus the deposit. We made a fuckin' deal, muthafucka."

"No, Niggas. We's done the shootin'. We's takin' the heat, So, we's is takin' all the fuckin' money."

At that moment, Downtown, who was known for having an uncontrollable temper, began to pull out his Glock 9MM handgun. He didn't get the chance even to pull the trigger and fire off a round when the Satan's Disciple gang member started shooting his AK-47 at the four Black Cobras.

He got off at least fifty rounds, shooting the four gang members all over their bodies and heads, with blood splattering everywhere. By the time the shooting was over, their blood was splattered all over the garage, the Rolls Royce, and on the door of the garage and the concrete floor.

At that moment, Lil' Bro took the briefcase filled with cash, closed and locked it. The four Satan's Disciples then shut off the light of the garage and locked the garage door. The four Black Cobras were dead, their mutilated bodies scattered in the empty garage on North Keeler Avenue.

The four Satan's Disciples got into their late-model Cadillac Escalade parked on the side street and quickly left the murder scene. The red blood from the mutilated bodies of those rival gang members had now almost completely covered the floor of the garage.

The vacant garage was now black and silent.

The only other sounds in that dark garage were the flies and other insects that were beginning to buzz around, accumulating on those four, mutilated dead bodies.

And the faint beeping sound from Two-Bit's cellular phone.

CHAPTER FIFTEEN
DETECTIVE PHILLIP DORIAN - AUGUST 7TH

Detective Dorian was sitting at his desk, eating his Subway sandwich at the Sixteenth District Area Five in Jefferson Park. It had been a slow morning that day, and he was finishing up some prior case paperwork when he received a phone call at a little after one o'clock in the afternoon.
"Detective Dorian speaking."
He was trying to answer his desk phone with his mouth still full of the last bite of my turkey sandwich.
"Phil? It's Tommy," said the voice on the other line.
"What's up to Tommy? How's it going?"
"Great, Phil. Except we've got some victims here at 1406 North Keeler, and we don't have any spare detectives to come over and help us. Can you come over?" he politely asked.
"Victims? How many?"
"Four of them, Phil. Four African American men in their twenties and thirties. Looks like a gang-hit."
"I don't know, Tommy. I just finished my lunch, and I'm not sure if I'm in the mood for..." Dorian said, trying to joke with his partner.
"Can you get here quick? We could use your help." Dorian was surprised at the urgency of his partner's voice. He sounded way too serious.
"Ok, Tommy. I'll be right over."
He dusted the breadcrumbs off of his desk and grabbed his suit coat. He figured this was probably some alley gangbangers caught up in a drug deal gone south. Dorian had seen many of those lately. Some of the detectives in his unit have been helping over in the Seventh District in the Englewood neighborhood on the south side of Chicago, where the drug wars and the gang member bodies had been piling up. Dorian jumped

into his Crown Victoria police car and sped over to the Garfield neighborhood. With the sirens on, he was at the North Keeler address in less than ten minutes.

Detective Tommy Morton was anxiously awaiting his arrival at the driveway of the home. The patrolmen had already posted the crime scene tape around the house, and there were Chicago EMT Units and several more police cars parked in front of the crime scene.

"Hey, Tommy, what do we got?" I said as we shook hands.

"Hey, Phil. You have a little more experience in these kinds of murders. "

"What kind of murders are we talking about?" he innocently asked.

"Gangbangers...four dead ones. Come with me to the garage."

He followed Detective Morton around the house and to the garage in the back facing the alley, where there were several other patrolmen and a couple of guys from the Chicago Fire Department.

He was shocked at the gruesome murder scene.

In the middle of the garage were the four shot-up, mutilated bodies of Black Cobras gang members. Dorian immediately recognized one of them, lying on the floor in front of the garage's toolbox. The other three were scattered around a newer model, black Rolls Royce, which looked like it had absorbed several rounds of bullets around the car's chassis and windshields. Three gang members had weapons in their hands, while the gang member, Two-Bit, was shot up, disfigured, and lying face up.

"Welcome to the O-K Corral," Morton said, while the other detectives were outlining the bodies and marking off where the bullet shells were discovered.

"Or the street gang version of the St. Valentine's Day massacre," Dorian answered.

"What do you think happened here?"

"Looks like some sort of drug deal gone wrong. But the strange thing is, there aren't that many drugs here. There are some traces of cocaine in the back seat, and a manilla envelope with eight thousand dollars in cash stuffed under the front seat."

Dorian looked around, starting to observe the stench of the tangled, murdered dead bodies.

"These guys have been dead for a while."

"Yes. Probably over thirty-six hours," Morton responded.

Dorian kept looking intently at the dead bodies, seeing other gang members that he might recognize. One of them was wearing a black sweatshirt hoodie with some gang logo on it, which revealed their gang affiliation.

"Who reported this?"

"A real estate agent. The house is vacant and is on the market. The real estate saleswoman had a showing this morning and immediately noticed the stench coming from the garage. She called it in, and we have her in the squad car right now. She's pretty shaken up."

"Nobody heard anything?"

"We have some patrolmen scouring the neighborhood for any witnesses. So far, no one has said that they heard anything."

Dorian shook his head.

"What kind of weapon was used; do you think?"

"An AK-47 assault rifle, probably with a bump stock of some kind."

Dorian continued to walk around the garage, wearing his mask and latex gloves. Most of the victims were so shot up and unrecognizable that it would probably take some prints and their dental records to make an identification.

The Chicago P.D. Crime Scene Investigation had just arrived, and they were taking prints and blood samples from the victims. Dorian noticed that each one of the victims had handguns, so he ordered the CSI investigators to collect their guns and place them in plastic bags for testing. They also checked for their identification both in the Rolls Royce and in their wallets. From the driver's licenses that were found, their identities were the following:

James Harding, 32, of Chicago (aka Two-Bit)
David Coolidge, 29, of Chicago (aka Downtown)
Vyto Jones, 27, Homewood (aka Mickey-Cash)
Gino Lewis, 25, of Maywood (aka Gigi-Blow)

It was a gruesome crime scene. One of the victims, Two-Bit Harding, had his face shot up so severely that his eyeballs had been blown out of their sockets and brain matter had spilled onto the concrete garage floor. The others were equally unrecognizable. It was as though the shooters took special pride in making sure that all of the bullets had been aimed at their heads. Their torsos were equally shot up, as there had been approximately over one hundred rounds of bullets shot into the four victims.

There was a pool of blood everywhere around each of the bodies, which had spilled underneath the Rolls Royce and under all four tires of the car.

Tommy kept shaking his head as Dorian kept staring at the corpses in total amazement.

"These bangers have turned murder into an art form," observed Detective Morton.

Detective Dorian continued to study the victims, trying to process the whole murder scene. He had not seen such a gruesome crime scene since investigating those 'Pedophile Priest Murders' two years ago.

Dorian and Morton continued to stare at the four dead bodies, still dripping blood onto the garage floor.

"Have you interviewed the real estate lady?" Detective Dorian asked.

"Yes. Her name is Rita Neri, and she has an office in the city. This house has been on the market for several months now, and the owners moved out last month."

"Do we have the names of the owners of this property?"

"Yes...a polish couple named Andrej and Bozena Karponowski."

"Let's try to contact them and find out what they know."

Morton walked over to the service entrance door next to the garage door. He looked at the doorknob intently while CSI dusted it off from prints.

"Phil, this door lock has been picked open. Looks liked the doorknob wasn't working."

Dorian walked over to the door and played with the door lock, noticing that the doorknob had been tampered with.

"These shooters probably gained access to the garage knowing that no one was home at the time and used it as their meeting place," Dorian observed.

He kept staring at the bodies, then walked around the garage, looking for any other apparent clues.

"So, this probably wasn't a drug deal."

"No, Phil, I think it was some kind of meeting gone wrong, probably between different gangs in the neighborhood," Morton replied.

"These guys are Black Cobras. Who would the other gang members in the area be?" Dorian inquired.

"The only ones I know about in this area is a small gang called Satan's Disciples. There is another small gang called the Black Saviors, but those guys aren't ballsy enough to pull off a bloody massacre like this."

"Why?"

"They're all a bunch of black, young punks. They're into selling heaters, blow, and street candy. They're not bold enough to take out some big-time gang members like these guys."

Dorian glared at Morton for several long seconds.

"Two-Bit and Downtown are big-time with the Cobras, right?"

"Oh yeah. These guys are 'Big-Dog' Phillips' special boys. They're pretty tight with the head of that gang."

As the coroner's office came to collect the bodies, Dorian and Morton stood outside when they received an unexpected visitor.

It was the Channel Eight News Truck with 'you-know-who.'

"Well, well...look who's here," Dorian observed as the familiar news reporter arrived with his microphone cameraman.

"Yep...where there's shit, there's flies," Morton sarcastically said, verbally expressing his contempt for the Channel Eight newsman.

Chaz Rizzo smiled as he shook hands with both detectives.

"You guys never miss a trick. Always taking a shot at any poor bastard trying to make a living." Rizzo answered, putting another one of his Marlboro Lights in his mouth.

He then walked closely to Tommy Morton and asked him for a light, knowing that he was an intense smoker like he was. Detective Morton only managed to shake his head at the news reporter as he lit up his cigarette.

When it came to sleazy news journalists, Chaz Rizzo was in a class all of his own. He always seemed to be on the look-out for violent news stories, brutal killings, and especially gruesome homicides. Chaz Rizzo's news crew seemed to concentrate on mobbed-up murder victims, sliced up pedophile priests, or shot-up gangbangers. In Chicago, when it came to violent murders, Rizzo was always on top of it.

"I'd be careful if I were you," Dorian said.
"There is a lot of blood in there. I don't want you to ruin that beautiful Valentino suit that you're wearing."

On that day, the Channel Eight news reporter was wearing a black, Valentino pin-striped suit, crisp white shirt, and a fancy, bright orange and black tie, which he probably paid over a thousand bucks for at some overpriced tie shop on the Gold Coast.

"I wouldn't walk in there with that tie, Chaz. You might scare up those gang-bangers laying on that garage floor."

Rizzo smiled at the detectives, knowing that they were extremely jealous of his wardrobe expense account.

"So what do we have here? A cash payoff went bad?" Rizzo remarked.

"Why are you assuming it was a cash payoff?" Dorian immediately asked.

Rizzo smiled that grin of his after laughing that girly-giggle that always got on Dorian's fucking nerves.

"Gang-bangers don't meet up at vacant, residential garages to do drug deals, Philly. They like clean, well-lit warehouses or garages like this one, where everybody looks like they're all legit. Those cash drug deals are done on the street, not in residential neighborhoods," Rizzo commented.

"That's what I like about you, Riz. You've got all the fucking answers, as usual," Morton replied, knowing deep down that Rizzo was probably right.

Rizzo smiled, taking a long drag from his cigarette.

"I hear they're all Black Cobras. Have you guys heard from Big Dog yet?" he said, looking at both detectives.

"No, not yet. But I imagine we're going to," Dorian replied.

Rizzo smiled, finishing his cigarette then motioning his cameraman to a location where he could do his live news feed.

Dorian and Morton had not had time to consider the ramifications of the murder of these four Black Cobras. They both knew that whenever there was a murdered gangbanger on Chicago's streets, it always started a street war where lots of blood was spilled and innocent victims killed.

Sometimes, those innocent victims were young children, haplessly getting in the way of their random shootings. It was a sure bet that when the head of the Black Cobras got the news of his dead associates, the reprisals would be swift, deadly, and vicious.

"Let the gang wars now begin," Rizzo sarcastically stated, as he turned on his microphone to begin his live feed.

Dorian and Morton looked at each other, and their faces were now covered with fear. The gangland wars between the Cobras and every other city gang were about to get very ugly. It was as if someone had turned up the gas burner, as the senseless violence was now about to start.

The crime laden communities and low-income neighborhoods of their city were about to become more violent, from the racially tense northside to the broken, poor westside, and way down to the rat-infested southside.

Both detectives knew that the streets of Chicago were about to get vividly painted with blood.

CHAPTER SIXTEEN
MISTER K'S COFFEE SHOPPE- LATE NIGHT, AUGUST 9

The small, dingy coffee shop at 2050 W. Belmont Avenue on the northside of Chicago was one of those twenty-four-hour 'greasy-spoons' that served breakfast at all hours of the day and night. The restaurant's pungent aroma was a cross between the smell of fried sausage, over-cooked bacon, and burnt toast. It still had it's a neon red and white sign from the 1960s, where the 'M' letter of the 'Mister K's Restaurant' was always half-lit and blinking. It was an older, conspicuous little joint with seven or eight booths and a few tables scattered in the middle. The floors always looked filthy, no matter how much detergent and bleach they used to wash them. The dark, brown, and gold wallpaper hanging on the walls looked like it had been heavily glued back in the seventies, and there was still a jukebox in the corner with an 'Out of Order' sign taped on it.

Although it was usually vacant and empty of patrons at eleven-thirty in the evening, it was a perfect meeting spot for politicians, ward bosses, and family capos who wanted to stay under the radar of anyone wishing to keep track of their whereabouts.

Gus Kostopoulos, 76 years old, had owned the restaurant for over fifty years and operated it along with his wife of fifty-five years, Olga. She managed to move slowly across the dining room to take the patron's orders while he was the short-order cook in back. Other than a Latino named Juanito helping them in the kitchen, they pretty much ran and operated that old, seedy coffee shop by themselves.

On that muggy August evening, a tall, burly African American man walked into their restaurant. He was wearing a large, short-sleeve, blue and white top that could have passed for a bowling shirt, baggy jeans, and a dark, black leather cap covering his bald head. The man looked to be in his sixties and was good friends with the owner.

"How's it going, Gus," the man yelled out as he sat down at a booth within the darkest corner of the restaurant.

"Hello, Mr. Wally," the old man said with a slight Greek accent from the back kitchen. His waitress wife came out to bring him a cup of black, freshly brewed coffee.

"Hello, Mr. Wally," the old woman said. "The usual?"

"Yes, please, Olga."

"Is there another coming?"

"Yes, Olga. He should be here shortly."

She brought out two glasses of ice waters and another empty coffee cup for the man's guest, along with some silverware wrapped tightly inside a white, paper napkin.

There was no one else in the restaurant, and the older patron liked to have his clandestine meetings at that location for that very reason. It was usually void of any patrons late at night, and it was under the radar.

But most of all, Gus Kostopoulos knew how to keep his mouth shut.

Chicago Police Superintendent Walter Byron, or 'Mr. Wally' as he was called there, loved coming into this greasy joint late at night to relax and have a late-night breakfast. He usually got hungry every evening after ten o'clock, and he would instead make the drive from his Lincoln Park home to the Belmont and Damen Avenue location for a late-night snack. He never wanted to bother his wife to make him a late-night breakfast after cooking a large dinner for him at six o'clock.

He had no sooner taken a sip of his black coffee when he heard the ring from the opening of the entrance door. His guest had arrived on time, as always.

Gus peered over the kitchen into the dining room to see who had just come in. When he saw who his next patron guest was, he immediately knew what he had to do.

The older man walked out from behind the kitchen counter and locked the front entrance door. He turned the 'Always Open' sign around to say 'Sorry, We're Closed' at the front window, then dimming the lights and pulling down the restaurant's shades.

Kostopoulos had the routine memorized, and they all knew the drill:

Quickly make their food orders and serve their two guests. They would then all sit in the back-utility room near the rear door with the radio on so that they wouldn't hear their private conversation.

Gus had been doing this 'fake closed coffee shop' routine for many years. For an extra hundred-dollar bill and a large cash tip for his wife, he would perform this drill for anyone important, including a politician, ward alderman, or mob boss within the City of Chicago who needed his coffee shop space for privacy late at night.

The well-dressed man, wearing a tieless white shirt and a dark blue, pin-striped suit, sat down at the booth across from Mr. Wally.

"What's up, Eddie?"

The man smiled as Olga filled up his empty coffee cup with fresh coffee.

"The usual, Mr. Barrett?"

"No, Olga, just give me a croissant. I can't eat late at night like this guy," as he smiles at Byron.

Alderman Eddie Barrett was texted on his 'burner phone' by someone within the Chicago Police Department earlier that morning. The text simply said '2050 1130," which was the same code that they had used when they carried around pagers many years ago. When that code was texted to either one of them, it usually meant that they would meet at 2050 West Belmont at eleven-thirty later that evening. This time, Chief Byron texted Alderman Barrett, in which he responded with the letter 'K' earlier that morning. Both burner phones were registered to their employees within their immediate staff. They routinely interchanged these burner phones often, using different names, different phone numbers, and various cellular phone carriers.

This was the first private meeting between the two of them since the assassination of Mayor Kollar, and the two of them had a lot to talk about.

They made some small talk about the hot, humid weather and baseball scores.

"How about those Cubs?" Byron immediately asked as Olga had brought out their food.

"They're getting as bad as the Sox," Eddie observed, inserting some butter into his croissant with a butter knife.

"Been to any Sox games?" the Chief asked.

"Not lately. Since the 'Man-Hater' was aced, there had been no time for baseball games."

Both Eddie and Mr. Wally referred to the late mayor as the 'Man-Hater' since she had been elected to office.

"Are you catching any heat?" the police chief asked.

"No, not really. The media has been snooping around, and several reporters have been clamoring my office for interviews, but nothing severe. How are you handling your detectives?"

"I've got Detectives Dorian, Morton, and Romanowski working on the case, and I've been keeping a tight leash on all of them. Every time they get too close, I pull them back and stall them. I've got to keep these guys on the case investigating, so when the FBI is called in, they will be able to say that they did their due diligence."

"When do you think the feds will be called in?"

"When this homicide case gets cold enough for everyone to come to the same conclusion and back off."

Mr. Wally took another sip of his black coffee.

"Eventually, the case will be ruled as an 'unsolved homicide,'" Byron answered.

"Wally, are you fucking nuts? I told you nobody is going to accept the mayor's assassination as an 'unsolved homicide.' I told you before. We need to throw that fucking gang-banger under the bus."

They were both silent for several long minutes.

"I can't, Eddie. I gave them my word. If we throw the Black Cobras under the bus, it's going to start a street war between the gangs and the coppers that will escalate out of control."

Another silent moment.

"Did they get their money?"

"Yeah, the other night. One of my detectives was parked in the garage and observed the handoff."

Chief Byron then smiled.

"Your boy, Javier, took a shot at my detective as he was pulling out. That could have gotten messy."

Eddie Barrett smiled.

"Don't worry, Wally. I'll take care of Javier."

Mr. Wally smiled while he began eating his three scrambled eggs, hash browns, four links of sausage, and some wheat toast.

"How the fuck do you eat so much food at this late hour?" the alderman asked.

"The same way you can drink your Jack on the Rocks all fucking day?" the chief responded.

Eddie laughed.

"I guess we both have some bad habits that are going to kill us."

A silent moment as they both shook their heads.

"If somebody else doesn't kill us first," Wally responded with his mouth full.

They both sat there while Eddie Barrett drank his coffee and watched the City's Top

Cop devour his breakfast at almost midnight. The alderman then brought up the subject again, knowing that the conversation was going to get contentious.

"Wally, we need a patsy."

"No, Eddie, we don't. We can keep this murder unsolved. This city has dozens of them every week."

"Not when it comes to the Mayor's assassin. The feds, the media, and city activists are hot on solving this case and trying to figure out who the murderer is. They're not going to let up."

"Look, Eddie, we've got nothing to worry about. We don't even know who the assassin is," Wally said.

"We farmed it out to the Cobras, remember? They said they would find a member from the gang to pull it off," he reminded the Alderman.

"We're completely insulated. You don't know who did it. I don't know who did it. And the head of the Black Cobras, 'Big Dog' doesn't even know who did it."

Chief Byron took the last bite of his wheat toast.

"As a matter of fact, he didn't know anything about it. He only just recently found out that someone in his gang was involved. And he's not too happy about it."

Eddie Barrett looked at the Chief of Police.

"And how the fuck is that going to play out?"

"He's out on bail right now. You said you would help me get his charges thrown out on a disqualification if he looks the other way."

"Well yeah, if he does look the other way. If he's pissed about one of his gang members taking out the Mayor, then he may not be too willing to look in the other direction."

"He has no choice, Eddie. The alternative is his spending the rest of his life in Menard Prison downstate."

He was cleaning his plate with his toast, finally finishing his late-night breakfast.

"Don't worry, Eddie. He'll play ball."

Another silent moment.

"And besides, we really don't know who took out the 'Man-hater' now, do we? And we really don't know if his gang is even involved. The more stupid everyone remains, the better," Byron reasoned.

Eddie Barrett was silent for several long minutes. Byron could tell that his wheels were turning.

"You know, if you knew your history, you would know that every political assassination and every successful plot to take out a person in power has to have a patsy. 'The Outfit' always has a patsy when taking out someone important," the alderman explained.

"Look at the Kennedy Assassination? Who was the patsy there when they captured Oswald?" Eddie asked, sounding like a high school history teacher.

Chief Byron was quiet, wiping his mouth and not listening to Barrett.

"Jack Ruby. And who was the patsy when Martin Luther King was killed?"

More silence.

"James Earl Ray."

They both glared at each other for several long seconds.

"You better brush up on your history Wally," as the Fourteenth Ward alderman poured himself another cup of coffee from the miniature coffee pot that Olga had left for them at their table.

"We fucked up, Wally. We should have figured out who the patsy was going to be before putting this operation together."

"It's not necessary now, Eddie. The less that we know right now, the better."

"Not if the Black Cobras start getting pissed off."

"Leave the Cobras up to me, Eddie. I can handle them. The only thing we gotta do right now is to stay stupid. The less that we all know, the better."

Eddie Barrett pulled out a wade of cash with that comment and left three hundred-dollar bills for their usual twenty-dollar breakfast bill. He then got up and grabbed his cell phone and car keys that he had placed on the table earlier.

"Let's hook up next week, Wally. Keep me apprised of what's going on," he said, shaking his hand.

As he got up and walked toward the door, he loudly said to the police chief.

"Start shopping for a patsy."

He then exited the restaurant, and quickly walked to his car, parked half a block away.

Wally cleaned off his bowling shirt and got up to leave, thanking the restaurant's proprietor.

"Thanks again, Gus. Left you some money on the table."

"Thank you, Mr. Wally."

He quickly walked out of the late-night restaurant, walking in the opposite direction as the alderman as he located his late-model Ford Escape. As he walked, he considered Eddie Barrett's suggestion in trying to find a patsy. He wondered who he could throw under the bus and use as a patsy in the murder assassination of Mayor Kollar?

He reached into his front pocket before unlocking his car and pulled out his cellular phone, shutting off the 'record' button. He noticed that his cellular phone said '38 minutes, 41 seconds', the length of their late-night meeting at Mr. K's Restaurant.

Chief of Police Walter Byron had secretly recorded his meeting with the Fourteenth Ward Alderman, a practice he had been doing for the last three months of covert meetings with Eddie Barrett. Knowing the alderman and his ruthless reputation, he had to protect himself.

Just in case Barrett got any crazy ideas and decided to do something stupid.

Just in case the alderman decided to implicate the police chief in this assassination plot and try to wash his hands.

Just in case he got dragged into this murder plot and was accused of hiring the assassin himself.

A patsy, he laughed to himself.

Who else would make a better 'patsy,' a better murder accomplice than Eddie Barrett himself?

Chapter Seventeen
Franklin Street Café - August 11th

It was a wet and rainy summer afternoon, as I had been sitting at my usual table at the Franklin Street Café on the corner of Lake and Franklin Streets. The Chicago Tribune Building was several blocks away, but I needed to go elsewhere to get some work done. I had to work on this Kollar story, away from all of the newsroom interruptions that had been going on all day. I needed a break from the news studio to escape somewhere in the city where my assistant editor and my desk phone wouldn't find me. For almost an hour, I managed to work in a small, cramped little booth in the corner of the restaurant. My laptop was open, and my notes were scattered across the table while the waitress politely interrupted me now and again to check on me.

I had been coming into the Franklin Street Café for years, and it was my hide-a-way from the Chicago Tribune. It was a small, eight table coffee shop, no larger than a thousand square feet, amply hidden away amongst the modern skyscrapers, high-end retail stores, and glitzy, over-priced restaurants of North Wacker Drive.

"Another piece of pie, Larry?"

"No thanks, honey," I managed to reply to Gloria, an older brunette waitress with excessive tattoos painted across her right arm.

"Your banana cream pies are amazing today," as I was so tempted to have another piece.

"Make 'em just for you, darlin'," she flirted, pouring me another cup of freshly brewed coffee.

"I'll check back with you later. You never say 'no' to me twice," she winked her eye.

She was right. I never got out of there without having at least two or three pieces of their homemade pie specials.

The coffee shop was just far enough away to where I could run back to the newsroom if I were needed back at the office. My assistant editor, Tom Olsen, knew I was at my favorite coffee shop working away, but he didn't mind. As long as I made my deadlines, he was okay with wherever I brought my laptop. I even tried working at the North Avenue Beach once, but the excessive, blowing sand got into my Dell laptop, costing me nearly four hundred dollars in computer repairs.

I knew everyone at that coffee shop, so they allowed me to sample their pie specials and consume several pots of coffee in return for using that corner table as my satellite office. I had written many of my feature articles at that corner table over the many years of working there, and I had threatened to take that old wooden table with me whenever I retired.

I had been working on my investigative article, which was had a deadline of eight o'clock that night, struggling to connect all of the dots and piece what information I had regarding the potential assassins to Mayor Kollar. The list of political enemies was so extensively long, and I honestly didn't know where to start. Whatever information I had gathered together had mostly come from Chaz Rizzo at the funeral. His hard finger pointing to the Fourteenth Ward didn't have any legs, and there wasn't enough substantial proof or any hard evidence. Until I knew which direction I was going as far as this story was concerned, I had to be very careful with how I worded the long list of suspects.

It was almost six o'clock when a familiar face walked into the coffee shop while I was taking a sip of my third cup of coffee. Her face looked familiar, and I knew I had seen her somewhere before. She was a tall, slender brown-haired girl, wearing a beige raincoat with its belt dangling from the back. Her Italian high heeled shoes perfectly matched her tanned, shapely legs. For several long seconds, I couldn't take my eyes off of her.

"I'll have a ham and cheese croissant sandwich and a large cappuccino to go, please," she asked the attending waitress taking orders at the cash register.

"Of course. That will be $14.35," Gloria, the waitress replied, now making eye contact with me while processing her credit card.

The gorgeous young lady turned around and noticed me sitting in the corner of the coffee shop. She smiled and acknowledged me, then turned back around to sign her credit card receipt.

"It will be about fifteen minutes for that, ma'am."

"That will be fine," she said.

As she put her credit card back in her purse, she turned and looked at me again, as if she had seen me somewhere before. By that moment, I realized who she was, and I had to pinch myself.

Today was my lucky day, I thought to myself.

She then walked over towards my table.

"Haven't I seen you somewhere before?" she innocently asked. Her piercing hazel brown eyes and her Courtney Cox good looks were mesmerizing.

At that moment, I stood up and brushed off the crumbs from my last two pieces of banana cream pie off of my short sleeve shirt.

"Yes, you're that reporter from CNN, correct? I think we saw each other at Northwestern Hospital when Mayor Kollar died last week."

"Yes, that's it. You were there as well. I remember you now," as we both smiled. Her incredible beauty was captivating.

I then extended out my hand.

"I'm Larry McKay, with the Chicago Tribune."

She accepted my handshake offer and gave me her right hand in return, which displayed a Piaget gold watch and a diamond bracelet. I also noticed that her right hand displayed a very expensive ruby ring and another gold bracelet of some kind.

But her ring finger was vacant.

"Pleased to meet you. I'm Talia Bowerman with CNN."

"The pleasure is mine," I graciously replied,

"Please sit down," inviting her to sit at my make-shift desk, as I suddenly noticed a banana crème pie stain on the left side of my white shirt.

She was wearing an Ann Taylor black suit coat and skirt, which professionally matched her button-down white blouse. It was unbuttoned just low enough to tease you with her cleavage. Her business suit did a terrible job of hiding her incredible, sensuous figure, covered by a beige raincoat. You didn't need a Northwestern MBA to figure out that she spent a lot of time in the gym.

"I see you've discovered my private office," I snidely remarked, trying in vain to start up a meaningful conversation.

"Yes, I have indeed," she smiled.

"I usually come here and pick up a sandwich and a cappuccino before walking over to Union Station to catch the 6:47 train."

"Do you live in the suburbs?"

"No. I take a class twice a week at DePaul University. I'm working on my master's degree," she replied.

"Well, you should get a slice of their banana cream pie today. It's to die for," I explained, trying to keep the conversation going.

At that moment, I felt like that banana cream pie stain was loudly jumping off my shirt for everyone in that snack shop to see, especially my new CNN friend.

"Perhaps next time," she said, making eye contact with my shirt stain.

"Is your office nearby?" I asked, even though I already knew where her CNN satellite office was.

"Yes, our Chicago Bureau is located on North Michigan Avenue, not very far away from the Tribune building," she explained.

"Yes, right near Trump Towers," I said, pretending that I cared about where her newsroom office was.

Her news bureau was just close enough to my newsroom office to make trouble. I had walked past the CNN Bureau in Streeterville many times before, and I was very familiar with her local office location on the seventh floor of her 435 North Michigan Avenue building. I briefly fantasied about kidnapping her for lunch one day, enjoying a 'nooner' and having her back at her desk by one o'clock. At that instant, I was trying very hard not to make it look obvious while I was undressing her with my eyes.

There were a few silent seconds as I was struggling to continue the conversation.

"Are you working on the Mayor Kollar story?" I asked, figuring that she was the CNN correspondent covering the event.

"Yes. We've been working on the story now for quite some time, but we're not coming up with any real leads."

"Really? Nobody has pointed you over to the Fourteenth Ward?"

She looked at me somewhat puzzled.

"The Fourteenth Ward? Do you mean Eddie Barrett?"

I smiled my famous Felix the Cat cartoon grin, making her think that I knew something that I didn't know anything about. That was a sordid journalism trick that I learned from my buddy Chaz Rizzo.

"What's the connection there?" she inquisitively asked.

At that second, I should have withheld what little information I knew about Eddie Barrett for ransom, in exchange for making that 'nooner' fantasy of mine come true.

"Fast Eddie has had it out for Kollar ever since she sic'd the 'Federales' on his office several months ago. They were anything but Facebook friends," I volunteered.

"No love lost, huh?" she smiled. "Yes, I did hear that," Talia continued.

"I've also heard that there was quite a bit of animosity with the Chicago Police Department and especially, Chief Byron, and the Mayor's office."

"Really," I laughed, thinking that her suggestion was initially rather amusing.

"So, you think the Chicago P.D. Superintendent is crazy enough to take out the Mayor of Chicago in the middle of the day on a Sunday afternoon?"

"There are whispers to that effect, yes," she explained.

It took all of my inner strength to keep from chuckling, as the mere suggestion of the city's top cop taking out the Mayor of Chicago was laughable at best.

"Wow, we're really stretching this now, aren't we?"

"This is Chicago, Mr. McKay. Anything is possible in the Windy City," she replied.

"Did you forget about Chief Byron's little incident last summer?"

I then remembered the story that broke about Chief Byron getting stopped on Western Avenue by a Chicago copper one night last summer. He initially seemed to be driving under the influence of alcohol and had one of his young, white female associates in the front seat. Her blouse was barely buttoned, and her hair was severely disheveled. Chief Byron's pants were still unbuckled and barely covering his legs.

It didn't take a driving instructor to figure out that the woman was probably giving him oral sex while trying to maneuver his vehicle, which would have explained his erratic driving that evening.

It wouldn't have been any real news, as the patrolman decided to play 'catch and release,' being that Byron was 'happily married' and the women in the front seat of his car was forty-four-year-old Alyssa Florentine, the wife of the very powerful Twelfth Ward Alderman, Michael Florentine.

The incident came over the police radio blotter, so we all knew that Chief Byron was pulled over for driving his car recklessly down Western Avenue. But out of respect for Byron and Alderman Florentine, we were told initially at the Tribune to ignore the incident.

That is until Channel Eight's sleazy Chaz Rizzo broke the story.

The Chicago Tribune then ran with it as front-page news. Mayor Kollar was livid, and she privately admonished the Chief of Police for showing impaired judgment and a tremendous lack of professionalism.

The next day, Chief Byron, dressed in his full top-cop regalia, held a news conference at City Hall for the news media. His excuse was that he was driving the alderman's wife home from a political function they had both attended that evening. His erratic driving was because he was under some very potent heart medication.

Everybody in that room at City Hall saw right through Byron's line of bullshit. I was standing right next to Chaz Rizzo while Chief Walter Byron was publicly making excuses as if he were trying to talk his way out of a DUI ticket.

"They were both fucking drunk on their asses, and Florentine's wife was sucking on his 'slong' while he was driving," Rizzo loudly whispered under his breath, making sure I was the only one who could hear him.

"Is that what you're going to say on your live, six o'clock newsfeed tonight?" I kiddingly asked him. We were both laughing about it, knowing that we could never report that kind of incident about a public official in the news media.

Until the moment of Mayor Kollar's assassination, Chief Byron's job was on the chopping block and was definitely in jeopardy.

"Well then, maybe," I replied to the beautiful CNN reporter.

"But there are a lot of people in this city that have a motive. Trying to figure out which one is the real issue," I said while trying very hard to keep my eyes where they belonged.

"Indeed," Talia replied.

At that moment, our pleasant conversation was unpleasantly interrupted.

"Your croissant sandwich and large cappuccino, ma'am," Gloria said noisily, making sure that we ended our enticing little visit at my corner office.

"I've got to go," as she hurriedly got up and extended her hand. "Hope to see you again."

"I'm usually here a few days a week, whenever I'm trying to escape the wrath of my assistant editor."

She then walked to the counter and grabbed her dinner in the brown paper bag. Smiling, Talia made eye contact and waved again to me one last time while pushing the glass door open and quickly walking towards Union Station.

For about ten seconds, I was utterly mesmerized. I was fascinated by the beauty and charm of that CNN reporter, and I had to shake myself back into reality. Of all of the places that I could have encountered her, it seemed so unusual that she had chosen this hidden, discrete little coffee shop to find me. I found it so bizarre because hardly anyone even knows that this little place even existed, let alone encounter another fellow reporter at the Franklin Street Café.

"Are you thinking about cheating on me?" Gloria smiled as she approached me at my table, pouring more fresh coffee into my cup. We enjoyed kidding and flirting with each other whenever I was there.

"Does she come in here often? I've never seen her here before."

"Neither have I," Gloria replied. "Maybe she's stalking you," she winked her eye.

I smiled, taking another sip of my fresh, black coffee.

"That's for another fantasy," I remarked.

At that moment, I never once believed that any of my thoughts or fantasies about CNN's Talia Bowerman would ever come true.

CHAPTER EIGHTEEN
A SECOND CHESS MATCH- AUGUST 12TH

It was a cooler evening for a summer weeknight, as Little Tony found a convenient spot to park his black Maserati on West 79th Street. It was a Wednesday night, and Little Tony had promised Fr. Fitz that he would be over his rectory at St. Simeon Church for their weekly 'cenetta.'

He had thought seriously about canceling their weekly date that night. Although he appreciated the great food and the parish priest's camaraderie, the Chicago Mafioso certainly didn't need the sociology lecture. Although DiMatteo was acutely aware of the sociological problems that were going on in the city, he didn't need to be told by the activist priest how he could get personally involved in fixing them.

Little Tony had enough problems. He was running a successful food distribution business, with shipping hubs in several different United States locations. Tony had his hands full with the gambling machines and the various juice loans he had on the streets. And now, with all of the CBD and marijuana retail stores that were opening up throughout the state, he was in over his eyeballs in high-interest loans. DiMatteo had gotten involved in financing several of these various cannabis retail stores throughout the Chicagoland area, for which he also had a piece. He didn't want, nor did he need to get involved in solving the city's social and political unrest.

Tony walked up the front steps and rang the doorbell, in which the rectory cook and long-time housekeeper, Mrs. Valenti, quickly answered the door.

"Ciao, Signore DiMatteo. Come stai'?" she asked him how he was in their native Italian.

"Molto bene, Signora. Dove' stai Padre Fitz, per favore?" he politely asked where Fr. Fitz was, as she conveniently answered the door for him.

"Si sta preparando per la cena", she replied, "Sarà giù a breve."

Mrs. Valenti explained that Fr. Fitz was getting ready for dinner and that he would be downstairs shortly.

She took his sport coat as he promptly sat at their expansive dining room table. There was already bruschetta, freshly baked bread, and one huge antipasto tray, including various cheeses, different types of olives, and giardiniera. Other lunch meats were arranged neatly on the large silver platter, including mortadella, salami, and soppressata.

Little Tony wanted so badly to help himself to Mrs. Valenti's initial dinner spread but knew that it would be rude to begin without his gracious host.

"Would you like some wine?" Mrs. Valenti asked him in Italian.

"Absolutely."

She had a large gallon of Carlo Rossi Paisano red wine on the table, which she quickly opened and poured a glass for the Chicago Capo dei Capi.

"Are you sure you don't want to come and work for me, Signora? I will pay you to double whatever Fr. Fitz is paying you," Little Tony aggressively offered.

"No, grazie," Mrs. Valenti loyally responded.

"Fr. Fitz is very, very good to me. Besides, I feel like I am doing God's work when I am here at this rectory," she humbly replied.

Little Tony smiled while sampling his glass of Carlo Rossi red wine.

"Well, when you get tired of working for the Lord and want to make some real money, you know where to find me," he answered in his usual snarky voice.

At that moment, Fr. Fitz arrived at the rectory dining room to greet his beloved guest.

"Are you trying to steal my incredible cook again, Tony?" Fr. Fitz kiddingly asked as the two of them gave each other a courtesy hug.

Fr. Fitz was wearing a long sleeve Oxford white shirt, blue jeans, and dark brown loafers. He looked very comfortable and had been looking forward to his dinner date with Chicago's most powerful mafioso.

"America is a country of opportunities, Father," Little Tony answered, as Fr. Fitz sat down at the table and poured himself a tall glass of red wine.

He smiled and said, 'Salute' in flawless Italian. Fr. Fitz had learned fluent Italian when he was studying at the seminary and spent several months living and working at the Vatican in Rome.

"Hai fame? Signora Valenti ha preparato un pasto incredibile per noi," Fr. Fitz said in Italian, showing off his ability to talk and communicate in DiMatteo's native language. He had asked Little Tony if he was hungry, acknowledging that Mrs. Valenti had prepared a wonderful meal for the two of them.

"Father, I'm impressed. You can even speak my native language fluently. Are you looking to be my new consigliere?" Little Tony joked.

"I was a seminary student in Rome for several months, Tony. It's a beautiful language, and I enjoy practicing with anyone who knows how to converse in Italian well."

"I'm impressed, Father. What other languages do you know?"

"I speak four languages, Tony. Besides English and Italian, I can also speak Spanish and French fluently," he responded.

"When you're a parish priest in an active neighborhood such as this one, knowing other languages comes in handy."

"I'll bet, Father. There must be a lot of gang members in this neighborhood who speak fucking French," he joked.

The two of them laughed as Little Tony poked fun at the priest's last statement. It was amazing how quickly the two of them got along and felt comfortable with one another. Although Little Tony knew that Fr. Fitz liked to preach to him regarding 'good and evil' and his responsibilities to the community, the Mafia boss felt incredibly comfortable. Little Tony and Father Fitzgerald got along as if they had known each other for years.

Tony DiMatteo missed the close relationship that he used to have with Monsignor Joseph Kilbane. He had always felt that as long as Monsignor Kilbane was around to make sure Tony had the Lord's best intentions in mind, that he had a fighting chance of 'getting through the pearly gates.'

Monsignor Kilbane always knew that he had free access to Little Tony's checkbook when it came to charitable causes and squeezing him for donations. With Kilbane, Little Tony had donated millions of dollars to charities, food banks, and orphanages in dire need in the Chicagoland area.

Little Tony and Father Fitz had started to develop a very amicable friendship. He allowed the parish priest to make suggestions and comments that most laypeople would never get away within his immediate circle.

They began making small talk for over an hour, as the two of them enjoyed coniglio arrosto con patate (roasted rabbit with potatoes), stuffed red peppers with rice and meat sauce, aranchini (fried rice balls), farfalle pasta with shrimp and vodka sauce, and assorted pastries and desserts after dinner.

They were finishing their espresso coffees within an hour when Little Tony and Fr. Fitz got up from the dinner table. They then walked over to the living room, where the chess table and the large red velvet chairs were waiting.

"Shall we?" Fr. Fitz formally invited the Chicago Capo.

"Sure, Father. But we're playing for your cash envelope again, right?" Tony winked his eye.

"No, Tony, per your suggestion. We are playing for fun this time."

"Good," he said, as a grabbed a black pawn and a white pawn and hit them in each one of his closed fists. Fr. Fitz picked Tony's left hand, which disclosed the black pawn. He would play black, while the parish priest would play white and have the opening move. This time, there was a time clock next to the chessboard, which wasn't there the last time they had played.

"We're playing with a game clock now, huh, Father?"

"Yes, I didn't want you to think that we were going to take this game lightly."

"Good. I don't want you to throw the game like you did the last time."

Fr. Fitz only smiled. He knew that he couldn't continue to lie to his friend regarding his intentions the last time they played.

Fr. Fitz made the first move.

White – e4.

Then Tony's move.

Black – c5.

Fr. Fitz moved, then hitting the time clock.

White – Nf3.

Each player strategically moved their chess pieces before hitting the time clock.

Black – d4.

White – Nc3.

Black – Nf6.

By analyzing the first opening moves, Father Fitz immediately knew what game playing strategy Little Tony was using.

He was using the 'Sicilian Defense' method, a series of chess moves developed back to the late 16th century by the Italian chess players Giulio Polerio and Gioachino Greco. This is an aggressive method in which the chess player immediately goes on the assault by assertively using his knights in his opening moves to attack his opponent.

The Sicilian is the most popular and best-scoring response to white's first move. It is statistically a more successful opening for the chess player because of the high success rate in advancing the chess pieces aggressively across the board.

"I'm impressed, Tony. You're using the Sicilian Method in your opening moves."

Little Tony smiled.

"Thanks, Father. I've been reading up on chess in my office."

Father Fitz was amused, smiling at Little Tony.

"Have I created a monster? I'm thrilled that you are taking our chess matches so seriously."

Little Tony glared at the parish priest.

"I don't like to lose, Father."

Then Fr. Fitz made his move.

White–Be3.

The grandmaster used another method to counter black's Sicilian Method, called the English Attack.

This chess method was popularized by the English chess grandmasters Murray Chandler, John Nunn, and Nigel Short in the early 1980s. This is a counterattack method in which the player uses his bishops to strategically deflect the offense position, which the player uses to defeat his opponent.

The two players continued to move their chess pieces across the board, hitting the timeclock after every move. The game's intensity had suddenly risen as the two players realized how well and intelligently each player was moving their game pieces.

After ten minutes or more of intense playing, Fr. Fitz decided to break the silence.

"Have you thought a little more about what we discussed last week?"

"About what, Father?" Tony was playing stupid, still immersed in their chess match.

"My suggestion regarding your getting involved in bringing peace to all of the city violence."

"It's not my problem, Father."

Fr. Fitz looked at Little Tony.

"It is your problem, Tony. This problem belongs to all of us."

Little Tony then glared back at Fr. Fitz, as if to almost mock him.

"What the fuck do you want me to do, Father? Go marching down State Street arm in arm with the new mayor singing 'Kumbaya'? Who the fuck do you think I am? Martin Luther King?"

The priest then raised his voice.

"No, Tony. But any action that you and your family take in keeping the peace and defending these businesses that are getting looted will make these violent protesters think twice before turning peaceful demonstrations into violent ones."

"And how the fuck do you suggest that we do that? Do you want me to put two wise-guys standing next to their cars on running boards with machine guns? This ain't the fucking Roaring Twenties and Prohibition, Father."

"I'm not advocating that, Tony. I'm only suggesting that you initiate some sort of security program for all these high-profile retail stores that are experiencing all of this looting."

Father Fitz then shut off the game clock, now realizing that the two of them were now about to engage in a fierce and very crucial debate.

"You need to get involved."

"Involved by doing what Father? Putting hitmen in front of all of these stores and shoot to kill anyone who tries to break their fucking windows?"

Fr. Fitz smiled.

"That would be a good start."

"Are you fucking kidding me? We can't do that, and you know it."

"All you need is one instance, Tony. One situation where a loud and direct message is communicated to all of these 'BLM' protestors and gang bangers who are using this social unrest to inflict damage and hurt anyone and everyone who gets in their way. The coppers can't retaliate. They can't use their guns. The business owners aren't equipped to do anything either," Fr. Fitz reasoned.

"You and your family are the only ones who can successfully defend these local businesses and restore peace in the city."

Little Tony looked at the activist priest.

"And you're okay with this, Father? You're supposed to be preaching peace and love and forgiveness. Not sending gangsters into the city to shoot up violent protestors."

"I'm not advocating violence."

"Oh, really? Then what the fuck are you doing then? You just said that shooting them up would be a 'good start.'"

"I'm saying that we need to protect the innocent citizens of this city and maintain law and order. The Chicago P.D. can't do it anymore. We need some totalitarianism in our city right now. The only ones capable of inflicting any authority against those bringing violence and evil into our city is 'The Outfit.'

"Even if we shoot to kill?"

Fr. Fitz was silent for a moment.

"You're abolishing Satan."

"I think you've been mixing too much 'grappa' with your vino on Sundays, Father. You're not fucking thinking straight."

Fr. Fitz looked amused as Little Tony started laughing.

"I gotta tell ya, Father. You're something else. You're nothing like the priests I grew up with. All the fucking Catholic priests that I know still believe in the 'thou shall not kill' commandment."

Fr. Fitz loudly retorted.

"And you have never broken that commandment, Tony?"

"That's none of your fucking business, Father," he now said in an angry voice.

"Whatever sins I've committed have nothing to do with you," Little Tony loudly replied.

He was now starting to get very irritated and angry with this priest. Little Tony had never been confronted by anyone regarding his past sins, his lifestyle, or especially, the number of bastards he's had to make disappear that may have gotten in his way over the years.

Fr. Fitz dialed it back a notch, realizing that he was now backing Chicago's most dangerous gangster into a terrifying corner.

"Look, Tony. I am not implying that you 'rub out' anyone. I am only suggesting that your family get involved in restoring law and order into this town. The City of Chicago and the Chicago Police have entirely lost control."

Tony then laughed at the parish priest.

"And after we rub out all of these asshole gangbangers and all of these violent rioters and looters that are destroying the town, then what? Do you think anyone in City Hall is going to fucking appreciate it?"

He paused for a moment.

"Do you think they're going to erect a statue of me in Grant Park?" he snickered.

"Oh, I know. Maybe the Mayor will give me a key to the fucking city!"

For several long seconds, they were both quiet as the two respected men stared at each other.

Both of these individuals were Chicago icons, and both men had different means and methods of their ideas of how to restore peace and create social change in their respective professions.

"You and your family are the only ones who can bring peace and respect back to Chicago."

"Why me, Father? Why not somebody else? Why don't you hook up with somebody else in 'The Outfit'?"

"Because you're the Capo dei Capi, and you're the only wise guy that I know who has any integrity."

"There are no wise guys with integrity, Father. That's why they call us 'wise guys.'"

The two of them were silent for several moments.

"Forget about it, Father. We don't need the heat right now. Besides, they'll immediately figure out right away who is behind all of this and what we're doing."

Fr. Fitz smiled at his chess adversary.

"Not if you do it right."

The two of them looked at each other as if Tony were unable to talk. The priest could tell that the wheels inside of Little Tony's head were turning.

Fr. Fitz smiled as the two of them had suddenly lost interest in finishing their chess game.

"I don't think I have to tell you what to do. But I do believe that you probably have a lot of clients who require your special 'security services.'"

Tony smiled back. He was utterly amazed and astounded at what he was hearing from Fr. Fitz.

This was a priest who had no qualms about implementing 'an eye for an eye,' like in the Old Testament. Fr. Fitz was a very religious man who realized the dangerous capabilities of those worthless criminals with 'satanic tendencies.' Fr. Fitz was a man of the cloth who recognized long ago that those demonic souls who represented and inflicted death and violence onto innocent victims needed to be harshly dealt with.

Fr. Fitzgerald believed that the kingdom of heaven was peacefully ruled by those angels who mightily waived their long shiny swords. He was not afraid of violence. Fr. Fitz knew that there was a time and place for everything in society, especially when it came to exacting revenge on those who stole the lives of innocent victims.

Several years ago, there was a time when Fr. Fitzgerald's political viewpoints on capital punishment ran against the mandates and the Roman Catholic Church's laws.

In 2001, an African American man brutally killed two young little girls after capturing and raping them. They went missing for several weeks, as Chicago P.D. detectives were scouring the city to find those missing little girls, ages ten and twelve. When their mangled, mutilated bodies turned up in an abandoned crack house in Englewood, DNA results lead them to the capture of their perpetrator.

The alleged killer and rapist plead the insanity defense, and he was sentenced to life in prison with the possibility of parole after twenty years.

Fr. Colin Fitzgerald took personal offense to this dangerous criminal's prison sentence. He led a protest downtown to the Dirksen Building on North Dearborn Street, with over a thousand pro-death penalty activists and demonstrators marching behind him. He and his followers demanded the reinstatement of capital punishment in the State of Illinois, commanding that the death penalty be immediately declared against this child rapist and murderer. That perpetrator had killed those two young girls.

"A lifetime prison sentence is not the correct punishment for first-degree murder. A lifetime in prison will never deter those criminals who wish to take another human being's life, especially when they are two young, innocent victims who had their whole lives ahead of them," Fr. Fitz was quoted in the papers.

His far-right political viewpoints on subjects like capital punishment brought him a considerable amount of public criticism by various Catholic clergy, especially Chicago's Cardinal Markowitz. He was publicly admonished by the Archdiocese of Chicago and was restricted from public speaking to the media or conducting any more public demonstrations for several months.

Fr. Fitz was mostly banned from overtly broadcasting his extreme right-wing political opinions.

But Little Tony liked Fr. Fitz. He was becoming very enamored with this activist priest.

Fr. Colin Fitzgerald had the drive, the determination, and the moxey of a 'war-time consigliere.'

"Are you sure you're a Catholic priest?"

They both smiled at each other.

With that comment, Fr. Fitz offered his hand as a peace offering, knowing that their political conversation that evening had gotten a little contentious.

Little Tony smiled as he shook his hand.

"It's a good thing you resigned this game, Father. I was kicking your ass anyway," he said in a cocky voice.

At that point in the chess match, they had completed twelve moves. With two captured white rooks, a bishop, and three pawns, Little Tony was about to secure the white queen.

Fr. Fitz then started rearranging the chess pieces back to their starting positions on the chessboard.

"Perhaps we can play a new chess match next week, Tony."

The Capo dei Capi smiled as he rose from his chair and began to find his way out the door.

"It's been an interesting game, Father. And a very interesting conversation. Thank you for the wonderful dinner. And say goodbye to Mrs. Valenti for me."

"I will. Thank you for coming as always, Tony. Next week, I'll beat you for sure."

They both smiled at each other and shook hands. He then exited the front door of the rectory and got into his car parked on 79th Street. Fr. Fitz turned the porch light on as Tony left his black Maserati onto oncoming traffic.

Fr. Fitzgerald was extremely pleased with the way he was slowly gaining Tony DiMatteo's trust. He could tell that Little Tony enjoyed their chess matches, while the chess grandmaster held himself back on several moves. Although he was very familiar with Tony's gambit strategies, he wanted to continue to entice him into coming over to play him every week.

Fr. Fitz was giving the Capo dei Capi just enough slack to allow him to feel confident at playing him in the game of chess, a game that he was indeed a master at playing.

But winning over Little Tony DiMatteo's trust and confidence was far more critical than beating him in any damn chess game.

CHAPTER NINETEEN
PICKING UP THE CHESS PIECES - AUGUST 14TH

It was raining hard outside, and the robust and intense drizzle against the windowpane was incredibly distracting. Wacker Drive looked as though it was underwater, and the torrential rain was overflowing the main street and was starting to spill onto the sidewalk. The monsoon-like weather had been forecasted all day and wasn't supposed to let up until late in the evening.

I was sitting at the Franklin Street Café that afternoon, trying to put the finishing touches on my Mayor Kollar story. I had put some of the puzzle pieces together but investigating and finding the actual assassin was still a long shot. It was already the middle of August, and the Mayor's assassination had occurred almost four weeks ago.

It was a jigsaw puzzle, indeed. The Chicago P.D. had a long list of suspects but not actual clues about who pulled the trigger. I had several at length telephone calls with Detective Romanowski and Detective Morton, but they were not ready to announce anything that would lead them to the actual shooter. According to the detectives and their intense investigation, no one had seen anyone leaving the vacant gray house next door on that Sunday afternoon.

The same questions kept turning over in my mind: How could a shooter with a high power rifle assassinate a public figure at her home in the middle of the afternoon? With no witnesses, no evidence, and no DNA traces at the crime scene? How could the Chicago P.D.

not have taken extra precautions when they realized that the house next door was vacant?

I asked that same question to Detective Romanowski, and that seemed to arise his suspicions. We looked into that situation together and traced the owner of that house next door to a land trust registered and to an attorney's office in Arlington Heights by the name of Silverio Vitello. Finally, we traced the address of that house to a real estate office management firm, for which that attorney was also the registered agent.

I had called Mr. Vitello yesterday, and he stated that the Sapphire Management Group handled the management of that house on 3557 W. Shakespeare. He refused to give me any other information until Detectives Morton and Romanowski paid him a little visit this morning. It turned out that there was a month to month lease on that house for the amount of $1,850 per month, and it had been paid for three months in advance by someone using a currency check for the amount of $5,550 back in May. But no one lived in the house, and there was no furniture or other belongings inside. It was as if someone had paid for that house to be empty next door to the Mayor's home.

But who would want that home empty for June, July, and August? Especially during the summer in Logan Square in Chicago? Was there anyone entering and leaving that house? I had a hunch, so I decided to knock on some doors.

I interviewed an older lady named Elsa Canale, who looked to be in her late seventies and lived alone across the vacant house. She turned out to be an excellent witness, as, like most elderly residents, seemed to have nothing else better to do than to stare out of her front window, drink coffee and take note of any activity going on in the neighborhood. She had stated that there had been a significant amount of police activity going on in that house *prior* to the mayor's assassination.

"Yes, sir," the older woman said.

"I saw several unmarked police cars parked in and around the Mayor's house and that house next door, and I even saw several policemen entering and leaving that house."

"You saw Chicago patrolmen entering that house before the assassination?"

"Yes, sir," she replied.

"Did you see anyone coming in or out of that house on the same day as the Mayor's assassination?"

"No, sir. During that day and several days prior, I didn't see anyone going in or out of that house."

Why would the Chicago Police Department be entering and leaving that house before the assassination? But then, a few days prior, no activity? That immediately made me suspicious. Was the house next door used as a stakeout location for the Chicago P.D. for security purposes? That would have been normal in providing additional security to the Mayor's home. But why was it leased for only three months, using a cashier's check from a currency exchange?

The cashier's check was drawn on May 22nd from a currency exchange located at 7121 West Archer Avenue in Chicago.

When I researched the currency exchange address yesterday, I immediately made a phone call that afternoon to my detective buddy Detective Romanowski at the Eighteenth District.

"Romanowski," he answered his desk phone in his usual, excitable voice.

"Denny, it's McKay. I did some research on that currency exchange where the check was drawn last May. Take a wild guess where that currency exchange is located?"

A moment of silence.

"Please don't say the Fourteenth Ward."

"Bingo."

"Eddie Barrett's ward? Just fucking beautiful," Denny replied.

"Who is the owner of that currency exchange?" I eagerly asked.

There was a ten-second silence over the telephone, and I could hear the wheels turning in Romanowski's head.

"If I'm not mistaken, that currency exchange is part of a large group of exchanges owned and operated by a guy by the name of Chris Bucaro."

"Really?"

"I only happen to know that because we had to do a stakeout along with the FBI last year on a contractor who was cashing a large number of checks there, and the owner wasn't too keen on allowing us in. We had to go into court and get a subpoena."

I had heard the name before, and more bells were going off and ringing in my head.

"Isn't Bucaro mobbed up with the DiMatteo Family?"

"Yes, he is. Some time ago, we found out that the DiMatteo's had financed his operations for several years, and many of these sketchy transactions go through Bucaro's currency exchanges. He has fourteen of them scattered around the city."

"So, a cashier's check from one of Bucaro's currency exchanges, who happens to be connected to the DiMatteo Family..." I summarized.

"Yes," Romanowski replied, following along.

"And this a currency exchange that is located in Eddie Barrett's Fourteenth Ward, which was used to pay for a short-term, three-month lease for a house next door to the Mayor's home..."

"Yep, sure looks that way."

"And, according to Mrs. Simpson, the African American lady who lives across the street, says that she saw Chicago P.D. patrolmen going in and out of that house for several weeks before the Mayor's shooting..."

Romanowski was suddenly silent.

"And according to the neighbor across the street, she says that the police had..."

"How old is this lady?" the detective interrupted me.

"She looked to be in her late seventies," I replied.

"And you think that this old lady had got enough marbles to notice CPD coppers going in and out of that house?"

"Denny, she seemed pretty sharp."

"Did she notice anyone going in and out of that house on July 19th, the day of that shooting?"

"Well, that's what is so weird, Dennis. She notices all of this activity going on until the last day before the Mayor's murder."

A long silence over the telephone.

"McKay, let me call you back."

He then abruptly hung up the phone.

My conversation with Romanowski took place around three-thirty in the afternoon. Around 4:45 pm, I tried to call him back but got his voicemail, and for some odd reason, the detective didn't call me back.

Now I was suspicious. It wasn't like Romanowski to end a phone conversation abruptly and not return my call.

Early the next morning, I decided to pay him a visit at 1160 North Larrabee Street. I parked my car in the Chicago Police Department Eighteenth District parking lot and approached the desk sergeant.

"What's up, McKay? Long time, no see!" The gruff, six-foot, two-inch desk sergeant happily greeted me as I walked through the front door. Desk Sergeant Linda Bailey was a very tall, not very pretty police officer in her late fifties, whose physical appearance could probably scare most career criminals into going straight. I never had the nerve to ask her if she had a sex-change operation, as there were remnants of her five-o'clock shadow starting to crop up on that early Wednesday morning.

"Nice to see you too, Sarg. How many bagels am I going to have to bring to get in front of Detective Romanowski this morning?" I eagerly asked.

"I would say your chances are pretty low, considering that you've walked in here with your hands empty. The detective is in a meeting right now and will probably be another half hour or so."

I looked at my watch and noticed it was almost eight o'clock.

"So then...what will it take?" I politely asked.

"If you come back here with a couple of sesame seed bagels and a large, black coffee from Dunkin' Donuts, you might be able to get five minutes of his attention," she suggested.

"And while you're at it, get me a large coffee too...cream and sugar."

"Sure thing, Sarg."

I jumped back into my car and arrived back twenty minutes later with a small bag of sesame seed bagels, a tub of cream cheese, and two large coffees. Romanowski had just finished with his meeting, so I had timed it just right as she sent me in the right direction to his office.

"What's up, Detective?" I brightly exclaimed, bearing gifts.

I set his coffee and cream cheese bagels on his cluttered desk, hoping to get some respect and, maybe, some critical information.

"McKay, you couldn't wait for me to call you back?" he asked in his ordinarily gruff voice.

"And risk the chance of your getting in bed with another reporter? Come on, Denny! I want you all to myself," I joked.

"Yeah, right, McKay. You come waltzing into my office with coffee and bagels, expecting to pump more information out of me on the Mayor's assassination," Romanowski graveled loudly, as he didn't waste any time assaulting the Dunkin' Donuts bag of goodies.

"Would you like me to lie?" I said with a smile, hoping that my chirpy, bouncy sense of humor would charm him into giving me some information.

He reached into the bag, grabbed a sesame seed bagel, and slapped on some cream cheese. Romanowski then quickly devoured it as though he were going to the electric chair.

"Thanks, McKay," he replied, remembering to wish me a 'good morning' as well. After he took his first gulp of coffee, I watched the caffeine do its magic.

"So, what can I do for you, McKay?" he asked in a charming voice.

I looked at him suspiciously. Why was he suddenly playing stupid?

"Come on, Denny. Cut the crap. Why didn't you call me back yesterday?"

He looked at me emphatically, as if I had no business asking him any questions.

"I didn't hear back."

"Back from who?"

"I called Central Operations over in the Twelfth District. I figured they would have some information on why there was so much police activity in that house next door to Kollar's," the detective answered.

"Nobody contacted me."

I glared at him for several long seconds, as neither of us said a word.

Romanowski grabbed another bagel, and using his formal manners, scooped some cream cheese with his finger and used it as a utensil.

"Don't you expect them to call you back right away?"

"Not usually," he replied, inserting a large portion of that bagel in his mouth and trying to talk with his mouth full.

"And you're not suspicious?"

"No," he said with his mouth full. "They usually take their time returning phone calls."

"Even when you're trying to complete an investigation?"

He squinted his eyes at me as if I had no reason to question the Chicago Police Department's top brass.

Something was up, and I could tell Romanowski wasn't telling me everything. Earlier in the week, he said that he was working alongside Detectives Morton and Dorian, so I decided to play them up against each other.

"I was just at the Sixteenth District. Your buddy Tommy Morton asked me to pick him up some Marlboro cigarettes on the way in."

"Oh, really?" Still talking with his mouth full.

"Yeah, Morton thinks the CPD was renting that house for surveillance purposes."

It was total bullshit.

"Really? Morton said that?" Detective Romanowski started getting upset, his face turning three shades of red.

"Yeah, Tommy said that CPD was using that house for a while to keep an eye on any suspicious activity going on at Mayor Kollar's house."

"Fucking Morton shouldn't have told you that. That was classified information."

I smiled to myself, knowing that I had gotten him to admit something that he wasn't about to confirm or tell me otherwise.

"So, how did an assassin get into that house without the CPD coppers knowing about it?" I point-blank asked him.

There were several long moments of silence, as Romanowski had suddenly realized that his Dunkin' Donuts goodie bag was empty, and he no longer had any more fresh bagels to munch on.

"You're annoying me, McKay. I'm busy."

"You're holding out on me, Denny. I'm not feeling the love here."

"What the fuck do you want from me, McKay? As soon as I start asking Central Operations questions, they tell me that whatever was going on next door is classified information. So, all of a sudden, I'm supposed to stop asking questions on an investigation that we were assigned to investigate by Superintendent Walter Byron himself."

I looked at him with a half-smile on my face.

"And you and Morton are okay with this?"

A long moment of silence.

"No, McKay. I'm not. But I've also got twenty-three years invested here, and I need my pension. So, I do what I'm told."

I got up from the chair I was sitting on in front of his desk and grabbed my car keys.

"You surprise me, Denny. I always figured you as a straight shooter who didn't get pushed around by the Top Brass. There's a lot of unanswered questions here, and all of a sudden, you're not very hungry to get them answered."

He glared at me, initially not saying a word. By the look in his eyes, I could tell there was so much more information that he wanted to say to me and that there was so much more that needed to be investigated. The Top Brass was suddenly tying up his hands, and Detective Dennis Romanowski was forced to look the other way.

"You need to leave, McKay. I'm busy here," he only answered.

I smiled and shook his hand, leaving his office without saying another word that morning.

As the rain kept coming down that afternoon, I continued to bang out what little information I knew about the assassination plot to kill Mayor Kollar. Should I mention the house next door was temporarily being rented out by an unknown party, where the Chicago P.D. had full and total access?

At that moment, a gorgeous brunette came into the Franklin Caffe' holding a red umbrella over her head as if to unsuccessfully keep the pouring rain from getting her dark business suit all getting wet. As she walked up to the counter to order her croissant sandwich, she turned and looked at me. Her eyes seemed to gleam as though she was excited to see me sitting at the corner working on my laptop.

"How much are they charging you for rent here?" Talia Bowerman eagerly asked as she walked even closer to my makeshift office.

"It's a beautiful arrangement," I smiled back, noticing that her business attire had gotten significantly wet from all of the rain.

"I work, and they give me coffee and pie all day."

"Sounds like a beautiful thing," she smiled. I was utterly mesmerized at that moment, not being able to take my eyes off of her. There was something about her that was enthralling. She was dressed impeccably, wearing a warm, blue blouse unbuttoned half-way along with her curvy figure. Her flowing, dark, curly brown hair complemented her attire, as her tanned, shapely legs looked so perfectly, showing off those black, Zanotti high heeled shoes.

"Class tonight?" I asked.

"Yes. I need to get some homework done on the train."

As she stood there, I became a little nervous about trying to make conversation with her. I wanted to know more about her, to get her phone number, and to go past the awkward stage of getting her to pay more attention to me as I sat there in that little booth of my favorite coffee shop.

I could immediately tell that Talia Bowerman was not your average, friendly, run-of-the-mill acquaintance that was going to let me wine her, dine her, and have my way with her. This was a very classy, lovely lady. If anything, she seemed quite the opposite.

She was the kind of girl who enjoyed the mystery, who prided herself on being elusive, who got a thrill playing the mental chess games that go with every phrase, every sentence, every word. She was the kind of woman who challenged your whole thought process, the kind who knows that a single strand of her dark, wavy long hair could pull a thousand and one ships. She spoke with confidence, had the look of a Hollywood starlet, and had enough 'moxey' to let you know that she could probably beat you at your own game.

"How's the investigation going?" she eagerly asked.

"Very slow. How about you?"

"Everybody is pretty tight-lipped, especially the coppers."

Another awkward moment of silence.

"Would you like to sit down?" I asked, moving some of my computer bags off of the chair across from the make-shift desk.

"No, Larry. I'm running late for my train."

"Too bad," I said. "There's a nice slice of cheesecake and a cup of coffee with your name on it. Would go great with a rainy wet day like today," I suggested, knowing that I was very forward.

She smiled at me as the waitress announced her croissant sandwich and her cappuccino coffee to go was ready for her to grab and run.

"Next time, Larry. I promise. I need to get to class tonight," she said.

As she grabbed her goodies in the brown paper bag, she bee-lined it to the door, awkwardly pushing her umbrella to open before going outside in the rain.

"Hope to see you again," I said as she was about to leave. "I'm holding you to that promise."

Then she smiled and waved.

"I can't wait," she responded, waving me off as she exited the front door onto the pouring rain.

I smiled to myself as she continued to walk towards Union Station quickly. I hoped that maybe the next time I saw her, we could collaborate our information to complete this story. Perhaps there was a chance of having a journalist-partner in investigating this news article. Maybe there was a dinner date in the future.

As she walked away in the rain, I instinctively continued to stare at her walking away, holding her umbrella and strolling southbound on Wacker Drive in the drizzle.

At that moment, seeing her once again would be a dream come true.

CHAPTER TWENTY
MORNING HEADLINES - AUGUST 15TH

I had just arrived at my desk that morning when my desk phone was already ringing off the hook. I already knew who it was, as I had not even had a chance to grab my cup of coffee from the cafeteria that morning.

I looked over at my assistant editor's office, and I could see him waving me in from his large office window, looking over the newsroom. I held up my index finger, then made a motion with my left hand, indicating that I desperately needed my cup of caffeine. Assistant Editor John Olsen gave me a dirty look as I quickly went into the cafeteria and raped Mrs. Folger for that last cup of coffee sitting in the coffee pot.

The standard rule in the newsroom was that the last person to empty the final coffee cup had to make a new fresh pot, so I was obligated to throw another packet of ground coffee into the coffee maker. As the new pot was percolating, I could hear my desk phone ringing again from the other side of the office.

"Are you fucking nuts?" I immediately asked my editor as I walked into his office.

"Why are you blowing me off, McKay? I needed you in here right away!"

"Don't get your panties in a bunch, boss. I'm allowed a cup of coffee when I come into the newsroom, being that I was here banging out that story until past eleven o'clock last night."

Assistant Editor J. Thomas Olsen was smiling while making eye contact at the morning edition of the Chicago Tribune that was sitting on his desk with the front-page headlines:

Snipers Nest Leased By CPD

"My fucking phone has been ringing off the hook all morning," Olsen smiled, looking pleased with the product of yesterday's journalistic efforts.

"Oh really," I grinned as I sat down in front of Olsen's exceedingly immaculate antique desk.

I sometimes wondered when walking into my editor's office if he was the combined, demented version of the 'Odd Couple.' He looked and dressed like Oscar Madison but had the obsessive-compulsive disorder tendencies of Felix Unger. He was continually rearranging the objects on his neatly situated desk as if the particular arrangement and placement of his paperweights or pen holders had more significance over another.

Olsen was also a true believer of 'feng shui,' which is the Japanese philosophy of rearranging the furniture and living space to create a healthy balance within the natural world. As many people know, the goal of feng shui is to harness positive energy forces and establish harmony between an individual and their particular environment. Tom Olsen would often rearrange his office from time to time, believing that the positive flows of energy had more particular significance with where and what direction his antique desk and file cabinets were facing in his office.

All of this was just another testimonial of how mentally fucking sick this poor bastard really was.

"Chief of Police Walter Byron left me two nasty messages this morning."

"Really?" I said, sounding surprised.

I always enjoyed it when my front-page articles and headlines created controversy. I can't deny that I still got a 'hard-on' from watching all of the desk phones in the newsroom light up whenever I put out a front-page news article the day before.

"Byron is going to put out a press statement, calling our journalistic reporting 'irresponsible' and denying any connection between the CPD's leased house next door to Kollar's and the sniper."

"Well, we knew that was going to happen," I commented.

Tom Olsen smiled as if there was more. He pulled out a Lucky Strike cigarette and, while leaving it unlit, began twirling it around his mouth.

"He also wants your fucking head."

"Did you tell him to stand in line?" still trying to enjoy my first cup of now very lukewarm coffee.

Olsen placed the morning edition of the newspaper on another side of his neatly arranged desk, then started fidgeting with his paperweights.

"Byron probably put out a bounty on you, so I wouldn't go racing down Milwaukee Avenue anytime soon," Olsen warned, knowing that I often took Milwaukee Avenue home when the Kennedy Expressway was jammed up with traffic.

It wasn't unlike the Chief of Police Walter Byron to have his patrol officers pay extra attention to any Chicago Tribune reporter who wrote a derogatory article about either him or his beloved police department. I remember writing a critical news article regarding the Chicago Police Department a few months ago.

I made the mistake of associating his police department with the 'Keystone Coppers,' criticizing them for their lack of power and force with the increasing gangland activity and renewed violence in the city. A Chicago Police patrol car began following me going northbound on Milwaukee Avenue and didn't turn off until I almost arrived at my home in Sauganash. I was driving my BMW five miles under the speed limit, doing a mental check of any traffic violations that I could be busted on while that Chicago copper was tailgating me all the way home. Afterward, I mentioned this to Olsen, who got a kick out of it.

"Yeah, you're probably right. I'd better take the CTA for the next few weeks," I joked, both of us knowing that I wasn't much of a mass-transit commuter.

"So, how's your investigation going regarding all of the new city violence? You haven't put out another article since that 'Chicago Up For Grabs' headline you did a few weeks ago."

There had been several riots and lootings on Michigan Avenue and the surrounding Chicago Loop vicinity that past week. This violence was instigated by new 'Black Lives Matter' protests, led by a large band of Antifa protestors.

"I know. I've been way too busy with this Kollar Assassination, Chief. Still trying to ascertain the connection between the Chicago PD and this sniper at large."

"You may want to back off on that for right now. Until the Chicago P.D. starts making any arrests or comes up with any suspects, you may be spinning your wheels and wasting your time."

I nodded my head, now finishing my black cup of coffee and looking for more.

"Yeah, boss, but what I really can't understand," I pointed out, "is why the CPD detectives assigned to this investigation keep backing off wherever they get any new clues to solving this case?"

Olsen looked at me, his mental wheels turning over and spinning on all gears.

"Are you talking about Romanowski, Dorian, and Morton?"

"All three. It seems like every time I start getting too close to the truth; they stonewall me."

"Maybe Byron has a leash on them," Olsen observed.

"Maybe he's trying to slow down the investigation, making sure that they have all their 'ducks in order' before jumping to any conclusions," he concluded.

"But what would be the point in doing that? They're under a tremendous amount of pressure to solve this case. I would think that the sooner they can arrest a suspect, the sooner they can put this case to rest and stop all the heat from City Hall," I reasoned.

There was a moment of silence, as we both were deep in thought.

"Well, as we stated for the record, there is no definite connection with the CPD and the sniper, just because the bullet that killed Kollar came from that house next door. It's not unusual for the CPD to lease out adjacent properties for security purposes, and you pointed that out in your article last night," Olsen reminded me.

"Yeah, boss. But why slow down the investigation? It's as if as soon as the CPD detectives come up with another valuable clue, the 'Top Brass' push the detectives in another direction, almost as though they're purposely trying to distract them," I pointed out.

Another silent moment.

"What does your buddy, Romanowski say?"

"He's playing his cards close to his chest. But I've known him long enough to know that deep down, he's getting pretty frustrated. He doesn't want to make any waves."

Olsen picked up another glass, decorative paperweight and put it down on the other side of his desk.

"Your pallie needs to grow some balls."

"My pallie is trying to protect his pension," I quickly answered.

At that moment, I felt my cellular phone vibrating in my back pocket. As I pulled it up and looked at the caller ID, I immediately smiled.

It was Detective Romanowski.

"I'll call you back," I immediately answered, then hung up the phone.

"Speaking of detectives without balls," I smiled, indicating that the cell phone call was from Romanowski himself.

"Okay, McKay. Let me know what else you come up with," Olsen said in closing.

"And like I said, don't go speeding down Milwaukee Avenue," he jokingly smiled.

I got up from his chair and threw out my empty styrofoam cup into his steel circular file next to his desk. I then began dialing Detective Romanowski's cell phone number as I was returning to my cubicle.

"Are you out of your fucking mind?" was the detective's immediate greeting as he answered his phone.

"Good morning, Dennis," I replied.

"I've got your 'Good morning' right here, you crazy fuck," the detective responded.

"I'm beginning to believe that you're pretending to be dumb now and again isn't just an act after all. You *really are* this fucking stupid," Romanowski chastised.

"I didn't put anything in that article that we didn't already verify," I said in my defense.

"Yeah, but by putting that leased house in the papers makes us look fucking bad, not to mention that you've compromised the investigation," Denny replied.

"What investigation, Denny? You 'Three Stooges' haven't come up with shit!"

"Just because I haven't shared all of our 'intel' with you doesn't mean we haven't uncovered anything."

There was a three-second pause.

"Do you have any idea how much my butt hurts this morning? Byron has been busy reaming my ass over the phone."

"I'm sorry, Denny. I didn't mean to throw you in front of the bus. I only mentioned your name in the article once," I said.

"Once is one time too many, dumbass. You know I don't like my name in the papers, especially when it's misspelled."

"What?"

I picked up the Tribune article and read it over closely while still on the phone. Even though I had spelled the detective's name correctly in my final submission, it had somehow been wrongly typeset and somehow misspelled. My news article referred to the Chicago detective from the CPD Eighteenth District as Romankowski' rather than Detective 'Romanowski,' with the insertion of an extra letter 'k.'

"Blame the printers, Amigo. I spelled it right when I submitted it last night."

"You were never any good with 'pollock' names," he replied, his voice now calming down to a mild snicker.

"Well, Denny, at least you have some deniability," I chuckled. "You can always say it wasn't you."

"Fat chance of that, you fucking idiot."

Still holding my cell phone next to my ear, I was walking back into the newsroom cafeteria, ready to attack my second cup of coffee. I was forced to use a styrofoam cup on that morning, as my ceramic 'Go Chippewas' coffee cup had accidentally been knocked off of my desk the day before and broke into a million pieces.

"So, does this mean that you're banning me from the Eighteenth District?"

"Absolutely. It's going to cost you more than a dozen fresh bagels to ever to walk back in here again," Dennis reprimanded.

There was a moment of silence as I was slurping my freshly brewed coffee very loudly over the phone.

"So, what's Little Tony been up to?" I eagerly asked, knowing that the Chicago P.D.

has had a patrol car staking out him out in his food warehouse's parking lot on South Ashland Avenue.

"Why do you ask?"

"I'm snooping around for another story."

"Call Detective Dorian. Little Tony is on his radar."

"Yeah, right. You know Phil Dorian won't give me the time of day."

"For good reason, you dumbshit."

There was a slight pause in Detective Dennis Romanowski's voice.

"From what I've heard from Dorian, it's been a boring stake-out. Little Tony seems only to be going back and forth from home to work, day in and day out," Denny responded.

"You're right. That is boring."

Another pause.

"Except for Wednesdays."

"What happens on Wednesdays?" I innocently asked.

"For some odd reason, during these past few Wednesday nights, Little Tony has been going to the St. Simeon Rectory on 79th Street and spending several hours there."

"Really?" I asked. I was now suddenly very interested in this strange new activity.

"Is he attending mass at St. Simeon?"

"Doubt it. If he's not going to his neighborhood church in Bridgeport on Sundays, why would he be hanging around St. Simeon on Wednesday nights?"

There was a long silence on the phone, as the two of us were deep in thought. Maybe he was suddenly interested in bible studies at St. Simeon Church with the church pastor?

Then I remembered who the church pastor was at St. Simeon Church.

"Isn't that Fr. Fitzgerald's church on 79th Street? That community activist priest who's always trying to get his name in the papers?"

"Yes, it is."

I suddenly became wary as a light bulb went off in my head.

"I'll talk to you later, Denny."

As I hung up the telephone, the wheels started spinning in my head. I jumped on the internet and started researching all of the recent news articles that I could find regarding Anthony 'Little Tony' DiMatteo and Fr. Colin Fitzgerald, the St. Simeon pastor.

I found the recent obituary of Little Tony's mother, Carmela DiMatteo, on the internet, who had just died during the last week of July. And like all Catholic obituaries, it listed who the presiding priest would be over the ninety-four-year-old's celebration of life at the Our Lady of the Nativity Church in Bridgeport:

None other than Fr. Colin J. Fitzgerald.

Was he going to St. Simeon for spiritual enlightenment and bereavement counseling? Was Little Tony suddenly embracing his Catholic faith and discovering his mortality and Christian morals later in life?

With anybody else, those would have been very viable explanations. But for anyone who knew Little Tony and his dangerous reputation in town, going to catechism and 'Discovering Jesus' could never logically be on Capo dei Capi's agenda.

And Fr. Fitzgerald's reputation as a social reformer and a pro-death sentence activist made me even more suspicious. Fr. Fitzgerald was very well known for his very vocal 'eye-for-an-eye' philosophies, which have always been in sharp contrast to the Roman Catholic Church's religious doctrines.

I would later discover the connection between DiMatteo's visits to the St. Simeon Rectory and the sudden surge of upcoming violence that was about to plague Chicago.

CHAPTER TWENTY-ONE
FRIENDS IN WAITING -LATE NIGHT AUGUST 16TH

That hot, summer evening in the middle of August only continued to get hotter, as the sweltering evening temperatures exceeded ninety-five degrees. The city's humidity was almost overbearing, as one needed a cold bottle of water only to walk outside.

There had been some bantering of some social unrest posted on some of the Facebook and Instagram accounts to the effect that there would be some social unrest that evening.

The previous Saturday evening, there was an incident involving the killing of a young, African American man in the Auburn-Gresham neighborhood by one of the Chicago Police patrolmen. Two squad cars responded to a robbery in progress at a convenience store at the corner of 83rd Street and Loomis.

When two of the would-be robbers exited the store, the police had ordered the criminals to 'Freeze' and to 'Drop Your Weapons.' One of them, a twenty-six-year-old man named Antonio Barnes, drew his gun and took a shot at the officer. The officer, feeling that his life had been threatened, shot back, hitting the man in the chest, and instantly killing him.

It was only a matter of minutes before the victim's shooting was reported on Channel Eight Eyewitness News. Their star reporter, Chaz Rizzo, was at the crime scene within thirty minutes of the incident.

Before the shooting, the reporter had a prior engagement at the Il Quartino Ristorante on North State Street. Rizzo was on a first date with one of his frequent Match.Com hookups when he had to run out of the restaurant to cover this young man's horrific killing on the South Side.

"This is Chaz Rizzo, Channel Eight Eyewitness News. There has been a shooting death of a 26-year-old male in the Auburn-Gresham neighborhood. The victim was one of two African American males attempting to rob this convenience store on the corner of 83rd and Loomis tonight. The police arrived, guns were drawn, and the victim was shot once in the chest. He was taken to Chicago-Western Hospital, where he was pronounced dead."

Chas Rizzo went on to report the incident and interview several eyewitnesses. They were all African American, and they all said the Chicago patrolman drew his weapon first and that they didn't see the victim draw his gun. Another eyewitness stated that the police officer had ample time to stop or 'taser' the victim without using deadly force. The patrolman's life was never in danger, according to the nearby eyewitnesses there at the scene.

One of the community activists was interviewed on the air for his comments. He was an African American named Lester Andrews, and he stated on all the newscasts later that evening that this killing was another example of Chicago's police brutality. Defenseless, African Americans are *viciously being murdered* by the Chicago Police force.

It was all over the news and social media that Saturday evening that an innocent black man was shot and brutally killed by the Chicago police.

The new Mayor of Chicago, Ray Sanchez, conducted a news conference the following

Sunday afternoon, expressing his extreme disappointment in the Chicago Police Department. He demanded the officer's body camera video be immediately released to the news media to demonstrate exactly what had happened.

By the time the Superintendent of the Chicago Police had released the information from the officer's body camera later that day, it was too late.

The 'Black Lives Matter' groups and other Antifa activists within the city began their protests in front of Chicago's City Hall. There were hundreds of people downtown, protesting the 'brutal' police shooting and demanding that the City of Chicago now 'defund' the police department.

Little Tony DiMatteo was sitting in his living room in Bridgeport that Sunday morning, reading the newspaper and enjoying his usual cup of double espresso. He had just worked out at the gym in his office on South Ashland Avenue but decided to return home early that summer day in August. He and his wife, Angelina, had promised that they would be at his sister's house on Grand Avenue to celebrate his brother-in-law, Antonio Fazio's eightieth birthday that Sunday afternoon.

His sister, Costanza, was expecting the whole family to be over for dinner at her house at one o'clock. Of course, Little Tony knew that his sister never took 'no' for an answer. His wife was at church over at Our Lady of the

Nativity and usually didn't come home before eleven o'clock.

Because he never liked to talk business when he was at home, Tony decided to make an exception and called his consigliere.

Little Tony turned on his 'burner phone.'

"Sal, are you fucking watching this shit?" Tony asked his trusted associate, Salvatore Marrocco.

"This killing is all over the fucking news. Now these 'Black Lives Matter' people are starting trouble again. They're already fucking protesting over at City Hall."

"Yeah, I saw Chaz Rizzo on the news last night."

"Yeah, and nowhere does any one of these dumb mother-fuckers say anything on the news about this black guy fucking drawing his gun first at the police officer."

"Yeah, I know Tony."

Little Tony was quiet for several long moments.

"How quickly can you assemble the drivers at the warehouse."

"I can get most of them there by two o'clock."

The consigliere knew not to be very specific or inquire about any details regarding the Capo dei Capi's request. The two of them never trusted any cell phones or even the burner phones they regularly used. They knew that their means of cell phone communication could never entirely be relied upon as fully secured.

Little Tony was quite familiar with having his telephones bugged, and he was always meticulous about what he said over the phone. Marrocco was only told to assemble about one hundred of his men to get together for a meeting.

Little Tony had been thinking long and hard about Fr. Fitz's proposal. He thought the priest was out of his mind at first, especially when the pastor brought the subject up again during their chess match last week.

Maybe, this priest wasn't so crazy.

That afternoon, Little Tony and his wife were just finishing dinner at his sister's house on Grand Avenue when he had to excuse himself.

"Connie, see if one of your sons can take Angelina home. Something just came up at the warehouse," Tony ordered her sister.

Despite her protests, Little Tony got into his black Maserati and drove southbound to his tomato distribution company on South Ashland Avenue.

When he arrived at 2:15 pm, almost one hundred of his teamster's truckdrivers were assembled at the warehouse, just as Sal Marrocco had promised. As he walked into the warehouse, he greeted several of his employees and called over his consigliere.

He pulled Marrocco into his office upstairs, and they were in a conference for the next twenty minutes or so, as he gave his trusted consigliere his marching orders.

Little Tony DiMatteo had a plan.

It was almost seven o'clock on that Sunday evening, and the rioters, activists, and 'Black

Lives Matter' groups were in full force, marching everywhere in the Chicago Loop. The Chicago Police Department spokesman reported that the officers involved in the Auburn-Gresham neighborhood incident shot and killed the suspect who was firing at them during the convenience store robbery. But these statements did not affect the citywide chaos in the area, with crowds lashing out at what they called extreme police actions.

None of the news media had correctly reported the incident, emphasizing that the Chicago robber had been killed at the police's hands, without including the cops being shot first by the victim. The Chicago P.D. kept saying that the news media's misinformation was sparking widespread outrage, causing a complete and total distrust in the community.

Meanwhile, word of the incident left outrage behind. Videos were being broadcasted, showing crowds gathering in front of several upscale stores on Michigan Avenue, and about an hour later, and more police flooded in.

Several rioters were busy looting and smashing store windows, justifying their actions as 'reparations' that were owed to all African Americans from the injustices of slavery over two hundred years ago.

The crowds of over three hundred rioters were now getting aggressive. There were more tense moments amid clashes with the police. The word had spread on social media that the person the officers had shot was a young boy, not a 26-year-old violent male criminal.

Hundreds of people smashed windows, stole from stores, and clashed with police in

Chicago's Magnificent Mile shopping district and other parts of the city's downtown.

A crowd of people began to approach the Jewelers Row district on South Wabash, where several other stores in the area had already been vandalized and looted.

A red Chevrolet van pulled up in front of the jewelry store at 17 South Wabash. In front of the store, two large burly gentlemen, Tony Campana and Joe Rogelio. They were sitting on their lawn chairs drinking their espressos and relaxing, totally oblivious to the nearby violence going on around their immediate area.

As three young, African American boys quickly got their vehicle with baseball bats and sledgehammers in hand, they had immediately approached the jewelry store's front door entrance and storefront. The three young boys stopped and momentarily looked at the two, burley gentlemen.

Still holding his espresso in his hand, one of the men, Joe Rogelio, calmly smiled and exclaimed,

"Yous' guys shouldn't go in there if I was you."

Laughing at the two men, the three youths broke the front door and the window and proceeded to enter the jewelry store. They started smashing several display cases, which only had some very cheap costume jewelry lavishly displayed with exorbitant fake price tags.

When the second display case was broken, two large men dressed in black and wearing ski masks came out from the back of the store, holding AK-47 semi-automatic rifles.

"YOUS' GUYS WERE FUCKIN' WARNED," one of them screamed as they both fired their automatic weapons into the three black youths, firing off over one hundred rounds.

Their blood and brain matter was now splattered all over the walls. Pieces of their flesh had been brutally shot off, scattered on the carpeted floor and the display cases that they were attempting to smash and grab. Their young faces were completely bloodied and unrecognizable, as bullets were fired into their heads, their arms, their legs, and throughout their torsos.

Another black youth, who was sitting in the red van, came out to see what was going on. Both of the burly men were still sitting on their lawn chairs, calmly drinking their espressos.

"Yous' guys were told not to go in there," Tony Campana said.

Another young black man came out of the van. This one was armed. Before he could draw his weapon, Joe Rogelio stood up from his lawn chair and shot the young black kid between the eyes, with the youth's gun still in his hand.

Now Campana stood up from his chair as the other black youth observed the whole incident in horror.

"Look what yous' guys did. Yous' guys made me spill my coffee."

The witness, obviously scared to death, retreated into his van and quickly sped off.

Within minutes, several police squad cars were in front of 7 South Wabash Street.

"What the hell happened?" one of the patrolmen asked.

Inside the jewelry store, there were three dead youths lying face up, their bodies wholly shot up from multiple gunshot wounds. The two burly men managed to drag the other doomed black kid inside the store, in front of the door, before the police arrived.

As the several patrolmen were gathering in front of the jewelry store, the two men were still sitting in front of the store, drinking espresso. They had a large thermos filled with their favorite Italian coffee sitting between their lawn chairs.

"We ain't seen nuttin'," one of the men said, as the patrolman continued to survey the violent killing of the four black youths. One of the patrolmen noticed that the jewelry store's surveillance cameras had been shot at and were dislodged and not working when the police arrived.

As it had turned out, Little Tony targeted sixty-seven jewelry stores within the Chicago Loop and the surrounding areas, and they had immediately staffed them with his version of 'security guards' or the DiMatteo Family's very experienced 'associates.'

Earlier that Sunday, Sal Marrocco called the jewelry store owners he had on his speed dial list and e-mail directory. He predicted that there would be massive looting that evening and asked them if they needed 'extra protection.' He knew that there would be rioting and violence that Sunday evening from what had previously happened in months past.

As Fr. Fitz had initially suggested, Little Tony's underworld business would greatly benefit from the additional protection and security services that he would be able to provide to any of the local business owners who were getting tired of replacing windows, restoring merchandise, and filing insurance claims.

Both he and Sal Marrocco predicted that the city's jewelry stores and the Chicago Loop would get looted first. He knew that the 'protection fees' that he was charging the sixty-seven jewelry stores in the Chicagoland area would be money well spent on 'security protection' on that violent Sunday evening.

Later that night, Little Tony waited up for his consigliere's phone call on his burner phone. He was sitting on his Lazy-boy chair, enjoying a glass of wine, and watching the news. When Marrocco called at about ten o'clock, he told him of the incident at 7 South Wabash.

Little Tony smiled and loudly reacted, "I love this fucking priest."

He referred to Father Colin J. Fitzgerald, and the Capo dei Capi couldn't have been more pleased.

The Channel Eight news trucks were now in front of the vandalized jewelry store, with white sheets draped over the four victims.

Chaz Rizzo was already standing in front of his Channel Eight news truck, preparing and waiting to do the news feed for the ten o'clock news. Police detectives were now swarming around the area, as Detective Tommy Morton from the Sixteenth District arrived in his squad car at about ten-thirty.

"Good evening, Detective," Rizzo smiled, trying to greet the Sixteenth District detective respectfully. Rizzo had known Morton for a significant number of years. Detective Morton only nodded his head at the news reporter.

When the patrolman briefed him on the jewelry store victims' circumstance, Detective Morton already knew that he was in over his head.

He immediately knew right away, from the identification of the two burly men that were sitting in front of the jewelry store, that this shooting incident was something completely different and unusual, like nothing he had ever seen before.

He then called his partner, Detective Philip Dorian, on his cell phone at home.

"Good evening Phil, sorry to bother you tonight," he immediately apologized.

"We have four dead youths in front of the jewelry store at 7 South Wabash. One of them was shot point-blank in the head. The other three were shot up with what looks like bullets from a couple of AK-47's."

Dorian, who was barely awake and was watching television in his West Loop loft, suddenly had alarms loudly going off in his head.

"Any idea who did this?" he asked Morton, thinking that it could be a gang-related incident.

"The two guys we picked up are Teamsters from the Local 705. There are both drivers for DiMatteo Tomato Distribution on South Ashland," Morton explained.

"They were sitting on lawn chairs drinking coffee in front of the jewelry store and watched the whole incident happen," Morton described.

Dorian was surprised.

"What the fuck were two Teamsters truck drivers doing in front of a jewelry store on

South Wabash while the rest of the city was getting looted?"

Morton hesitated to respond.

"They said that they were only observing the crowds and that they warned the deceased men not to enter the store."

As it turned out, both of the men who were sitting outside of that jewelry store on South Wabash were indeed Teamsters, union truck drivers for the DiMatteo Tomato Distribution Company.

Anthony Campana and Joseph Rogelio were both trusted associates of the DiMatteo Crime Family. Both men were taken into custody by the police and brought down to the Chicago Police Department District One on South State Street. They were questioned extensively and held overnight. Neither refused to volunteer any information, only insisting that they 'didn't see nuttin'."

Their criminal attorney, Michael Prescott, who recently had been retained and was now on the DiMatteo payroll, arrived at the police precinct early on that Monday morning. He skillfully pleaded that the negligent youths were initially warned by the 'security guards' not to trespass or enter the jewelry store.

When they smashed several display cases and had weapons in their hands, the store's security had the right to shoot them to defend their property and safety. It didn't matter that three of the four criminal youths were brutally shot up and mutilated with AK-47 automatic rifles. The two gunmen then immediately escaped from the jewelry store using the back-door exit.

And, of course, the two security guards sitting on their lawn chairs drinking their espressos throughout the whole incident had no idea who the gunmen were. Campana and Rogelio were quietly released that Monday morning, without any media coverage or fanfare.

In reality, Phil Dorian knew what had happened and how those truck drivers had coincidently been there in front of that Jeweler's Row store on South Wabash. There were several long moments of silence on the phone.

"Phil, are you there?"

Another moment of silence.

"Yeah, Tommy, I'm here."

They now were both silent, as Dorian was deep in thought.

"What do you make of this shit?" Morton eagerly asked.

After another moment, Dorian smiled as he answered his partner's question:

"I think Little Tony is a fucking genius."

CHAPTER TWENTY-TWO
THE BOYS CLUB- THE DAY AFTER

On that warm summer night, the air conditioning in my townhouse was going full blast as I was relaxing on the couch with the television blaring. I had just arrived home that Sunday night from visiting with my mother that day, and it felt nice to fall asleep and relax once again on my own, comfortable couch. The family room of my townhouse felt so relaxed, cool, and comfortable. In fact, it was almost freezing. I couldn't remember if I set the thermostat on my air conditioner on either 'meats' or 'frozen foods.'

It had been a very peaceful, relaxing weekend. I spent most of that day at my mother's house in Norridge, cutting her grass and piddling around the house with different odds and ends chores that she needed to be done. She had made farfalle pasta with Bolognese sauce for our Sunday dinner, and I was still stuffed from my mother's homemade cooking.

I was practically half-asleep on the couch when the ten o'clock news came blasting out of the big screen TV with a shocking bulletin:

Channel Eight Eyewitness news has just learned of four youths, ranging from ages fifteen to eighteen years old, have been brutally killed inside the Mancini Jewelry store, located on 17 South Wabash in Jewelers Row. The youths were attempting to break in and loot the store when some security guards with AK-47 semi-automatic rifles violently shot the four African Americans. Two men, who were acting as security lookouts, were arrested by the Chicago Police Department. Their names are Anthony Campana and Joseph Rogelio, known union teamsters and work for the DiMatteo Tomato Distribution Company on South Ashland Avenue. The names of the murdered victims have not yet been released.

I suddenly stood up from my couch and glued myself to the Channel Eight newscast, trying to absorb as much information as I could. There had been some anticipation of some downtown riots and looting that many thought would occur over the weekend. I had heard that several businesses had boarded up their shops in anticipation of the civil unrest.

Mayor Ray Sanchez and the Police Superintendent Walter Byron had requested that additional police forces begin patrolling the Chicago Loop area that weekend, as I was sure that the Jewelers Row area was well patrolled at the time of the incident.

The newscast stated that the two men arrested had sat in front of the jewelry store as lookouts as if they were anticipating the jewelry store to be broken into and robbed. The news reporter mentioned something about some security guards inside the store who did the shooting.

At that point, I was suspicious. Two burly truck drivers, who were Teamsters, were employed by the DiMatteo Tomato Distribution Company. Anyone who was a 'mob watcher' in town knew that most truck drivers in the Teamsters Union had a connection to the DiMatteo Family. It immediately sounded like the jewelry store owner was connected to Little

Tony DiMatteo or hired him that evening to guard his jewelry store in case of looters.

I went to the newsroom early the following Monday morning, and I knew that I would be covering this story for the paper. If the DiMatteo's were involved in this shooting incident, I knew where I had to go and who I needed to meet to get my information. I decided that I needed visit some 'friends' later that morning.

It was about ten o'clock on that Monday morning when I parallel parked my car on West 31st and Morgan Streets in Bridgeport. There was an unmarked, red brick building that many in the neighborhood knew was a social club. Some of 'The Boys' hang out there, and I was looking for one 'wise-guy' in particular.

The faded address of 1013 West 31st Street was barely readable on the unmarked, red-bricked building near the railroad tracks. It had been an unassuming social club for the last thirty years. I liked to call it a 'man-cave for Bridgeport grease-balls,' where many Italian men hung out there to play cards, drink espressos, watch football, and enjoy the Italian soccer games all day long. Some would spend hours on the gambling machines in the back room, while the rest either played cards or craps in the other room. It was sort of a 'mini-casino' there, and most of the local 'grease balls' found it to be a great place to hang out to escape their homes and their nagging wives.

When I opened the entrance door, probably two dozen or more guys were sitting and standing around the bar, with all of their eyes looking directly at me. I felt like an alien as if I was deformed with three-eyes, as I casually walked up to the bar.

"Espresso doppio," I loudly ordered, knowing that in a place like that, you never asked for 'cappuccino.'

"Molto bene," the barista answered, assuming that I was Italian.

I looked around the room, finally locking eyes with the very man I was looking for, playing cards in the corner.

Marco 'Crazy Eight' Incandella was a large, barrel-chested, older man in his late fifties, barely five feet, seven inches tall. He had a large double chin and probably weighed no less than three hundred pounds, always wearing a large sweatshirt hoodie to cover his protruding stomach.

They called him 'Crazy Eight' for two reasons: The first reason was that he only had eight fingers, having lost his index and middle finger on his left hand from a violent mob hit gone wrong. The second reason was quite apparent; the man was definitely crazy.

There was a story several years ago that he was once in a card game with another man, Pat Brandonisio, who refused to cover his $500 marker, spitting on Crazy Eight's face when he asked him for the money.

That was probably not a very wise decision on Brandonisio's part.

Crazy Eight went ballistic. They say he chased him with a hunting knife down 31st Avenue in Bridgeport in the middle of the day until finally catching him hiding behind some garbage cans in a backstreet alley.

The DiMatteo hitman was also well known for his culinary skills with a butcher knife. He immediately emasculated him, cutting off his penis and shoving it into his mouth. He then continued to stab him to death while his genitals were still in his mouth until his face and body were decimated beyond recognition. Brandonisio's s homicide was another one of many unsolved murders in the Bridgeport neighborhood.

In Bridgeport, the Italian phrase 'omerta' (the code of silence about any criminal activity and refusal to give any evidence to the authorities) is still a practice that is religiously followed in the Southside neighborhood.

Marco Incandella was an enforcer and a high-ranking lieutenant in the DiMatteo Family for many years. He was considered third in charge regarding his family ranking and was an understudy to the family consigliere, Sal Marrocco. Incandella was very close to the family capo, Anthony 'Little Tony' DiMatteo.

Crazy Eight Incandella was the one in the DiMatteo Family who made things happen. Having written some news stories and investigated several mob incidents over the last thirty years in Chicago, I met Incandella many years ago and forged a good friendship with him. Crazy Eight was my 'go-to' guy whenever something was going on with the Chicago Outfit, especially in the DiMatteo Family. He took personal control of all of the illegal activities that the DiMatteo's were involved in. Crazy Eight liked to say that he worked in the DiMatteo Family's 'accounts receivable' department.

I waited for my espresso and walked over to the table where he played some Italian card game with an Italian deck of cards. He was sitting with three other enormous 'gorillas,' pretending not to know who I was.

"Hey Craz', what's going on," I casually said, trying to get him to take notice of my presence.

"In a few minutes, Larry. I'm busy here," as he slammed a few cards on the table and rattled out some Italian swear words I had only heard from my mother when I was a little kid.

Being half Italian from my maternal side, I was very familiar with Italian phrases and vulgarity when growing up near Belmont and Central Avenues. My mother, who spoke fluent Italian, directed her obscene, Ivy League repertoire at my innocent Scottish father. She was a brilliant 'wordsmith' of sorts. In both languages, she could insert and put together swear words into names and sentences that I never thought were even possible.

I watched him finish playing their card game while I sat at another empty table. I was still feeling all the other sets of eyes staring back at me, practically 'burning holes' into my skull with their x-ray vision.

"Catzo di Mama" Crazy Eight loudly yelled out as he threw his failed hand of cards on the table. He threw out a twenty-dollar bill, then got up and smiled at his 'gorilla' friends, who were all too happy to take his money. Incandella then walked over to my table where I was sitting.

I immediately got up to shake his hand, but he was all too eager to pull me towards him and kiss me on both cheeks.

"Hey, what's up, McKay?"

"Hey Craz, how are you?"

"Great. Hey, I read that article you wrote on the Mayor a while ago. I was impressed. It was very 'articulate.'"

I was shocked that Crazy Eight even picked up and read the paper, let alone critique a news article that I had written. I looked at him strangely for a minute, then realizing that he was using an unfamiliar fifty-cent word and had no clue what it meant.

"Articulate? Do you mean to say 'eloquent'?"

"Oh yeah, that's it. You know what I mean, McKay. It was a nice article."

Crazy Eight sat back down and ordered us both another espresso. We then exchanged 'how are you's' and talked about his grown-up kids and miserable marriage. After a few more minutes, Incandella broke the ice.

"So, what's up, McKay?"

"Craz, do you know anything about that shooting incident on Jeweler's Row last night?"

Incandella paused and looked at me for a moment, as his dark, olive leather skin started to turn red. He then looked around the room.

"No," he bluntly said, as he looked at me straight in the eyes while finishing his coffee. His blank, cold stare almost looked scary, as we both knew he wasn't telling the truth.

"What do you mean, 'no'?" I pressed.

"McKay, I just told you. No. No means no. I don't know nuttin'."

Incandella looked at me again, and I could tell he was starting to get uncomfortable with the conversation. I decided to let the silence sink in as I was finishing my second cup of espresso. I then suggested that Crazy Eight and I go outside and talk.

As he followed me out to the back of the building where the parking lot was located, I suddenly realized that I was asking some very personal questions to a terrifying guy like Marco 'Crazy Eight' Incandella. He had quite a vicious reputation and allegedly had several violent hits of his own under his belt. Being in the middle of Bridgeport, standing outside in a back-parking lot on an early Monday morning in the summer was probably not such a good idea.

"Look, McKay. You can't come in here and start asking 'dems kind of questions about whatever you hear on the fucking news," he explained with a very stern tone in his voice.

I looked at him, figuring I could get him to calm down with my usual, relaxed 'reporter's charm' without him getting too excited.

"Come on, Craz. I'm not trying to start any trouble here. It's just that I'm going to be assigned to covering this story, and I need to find out exactly what happened before some other reporter blows it out of proportion."

"Just because some kids got blown away last night doesn't mean it had nuttin' to do with us. We had nuttin' to do with those kids getting' blasted."

"Cut the bullshit, Craz! Two of your guys got picked up while standing guard at that jewelry store last night, who just happen to be union Teamsters. Everyone in town knows that your family has most of those drivers on your payroll."

"I don't know what you're talking about, McKay."

Crazy Eight was now starting to get agitated as if I was stirring an angry rattlesnake with a long stick. I looked at him for several long, silent seconds.

"Okay, Craz. Have it your way. I'll write the story based on whatever street gossip and information I get from District Sixteen police detectives. When the subject of the DiMatteo Family gets brought up, I won't sweep anything under the carpet," I said in a booming and assertive voice.

Crazy Eight started glaring at me, wondering if I had just found my new set of balls. I guess it took a lot of guts for me to start talking to him loudly, so rudely, and in a very condescending tone of voice.

"I'm sure Marrocco and Little Tony will love seeing your family's name in the Chicago Tribune tomorrow," I pointed out. "and there won't be a damn thing that I can do about it."

Crazy Eight was now giving me a dirty look.

There were more moments of silence, as the noisy traffic on 31st Street was starting to get congested and backed up on that Monday morning. The noise from the stream of traffic would have easily deafened the sound of any gunshot blast.

"Okay, McKay. But I'm only telling you this out of respect for our friendship. I know you're going to be discerning."

I immediately knew that the gangster was getting his fifty-cent words all mixed up again.

"You mean discrete."

"Yeah, that's it."

I only nodded my head.

"Don't blab out nuttin' stupid about the family."

"I promise, Craz. I will make sure your family's name doesn't get into the papers."

Another silent moment.

"Our family is now in the security guard business. We're going around our stops and asking if they need additional security services for a big bump in the street tax."

"Really?"

"Yeah, with these downtown riots and lootings going around, we're standing watch outside of our street stops and guarding their places, makin' sure nobody breaks in."

"Okay, so what happened last night?"

"The story I heard was Joe Rogelio, and Tony Campana were standing watch in front of Mancini's Jewelry when some black kids in a red van pulled up with sledgehammers and baseball bats. They were verbally warned not to go inside and break anything, but they didn't listen. Those dumb fucks decided to go inside anyway and started looting, busting up cases, and stealing shit."

"Okay, then what happened."

"They were told to stop and leave by two of our guys who were sitting in the back room with their loaded pieces. When they wouldn't leave, those kids got blasted."

I stood there in the back of that red brick building, totally shocked at what I was hearing.

"Since when did you guys start guarding your stops from looters? Who put this idea into your heads to start doing this shit?"

Incandella started glaring at me again, wondering now if he should stop talking to a news reporter.

"You guys know that's only looking for trouble. It's was only a matter of time before somebody got hurt," I pointed out.

"And why would you guys be shooting at a bunch of teenagers anyway? Killing them no less! You guys couldn't just scare them away?"

"Look, McKay, I've told you too much. I'm going back inside."

"Wait! Tell me how these security services got started. Was this from the Capo? Where did all of this start?"

Incandella looked at me again, ready to turn his back on me and to walk back into the boys club without answering any more questions.

"We're done here, McKay."

"Come on, Craz. Throw me a bone here. Where is this shit coming from?" I innocently asked the family 'made-man'.

"Has Little Tony had a sudden 'divine intervention' somewhere? Has someone from the 'powers that be' been telling him he's gotta start protecting his customers and his stops?" I naively asked.

Crazy Eight's eyes suddenly bulged out from out of his head.

"Divine Intervention? How did you hear this?"

I realized that I suddenly hit a nerve. I decided to bullshit and pretend that I knew what was going on. Marco Incandella was an easy target to pump out information.

"Well, yeah, Craz. The whole city knows that Little Tony has found Jesus since his mother died," I said.

I had no idea what I was talking about, and it was all complete bullshit. Crazy Eight looked at me even more intently, now wanting to set the story straight.

"Look, McKay, just because the boss has been going to St. Simeon's once a week doesn't mean he's a religious freak now. He only goes there for business," he said very nervously.

I looked at him, now knowing that I had him on the hook. I realized at that moment that I was barking up the right tree.

"Business? What kind of business does the Capo have at St. Simeon's Church?"

I immediately thought about Fr. Colin Fitzgerald, who was the pastor there at St. Simeon's Church. Fr. Fitz was also a very energetic political activist, holding his neighborhood demonstrations and conducting news media rallies on his church doorsteps regarding any new political happenings that are going on in the city. I was there once covering a story on a rally Fr. Fitz was conducting last year on the late-term abortion laws recently passed in Springfield.

"It's none of my business what the Capo does on Wednesday nights at church, McKay."

"He must be doing a lot of praying," I assumed.

Incandella laughed.

"No, he ain't praying. He's been reading a lot of books on chess."

"Books on chess?"

"Yeah. When he's in his office at the warehouse, he's got a stack of chess books sitting on the corner of his desk when he's not barking out orders."

"You're kidding?"

"Yeah, he's even got a chessboard set up in his office. The boss and Sal Marrocco have been playing chess every day at lunchtime."

I started shaking my head in disbelief.

"All the guys in the warehouse are laughing about it. The boss has offered to double their paychecks to anyone who can beat him in a game of chess."

I started to laugh to myself at this new revelation. While all of the other capos from 'The Outfit' are playing golf at the Medinah Country Club at a $1000 a hole, Little Tony is boning up on his chess game.

The street hood suddenly got nervous, afraid that someone would see us talking together outside the back parking lot.

"You gotta go now, McKay. You've overstayed your welcome."

Crazy Eight then walked back into the boys club to finish his morning card games of 'Scopa' and 'Briscola' with the rest of his gorilla friends.

Books on Chess? Meetings at St. Simeon's on Wednesday nights? What the hell was going on? What was the connection, and what did it have to do with the DiMatteo's going into the armed security business on Chicago's streets?

Judging by the nervousness displayed by Crazy Eight Incandella, I had a distinct feeling that I was definitely 'barking up the right tree.'

Chapter Twenty-Three
A Nice Little Visit- August 18th

Detective Dorian pulled his squad car into the DiMatteo Tomato Company's parking lot, and Detective Tommy Morton was already there waiting for him. They both got out of their vehicles on that Tuesday morning and looked around the area before entering the building. Detective Dorian had developed a habit of looking around for surveillance cameras whenever he pulled into a strange parking lot.

"Wave to the cameras," he mentioned to Tommy Morton, as they walked around the parking lot. An unmarked squad car was already parked on the southwest corner of the lot, and they walked over to the black unmarked car. The Chicago P.D. had made it a point to keep an unmarked car parked at the DiMatteo Tomato Company over the last several weeks, especially now since the downtown looting started on Sunday night.

Dorian figured he would ask the stakeout patrolman Mike DiNatale some questions. He took turns with another officer over the last several weeks as they kept an eye on Little Tony. They maintained a detailed account of when and where Little Tony was going and whatever his activities had been. Dorian asked the patrolman to give him a detailed report over the last forty-eight hours, and he casually mentioned that DiMatteo was basically either at work or going home.

"It's been a pretty boring stack-out. This shit is getting old," DiNatale said, drinking his coffee.

"Any chance he may have ditched you, or taken a decoy vehicle and gone elsewhere?" I asked.

"How? He only has two cars, his Maserati and his Mercedes Limousine, and they've had both cars staked out and accounted for."

"Any chance he might have slipped away from you?"

"No way, Phil. We've been watching him 24/7. He's hasn't gone anywhere or done anything unusual," he said.

There was a five-second pause.

"Except on Wednesday nights. Little Tony looks like he's found Jesus. He goes to the rectory at St. Simeon for a few hours every Wednesday."

"What the hell is he doing there?"

"Don't know, Phil. Maybe he's going to Catechism."

Morton and Dorian just looked at each other and shook their heads. He picked his cell phone and called his district office to give them an update.

"Thanks, Mike," he casually mentioned to the patrolman.

"How long do you want to stake out this guy?" he asked.

"Not much longer, maybe a few more days. But I'll let you know," Detective Morton replied.

They both walked into the DiMatteo Tomato plant and flashed our stars to his warehouse manager, who directed them to Tony's office up on the second floor. When they walked in, his dark-haired secretary was already expecting them in the reception room.

"Mr. DiMatteo will be right with you," she mentioned.

Morton and Dorian sat down and waited for probably thirty minutes or more, as they were both offered espressos and whatever other stale goodies they had laying around in their expansive, multi-million-dollar warehouse building.

They were both expecting DiMatteo to be in one of his cocky moods as he finally appeared out of his office.

"Well, well...if it isn't Starsky and fucking Hutch. Don't you guys ever get tired of doing fucking reruns?" he asked in his usually very charming demeanor.

Dorian remembered that Little Tony would be muted in the English language if he couldn't recite his descriptive, colorful Shakespearean poetry.

"Morning, Tony, it's nice to see you too," Dorian replied, figuring he probably already knew why they were there.

"You guys must be lost. Maybe you need some fucking coffee to help rejuvenate yourselves and find your way back out to the parking lot where you have that other copper schmuck sitting in his unmarked patrol car," Little Tony said, cocky as always.

"That's okay, Tony. We figured you were overdue for another visit," Detective Morton replied.

Little Tony smiled for a moment as his executive receptionist handed him another refill of his double espresso with a small shot of sambuca.

"Have you guys ever seen my beautiful warehouse?" he eagerly asked.

"Yes, Tony. We saw your warehouse the last time we were here," Morton said.

"Oh, yeah. That's right. Yous' guys were looking for that monsignor priest guy a few years back," DiMatteo casually observed.

"Yes, Tony, your childhood friend, Monsignor Kilbane, whom you helped make disappear," replied Dorian.

Little Tony laughed out loud.

"If I helped make him disappear, don't you think I would have disappeared with him? What makes you think I would stick around here and subject myself to all of you goddamn copper's fucking harassing me and my employees?"

They were both referring to Monsignor Joseph Kilbane, who was once the chief of staff for the Cardinal and the Archdiocese of Chicago. Two years ago, when the 'Pedophile Priest Murders' were going on in the city, Monsignor Kilbane was considered a prime suspect in those serial murders. There was an alleged scheme hatched by Kilbane and the Archdiocese to 'kill off' four older pedophile priests for their insurance policy proceeds. Since Kilbane and DiMatteo were childhood friends, and both grew up in the Bridgeport area, they had a very close relationship, and the authorities always figured that DiMatteo was involved.

Detective Dorian was suspicious that DiMatteo helped Kilbane 'suddenly disappear' and shipped him off to a remote island in the Caribbean called Labadee. The Chicago P.D. has known of Kilbane's whereabouts for some time but has not extradited him since there are no extradition treaties between that remote island and the U.S. government.

"I'm just a businessman, trying to make a living here," he said in his cocky, Joe Pesci tone of voice.

Detective Dorian smiled. He was all too familiar with Little Tony's wise-guy attitude and his sarcastic mouth.

"That's because you're not the cabana boy type, Tony. I can't see you walking around with coconuts and a grass skirt," Dorian replied.

"That's a scary thought," Detective Morton chuckled.

Tony only smirked while taking another long sip of his juiced-up espresso.

Philip Dorian had known from experience what he was dealing with, and he always made sure he brought along his 'A-Game' whenever he was interrogating Little Tony.

The DiMatteo family capo was a cocky, arrogant, mega-rich Mafioso who knew criminal law better than most law school professors. Before this meeting, Dorian knew that Little Tony would probably 'toy' with both of them until he got tired and bored. The Capo got his 'rocks off' talking smart to detectives and coppers. Unless someone were quick-witted enough to keep up with his disrespectful bantering, DiMatteo would verbally embarrass them and have them for breakfast.

Dorian had a cocky smile on his face as Little Tony glared at him for several silent moments. He now knew that the authorities were wise to his little scheme with Kilbane.

A large, heavyset man then came into the conference room.

"You guys remember my controller, Sal Marrocco," he introduced them as he shook their hands. As they started exchanging pleasantries, Dorian immediately noticed the shiny, red cross gold ring that he was wearing on his right hand.

"Still wearing my favorite ring, huh, Sal?"

At that moment, Little Tony interrupted the conversation.

"Did you fucking guys come in here ask questions or to buy fucking jewelry?"

"I've always liked that ring," Morton said. He was referring to the ring that all of the Society of the Rose Crucifix members used to all wear before most of them were all killed in a self-induced explosion on Division and Ashland a few years back. The Chicago P.D. always suspected that Marrocco was a member of that secret society. Still, he was not at that abandoned church for some odd reason when it suddenly exploded a few years ago with Detective Dorian inside.

Dorian was lucky to escape with his life. All of this was related to the Pedophile Priest Murder investigations that Dorian was involved with as the lead detective.

"Thanks," Marrocco replied in a deep, raspy voice.

By now, DiMatteo was getting frustrated.

"Okay, girls, the socializing is over. What the fuck do you two schmuck boys want? We're trying to run a business here."

"We just wanted to come over and give you our congratulations on your new business, Tony," Dorian sneered.

"What new business?"

"The security business, Tony," Dorian reiterated.

"The 'let's sit on our lawn chairs while we watch some looters get blown away in a jewelry store' business. Very unique," Detective Morton chimed in.

Little Tony glared at the two detectives.

"I don't know what you fucking guys are talking about."

"Of course, you don't, Tony," Dorian replied.

"Why would two of your teamsters be sitting in front of a store at Jeweler's Row drinking espresso while some gunmen with AK-47 rifles were waiting in back to obliterate four young, black robbers breaking into a jewelry store and intentionally looting it?"

"I don't know. Why don't you go and ask the store owner?"

"We did. He's as good at 'playing stupid' as you are, Tony. You must be teaching a particular course on 'How to Talk to Coppers – Intermediate 201'."

Tony chuckled. "I see you're on the ball today, Dorian. Did you come up with that line all by yourself, or did one of your faggot detectives help you with that one?"

"Never mind, Tony. Those murders have your name written all over them. Even those Teamster truck drivers are your employees, Tony. Then you send over your hot-shot criminal attorney to go fish them out of jail."

"Who? Michael Prescott? Yeah, he's pretty fucking good, isn't he?"

"That was your Broadway show, Tony, and you know it!" Dorian started to raise his voice.

At that moment, Little Tony DiMatteo started to lose his temper.

"You know, I love you fucking coppers! Instead of coming in here and thanking me, you assholes come into my building and make accusations," he loudly retorted.

"I didn't see any of you fucking coppers doing anything to protect those businesses from getting robbed and looted. You fucking guys were all standing around with your thumbs up your asses while those little fucking punks were breaking windows and stealing merchandise!" Little Tony was now raising his voice.

"So, you were involved?" Detective Morton now said, accusing Tony.

"I didn't say that. But whoever was involved in providing security for those jewelry stores, yous' guys should be shaking his fucking hand and kissing his ass for bringing some law and order into a very volatile situation," DiMatteo added.

"No thanks to that fucking mayor!"

Dorian then looked at Little Tony, lowering the decibel of his voice.

"Did you have to kill them, Tony?" he softly asked.

"You could have just ordered your men to scare them away. You didn't have to kill and obliterate them with over one hundred rounds of machine-gun bullets."

Little Tony smiled, still holding his almost empty espresso cup.

"I'll bet all of those little punk bastards are thinking twice about looting and robbing another jewelry store," Tony said.

Dorian looked at Little Tony, now stepping a few feet closer.

"No, Tony. All you did was raise the stakes of an already out of control poker game."

He then asked Little Tony, in an almost silent whisper.

"Who were the gunmen, Tony?" the detective simply asked.

"Again, I don't know what the fuck you're talking about," Tony insisted.

Morton and Dorian both looked at each other and shook their heads.

"Well, Tony, all you did make a bad situation even worse. Because the violent gangs are now going to be involved in robbing and looting these stores, and they're going to be armed with bigger and better AK-47 machine guns than any of your security guys will have, Tony," Dorian patiently explained.

"All you did was anger the gangs in the neighborhood. And they're not going to waste any time talking to any of your truck drivers sitting in lawn chairs in front of a jewelry store drinking espressos."

Little Tony only smiled as he set his now empty espresso cup down on the conference table.

"Let them bring it on, Dorian. Someone has got to start cleaning up this goddamn city. And if you coppers and the fucking mayor can't do it, then maybe a 'security company' who shoots first and asks questions later will," Tony said with a cocky tone in his voice.

"When the outfit was running this fucking town, you didn't hear about any of these uncontrollable riots and all this lawless looting going on in the City of Chicago. That's because these motherfuckers were all too afraid. Because they knew that the minute they got otta' of fucking line, they would get a bullet in their fucking heads and end up face down in the Chicago River."

Sal Marrocco, the controller and alleged consigliere to the DiMatteo Family, stepped in to quiet his boss.

"You've said enough, Tony," as he looked at the two detectives.

"If you guys still want to talk, we need to bring in our attorneys. Otherwise, this little visit is over, gentlemen."

Dorian and Morton looked at each other, knowing that they would have to get a subpoena to bring DiMatteo down to the Sixteenth District if they needed him to answer more questions. The two of them started to walk towards the conference room door.

As they were leaving, Dorian said some poignant words to Little Tony.

"Since you've elected yourself as the new sheriff in this town, make sure you have lots of armed deputies and cowboys to back you up, Tony," Dorian warned.

"This could be a very horrific war with lots of dead bodies...a bloody war that nobody is gonna win."

Little Tony only smiled.

"Tell the Chicago Fire Department to get their dive teams ready," he said as the two of them were exiting the door and walking out of the conference room.

"There's gonna be a lot of dead bodies in the Chicago River."

CHAPTER TWENTY-FOUR
THE RIGHT TO KILL -AUGUST 21ST

That summer afternoon was bustling with traffic in front of 2650 South California, as the Cook County State's Attorney Douglas Janes sat at his desk in front of his third-floor picture window. It had been a busy summer for the State's Attorney's office. With all of the looting, rioting, the recent assassination of Mayor Kollar, and now killing four black looters in Jeweler's Row, the prosecutors have been busy.

State's Attorney Doug Janes had been the head of the Cook County Attorney's Office for the last five years. With more than 700 attorneys and more than 1,100 employees, the Cook County State's Attorney's Office is the second-largest prosecutor's office in the nation. The office is responsible for the prosecution of all misdemeanor and felony crimes committed in Cook County, one of the United States' largest counties. In addition to direct criminal prosecution, Assistant State's Attorneys file legal actions to enforce child support orders, litigate to protect consumers and the elderly from exploitation and assist thousands of victims of sexual assault and domestic violence each year. The State's Attorney also serves as legal counsel for the government of Cook County. Overseeing all of these activities was an all-consuming job indeed for any State's Attorney.

Doug Janes was exhausted. His twelve-hour days included an intense schedule of judicial meetings, court appearances, press releases, and staff conferences, five days a week. Since his recent re-election into the office last November, Doug Janes had been busy scurrying against the late mayor's soft-line policies.

Until her assassination, the staunch Republican prosecutor had always been embattled with the mayor's policies on seasoned, career criminals. He was trying to find a compromise between Mayor Kollar's flexible, sympathetic platforms and Chief Byron's hard-core, right-wing procedures in arresting all of the recent violent perpetrators.

When those four African American looters were killed inside that jewelry store on South Wabash, that incident presented a unique opportunity for the seasoned Cook County prosecutor.

It is within the Second Amendment rights that protect all citizens' rights to keep and bear arms. The Supreme Court has consistently upheld that this right belongs to individuals in any instance of self-defense in their home or, in this instance, at one's place of work. While looters and rioters were busy breaking into businesses, causing extensive damage, and stealing merchandise, no one in Chicago was advocating the rights of those who wish to protect themselves and their livelihoods against these vandals.

That is until two Teamster truck drivers from the DiMatteo Tomato Distribution Company decided to camp out in front of a jewelry store at 17 South Wabash while the riots were going on around them, sitting on lawn chairs and drinking cups of espresso. The would-be looters were amply warned not to break into the jewelry store. And yet, four young African Americans ignored the two men sitting in front of the store. They busted the store's front windows and demolished two display cases with expensive jewelry before being shot up by the 'security company' with AK-47's.

    A rocket scientist didn't need his calculator and chalkboard to figure out who was behind all of this. Little Tony DiMatteo and the DiMatteo Family was obviously behind the whole incident, using force and encouraging his retail customers to use violence against any intruders looking to vandalize their stores.
    But was it self-defense or just cold-blooded murder?
    Had Mayor Janice Kollar still been alive, she would have showered the DiMatteo Family with subpoenas and injunctions, forcing the State's Attorney's office to prosecute the jewelry store owners, the two truck drivers, and possibly, Little Tony himself of first-degree murder.
    It became quite evident that while Janice Kollar was alive and occupied the Chicago Mayor's office, that all rioters could conveniently hide behind the Mayor's office and vandalize any retail stores at will, concealing themselves behind the 'Black Lives Matter' protests. But now that Kollar became a victim of the very violence she was trying to control, all hell was breaking loose in Chicago.
    It was now up to the Cook County State's Attorney's Office to uphold the law.
    But to what degree and at what length?
    The personal opinion of conservative Republican State Attorney Doug Janes was that any 'Black Lives Matter' protestor

equipped with a crowbar, sledgehammer, or even a firearm, should not be treated as a peaceful protestor at all, but as a violent criminal. Any violent act that they commit while protesting in the name of BLM discrimination was not a peaceful protest at all, but a violent act of crime. These so-called Antifa protestors needed to be accountable for their vicious, destructive actions and prosecuted accordingly.

With Janice Kollar now gone, Doug Janes could now take off his kid gloves.

There had been another incident at eight o'clock the night before on Harlem Avenue.

Two African American BLM protestors and would-be looters had broken into the Arezzo Jewelry store on 3118 North Harlem Avenue with crowbars, sledgehammers, and firearms. The front door was broken into, and several display cases with gold and diamond jewelry were taken. When the youths were warned not to enter the building by the security guard sitting in his car outside, he was ostensibly ignored.

Within ten minutes, two Chicago EMS Trucks arrived in front of the jewelry store. The two African Americans had been shot by an AK-47 repeatedly with over twenty rounds, both lying dead in a pool of blood.

Again, was this self-defense or cold-blooded murder?

At this point, the State's Attorney's office didn't care. Any protestor wishing to break into any place of business with the intention of robbing and looting would be risking their lives at their peril.

The only question that Janes now had was, 'why now'? Why was 'The Outfit' and its crime families suddenly taking an interest in Chicago's city-wide violence? Why were the crime families offering their services to defend their customers and their businesses violently? What was in it for them, other than an increase in their street tax? Who was spurring this on, and why now?

Doug Janes took out an Arturo Fuentes cigar, cut the end, and lit it up. That moment would probably be his only minute of relaxation before his phones would continue to ring regarding the 'senseless' killing of black youths. He had been receiving telephone calls all day from every peace-loving minister and African American politician who had made the BLM movement a part of their own personal cause.

Janes didn't care. He had put out a press release earlier that day, and he was smiling to himself. He knew that he could now stand up to those violent protestors, with the Chicago Police Department's backing and Chicago's syndicated crime families.

'Any BLM protestor who acts in any malicious or violent manner in an attempt to destroy and decimate property would no longer be treated as a peaceful protestor, but a violent criminal,' his press release said.

He received a laudatory email from the Superintendent Chief of Police, Walter Byron, supporting him and his office for taking a hard stand against the city's violent protestors.

Doug Janes continued to look out his picture window, blowing smoke circles and whispering to himself:

"May God have mercy on any 'Black Lives Matter' protestor with a sledgehammer or a crowbar in his hand."

CHAPTER TWENTY-FIVE
FAMILY INVOLVEMENT - SEPTEMBER 5TH

Frank Mercurio was sitting outside, overlooking the sizeable expansive estate of his Barrington Hills home. As was his usual routine, Frank enjoyed a cigar and a glass of his favorite bourbon whiskey. It was a warmer fall day in September, and after a hot, uncomfortable Chicago summer, the middle-aged crime family boss was enjoying the crisp, beautiful fall weather.

Mercurio had been a trusted underboss of Don Carlo Marchese and had been involved with the North Side crime family for over thirty years. He had assumed the well-established organized crime family's throne when Carlo Marchese was murdered a few days before Christmas in December 2018.

Marchese had been found hanging by a rope tied to the foot of a bed from the window of his eighteenth story hotel suite at the Blackstone Hotel in Chicago. The soft-spoken, low-key Mafioso was actively involved in importing and selling Vatican masterpieces from Rome in the black market. The potential buyers he had allegedly double-crossed finally did him in.

Frank Mercurio wasn't going to make the same mistakes that his previous boss had made in his business dealings in the underworld. They had an established scavenger and recycling business that had always been profitable for years, and he didn't need to get involved with any other activities that he wasn't familiar.

But as the family boss sat in his patio chair, smoking his cigar, something was definitely on his mind. His underboss, Raffaele 'Ralphie-boy' Raciti, kept him apprised of a rumor that was now occurring and was possibly, getting out of control.

He had heard that Little Tony DiMatteo had started a new 'security firm.' With all of the rampant violence and lootings occurring in downtown Chicago, he had heard that the DiMatteo Family had been 'hired' to provide protection services to all of the local jewelry stores in the city.

"That mother-fucker," Mercurio whispered loudly to himself as he took another long sip of his bourbon.

He knew that Little Tony had seized a new opportunity in providing protection and security services, and he was sure that they were making quite a financial killing. Although he was content in sitting back and enjoying his waste management empire's stable profits, Don Mercurio was curious. Was this a new business opportunity that their family should get involved in?

He had spoken about it to his underboss, and he was informed that many of their family 'associates' were getting the itch, meaning that they wanted a piece of the action. The Marchese Family had always resisted following the flow of other crime families that had gotten more involved in legal marijuana dispensaries and the illegal drug trades.

In past years, the Marchese's had sat back and watched the other crime families like the DiMatteo's, the Lucatelli's and the Roselli's, get rich on the drug trades were going on in the streets of Chicago. Carlo Marchese was always smart enough and patient enough to sit back and watch the other families make their mistakes. Those decisions brought on excessive heat from the authorities and especially the FBI. Every mob boss in Chicago knew that the Federal Bureau of Investigation was continually watching their every move.

Frank Mercurio had heard that four black youths were shot to death last month, trying to rob and loot a high-end jewelry store in Jeweler's Row during the summer Chicago riots. He had heard that the jewelry store had hired the protection and security services of the DiMatteo Family. Frank had also heard that the security watchmen, two of his Teamster truck drivers, were released from their jail cells the next day, as the prosecutors couldn't prove that they pulled the trigger.

"That mother-fucker," he said to himself again.

"Only a son-of-a-bitch like Little Tony could so brazenly guard a downtown jewelry store and get away with murder," Mercurio said to himself.

But somehow, through the legal savvy of DiMatteo's high-profile attorney, Michael Prescott, both of them were able to walk out of their jail cells scot-free.

"Buon Pomeriggio," his underboss greeted, wishing Frank Mercurio a good afternoon. The man kissed him on both cheeks as he approached the beautiful, stone-clad courtyard of the Mercurio estate.

Mercurio nodded his head as he sat back down on his chair, taking a long drag from his Cohiba cigar. He had asked his underboss to come over and discuss some pressing matters, and the new security services being offered by the DiMatteo Family was one of them.

Ralph Raciti was now a trusted advisor and underboss of the Mercurio Family. He moved up the family hierarchy ranks over many years since being a street tax collector from the Grand Avenue neighborhood, near the West Loop.

The two of them sat there in silence for several long minutes, as one of the servants had brought over two espresso coffees for both of them to enjoy.

Breaking the silence, Raciti then immediately spoke, "You wished to talk to me?"

Mercurio, wearing a casual, beige windbreaker jacket and light khaki pants, could have passed for one of the servants that day. The head of the crime family enjoyed keeping a casually low profile, and he seldom enforced his family authority unless necessary.

"We need to address this situation with our friends," Mercurio started the conversation.

"Regarding DiMatteo's new business? Yes, I heard about it."

"What do you think about all of this?" Mercurio asked his underboss, taking a long drag from his Cohiba.

"You mean DiMatteo getting into the security business? It's interesting," Raciti smiled as he made himself comfortable on one of the outdoor patio chairs.

"I hear that he's got these jewelry stores begging for protection and getting over 'Ten-G' a pop," said the underboss, as one of the housemaids brought a glass a bourbon outside for him to enjoy.

"That's great money, boss. The DiMatteo's always had trouble collecting the street tax before. But now, with these new 'security' services that they're offering these jewelry stores, they seem to be throwing money at them."

Mercurio took another long drag of his cigar and looked out at his expansive estate without making eye contact with Raciti.

"What kind of heat are they catching?" he asked.

"You saw what happened, boss. They picked up the two of DiMatteo's guys that were sitting in front of the jewelry store and tried to get them on murder and assault charges, but they both walked."

As Raciti was explaining this, Mercurio continued to shake his head.

"When those kids broke into that store with sledgehammers and baseball bats and started breaking up the display cases, the guys inside opened fire on them. The owners had the right to shoot them dead because they felt threatened."

"Yeah, but it wasn't the owners doing the shooting. It was DiMatteo's boys, from what I heard."

"Yeah, boss. That's what I heard too."

The two of them were silent for several long minutes.

"What kind of money did they pay Little Tony and his boys that night?"

Raciti thought about it for a moment.

"I heard they doled ten grand in cash."

Another silent moment.

"That's better than any street tax," Ralphie-boy observed.

A few more silent moments.

"What are the other families doing? Who else is getting involved in this?"

"I heard the Lucatelli's are starting to go out and visit these jewelry stores and some of these larger retail places that have been getting robbed and looted. Some of them are forking over the dough for protection. Their offering to discount DiMatteo for protection services," Ralphie stated.

"Fucking Little Tony can't be too happy about that," Mercurio smiled.

A few more silent moments.

"So, what do you think? Should we start going out to our stops?"

Raciti was silent for a moment.

"The only ones we're going to be able to shake down are the jewelry stores, and that's only if we can undercut the DiMatteo's. We gotta hope that the 'G' doesn't start snooping around, 'cuz this ain't going to be easy to keep quiet."

It wasn't the Marchese Family's style to follow the other crime families' actions when getting involved in different street activities. Don Carlo would frown on that kind of thinking. The family had always done very well with forcing their customers to pay them to provide their dumpsters and roll-off containers for garbage pick-up. They had always done well in years past.

But with the increased competition and the other families 'muscling in' on their customers, clients, and businesses, and now offering 'security services,' Mercurio knew that he couldn't just idly stand by and do nothing. Their street income was starting to take a hit, and they were not collecting the kind of income and street tax that they had been able to gather in the past. This new 'security service' was a commodity that all of his clients would start to demand, and he knew that his family would have to step up. He had to protect his customers. He had to protect his business interests. He had to defend his North Side turf.

Frank Mercurio took another long swallow of his bourbon and took a final drag from his depleted Cohiba cigar, blowing smoke circles into the warm, fall air.

"Then fuck it. Tell the boys to go out and start making visits to our stops, especially the jewelry stores. We'll charge 'em half," Mercurio loudly ordered.

"If Little Fucking Tony can get away with this shit, then we can too."

They both smiled as they finished their drinks, rattling the ice cubes in their crystal drink tumblers.

The Marchese Family now knew that a street war for clients needing protection would erupt between the Chicago crime families.

The next day, the Marchese Family members, including their 'street soldiers,' started visiting all the jewelry stores and larger retail establishments on the North Side. They offered them 'security services' at discount prices, far below the going street tax rate of ten thousand dollars per store. Many of the vendors happily agreed to pay, knowing that the cost of vandalism and repairs would far outweigh any street tax being paid to the Marchese Family.

With the Lucatelli's and the Roselli's now hustling their customers for security services as well, the word was getting out that the Chicago families were now 'all in.' The Chicago underworld was now fully involved in fighting off the ruthless looters and gang member rioters inciting Chicago's citywide violence.

The word of the other crime families' involvement in these 'security services' quickly got back to Little Tony DiMatteo and his consigliere, Sal Marrocco.

On that Tuesday morning, Little Tony arrived at his warehouse at five o'clock for his usual workout routine at his gym. Consigliere Sal Marrocco was waiting for him on his workout bike. Marrocco had on his regular black and red workout sweats and a large white towel around his neck. He watched Little Tony climb onto the bicycle next to him as they both exchanged their usual morning greetings.

"How did you sleep last night?" Marrocco immediately asked.

"Like a baby. Why?"

"Didn't you hear?" Marrocco asked.

"Hear what?"

"The Marchese's are hitting the streets, trying to hustle clients for their 'security' services."

"Really? The Marchese's are now in this shit too?"

"Yeah. I guess they're following the Lucatelli's s and Roselli's. But they're now undercutting their fees, big time. And they're throwing in extra disposal and waste services too," Marrocco mentioned.

He was now peddling his stationary bike at a higher rate of speed, trying to talk while out of breath.

Little Tony calmly looked at him.

"I'm surprised. The Marchese's usually don't do that shit," shaking his head.

"Boy, ever since Don Carlo got whacked, they've been doing a lot of things different."

There were several moments of silence between them as they began to accelerate and decelerate their stationary bicycles.

"You know what's going to happen now? If we don't watch ourselves, all of this is going to start a fucking street war," Marrocco observed.

"Yeah, I know," Little Tony responded.

"Somebody is going to get pissed off, somebody is going to get mad and shoot somebody else, and the whole fucking war is gonna start up again."

A moment passed as Little Tony was thinking.

"We haven't had a street war in the last thirty years, since the '90s, and now we're gonna start shooting at each other again over these fucking security services," he astutely observed.

The two of them continued to do their spinning on their bicycles for almost twenty minutes, and neither one say another word.

Finally, Little Tony slowed down his peddling and looked directly at his trusted consigliere. He then made a very loud observation, verbally second-guessing himself.

"Maybe listening to that fucking priest was a big mistake."

CHAPTER TWENTY-SIX
SCENES FROM A SUSHI RESTAURANT-SEPTEMBER 8TH

I was working at my satellite office at the Franklin Street Café, trying to put a story together for tomorrow's deadline. It was the beginning of the autumn season. The Indian Summer was more than tolerable for anyone looking to get their last enjoyable days of warm, pleasant weather in Chicago.

I was on my second piece of coconut cream pie, had probably consumed half a pot of fresh coffee, and it wasn't even four o'clock yet. Between the Kollar murder case and the Fr. Fitz-Little Tony scenario, I felt like I was spinning my wheels on both investigations. Each inquiry had a missing puzzle piece, a reluctant witness, or a half-cocked theory that just didn't make any sense. I was trying like hell to prove my various notions and ideas for each situation but kept hitting brick walls. On that day, I probably ate more coconut cream pie out of frustration, trying like hell to string a paragraph of words that would make any sense.

At about four-thirty, she walked through the door.

The object of my affections and my most secret fantasies entered the café, looking more beautiful than ever. Talia Bowerman held her dark brown leather briefcase with her laptop sticking out of hit, looking as though she was in a hurry. She had her long, wavy dark brown hair combed to one side, wearing an off-white Anne Klein business suit with a black, mostly unbuttoned blouse underneath. I could see her sun-tanned skin mingling nicely with her bright gold chain around her neck, dancing across her well-endowed cleavage. Her natural beauty was a sight to behold, and I immediately realized that I couldn't take my eyes off of her.

She walked up to the hostess and, this time, asked if she could be seated at a table. Talia had stolen my cue and decided to take up my rentable desk space suggestion at the Franklin Café as well. As she sat at the booth directly across from mine, I continued to glare at her until I caught her attention. While she was setting up her laptop, she finally locked eyes with mine and smiled.

"Hello, McKay."

"Hey, Talia."

"I decided to take your advice and find a place to work here rather than in my office. There were too many distractions there today, and I needed to break away from my boss. He's been brutal today."

"I know the feeling," I replied, still unable to take my eyes off of her.

At that moment, I continued to watch her unpack her briefcase when I decided to take a chance before she got herself settled.

"I have some room here at my booth if you would like to come over here and work. Maybe we could share some ideas on some of our stories."

She smiled, probably waiting for me to invite her all along.

"Are you sure that I wouldn't be disturbing you?"

"Not at all. At the rate I'm going, I've probably eaten more pie than I have been working. Maybe your being here can finally help me put together a legible paragraph," I replied.

She chuckled, then moved her briefcase and laptop over to my table and got herself settled.

"Coffee?" Gloria, the waitress, came over with a fresh pot of coffee in her hand.

"Absolutely," Talia replied. "Keep my cup filled."

I smiled as her cup was being filled.

"You're also a caffeine addict, I see."

"I drink way too much of it. And after seven o'clock, I replace my coffee cup with my wine glass."

"You're a girl after my own heart," I chuckled.

"Yes," she widely grinned as she opened her laptop and made herself comfortable.

"And I spend a lot of time running to the bathroom too."

"That's not surprising," I replied.

She turned her computer on and began to settle herself into her work, while I only managed to drool while glaring at her from behind my computer screen. She looked far more sensuous up closely, with her lightly dabbed rose color makeup and eye shadow that accentuated her alluring light blue eyes. Her resemblance to Cortney Cox was uncanny, as I expected Chandler Bing from 'Friends' to barge in on us with his usual cup of coffee from the Central Perk.

"So, how long have you been with the Tribune?" she started the conversation.

"Since college. I started with the Tribune when I graduated from Central Michigan

University in 1985. Been with them over thirty-five years," I exclaimed.

"Interesting. Someone with your lengthy background is usually an assistant editor somewhere. I'm surprised you're still a street-beat reporter."

"I still enjoy the excitement," I lied, even though a nice, comfy assistant editor's job had always appealed to me.

"How about you?"

"Was with the Wall Street Journal in New York City for several years. I went straight over to work for them when I graduated from Boston College in 1993. Then I worked for a local news station as their beat reporter until getting this job with CNN. Been with them for four years here in Chicago," she explained.

"You seem to enjoy it," I complimented her, still unable to take my eyes off of her.

"It's okay. The hours are somewhat grueling, and I find myself working all hours of the day and night, sometimes with a glass of wine in my hand," she clarified.

"Boston College, huh? You must be from out east."

"I grew up near Rochester, New York."

"Really? Very interesting. So how do you like being a Chicagoan?"

Talia began to gleam as if I had asked her a fascinating subject that she enjoyed talking about.

"This is such a beautiful city. I enjoy the downtown Loop, the restaurants, the bars, and all of the nightlife. Between Michigan Avenue, Navy Pier and Wrigley Field, I never get tired of discovering new places in this wonderful city."

I beamed, knowing that there were probably some new places that I could probably help her discover here as a Chicago native.

"Do you live here in the city?"

"Yes, in the West Loop, near Randolph Street. And you?"

"Sauganash neighborhood, in a townhouse just north of Petersen Avenue. On the north side of the city, where all the old, rich people live."

"Did you grow up around here?" she curiously asked.

"Yes. I grew up in the Belmont-Cragin neighborhood and went to St. Patrick High School. My parents later moved to Norridge."

"You're lucky to grow up in such a wonderful, exciting city. Rochester is nothing like here in the Windy City," she observed. "There is no better place in the Midwest than in Chicago in the summertime."

"Yeah, well, with all of the recent violence going on, I'm sure you would get some debate on that."

I could smell her sweet-scented perfume in the air as I was sitting there at the table. I began to wonder if she ever got tired of looking so classy and so damned gorgeous. My mind began to speculate on how many ex-husbands, boyfriends, and broken hearts she had left back in New York.

We were starting to settle in and get comfortable with one another and the conversation, making more small talk, and discussing different current events that had been recently happening. The waitress came to our table and brought over another fresh pot of coffee when I finally got up enough guts to make my move.

"How do you feel about blowing this coffee shop and going off somewhere for dinner?" I felt myself getting nervous asking that question, and I could feel droplets of sweat starting to drip down my back.

She smiled and thought for a moment.

"I should finish this story. I need to submit it tomorrow morning."

"Come on, Talia. We can't both live on pie and coffee all night. We've got to go out and get some dinner somewhere, don't you agree?"

Talia then looked at me and smiled. I immediately knew that I probably liked me as well, as her alluring light blue eyes had me in a hypnotic spell.

"Okay, Larry. I can go out for a little bit. But I have to work on this story. As I said, it has to be finished by the morning."

"I won't keep you from your work, Talia."

"Okay, what did you have in mind?"

I had a taste for sushi that night for some odd reason, so I thought going to some oriental Japanese restaurant downtown somewhere might appeal to her.

"Do you like Sushi?"

"I love Sushi."

"Okay then, there is a great Sushi restaurant called Momotaro on West Lake Street, which is about ten minutes from here. We can grab a cab, bring along our stuff, and go there for dinner. What do you think?"

Her eyes gleamed, and I knew right away that I had her. My heart started racing at two hundred beats a minute as we gathered our laptops, and I left some cash on the table. We then went outside of the Franklin Café and caught a taxicab. As she climbed into the cab first, I couldn't help but notice her gorgeous, shapely legs and looked so sumptuous in those Zanotti black, high heel shoes.

As we made small talk in the taxicab, she looked more excited than I was. She mentioned that she had just celebrated her forty-ninth birthday a few weeks ago and wasn't looking forward to the big one next year. I reassured her that turning fifty was nothing compared to my milestone birthday in a few years. The taxicab kept weaving in and out of traffic, and after abruptly stopping at several stoplights, we had finally arrived at our destination at 820 West Lake Street.

As we both got out of the cab, she wrapped her arm around mine as we entered the restaurant. Greeting the hostess and immediately showing us to our table, I suddenly felt like we were a couple, looking forward to getting to know her better. I was drenched with anticipation as if I was living through an incredible fantasy that was about to come true.

Talia asked the waiter for an Old-Fashioned cocktail, while I ordered a Sapporo Japanese beer. We then ordered three sushi rolls, and our conversation became even more lively.

"So how is your investigation going?" she asked, as she was taking a long sip of her Old-Fashioned cocktail.

"Which one? I'm hitting brick walls on both ends."

"Yes, me too. My only suspicion is that Chief of Police Byron has his hands dirty in this whole thing, but nobody is talking, certainly no one in the Chicago P.D," as she took another long sip of her cocktail.

"Let's start with the mayor's assassination," Talia suggested. "Where are you at with that?"

"Well, the only thing I've been able to ascertain was the Chicago P.D. was renting the house next door to the Mayor's home and that several coppers were going in and out of that home up until the day of her murder. No one saw anyone leaving the house after Kollar was shot, but that doesn't mean that someone could have conspicuously run out of there with a collapsible rifle," I recited, telling her what I know.

"How could someone run out of that house without the police noticing, seeing that they were providing security detail for Mayor Kollar," Talia asked.

"Maybe they did see someone running out of that house, and perhaps, they looked the other way," I suggested.

There were about ten seconds of silence while my theory sank in. This would tie into her hypothesis of Chief Byron knowing more about the mayor's assassin's identity than what he was letting on.

"So that would confirm my theory, Larry. Mayor Byron knows more than what he's letting on."

"Okay, so we have a nice little cover-up going on in the Chicago Police Department," I ascertained.

"Are you going to run with that in your article tomorrow?" Talia asked.

I smiled at her as she was putting her left hand on my leg.

"I will if you will," I jokingly suggested.

She put her hand out to shake mine. "Deal," she said, as she raised her glass, and we made a quick toast.

The waiter brought over our entrees, and we watched each other have fun while struggling to use our chopsticks.

"I'm so used to Italian food," I joked.

"I'm half Italian from my mother's side," she mentioned. "My father is English and Scottish."

"Really? That's a coincidence."

"Why?"

"My mother was born in Rome, and my father was Scottish. He passed away a few years ago from Parkinson's Disease," I mentioned.

"I'm sorry."

"Thanks."

"Maybe we should have gone Italian tonight," she suggested. "We could have been twirling spaghetti instead of these chopsticks."

At that moment, she was rubbing my leg while handily using her Japanese eating utensils like a professional. By that moment, I was thinking about anything except what she was doing and how close I was getting to fulfilling all of my fantasies about her.

Talia was a beautiful, intelligent, hard-working journalist with an impressive background and a notable resume. She was not only gorgeous, but she was easy to talk to.

And so far that evening, she was laughing at all of my stupid jokes. Talia had a great sense of humor, and I could tell that she didn't take herself too seriously during our conversation.

"I understand eating fish is a healthy alternative when watching your weight," I exclaimed.

I was trying hard to change the subject, as all of her leg rubbings were starting to get me a little too excited.

"Yes, it is. I seldom eat red meat anymore. I eat a lot of fish and vegetables, and I try to get to the gym two or three times a week when I can," she replied.

"I wish I had the time. The pressures of this job and my divorce several years ago hasn't helped my weight. I've gained a few pounds over the past few years," I said as I was making an excuse, taking another gulp of my second Sapporo beer.

"It's hard, especially at our age. It seems like we work harder and enjoy our lives less as we get older. Our health and our waistlines seem always to take a toll," Talia replied, although by observing her youthful, fit, and trim figure, she had nothing to be ashamed of.

"When were you divorced?"

"Several years ago. My ex-wife decided she didn't want to be married to a reporter anymore. I guess I was spending more time chasing down leads for a front-page story than the time I was spending chasing her."

"I'm sorry to hear this," she replied, sounding very empathetic. "How long were you married?"

"Five very long years. Thank goodness we didn't bring any children into the world," I casually mentioned.

"How about you?" I asked.

"I was married and divorced twice. Once to a Wall Street stockbroker in New York while I was working for the Journal, that didn't last long."

"Oh, really."

"The second time was to an attorney, and we were married for several years. We never had any children, although I experienced two miscarriages. That, along with his variant girlfriends, took a toll on our marriage."

There was something wonderfully comfortable about Talia. She was extremely knowledgeable, easy to talk to, and a fascinating woman. She opened up to me so quickly, and I felt as though I had known her for years.

"So how is it that a beautiful lady like you isn't married now?" I pursued my questioning, feeling ambitious after finishing my second Sapporo.

"I've had lots of prospects and have had more than my share of relationships. But I get very nervous when the subject of marriage comes up again," Talia replied.

"Why aren't you married again?" she asked.

"I keep getting into relationships with the wrong women. At my age now, I'm much better off alone. The only woman I have to worry about right now is my mother. She's eighty years old, and I run over to visit and look after her two or three times a week, especially on Sundays."

We sat there and finished our dinner, making more small talk about the vast differences between living in Rochester and Chicago. I discovered that she was a huge New

York Rangers fan and followed the team and their scores during the hockey season

"We're rivals," I jokingly said. "I go to about a dozen or more Blackhawks games every year."

After paying the dinner check, we exited the restaurant, and we carried our laptops and workbags and went for a long walk on West Lake Street to Randolph Street. We walked together, very closely, and I grasped her hand while we wandered together along Randolph Street.

By then, we had walked back to her loft on North Morgan Street. It was almost 10:30 pm. Talia apologized, explaining that she had to finish her news story by tomorrow morning. Otherwise, she would invite me up. We entered the door of her building lobby, and we both stopped short of the elevator.

"I had a wonderful evening, Larry. Thank you so much for dinner and the wonderful walk back home."

"When can I see you again?" I eagerly asked, trying not to sound too anxious.

She displayed a big, wonderful smile as if there wasn't anything in the world that she wanted more.

"Whenever you like, that is, whenever I'm not trying to make a deadline," she beamed.

She grasped my hand and gave me a long, wet kiss on the cheek. We just stood in front of that elevator for over ten minutes, as I started to put my hand inside of her blouse, feeling her soft, gorgeous breasts. She smiled and then gently pushed me away.

"There are cameras here," she giggled.

I looked up, and sure enough, there were two cameras in the lobby getting a front-row seat on our mash and grab session.

"We'll finish this another time. Call me tomorrow," Talia said as she pressed the elevator button.

The door immediately opened, and she gave me one last long kiss, holding the door open with her foot.

"Good night," she whispered as the elevator doors closed in front of her.

I stood there, completely excited, and my hair all ruffled, wishing I could grab the next elevator up to her loft on the fourth floor.

My head was spinning. I had never felt so thrilled, so anxious, and so aroused, all at the same time. It was as though she was trying to get as close as she could to me, maybe even mentally seducing me, without ever lifting her baby finger. She was giving me signals that maybe, she was personally interested and that she perhaps, wanted to get intimate.

I couldn't remember the last time I had such a marvelous evening with such a beautiful woman as Talia. She had it all; beauty, intelligence, and plenty of class. But there was also a part of her that was a bit puzzling and Mysterious, as if she was holding back. Her beautiful, deep blue eyes seemed enigmatic, surreptitiously hiding something. There was more to Talia than what she was letting on.

I strolled out of her building lobby and onto North Morgan Street, walking quickly and skipping sidewalk steps as if I was a young schoolboy, and I just couldn't wait to see her again. I needed to call a taxicab or an Uber, but I was so excited at the moment, I didn't think I could sit still long enough for a ride back to the Tribune parking lot, where my car was.

On that night, I was a high school freshman who had just gotten his first kiss on a date with the most beautiful girl on the homecoming court.

On that night, every medieval, primitive emotion that involved the distrust and cynicism of a new relationship had totally evaporated.

On that night, every other thought of every other second on my mind involved my being next to Talia, kissing her, caressing her, and making love to her.

But there was still so much that I needed to learn about Ms. Talia Bowerman.

CHAPTER TWENTY-SEVEN
DISCOVERY- SEPTEMBER 9TH

It was damp, cold, and wet outside on that early autumn day in September. My Cole Hann leather loafers were soaked from the rain as I entered the Chicago Tribune building on Michigan Avenue.

The Weather Channel had called for non-stop thunderstorms for the next two days, and the city expected to get two to three inches of rain on that day alone.

I got into the newsroom early that day, knowing that I would have probably been better off working from home despite the weather. But I wanted to talk to the 'The Boss' and give him an update on Mayor Kollar's murder investigation after I met with Crazy Eight Incandella. I sat down at my desk and started to read and dissect my notes, putting some statements and sentences together while sorting out both of their conversations, trying to 'connect all the dots.'

There were so many open-ended questions regarding this case that I just didn't know where to start. The late mayor's enemy list was so extensive that it could have been any of those potential suspects. The long list includes Eddie Barrett and his cronies, members of Chicago's crime syndicate, and the gangbangers within the city, especially the Black Cobras. Even many of Chicago's fraternal police organizations may have had it out for her.

Was there anyone in the city who she may have not recently pissed off? Her management style was so abrasive; every time she had a press conference or made a statement to the media, there were her vocal opponents at every turn. Every time she made a political statement, she managed to insult someone. If it wasn't the conservative right-wingers with their sensible plan for the City of Chicago, it was the liberal left supporters with their broad-minded goals for aggressive growth and advancement within the city.

I decided to look into Crazy Eight's statements two weeks ago regarding Little Tony's church activities and his recent interest at St. Simeon's Church. The DiMatteo family hitman mentioned that Little Tony was going to church on Wednesdays and had a sudden interest in playing chess.

This statement took me entirely by surprise. With all of the legal and illegal activities that Little Tony was involved in, I found it hard to believe that he had any time to pursue a new passion for playing chess. Where did this new obsession come from?

Through the grapevine, I had heard that Little Tony's mother was an avid chess player before she began suffering from Alzheimer's Disease. There was extensive mention made of it at his mother's funeral, which Fr. Fitz had celebrated. Had Fr. Fitz used this pastime activity as a means to befriend Little Tony? And for what reason?

As I searched Fr. Colin J. Fitzgerald's name on the internet, I couldn't find anything unusual about him other than his education, his pastoral assignments within the Archdiocese, and his many, many political activities. Nothing I didn't already know.

Fr. Fitz was the 'Ralph Nader' of political causes within the City of Chicago and was a major thorn in the Archdiocese's side. There had been many public admonishments between Cardinal Markowitz and Fr. Fitz regarding his political activist rallies and media statements. There were even rumors that Fr. Fitz was considering breaking away from the Archdiocese of Chicago and conducting his religious crusades outside of the diocese. All this information was extensively covered in past articles and press releases by the Chicago Tribune, and none of these revelations was a surprise to anyone.

Just for grins and giggles, I searched a website that I had some moderate success with prior when doing some extensive background checks. HighSchoolAlumni.com was a website with archived pictures and yearbooks of high school class graduates nationwide over the last sixty years.

Colin John Fitzgerald was born the oldest of three children in the Beverly neighborhood on the Southwest side of Chicago. His first-generation parents were of Irish descent. He grew up in a very religious, devout Roman Catholic family where daily rosaries and weekly Sunday masses were never missed. His very Irish father, Patrick, was a desk sergeant with the Chicago P.D.'s Twenty-First District. His mother, Margaret, was a schoolteacher at St. Barnabas School and parish, where he grew up.

He played Little League baseball as a young child and was very active athletically before attending Marist High School on Chicago's southwest side.

Fitz was a member of the high school cross-country and track teams, the debate team and was in the Peter Chanel Club, a Marist high school organization for those wishing to enter the priesthood. He graduated with high honors in 1973.

He later earned his bachelor's degree from DePaul University in Sociology and then attended Mundelein Seminary. Colin John Fitzgerald was ordained a priest on May 22, 1981.

While perusing his high school yearbook online, I found another interesting fact: Fr. Fitz was the Marist High School chess club president. He had won several local and state chess matches, tournaments, and national championships. Fitzgerald reigned as high school grandmaster chess champion in the State of Illinois in 1972 and 1973.

Bingo. Fr. Colin Fitzgerald was a former chess grandmaster.

Upon looking into his background on the internet, Fr. Fitz was involved with several local chess clubs within the Chicagoland area and had participated in several competitive chess tournaments in the Chicago and Midwest areas.

Fr. Fitzgerald's social activism has also brought him media coverage throughout Chicago and beyond. He has often collaborated and associated with African American religious, political, and social activists. Under Fr. Fitz's leadership, the community of St. Simeon demanded the shutdown of many businesses specializing in drug paraphernalia. His parish also campaigned for the removal of tobacco and alcohol billboards from their neighborhood. When billboard owners refused to cooperate in the early 1990s, they decided to climb ladders and deface the signs.

In 2000, Fr. Fitz received international attention for encouraging his parishioners to buy time from prostitutes as a means of inviting the women into counseling and job training.

The Chicago Archdiocese largely distanced itself from Fr. Fitz's activities, to which he responded, "*How is what I'm doing not part of the gospel? The church leaders talk about evangelization. Well, if this isn't evangelization, I don't know what is.*"

St. Simeon raised several thousand dollars for his program, attracting many donors from outside their parish. St. Simeon has used similar methods to reach out to drug dealers.

He has been referred to as the 'Radical Disciple,' creating and generating controversy by inviting political activists such as Jesse Jackson, Al Sharpton, and others to speak at his well-attended masses. Although the Archdiocese of Chicago and especially Cardinal Markowitz have tried to distance themselves from Father Fitz and his activist activities, Fr. Fitz has continued to be a lightning rod for controversy.

So, we have Fr. Colin Fitzgerald, a native Chicagoland former grand chess master, who is the pastor of St. Simeon Church and a well-known political activist. In previous years, I also realized that the political activist pastor has often used his favorite pastime of playing chess to reach out to other community leaders and activists. It is even rumored that Fr. Fitz had often played chess with Cardinal Markowitz himself every week before becoming in his disfavor.

And now we have Little Tony DiMatteo, the Capo dei Capi of all of Chicago's crime families, who has a sudden interest in beating his warehouse employees in a game of chess. Crazy Eight Incandella said that Little Tony is at St. Simeon Church Rectory every week.

A coincidence, perhaps? Would he be praying the weekly rosary or attending a bible study on Wednesday nights? Could Little Tony have found religion and decided to become a good Catholic in his later years? I believed all of those possibilities for a total of about three seconds.

Fr. Colin Fitzgerald is a very active political advocate within Chicago. With the assassination of Mayor Kollar and all of the increased political unrest within the city, Fr. Fitz can't be taking all of this too lightly.

I decided to make a phone call to the St. Simeon rectory and contact the pastor for his comments.

"Hello, St Simeon's Parish?"
"Yes, I would like to speak with Fr. Fitzgerald, please."
"Whom may I say is calling," said an older women's voice on the other line.
"This is Lawrence McKay, from the Chicago Tribune."
A long moment of silence.
"What is this regarding, Mr. McKay?" A sarcastic thought went through my head:
None of your fucking business, lady. Just let me talk to the pastor, please.
"We are doing an article on the increased violence and rioting going on in the city, and we were interested in the pastor's comments,

being that he is a political activist and all," I managed to say to the guard dog secretary.

More silence.

"One moment, please."

I was on hold listening to elevator music for several long minutes until Fr. Fitz finally came to the telephone.

"Hello?"

"Fr. Fitzgerald? I'm Lawrence McKay from the Chicago Tribune. We are writing an article on the increased violence and rioting going on in the city, and we were interested in getting your comments, being that you are very active in the political scenes here in the city."

'I think it's a travesty, especially after our mayor was gunned down and assassinated in broad daylight several weeks ago. I think the violence in our city is unraveling the urban, authoritative controls that have been in place in our city for generations," Fr. Fitz stated.

I found it amazing how quickly and eager Fr. Fitzgerald vocalized his political and personal views, especially when speaking with the media.

"It is so shameful that these protest groups are hiding behind these 'Black Lives Matter' factions to violently destroy our beloved, beautiful city," he said.

"I am mortified by the aggressive, uncontrollable, violent crowds that are now assaulting and destroying Chicago."

He was indeed an outstanding, well-spoken politician disguised as a Catholic priest. I could tell Fr. Fitz enjoyed talking to the press.

"Your thoughts about the recent violence and especially, those four murdered youths who tried to vandalize that jewelry store on South Wabash the other evening?" I asked.

"I think it's shameful. We have now resorted to violence and ruthless murder in protecting our city and property," Fitz declared.

"Our young men are getting killed in all of this ruthless street violence. We've got to wrap our arms around our young brothers. We've got to love them," Fr. Fitz said as if he were getting ready to lead an intercity march.

"We've got to tell them they're worth too much to end up dead or in jail."

I attentively listened to Fr. Fitz address his emotional concerns to me in this telephone interview. It was as though he was expecting my phone call. Perhaps, Fr. Fitz had a press release written and ready to go for the first reporter that requested the activist pastor for his urban social views.

I then decided to 'turn the gas up on the stove.'

"There are rumors that factions of organized crime, and one criminal family, in particular, may have been responsible for the shooting death of those teenagers. What are your thoughts, Father?"

Fr. Fitz hesitated for a moment before answering.

"I think it's appalling and reprehensible that organized crime could be responsible for the shooting death of four black youths."

I then went for his throat.

"Did Little Tony make that confession to you last Wednesday night when he was at your rectory?"

There was then a frosty, ten-second silence where neither of us said a word.

"I think this interview is over, Mr. McKay," he coldly responded.

"Did you hear his confession last Wednesday night, Father? What was his penance? Or did you just advise him to get involved in the violent security business to maintain peace and social justice on the streets?"

"What Little Tony does in my church is none of your damned business, Mr. McKay."

I turned the gas up higher.

"I heard that Little Tony has been coming over to your rectory every Wednesday night for your weekly chess games, ever since the death of his mother last July."

There was no response.

"I hear that Little Tony has become quite an accomplished chess player, thanks to you and your chess skills, Father. Those must be exciting chess games, where you can try to checkmate him and get into his head," I mentioned loudly over the phone.

"We're done here, McKay."

I began verbally pushing him harder.

"I didn't realize that your religious and political ministry was part of the weekly chess tournaments at your rectory, Father."

I was starting to become very angry, as I was beginning to jump deeper into his shit.

"The crowds aren't coming to your political rallies anymore, Fr. Fitz. They're all too busy looting and vandalizing the city," I insinuated.

"So now you've resorted to pushing and encouraging organized crime families like the DiMatteo's to restore law and order in the city, no matter who gets killed in the process."

"Good-bye, McKay."

I began interrogating him even harder.

"You'd rather watch young black men violently die on the streets and maintain social order, something the police aren't doing a good job of anymore, right Father?"

I was beginning to enjoy cross-examining this hypocritical Catholic priest. His social, activist ranting and political lectures were starting to make me sick to my stomach.

"Fr. Fitz, you could care less how many young kids are dying in the streets!"

"That's enough, McKay," he replied in a loud, vindictive voice.

"Does the rest of the family know that you're the new DiMatteo Family advisor and legal counselor?" I loudly asked.

CLICK!

The activist pastor abruptly hung up the telephone, not wanting to hear any more of my interrogations about his weekly chess matches with one of Chicago's most dangerous crime figures.

Meeting up at Fr. Fitz's rectory every week tells me that Little Tony had found himself a brand-new best friend. My theory was that Fr. Fitz had befriended Little Tony using his extensive chess skills and was now very possibly, whispering in his ear.

With the new security activities of the Chicago Outfit and the killing of those young potential looters on Jewelers Row, I realized that, perhaps, Little Tony and Fr. Fitz could be doing a lot more than just playing chess on a wooden checkerboard.

Their toxic relationship suddenly reminded me of the historical dilemma in Russia back in 1914. Back then, there was a crazed cleric named Rasputin, who was a Russian, self-proclaimed holy man. He managed to push his vile, self-serving interests on Russia's royal family, especially Nicholas II, Russia's last czar.

I now had a suspicious feeling that Little Tony DiMatteo had now found himself a new family consigliere.

And this one defiantly wore a collar, a black cassock, and a gold crucifix around his neck.

CHAPTER TWENTY-EIGHT
THE GRAND MASTER - SEPTEMBER 26TH

Red and yellow autumn leaves were falling everywhere on West 79th Street, as the crisp fall air was slowly overtaking the late September weather in Chicago. It was jacket weather, as the temperature was barely in the forties. I managed to find a parking space and parked my older BMW vehicle down the street from St. Simeon Parish. I was eager to walk several blocks to the rectory of the popular, southside church.

I had read a publicized event that was going on at the church rectory, which was published in our Lifestyle section, and I was very eager to attend.

Even though I knew I wouldn't be welcome.

In front of the church was a large yellow sign with bright blue letters boldly displayed:

St. Simeon Chess Tournament
Saturday, September 26th at 1:00 pm

I had come to find out that our boy, Fr. Fitz, had started a church chess club several months ago within the parish and was hosting a chess tournament in the church rectory basement.

I was ecstatic. I had attended mass a few weeks before and tried to meet Fr. Fitz in-person to no avail. I then called his rectory office, trying to make an appointment. But the minute I had mentioned my name, his secretary immediately knew that I was a reporter and cut me off.

297

Fr. Fitz was a tough man to get in front of and was not about to make it easy for me.

He knew that I was a reporter after a story, and he also knew that it was only a matter of time before I caught up with him. He couldn't dodge me forever, even though we didn't hit it off during our telephone interview a few weeks ago.

As I walked into the rectory basement, two women were registering applicants entering the door. There was a line to register, and it looked as though over one hundred participants were getting ready to begin the tournament.

"May I help you?"

"Yes, how much is it to register?"

"Thirty dollars. Goes to a great cause."

"Great," as I handed her a twenty and a ten in currency from my wallet.

"Your name please?"

"Lawrence McKay," I replied.

She took my name down on a registration form, asking for my address and telephone number afterward.

"What is your level?"

"Level?"

"Yes. What is your playing level? Beginners, Intermediate or Advanced?"

I thought about it for a minute.

"Put me down for intermediate."

It had been several years since I played a chess game, but I remember playing it enough in high school and college to know my way around the chessboard. I used to have a roommate while living on campus at Central Michigan University who loved to play the game, and his excitement was infectious.

Before long, my fraternity brothers were playing for shots of tequila with every discarded chess piece.

"You're at Table 23."

"Thank you."

I grabbed my registration form along with a name tag and found my way around the spacious rectory basement until finding Table 23.

As I sat down, I noticed Fr. Fitz walking around the basement, greeting each of the chess players and discussing several opening strategies as they sat down at their respective tables. A young man, probably in his early twenties, sat down across from me and introduced himself.

"My name is Larry," as I stood up to shake his hand.

"Robert," he softly said as he sat down and fumbled with the positions of the beginning chess pieces.

He had light brown hair, was unshaven with a day-old beard, and thick brown glasses. He looked like a young chess master as he kept fidgeting with the chess pieces.

I noticed Fr. Fitz, approximately ten feet away from our table, staring at me from behind a crowd of several young players who were about to sit down.

He then walked over in my direction.

"You're Larry McKay from the Tribune, correct?"

"Yes, Father. It's so nice to meet you," as I rose from my chair like any normal gentleman to shake his hand.

There was a five-second delay as he finally accepted my handshake offer.

"You know, I should probably throw you out of here. Your intentions are anything except playing the game of chess."

"I was the chess grandmaster of my Sigma Phi Epsilon fraternity in college, Father," I notably informed him.

That was an exaggerated line of bullshit, as our frat house chess tournaments were only judged by the finalists who had consumed too many tequila shots and were still languid enough to strategically move their chess pieces.

"I do enjoy the game," I said to him, as he was looking at me suspiciously.

He then looked at my opponent and gave him a directive.

"Robert, could you exchange your seat with Table 32, please. I would like the pleasure of playing this gentleman."

"Okay, Father," Robert said as he got up and quickly walked over to the other table.

Fr. Fitzgerald then sat across from me, fidgeting with the chess pieces while waiting for the tournament to start. Chess piece fidgeting must be a relevant beginning strategy for tournament chess players.

Fr. Fitz then started the time clock.

It was my move first, as I moved my white pawn to C4.

"Would you mind if I asked you a few questions while we played, Father?"

"That's why you came here, isn't it McKay?"

I smiled at the parish-activist priest.

He then moved his black knight to C6.

"Fr. Fitz, you can't avoid me forever. I can assure you that our paper will publish an article regarding the DiMatteo Family's involvement in these violent shootings over the last month. You're sitting down with me, and having some input would, at the very least, reveal your side of the story."

I then moved my white queen to A4.

"What makes you think that I have anything to do with the DiMatteo's and these shootings?"

He moved his black knight to F6.

"Several of Little Tony's associates let the cat out of the bag regarding your Wednesday 'cenettas' and chess games."

Fr. Fitz glared at me for several long seconds.

"They all say that you're their new consigliere," I interjected.

Fr. Fitz immediately protested.

"That's total nonsense, McKay."

"We all know he's not in your confessional and that you're not getting his confession, Father. But my only question is: Why are you encouraging him to take violence against these rioters and looters in the name of peace in this city?"

I moved my white queen to A4.

"What makes you think that I would do that, McKay? I'm an ordained Catholic priest. I've been sworn in the name of Christ to follow the ten commandments and to preach peace to all of God's children. Encouraging 'The Outfit' to shoot up violent looters is not the way of Jesus and his followers," Fr. Fitz replied.

"Well yeah, Father. That's what I learned at parochial school."

He moved his chess piece—black pawn to B5.

"You never answered my question during our phone call the other day, Father. Why would you invite the most powerful Chicago mobster over to your home for a chess game?"

He looked at me in silence for a moment.

"What's in it for you?" I asked.

"Just another opportunity to save another man's soul, McKay," Fr. Fitz quickly replied.

He then amply changed the subject.

"What school did you go to?"

I moved my white bishop to G6.

"St. Joan of Arc in the Belmont-Cragin neighborhood. I graduated from St. Patrick High School in 1981."

He smiled for a moment.

"You went to Marist High School, right?"

"Right. I grew up in Beverly."

I smiled at him, hoping to break his thoughts and concentration from the chess game.

"Illinois Grand Chess Master, 1972 and 1973, correct Father?"

He looked at me, suspiciously for a moment.

He then moved his knight, taking my pawn at D4.

"Do you always do your homework on your journalistic subjects?"

I then tipped my cards, as I couldn't control my disdain for him any longer.

"Just the ones that are full of shit," I replied in a snarky tone of voice.

I just couldn't help myself.

This well-known radical Chicago activist conducted political rallies and protests on his church's front doorsteps. He went far beyond his means to usurp the corrupt political combine of the City of Chicago. He wasn't bashful to use any method available, including organized crime families and their infliction for violence. And he did it all while hiding behind the doors of his beloved St. Simeon Church, behind its lofty rafters and its beautiful, ornate stained-glass windows.

At that moment, I didn't realize how much I disliked this Catholic priest until I had finally faced him in person, looking at him straight in the eyes.

In contrast to his religious garments and his clerical collar, this man was *not* a Man of God. This man was a monster who got off controlling and manipulating others in the Chicagoland community for his beneficial gain.

Fitzgerald was a 'publicity junkie.' He was a toxic, manipulating narcissist who enjoyed broadcasting his self-image through the media as a Christian do-gooder, saving Chicago at any cost, which didn't exclude the blood of others.

As a reporter, I could tell that Fr. Fitz was very afraid of me damaging his pristine, God-fearing reputation. He didn't want me to smear his name in the papers.

"I would be careful if I were you, McKay. I know enough people at the Tribune that will gladly terminate your position as their veteran reporter."

"Really?" I remarked.

I moved my queen to A3.

"Yes, really, McKay. I've been asking some questions. You've got a newsroom reputation in this town as a troublemaker. That's probably why you've never been promoted from your newspaper desk job to the editor's office."

What a fucking son-of-a-bitch! This asshole had been checking up on me at the Tribune.

"I can make sure that you never get another job in this town again, McKay, except for maybe, writing obituaries."

A moment of silence.

"Or Hallmark greeting cards."

This fucking priest has balls of steel, I thought to myself. For about three seconds, I wondered how much time I would get in hell for throwing a right hook at this rotten, hypocritical priest-bastard.

"All of your senior editors say that you're more trouble than your worth, McKay. They keep you around because you're too old and you've been around too long to cut you loose. So, I would be very careful about what you print about me in your newspaper."

He then moved his black rook from one side of the chessboard and overtook my queen.

"Rook takes Queen."

"Check," he loudly said while hitting his stop clock.

I looked at the pieces on the board, realizing that I had been asking so many questions to the parish priest that I had lost my concentration in playing the game. I then moved my king out of harm's way, to no avail. I immediately knew the result.

Fr. Fitz then moved his bishop.

"Checkmate, McKay," the priest smiled as he rose from our table.

"You're now officially out of this chess tournament, Mr. McKay. I would kindly ask that you leave immediately, please."

Son-of-a-bitch, I thought to myself.

Not only did he beat me up in chess, but he threatened me with my job as a Chicago Tribune reporter as well.

I mildly got up from the table while grabbing my light fall jacket.

"So, Fr. Fitz...who is going to be saving your soul?"

At that moment, the treacherous look of evil on his face was invisibly piercing holes into my body. It was as if he were instantly condemning me to a deep, dark purgatory and sentencing me to a thousand and one brutal deaths.

"Our chess match is over," he reiterated.

"I'm sure we'll be talking again soon, Father," I said, ignoring his comment.

"You may want to check the news article I write about you for any spelling errors," I remarked.

"You know, like making sure that I spelled your name right and all," I said sarcastically.

I could now see boiling hot steam coming out of his eyes.

"Sometimes our computer spellcheck isn't always working. I could even send you a draft of the article for your review if you like, Father."

"Goodbye, McKay," as he immediately turned his back on me and walked away toward some other chess matches that were still going on.

As I walked up the steps of St. Simeon's Rectory basement, I thought about what Fr. Fitz had directly said.

Not only did the pastor borderline threaten me with my job, but I also realized that he was capable of doing far sinister, far more evil things behind the closed doors of his Catholic church.

Fr. Colin Fitzgerald was not just a man of the cloth. He was a very powerful, very narcissistic, very controlling man indeed. He appropriately used his political power as a means of threatening, manipulating, and influencing whoever he chose to control and complete whatever result he was looking for.

But why aim at the city's rioters and looters? As the city's foremost religious leader, why was he encouraging the city's criminal underworld, with its darkest element, to pass judgment on those unfortunate others? It was as though he was the one pulling the DiMatteo Family trigger on those violent street gangs himself.

Fr. Fitz was judge, jury, and executioner to anyone in the community whom he felt didn't walk a straight line. He was Sheriff Matt Dillon, and the City of Chicago was his own, personal Dodge City. The thought of his now initiating the evilest of deeds against me personally became a genuine possibility.

As the DiMatteo Family's unofficial new consigliere, Fr. Colin Fitzgerald was now capable of doing anything.

And that thought scared the living shit out of me.

CHAPTER TWENTY-NINE
THE CONFESSIONAL - OCTOBER 7TH

It was a warm, sunny Wednesday morning as worshippers walked up St. Simeon Church's steps for the early six o'clock mass. The early weekday service was popular among working Roman Catholics and commuters who took the bus or train to work in the Chicago Loop after mass and was heavily attended. Fr. Fitz had arrived early from the rectory that morning and entered the old, greystone church from the side door entrance. He greeted a few parishioners as he entered the sacristy and began putting on his green chasuble and holy vestments. Fr. Fitz enjoyed saying mass, as he found solace in this distraction from his stressful administrative and activist duties at Saint Simeon Parish.

The holy mass that weekday morning went quickly, as he recited a short sermon and dispensed communion to the eighty or so worshippers who attended that day. As was his usual routine after mass, he took off his vestments and walked over to the religious confessional in the church's rear. For the next hour, he was expected to offer his time and to hear confessions from the various parishioners who had attended services that morning. He had brought a prayer book along with him, as he usually did, to keep himself occupied in between acts of penance.

He had already heard the confessions of several people that morning when another well-dressed gentleman entered the confessional. As he entered the enclosed private chamber, the Pastor was only greeted with several moments of silence.

"Recite your trespasses before the Lord," the Fr. Fitz began, breaking the vast void. There were only more silent moments, as Fitzgerald tried to see who the man was that had entered his confessional. It was dark in the ornate, private room, where there were no lights available inside the church's closed chamber.

"Bless me, Father, for I have sinned..." a low, baritone voice in the confessional started.

There were more long seconds of silence.

"Go on, confess your sins, please," the pastor impatiently requested again.

"You never stop surprising me, Fitz. I never figured you for a mafia consigliere," said a bold, familiar voice.

"Who is this?"

"Do you have any idea what the hell you've instigated here in this town? Your little chess games with Little Tony DiMatteo have now started a crime war amongst the different families within 'The Outfit.' They're out there now, shooting thugs, street looters, and rioters. The gangs in this city, especially the Black Cobras, are now vowing revenge," as the rude dialog transpired from the other side of the confessional.

Fr. Fitz then smiled to himself as he immediately knew who it was.

"You couldn't come and see me after mass, Eddie? You had to come in and assault me in my confessional?"

Alderman Eddie Barrett smiled to himself.

"After all of the nasty things, you said about me in the papers. You're lucky that I'm even here at all."

The two men were more than familiar with each other and had quite a long history together. Not always good.

Barrett knew that, because of his currently contentious relationship with the political activist priest, Fr. Fitz would never agree to meet him privately. The Fourteenth Ward alderman had always been critical of the 'Radical Disciple's' methods and means of instigating public reaction and, in many cases, public turmoil.

Fr. Fitzgerald smiled to himself. It had been a very long time since he had privately talked to the Fourteenth Ward alderman.

Once upon a time, many years ago, the two political adversaries were once very good friends. When Fr. Fitz was assigned to St. Simeon Catholic Church as their new pastor twenty-five years ago, the church was crumbling. There were much-needed repairs and maintenance issues that required immediate attention. Eddie Barrett and his wife, who are still devout Catholics, attended several of Fr. Fitz's masses on West 79th Street, and the two had several friendly conversations after Sunday service.

When Fr. Fitz complained of the lack of funds for the church's much-needed repairs, unmarked white letter envelopes with large bundles of cash of at least five thousand dollars started suddenly appearing in the weekly contribution baskets.

Although Eddie Barrett never officially acknowledged the large cash donations, Fr.

Fitz had a good idea of who the anonymous cash benefactor was. On several occasions, Fr. Fitz embraced Eddie and his wife after mass, graciously thanking him for his monetary support.

But when Fr. Fitz became more active within the political community, he fell in disfavor with the Fourteenth Ward alderman.

Barrett felt as though the Catholic pastor should only be 'seen and not heard.' His media appearances and political rallies in front of his church became an embarrassment to Eddie Barrett and his city council. Their personal feuds and disagreements spilled into the newspapers and local newscasts, and the City Council publicly admonished the pastor for his radical, extreme political protests.

Needless to say, the miscellaneous cash envelopes into the church's weekly coffers suddenly dried up.

Fr. Fitz had publicly called Barrett and his cronies "Eddie and the Four C's," which stood for 'City of Chicago Council Criminals.' His reference to the alderman and his corrupt constituents sounded more like a 'doo-wop singing group from the fifties' than a political faction. Fitzgerald publicly pushed his Fourteenth Ward constituents to vote Eddie Barrett out of office during every citywide election.

The local media has since picked up on the antagonistic relationship between the two men. Their bantering, public political conflicts, and disagreements have mainly been advertised back and forth on the six o'clock news. Their contemptuous comments about each other have been publicized in the papers.

"You'll know when I'm coming here to assault you, Father. And by the way, I enjoyed your sermon this morning," Barrett said in a complimentary tone of voice.

"Thanks. But you didn't come up in line for communion this morning, Eddie. Were you not a good boy this week?"

"I'm always a good boy, Father. That's why you haven't seen my name in the papers lately, unlike you…"

"When your name is not in the papers, Eddie, I worry. I only know then that you're up to no good," the paster smirked.

"You know, Fitz, it's too bad that none of your parishioners understand and realize what a fucking hypocrite you are. You hide behind your pulpit and this confessional and preach peace and love to all of your parishioners. Then you're playing chess with Little Tony and enlisting 'The Boys' to start shooting up every black kid in town walking around with a crowbar and a baseball bat."

At that moment, Fr. Fitz got defensive.

"I've never preached to anyone to commit a murder or to take away a life, no matter how violent our city is."

He paused for a moment.

"I don't see you bastards doing anything about all of this violence and rioting going on downtown. The only thing you and your buddies are worried about is your loss of income from all of the brown paper bags you and your pallies were used to cutting up," the activist priest said. "Now that the feds are up your butts."

Barrett scoffed and sneered at the priest's insinuations.

"Mayor Kollar calling up the feds on your asses was the best thing she could have ever done before she was killed," Fr. Fitz reiterated.

"You know, Father, you weren't bitching and complaining about the city when your donation baskets were getting filled with fucking cash whenever you needed something done or fixed around here."

Fr. Fitz only smiled at his comment.

"Render unto Caesar the things that are Caesar's, and unto God the things that are God's," Fr. Fitz responded, quoting the Luke 20:25 gospel passage.

"That's what I love about you, Fitz. When it comes to fucking cash donations, you close your eyes and grab the bible with your left hand while your right hand is extended. You have no fucking scruples."

"Really?" Father Fitz reacted, shaking his head to himself in protest. He was starting to get a little angry now with his insulting remarks.

"Yes, really. You never cared how fucking dirty the money was, Fitz. As long as it ended up in your church donation basket."

"Eddie, why are you here?" Fr. Fitz impatiently responded, now getting tired of their abusive, confessional bantering.

"You need you to talk to your new buddy, Little Tony. He needs to back off on the street security. His nighttime 'cowboy patrols' are causing an inter-city war with everyone, including the cops and especially the other street gangs."

"I have no idea what you're talking about, Eddie."

"Cut the bullshit, Father. You're the one pressing the buttons right now, and I need you to tell Tony to back off."

There was a silent moment.

"You seem to be the new Windy City puppeteer, and you're the one holding all of the strings."

"Why would I do that?" Fr. Fitz protested.

"Your new buddy, Mayor Sanchez, has turned a blind eye to all of the city violence. All he's interested in right now is taking away your brown paper bags full of cash and keeping it all for himself," Fr. Fitzgerald argued. "And your pals in the Chicago Police are patrolling the streets wearing their own handcuffs. They're not taking any action at all in restoring any law and order on our streets," he observed.

The pastor paused for a moment.

"I've never, ever told anyone to kill anybody. I've only suggested that someone needs to take charge," he suggested.

"The coppers aren't doing it. The Mayor isn't doing it. And the corrupt politicians like you and your buddies in this town could care less. The gangs are too disorganized and are fighting amongst themselves. They're the ones thriving on all of this violence, with all of the inner-city rioting and looting. Who else is going to patrol the streets right now?"

At that moment, Eddie Barrett started to raise his voice in the confessional.

"And who the fuck put you in charge, Fitz?"

There was a silent moment as the alderman made his verbal point.

"Listen, Fitz. I've got a newsflash for you: Your only job is to run this fucking church. Your political bullshit rallies have only been one great big pain in all of our asses to everyone in the city council. You're a media press monger, and you get your rocks off seeing your name in the fucking papers. Who the hell elected you as the new Mayor of Chicago?"

"You certainly didn't, Eddie. Anyone in Chicago can do a better job running this town than that crooked Puerto Rican you and your buddies put in," the priest responded.

"Fuck you, Fitz," Eddie responded loudly.

"Keep your voice down, Eddie."

"Who the hell do you think you are, pushing your Mafia cowboys onto the streets and shooting up looters and gangbangers? Who the fuck put you in charge?"

Fr. Fitzgerald starting laughing, as he found amusement in Eddie Barrett's futile bantering and conversation in his confessional.

"I've never pushed anyone to do anything. But you know that this whole town is up for grabs right now, Eddie. You should have considered all of this before you and your boys decided to go out and 'ace the mayor.'"

A moment of silence.

"Is that why you're here in my church confessional, Eddie? Are you feeling guilty? Are you here to confess to her murder?"

A moment of silence.

"You should be ashamed of yourself, Eddie. Thou shall not kill."

"I didn't take her out, Fitz," the alderman objected.

"And if I had, I would have done a cleaner job than whoever shot her up in her garden on that Sunday afternoon."

"I believe that for about three seconds, Eddie. I don't put anything past you. You've got the biggest, largest pair of balls in town, and you are capable of doing anything."

The priest paused for a moment.

"I can't think of a single commandment that you *haven't* broken."

"Really Father? And you're judging me? You're the one who is..."

Before Eddie Barrett could finish his sentence, Fr. Fitz interrupted him and wrapped up his private 'confession.'

"Your penance is to recite the rosary every evening for the next ten days. Pray that the Lord will someday accept you again as one of His precious children into the Garden of Eden," Fr. Fitz directed the city alderman.

"In the name of the Father, the Son, and the Holy Spirit," the pastor recited as he crossed himself, holding his prayer book.

A moment of silence as Eddie Barrett, still a very religious man despite his numerous faults, also made the sign of the cross.

"You need to leave now, Eddie. And next time you decide to have a meeting with me, let's have one outside of the church confessional."

Eddie Barrett angrily opened the confessional door, loudly responding before his exit.

"I'm not done with you, Fitz. Remember what I said," he warned.

"Or the next time, you'll get your wish. Our next meeting will certainly not be in a church confessional," Eddie loudly threatened.

With that, Eddie Barrett angrily stormed out of the confessional. He slammed the chamber door so loud that the noise reverberated from the stained-glass windows of the southside greystone church. Several worshippers were staring at the angry alderman as he loudly exited St. Simeon Church. He walked down the church steps to his black Mercedes parked on West 79th Street, where his chauffeur was waiting.

"Get me the fuck out of here," he ordered his driver as the vehicle sped off into the busy morning traffic, going eastbound on West 79th Street towards the city.

The pastor gathered his prayer book and quickly walked out of the confessional chamber, walking over to the old church's front door. Several parishioners were still staring at the church's rear, witnessing the loud confessional drama between Fr. Colin Fitzgerald and Alderman Eddie Barrett.

He wanted to confront him face to face. He wished to admonish him again for invading his place of worship and giving him what sounded like a threat.

But most of all, he wanted to calm him down. He suddenly felt like he had missed his opportunity to make peace with one of the most powerful politicians in the city. Eddie Barrett invaded his church, his morning mass, and his peaceful place of worship.

He opened the old, antiquated walnut doors and walked down the steps of St. Simeon Church, looking both ways down West 79th Street, looking for his political nemesis and his once close friend.

But Eddie Barrett had abruptly left and disappeared. He was nowhere to be found. Fr. Fitz then walked back inside the church and, still grasping his prayer book, kneeled in the last pew at the church's rear and said a short prayer.

The pastor prayed for the Lord's divine forgiveness and understanding in his attempt to bring safety and peace to his streets and his neighborhood. He prayed that the killing and the street warfare would finally come to an end and that peace would one day return to his beloved city. He prayed for the end of the senseless violence in Chicago.

As he kneeled and said his prayers. Fr. Fitz realized that it was Wednesday and that he would have his usual visitor later that evening.

He then said one last prayer for Little Tony.

CHAPTER THIRTY
MEETING MRS. VALENTI-OCTOBER 9TH

I was sitting at my desk at the Chicago Tribune Building on that autumn afternoon, banging my head hard against the tabletop of my desk.

There had been a considerable amount of violence in the downtown loop during these last three months. The Black Cobras and Satan's Disciples had been going at it and killing each other, with many dead bodies and carnage on both sides. Finding a dead gangbanger in an Englewood alley on the Southside or in the Westside in the Hermosa neighborhood was becoming a daily news story.

Moreover, many large retailers, especially the Chicago jewelry stores, seemed to participate in 'The Outfit's' elite security services. The protestors turned looters were being shot at and killed once they entered and broke into those retail and jewelry store establishments. They were now going in there armed and ready for a shootout. A jewelry store on Michigan Avenue three days ago had been broken into, and the looters were armed and ready. Three people were shot and killed. One of them was a 'security guard' who had mob family affiliations with the Lucchese Family.

I was thoroughly frustrated. I just couldn't put it all together. No matter what leads I pursued, I was at another dead-end with this story regarding the Fr. Fitzgerald connection and Little Tony DiMatteo.

What was their real connection, other than playing chess on Wednesday nights? What did they talk about? What was the relationship between the DiMatteo Family and all of the recent city violence? Was Little Tony personally involved? Where did Fr. Fitz fit into all of this?

I had just got called into my bosses' office, and the boss wasn't kind to me at all.

"Where are you at with the 'Fr. Fitz-Little Tony's story?" my assistant editor Tom Olsen asked.

"I'm hitting some dead-ends, boss. Nobody seems to want to talk to me, and I can't get any information out of anyone."

"So, now what? Are we all supposed to cry like little girls because nobody wants to talk to us? Are we supposed to make up some bullshit and pretend we all work for the National Enquirer?"

I looked at him, whispering *'what a fucking jag-off'* several times under my breath. He knew all the difficulties I had getting anyone to go on the record regarding this story, and it was disappointing.

"I approached Fr. Fitz at his chess tournament at St. Simeon's Church last week, and I had a nice little chess game with the pastor," I stammered, trying to tell him that I was doing *something.*

"Did he admit to being a 'mobbed-up priest'? Did he tell you anything personal regarding his consulting Little Tony? What did you find out?"

I looked at him in silence for about five seconds. They were the longest five seconds of my life.

"I found out that he is an excellent chess player, but not much else."

Tom Olsen looked at me as though he were about to jump on top of his desk and directly into my shit.

"Are you fucking kidding me, McKay?"

There was another moment of silence.

"Look, McKay. Stop fucking around. You're a much better reporter than this. I don't need you to write me more 'Lord Byron' fucking memorial stories. I need a headliner, McKay!"

I looked at him, suddenly feeling motivated.

"Get back out on that goddamn street and find me a good fucking story on Fr. Fitz and our favorite Wise Guy. And don't come back in here until you hand me a worthwhile story. Otherwise, you will be writing Hallmark birthday cards."

As I walked out of his office, my ass was hurting. I felt as though I had just had sex in a dark, sleazy bathroom of some gay bar in Boys Town.

As I walked over to my desk, I grabbed my backpack, camera, and portable tape recorder. I had a hunch, and it was time for me to play my 'wildcard.'

It was about seven-thirty at night as I drove my car and parked it on West 79th Street. I decided that I would stake out the parish rectory over at St. Simeon's Church and try to come up with some additional information. There was one person in there that I knew could help me, and I had to play the waiting game.

At about nine o'clock at night, an older woman had left the rectory front door. I quickly got out of my car and approached her.

"Excuse me? Are you Mrs. Madeline Valenti?"

I had known her name because she had been quoted in a news article regarding Fr. Fitz's anniversary party as a Catholic priest several years ago. She was an older, Italian lady in her early seventies who was extremely loyal to Fr. Fitz.

"Who are you?"

"I'm Lawrence McKay, with the Chicago Tribune."

She looked at me, startled at first, then continued to walk towards her car parked several yards away.

"I don't talk to reporters."

I continued to follow her; my hand was in my jacket pocket, pushing the 'record' button of my portable tape recorder.

"What can you tell me about those weekly chess games between Fr. Fitz and Little Tony?"

She continued to keep walking, trying to ignore my questions.

"What are they doing together besides playing chess, Mrs. Valenti?"

She was still walking, trying hard to tune me out.

"Are you comfortable with your boss playing chess and befriending the most dangerous man in Chicago?"

She momentarily stopped. Mrs. Valenti looked at me but then continued walking.

"Mrs. Valenti, if you care anything about your boss, you'll talk to me. If something happens to your boss, who is Little Tony going to answer to? Do you think your boss is actually safe playing chess with Chicago's Capo dei Capi?"

"How is my talking to a reporter going to keep my boss safe?"

"By publicly alerting everyone, including the Chicago authorities, that Little Tony is responsible for the increasing violence that has been going on in the city right now. By running a story on your boss, it will put Fr. Fitz in a good light, showing everyone that he has been trying to counsel DiMatteo away from his life of violence."

It was all bullshit.

Mrs. Valenti kept walking. As she soon approached her car, she turned around and gave me a directive. She then looked at me with a shocked look on her face.

"I have to go home, and I have no time for reporters. But I will give you exactly five minutes."

"Okay. What do the pastor and Little Tony talk about?"

"I hear them talking about how the City of Chicago would be a much safer place if Chicago's 'Outfit' were in charge. Fr. Fitz tells Little Tony that he has a responsibility to keep the streets safe, and the only way to do that is to take care of all of the gangs and criminals that the Chicago P.D. can't shoot."

I wrote down highlights of the information she was telling me but knew that I had most of her answers tape-recorded.

Mrs. Valenti turned out to be a plethora of information. It was as if I had hit the 'play' button, and she kept talking and talking. The woman spoke about how she didn't trust Little Tony, and she suspected that if he ever got angry with Fr. Fitz, he would do whatever he needed to do to 'straighten out the situation.'

Little Tony confessed to 'rubbing out' a few rivals that had gotten in his way, but she couldn't remember who he was specifically talking about. At one point, Little Tony called Fr. Fitz 'his trusted consigliere.'

"Was Fr. Fitz trying to counsel the Chicago mobster?"

"No. Fr. Fitz told him that these gangs were possessed by demons, and the only way to bring peace into this city was by taking them out."

We stood in front of her car for over fifteen minutes, and she gave me more information about what was going on in those chess games than I could have ever gotten as a fly on the wall.

She then looked at her watch.

"I've got to go, Mr. McKay. You will not publish my name in your paper, yes?"

"Absolutely not, Mrs. Valenti. Your information with me will only be cited as an undisclosed source. I will not disclose your name to anyone. And I promise I will be kind to Fr. Fitz."

"Please. I am worried about him spending all that time with that 'criminale.'"

We then shook hands.

"Thank you, Mrs. Valenti."

As she got into her older Ford Bronco, I ran back to my car as fast as I could. I hadn't run that fast since I was ten years old, running away with that Playboy magazine that I had just stolen from the corner drug store under my winter jacket.

I got back to my townhouse in Sauganash and began writing my news story. I listened to the tape recordings of Mrs. Valenti several times, each time realizing and paraphrasing more and more information.

It was very obvious from what she was trying to tell me. Although Fr. Fitz was trying to come off as an innocent priest without any motive other than befriending Little Tony, it was quite apparent that he was 'throwing the rock and hiding his hand.'

Fr. Fitz had found in Little Tony DiMatteo a dangerous weapon that he could use at his disposal. He had brainwashed Little Tony and had him eating out of the palm of his hand. By the end of each chess game, Fr. Fitz had convinced Little Tony that any and all of his retributions against all of Chicago and its violent offenders were within God's sacred laws. He had convinced the crime boss that these gangbangers were demon's disciples and that they had to be swiftly dealt with accordingly.

Fr. Fitzgerald had now turned on a sadistic faucet that poured out blood. In the DiMatteo Family, he had found the tools that he needed to administer the well-deserved death sentences to those violent criminals who viciously lurked the streets of Chicago. The activist pastor no longer had to stage demonstrations in front of his church steps and protest unfit life sentences to those brutal criminals. They murdered innocent victims, especially the younger ones. By pushing and advocating store-front violence, he encouraged a sort of 'genocide' of ferocious, violent thugs and gangbangers responsible for most of the city's brutal crimes.

'Chicago's Criminals Beware' was the city's new mantra, and Fr. Fitzgerald was the Second City's most dangerous puppet master.

I went home in front of my laptop and started banging out this story, knowing full well that the parties involved would not be happy with whatever I reported in my news article. I knew there would be a backlash. I knew there would be repercussions and possible threats made.

I now realized that the flood gates of hell were about to break loose.

CHAPTER THIRTY-ONE
THE CHICAGO GAMBIT-OCTOBER 12TH

The wind was blowing hard against the tall windows of my favorite coffee shop on that breezy, autumn afternoon. At times, you could hear the wind whistling hard up against the glass as the rain intermittently began making large puddles on the sidewalks adjacent to Wacker Drive. It had been raining on and off all day and was starting to pour hard outside, making me realize that I was stranded inside of my favorite coffee establishment. I was being forced to enjoy wonderful slices of freshly baked banana cream pie while sitting there, trying to get some work done. But worse of all, I had my favorite waitress, Gloria, flirting and talking dirty to me while she kept my coffee cup aptly filled. The conditions were barely tolerable. It was a seemingly dreadful work environment, but somebody had to do it.

"More coffee, Hon?" she winked while filling my cup.

Gloria had on her usual light pink waitress uniform, with several of her blouse fasteners unbuttoned, making sure that I get a good look at her size 36-D cleavage. I began wondering if she was provoking me to guess the color of the Victoria Secrets bra she was wearing.

"Please. Thanks, Gloria."

"Did you want me to get you another piece of pie? Or can I make you a turkey sandwich?"

"Not now, Gloria, thanks."

I had been spending a considerable amount of time over these last three days working that 'Chicago Gambit' news story regarding Fr. Fitz and Little Tony, and it took me a while to put it together.

At the beginning of the article, I decided to get a little creative. I looked on the internet to find a chess poem, but nothing really caught my attention and communicated what I was trying to say. So after three cups of coffee and two pieces of banana crème pie, I decided to take a shot at writing something poetic, something I hadn't done since Mr. Shusterbaurer's English class at Saint Patrick High School over thirty-five years ago.

I headlined the news story with a very stark question:

Does the DiMatteo Family have a new consigliere?

I then opened the article with a simple poem that I composed, titled 'Chicago Gambit':

A gambit starts when war is declared,
The game may now begin.
A bishop moves, beyond its space,
The white pawn moves within.
As blood now drips on a checkered board,
Checkmate is now foreseen.
When a bishop kills a formidable knight,
...a black rook takes the queen.

The article then went on to discuss the weekly chess match between Fr. Colin J. 'Fr. Fitz' Fitzgerald, the former grand chess master, turned activist priest, and Anthony 'Little Tony' DiMatteo, the most powerful boss of the Chicago 'Outfit'. It elaborated on how the St. Simeon pastor befriended the Capo dei Capi and how the crime syndicate family had become more involved in the shooting deaths of looters and rioters that summer. The story made a rigid correlation between the violent summer events and how they fell in line with Fr. Fitz's well-known pro-capital punishment viewpoints.

I had called the DiMatteo Tomato Distribution Company and asked to speak with their CEO and chairman, Anthony DiMatteo. Naturally, he was not available for comment and did not return my phone calls, which I mentioned in the news story. The article was a little over two thousand words, and after all, was said and done, I felt very pleased with the news article. By eight o'clock that evening, I sent it over to my assistant editor, who decided to put the story on page two of the Chicago Tribune the next day after making a few minor suggestions.

I was in my office early the next Wednesday morning, trying to open my eyes to a fresh cup of Mrs. Folger's coffee. I couldn't have been sitting at my desk for more than ten minutes when my desk phone started ringing off the hook. Most of the phone calls, comments, and messages were laudatory, except a few aldermen from Chicago's City Council.

I received a cursory email directly from the Archdiocese of Chicago, not appreciating one of his priests being accused of being a 'made man.'

Most everyone commented about Fr. Fitz taking over the city's violent affairs since Mayor Kollar's assassination in to his own hands while using 'The Outfit' to take control of the town and distribute their own brand of justice.

At about eleven o'clock that morning, I was called into my assistant editor's office.

"I just got a phone call, McKay," Olsen started the first volley.

"Oh, really? I've been getting phone calls and emails all morning."

"Yeah, well, this one was special. Really special."

"Really?" as I sat down in front of his slovenly well-arranged desk.

"Ever hear of a guy by the name of Sal Marrocco?"

I pretended to be deep in thought, not wanting to let my assistant editor on that I knew precisely who Marrocco was. I had talked to him several times before in years past.

"Vaguely. He's mobbed up with the DiMatteo Family, right?"

It took all of three seconds to pull up his unforgettable image in my mind.

Salvatore Marrocco was the DiMatteo Tomato Distribution Company's financial controller and Little Tony's most trusted colleague. Sal was an older, heavy-set man in his late sixties, with over dyed jet-black hair and a mustache. He was very well educated, with an MBA degree from Northwestern University and a law degree from the University of Chicago. Although his corporate title was that of chief financial officer, he was better known as the 'Consigliere' of the DiMatteo Family. Little Tony consulted him daily regarding all business matters within the company and topics 'outside' of the DiMatteo Tomato business. Marrocco was quite valuable to Little Tony and was well paid for his diverse business knowledge, his understanding of the criminal and civil laws, and well-versed 'street smarts.'

"Duh," Olsen replied with a smile. "Your article has ruffled up some feathers over on South Ashland Avenue."

I was now smiling from ear to ear, knowing that my news article was the new talk of the town.

"You get your rocks off on this shit, don't you, McKay?"

I continued to smile without saying a word to my boss. He knew I always got a 'hard-on' after putting out stories like this in the paper.

"Am I on the mob 'hit list'?"

"Probably."

"Oh, goody-goody," I excitedly exclaimed, rubbing my hands together in anticipation.

Olsen only shook his head, figuring that only a whack-job reporter like myself would enjoy getting the attention of the city's most violent crime family.

"Marrocco is claiming that the DiMatteo Tomato Distribution Company is a legitimate business that doesn't get involved in the violent affairs of the City of Chicago. He's threatening the paper with a slander lawsuit."

"Did you tell him to stand in fucking line?" I smiled back at my editor.

"He claims that the whole story is without merit, and they are a 'legitimate company.' According to him, they had nothing to do with that violent execution that occurred on Jeweler's Row."

"No, kidding. Just like they don't know where Hoffa is either. Imagine that," I replied.

"They're all standing in line to take credit for that hit. Please don't tell me you want to do another article on Hoffa again," Olsen asked.

"No thanks, boss. I watched 'The Irishman' three times, and now I'm convinced that nobody knows what happened to him. Don't worry. I've got that one out of my system."

I did a news article on the Hoffa case almost twenty years ago, just after Frank 'The Irishman' Sheeran died in 2003. I had gotten a tip from my sources in the Detroit News that he had confessed to killing the Teamster's boss on his deathbed, but I couldn't verify his story. None of the DNA evidence from where he was supposedly shot and killed in that house on the West Side of Detroit tied into Sheeran's deathbed confession, so I dropped it.

"Marrocco is saying you have a very vivid imagination," Olsen replied.

"Really? And how does he explain two of his gorilla employees sitting in front of the jewelry store that night drinking espresso coffee while those kids were getting shot up inside?"

"He says that those two drivers lived nearby and were only concerned for their neighborhood. They knew nothing about the gunmen that were waiting inside of that jewelry store."

I laughed out loud at that one.

"Are you fucking kidding me?" I said with amazement.

"Marrocco says the incident was unrelated to the DiMatteo Family, and they expressed their deepest sympathies to the families of those ruthless gang-bangers that tried to loot up and destroy that jewelry store."

I continued to laugh at that ridiculous explanation.

"And for how many seconds are you buying that story?"

"Two or three, I haven't decided yet," Olsen smiled.

We both sat there silently for several long seconds, obviously very pleased with ourselves over how we had successfully investigated and put out that story.

"Needless to say, you need to watch your back, McKay. You can bet the farm that Little Tony and his family are not very pleased with you right now."

I got up and walked over to the Acqua-Fresh water cooler that was tucked in the corner of my bosses' office. I filled up the styrofoam cup and gulped down the cool, refreshing contents, thinking about how serious these new threats from the DiMatteo's could really be.

"I've been threatened before, boss. I can handle myself. Besides, do you think 'The Boys' are going to start taking out media newspapermen over every article they disagree with? Those days are long gone with Al Capone," I replied.

"You hope so, McKay. Just the same, watch your back. Like I've said to you before, take public transportation for a while. They still make car bombs, you know," he said while trying to keep a straight face.

I knew he was giving me these comforting words to make me feel better. As if I needed more excuses to lay awake at night.

"I think you've been watching way too many reruns of 'Casino' and 'Goodfellas,' boss," I smiled.

"Or 'The Irishman", he interjected.

Although we were only being threatened with a libel lawsuit from the DiMatteo Tomato Distribution Company, I realized while writing that article that there would be a distinct possibility that the crime family would be outraged. I knew there was a chance that they could take retribution towards any news reporter who brought out the truth regarding the Jeweler's Row incident in August. But my facts in that news story were spot-on, and my criticism was really aimed at Fr. Fitz. I pointed out several times in the article that he was using the Chicago crime family to accomplish his street smart, vigilante-style justice on the city's violent gangs.

And other than being excommunicated from the Roman Catholic Church, I really wasn't too worried at the time.

But in hindsight, I should have been very worried. Being excommunicated was the very least of my fucking problems.

As I was working at my desk that morning, the receptionist from the front office brought over a package that she had just received, hand-delivered to her desk.

"This package just came in. It's for you. McKay."

I looked at the brown-paper wrapped package that only said my name on it as the address:

Lawrence McKay – Chicago Tribune

There was no return address on it, and it was hand-delivered by one of those speedy delivery services. It was approximately twelve inches wide by six inches tall, and it smelled like powdered sugar. I could tell that it was a consumable food product of some kind.

As I tore open the brown wrapping paper, a white box with white string had been carefully tied around the box and was taped shut. Stamped on the corner was a fancy silver label that said 'Palermo Bakery' with a Harlem Avenue address and telephone number.

I untied the string and opened the box. There were twelve freshly prepared cannoli, green peanuts, white powdered sugar, and ricotta cream filling. They looked and smelled delicious.

Cannoli are Italian pastries consisting of tube-shaped shells of fried pastry dough, filled with a sweet, creamy filling usually containing ricotta, regularly a staple of Sicilian cuisine.

There was also a small white envelope with my name on it, written only as 'McKay' in black handwriting. I opened up the envelope, and I was surprised to read who it was from.

It simply said:

'Regards, The DiMatteo Family.'

I had heard of these gifts from the DiMatteo Family before and had heard several rumors of what these kinds of gifts meant to any lucky recipient.

At that moment, Tom Olsen, who probably saw food being delivered to my desk, eagerly came over to see what I had received.

"Hey Tommy," I innocently asked.

"I just received this box of fresh cannoli from some bakery on Harlem Avenue. The card inside simply says 'Regards, DiMatteo Family.'"

Olsen looked at the card, and without even asking, grabbed a fresh cannoli and shoved one inside of his mouth. The white powdered sugar splattered all over his dark shirt and tie.

"I just love cannoli," he managed to say with his mouth full.

I then looked at him, mildly annoyed that he was helping himself to my goodie box.

"What do you think this means?" I ignorantly asked.

He wiped his mouth off with his shirt and grabbed another cannoli to bring back to his office.

Before walking back, he turned around and casually mentioned:

"It means your fucking days are numbered."

CHAPTER THIRTY-TWO
RISTORANTE LO SCOGLIO-OCTOBER 13TH

It was little before three o'clock on that cloudy Thursday afternoon as I went back to the Franklin Café to see if I could get some more work done regarding the Kollar assassination. I was admittedly burned out, and I should have probably taken a day or two off before hitting it hard again.

I couldn't get that box of cannoli out of my head, and I couldn't get my head around the fact that perhaps, my life was in danger. I had left the box of cannoli in the cafeteria for everyone in the newsroom to enjoy, and I just ran out of there. I figured I was better off working somewhere else before receiving any more Sicilian death threats.

I was sitting there working for over an hour, consuming two slices of pumpkin pie and drinking large amounts of coffee. By four o'clock, my favorite CNN reporter walked into the Franklin Caffe' holding her famous red umbrella over her head, even though it had stopped raining outside. She walked up to the counter to order her cappuccino coffee. She then turned and looked at me, her eyes gleaming.

"I knew I would find you here," Talia Bowerman eagerly commented with bright sparkles in her eyes as she walked over and sat down at my makeshift office.

"I would think that they would have thrown you out of here by now."

"As long as I keep ordering pies and drinking coffee, I don't have anything to worry about."

"Congrats on your news article. It was very concise and well documented. I imagine the other news stations are going to be jumping on your story."

"Including CNN, perhaps?" I inquired.

"Including CNN, yes..." she slowly replied.

She sat down at my office while Gloria brought over her cappuccino, extra wet with another espresso shot.

"So, to whom do I have this honor then? Is this a social call or a business news media consultation?"

"That depends. I'm under some pressure from my news editor to do a newsfeed on your 'Chicago Gambit' story, so I would like to get your help if I could."

I looked at her and smiled.

"Well, you know this is going to cost you."

"I'm willing to pay a reasonable price," she quickly smiled while winking her eye.

"What do you have in mind?"

This was going to be way too easy, I thought to myself.

"How about if we start with a nice Italian dinner somewhere tonight?"

Talia smiled, looking pleased with the thought of ditching our journalistic newsroom responsibilities and playing hooky somewhere inside of a nice Italian restaurant.

"You'll never get a fight out of me over anything Italian," she replied, after taking another sip from her freshly prepared cappuccino.

I threw a couple of twenty-dollar bills on the table, then packed up our computers and papers. Within several minutes, we took a taxicab to one of my favorite restaurants in the River North neighborhood.

The black leather chairs and modern décor of the upscale restaurant blended nicely with the ambiance and the casual atmosphere of the Chicago River North neighborhood. Ristorante Lo Scoglio is a well-attended, contemporary nightspot for those wishing to enjoy its top-shelf martinis and avant-garde food menu, along with its classy, elegant dining room design.

"I've never been here before. Do you come here often?" Talia asked.

"Yes, it's one of my favorite places. The homemade pasta melts in your mouth, and the atmosphere is amazing."

She put her arm around mine as the hostess guided us to our cozy little table, which was next to the fireplace. We sat down at a quaint little spot next to a large picture window opposite Kinzie Street, facing all the hustle and bustle of that typical autumn evening in River North Chicago. We were given the wine list, and I immediately recommended the Belle Glos 2017 Pinot Noir Telephone & Clark vintage, which she was more than happy to try. I hoped that my being bold enough to immediately order an expensive bottle of red wine that our glasses would be well filled, and our conversation would stay light and breezy.

As we started to make ourselves relaxed and comfortable, she gazed at me and took a long sip from her wine glass.

"So, you must be feeling exhilarated taking your victory lap on the 'Chicago Gambit story. I like the way you opened up that article with that quaint little poem." she mentioned.

"Poetry has a subtle way of getting the point across when doing a feature story, especially on two thugs like Little Tony and Fr. Fitz."

"I like the way you opened up your story. You have a very descriptive style of writing. While reading your news media articles from the Tribune, I can see you're so good at what you do. Several reporters in my newsroom are very familiar with your journalistic reporting," she complimented as she sipped her wine. I was getting the impression that Talia had been doing some internet stalking.

"Yeah, well, I'm not that well-liked. If I were, I would be sitting in the assistant editor's chair by now. I've had more than my share of hits or misses too in this business."

"Well, you're not going to get any bad comments or feedback from me. You seem to be very well respected here in the Chicago media world."

"Thank you. Coming from a beautiful, sharp, take-no-prisoners journalist like yourself, I will take that as a compliment."

"Ever think about going into television journalism?" she asked.

"At my age? I think it's a little late for me. Besides, I have a difficult time dealing with the newsroom deadlines of a Chicago newspaper. I'm too old now to start waking up at four o'clock in the morning to be chasing down news stories with a cameraman to parts unknown."

"I agree. It takes a different breed. I'm still putting in my time doing these live newsfeeds with CNN. I'm told that this will slow down for me in a year or so, and they will start giving these news feeds to someone much younger," she winked, still holding her glass.

"Do you aspire to get a permanent news desk assignment? You would do well as one of those beautiful, sexy newscasters doing the six o'clock news," I complimented, now enjoying my Pinot Noir.

"Someday. I'm not going to lie. I would love a news desk assignment in front of the camera."

The wine was going down very smoothly, and I was enjoying our conversation. I was trying very hard to distract myself from locking my eyes with hers. Her warm, deep blue eyes were mesmerizing and could have melted every iceberg on any ocean. She then held up her glass and made a toast.

"Here's to the 'Chicago Gambit,'" she saluted, as we both raised our glasses.

After a few long moments, she hypnotically stared into my eyes.

"Did anyone ever tell you that you could pass for Rob Lowe?"

I didn't know if she was sincere or if the wine took an early effect on her 20-20 vision. I smiled, trying not to blush.

"Now and again," I only said.

"He's very handsome, you know," she only said. After spending several moments blushing, we engaged in a conversation discussing our brutal Chicago winters in comparison to Boston and her native Rochester, New York.

"So, how did you conclude that Fr. Fitz was the new crime family 'consigliere'?" she asked.

"I played chess with him."

"Really?"

"I tracked him down at a chess tournament he was sponsoring at his church rectory in September. So I entered my name, and I got to play Fr. Fitz. He's quite good."

"How interesting," she said with a smile.

"I found his name in the obituary when DiMatteo's mother died last summer. He was the priest presiding over the funeral. Knowing that he is so well known for his activist opinions regarding the death penalty and community violence, it wasn't hard to figure out that he was using Little Tony and his family as a weapon against the gangs." I explained.

We both took a long sip from our wine glasses.

"I also have a connection with one of DiMatteo's gorillas, and he informed me about their little weekly chess matches. After a while, I put two and two together."

"That was ingenious. I would have never put those theories together with the way you did in your news article. What has the DiMatteo Family had to say?" Talia asked.

"What did they have to say?" I asked.

"Well, yes...what has their reaction?"

I paused for a moment.

"Cannoli. They sent me a box of cannoli."

She glared at me for several long seconds.

"It's a Sicilian message letting me know that my life is in danger. They're not pleased, of course. Their controller, Sal Marrocco, is threatening a liability lawsuit against the paper, but nobody is worried."

We were both silent for a moment.

"You didn't Fr. Fitz in chess."

"Are you kidding? He nailed me in ten moves. Did you know that Fr. Fitz is a former grandmaster?"

"No kidding?"

"I found out that he was the Illinois Grand Chess Master in 1972 and 1973, while he was in high school."

Talia shook her head in amazement while sipping from her wine glass.

"Well, congrats again, McKay. You did a great job on that investigative story. I'm sure the other media stations will be picking up on your news article."

"Chaz Rizzo already called me about it, so I imagine he'll be doing a news feed on Channel Eight tonight. You know how much he loves those 'mob stories.' I'm just happy that I was able to crack the story before he did," I said while padding myself on the back.

A pause in the conversation.

"I have to say, Chaz Rizzo usually gives me and the Tribune credit when doing one of my news stories. Channel Eight is usually pretty good about that."

"We're not always that nice," she replied, referring to her CNN newsroom producers.

"Besides, Chaz Rizzo never impressed me. He's not all that," she loudly pointed out, as I poured another refill of Pinot Noir into her glass.

"You mean to tell me that Rizzo never asked you out?"

"Are you kidding? All the time! The man is incorrigible. I'm surprised the local 'Me-Too' movement hasn't nailed his ass to the cross yet over at Channel Eight. I've heard some juicy harassment stories about him from the other women reporters there. That man thinks with his 'little head.'"

I smiled, making sure that my glass was still full.

"That could be your next story."

"No, thank you. He's too creepy for me."

The waiter came over and put in our dinner orders while making sure that we were ready for another Belle Glos Pinot Noir at $79.95 a bottle.

"You won't mind if we mention your story on our newsfeed tomorrow, would you? We'll credit you as the reporter and the Chicago Tribune, of course."

"Of course, no worries."

I thought for a moment before I began formulating my words.

"So, tell me about your investigation into the Kollar assassination, Talia. Where are you at with that?"

I immediately noticed that her glass was empty, and I decided to make it my mission to keep her wine glass filled that evening.

She began to summarize, still enjoying the smooth, satin red Pinot Noir.

"As I mentioned to you before, you need to concentrate on the Mayor's enemies," she replied.

"Yes, but she had way too many of them."

"True, but you need to concentrate on the ones who had any power and muscle to take her out last summer. Who else was more qualified than the Chicago P.D. and their Chief of Police Superintendent, Walter Byron?"

I thought for a moment.

"I think he's a stretch, Talia. I don't think Byron has the kind of balls to take out the Mayor in broad daylight."

She took another sip of her wine.

"Not by himself, McKay. He had help. Lots of help. And he had to make all this look as though his hands are clean and that he wasn't involved."

We were both silent for several minutes, sorting out her Kollar assassination theories.

"So, you're assuming there was a City-wide conspiracy to kill Mayor Kollar?"

"I'm saying he didn't plan all of this alone. He's not that smart," she observed.

"Who else goes racing down Western Avenue while the wife of a Chicago alderman is giving him a blowjob in the front seat of his unmarked squad car?" she replied.

Talia then smiled as if to say, 'I know something you don't' before taking another sip. She then put her glass down on the table and made her final pitch.

"He had to have help. He couldn't have planned all of this alone," she summarized.

Another silent moment.

"Somebody...big," she emphasized.

I looked at her for several long moments. This woman was not only beautiful and smart, but she was also very intuitive. I figured her for the kind of woman who could manipulate her beauty and brains to get whatever it was that she wanted out of any man, especially when it came to conveying a story.

"Well, let me know how all of this works out for you. Personally, I think you are barking up the wrong tree."

"Really? Why?"

"It could be a mob hit," I theorized.

Talia laughed out loud.

"I think that you need to turn off those 'Godfather' reruns that you have been running continuously in your head," she smiled.

"' The Boys' didn't have an ax to grind with Kollar. And it isn't like them to get involved in a hit like that in broad daylight in front of her security detail at her house."

She took another sip.

"There had to be someone else working with Byron."

Another moment of silence.

"You mean like the gangs?"

Talia smiled but didn't say anything.

At that moment, the waiter arrived and saved the evening, bringing our entrée orders. She ordered the Branzino, Chilean seabass, while I ordered the special, the Pappardelle Con Sugo di Manzo. By then, my wine glass was now empty again.

Talia then grasped the Belle Glos wine bottle and poured the contents into my glass first, and then finished pouring the rest of it into her glass.

"Let's make a toast. To your excellent news reporting and your 'Chicago Gambit' story," smiling as she held up her glass.

I loudly said, 'cheers,' still staring at her gorgeous blue eyes.

We continued to make small talk about our jobs and our similar newsrooms, and we were both feeling buzzed from all of the wine.

It was turning out to be a chilly but beautiful autumn evening as the warmth of the adjacent fireplace near our table was radiating warm air across the room. I was enjoying our conversation while the pappardelle pasta was melting in my mouth. When the espresso coffee and desserts arrived, I asked the same question regarding the Kollar investigation.

"What is the connection between Chief Byron and the gangs? And which gang do you suppose was crazy enough to carry out this hit?"

"Definitely the Black Cobras. They've got the connections with the CPD and the gang members to pull it off. They're the largest street gang in Chicago," Talia said.

"The largest, but not the craziest," I pointed out.

"And they're not the most skilled when it comes to high-power rifles."

A silent moment while we finished our espressos.

"It had to take a sharp-shooter to make those shots from one hundred twenty yards away, and the street gangs are not known for being sharpshooters," I summarized.

Talia only smiled.

We both just sat there for several long moments, digesting all of this shared information. When the bill finally came, Talia offered to buy dinner, but I took out my American Express card and beat her to it.

I then helped her with her coat, and we both exited the restaurant. After calling a taxicab, we both entered the back seat, her hand now grasping mine very tightly. I was about to mention the address of the Franklin Street Café before she interrupted me.

"24 North Morgan Street, West Loop," she said, interjecting her home address to the cab driver.

I figured that we would drop her off at her house first while she held my hand tightly in the taxi's back seat. When we arrived, she leaned over and kissed me. It was one of those warm, wet, passionate kisses that guys only dream about when watching one of their favorite R-rated movies.

"Can I interest you in a nightcap?"

At that moment, I was speechless as I excitedly nodded my head.

I felt my heart start to race, knowing that I could finally have her all to myself for the evening. My hands were beginning to perspire, as I was both excited and nervous at the same time.

We entered the lobby of her apartment building together, her left hand tightly grasping mine. At that moment, she seemed to have this loving, adoring look in her blue eyes that I had never seen before. We both entered the elevator, and she pressed the button to the fourth floor. No sooner did the doors immediately close that Talia began kissing the corner of my mouth and planting long, wet kisses on my neck. I felt almost embarrassed, staring at the elevator cameras the whole time while she was kissing me.

"You do realize that we're on Candid Camera here, right?" I casually mentioned, not wanting the kisses to stop.

"I don't care," she whispered in my ear, "I've wanted to kiss you all night."

As the elevator doors opened, I had to briefly push her aside for the two of us to troll our way down the hallway to her room, number 4G. She inserted the key into the door's lock, and no sooner did the door close behind us that she began to attack me with a barrage of wet, moist, succulent kisses. Her lips still tasted like cherries, as the aroma of her perfume began to hypnotize me, feeling the perspiration running down the middle of my back.

"I've never made love to Rob Lowe before," she warmly mentioned.

"I've never made love to Courtney Cox either," I snidely remarked, as we both started giggling at the thought of two popular actors making love in her apartment that evening.

She started unbuttoning my shirt and began kissing my chest, planting wet, sensuous kisses up and along my shoulders and stomach. She started holding my gold crucifix, placing more kisses along my shoulders. She then unbuttoned her blouse, lifted her bra, and began pressing her incredible, well-endowed breasts up against my chest. From what I could briefly notice, her dark tan lines stopped where her amazing breasts began. They were absolutely gorgeous.

"I've had fantasies about making love to you in the middle of the day," I confessed between kisses. I wasn't sure if she even heard me.

"I would love to have a Nooner with you," she then whispered, kissing my neck and chest.

I finished taking off her blouse and her bra and began pressing my mouth against her rosy large nipples and breasts. We both began groaning with excitement as we finished undressing each other, and we simultaneously fell onto the freshly made bed. Her warm body felt amazing next to mine as I continued to place kisses and love bites along every part of her shapely, well-toned body.

We continued our lovemaking for what seemed to be hours and hours until our bodies were ravaged with exhaustion that evening. I remember thinking to myself, what a dream come true, to be making incredible love to the most beautiful, most alluring woman in Chicago. I could feel her sleeping, as her head, with her dark, flowing hair, was resting up against my chest. We were both falling in and out of romantic consciousness. I was trying very hard to keep my feelings and my thoughts to myself.

I did not want to blurt out the three words that always seem to scare women away after a romantic night of lovemaking, especially after the first time in bed.

We held each other close, staring at the window of her bedroom, holding her in my arms all night long. I couldn't remember the last time I had felt so emotionally satisfied. It was as though a peaceful feeling had transformed my soul, and it felt wonderful.

At that moment, I was trying very hard not to fall in love with the most beautiful news reporter in Chicago.

Chapter Thirty-Three
A Meeting With The Cardinal- October 15th

It was a cloudy, cold Thursday morning during that mid-week of October, as Fr. Colin Fitzgerald arrived at Cardinal Markowitz's Chicago mansion on North State Street.

His Eminence requested a meeting with Father Fitzgerald last week to discuss "some important issues" recently, which had transpired since the beginning of the summer. While Fr. Fitz had been associated with the St. Simeon Parish for over twenty-two years, he has consistently been a thorn on the side of the Archdiocese of Chicago. His avid political activism has brought about unwanted publicity and media coverage with the church, and the Cardinal had heard enough.

It was time to bring Fr. Fitzgerald into his office and have a 'Come to Jesus' meeting with famous community activist. The Archdiocese had censored the outspoken priest several times before, which only managed to quiet him down for a short time. But the recent rumors regarding the pastor's involvement with some organized crime families, the DiMatteo Family, in particular, had the Archdiocese of Chicago raising its eyebrows.

His Eminence was livid, to say the least.

Fr. Fitzgerald was aware of John Cardinal Markowitz's recent health issues that he had been suffering from. The Cardinal had recently been diagnosed with stage three prostate cancer. It had been announced in the press that his health was quickly deteriorating and that he had been undergoing chemotherapy treatments. His cancer treatments and health problems were also a concern to whatever His

Eminence had to say regarding Fr. Fitz's future as a pastor.

Fr. Fitz had threatened to leave the priesthood several times before to continue his local neighborhood activism. But when cooler heads prevailed, the Chicago Archdiocese and the rebel priest always managed to find some middle ground.

Fr. Fitzgerald parked his black Ford Escape within the adjacent parking lot and walked down North State Street to the massive, red-bricked Chicago mansion entrance. Its neatly manicured lawns, landscaped bushes, and oak trees complimented the black, wrought ironed fences surrounding its beautiful, park-like setting.

After checking in with several of the Cardinal's associates, he entered the ornate mansion and entered the large, lavish office of Cardinal Joseph D. Markowitz. His Eminence was sitting in a red velvet chair facing the window of his elaborate garden, which was now filled with the red and yellow maple leaves of fall. He was wearing a light fleece blanket around his shoulders as Fr. Fitzgerald knelt to kiss the Cardinal's right hand.

"Please sit down, Father," the Cardinal ordered as he rose from his chair and walked over to his decorative, massive oak desk. He coughed several times, clearing his throat, and then wiping his mouth with a white handkerchief. There wasn't any doubt that the Cardinal was not in the best of health.

"Father Fitzgerald, I called you in here to discuss some recent rumors which have arisen from your parish and some of your recent activities," His Eminence began.

"Reports and accusations that, quite frankly, seriously disturb me."

"What reports would those be, Your Eminence?"

Fr. Fitz now knew exactly where this conversation was going, and he was doing his best to play stupid.

Cardinal Markowitz glared at the parish priest, as he could see the anger and smoke coming out of his eyes.

"I understand that you are now a 'made-man.'"

At first, Fr. Fitz glared at the Cardinal, not understanding what he was talking about. He then started to chuckle at the Cardinal's reference until he began to explode.

"I fail to find any humor here, Fr. Fitzgerald!" Markowitz loudly responded. "There are recent, humiliating rumors that are going around about you and the DiMatteo Family."

"I can assure you that there is no truth in them."

"Really? The papers have reported that a certain parish priest from St. Simeon's Parish has had weekly chess matches with a certain Capo dei Capi on Wednesday evenings. Is this correct?"

The priest sat there, stoic for several long seconds, before nodding his head.

"Yes, Your Eminence, that is correct."

"So, Father, would you care to tell me what these meetings and these clandestine chess matches are all about?" Markowitz ranted.

Father Fitz sat there motionless.

"Are you having such a difficult time finding comparable chess opponents that you need to have a weekly chess match with one of the most dangerous organized crime members in the city?"

A silent moment.

"I understand that Little Tony has been your weekly chess partner since last summer."

"Your Eminence, I can assure you that I..."

"Don't interrupt me, Father!"

Cardinal Markowitz continued to glare at the parish priest while trying to reiterate his point.

"Do you actually know who you are dealing with? Little Tony DiMatteo, with his criminal activities and violent reputation, makes Satan and every evil demon from the deepest depths of hell look like innocent altar boys."

Fr. Fitz continued to stare at the Cardinal, not wanting to make the mistake of interrupting him.

"There are also rumors that you're encouraging some of these violent episodes that 'The Outfit' and especially, the DiMatteo Family has been involved with regarding some of these violent shootings."

"Your Eminence, I can..."

"Again, don't interrupt me!"

"There have been some violent shootings this past summer with these organized families taking out some of these looters and protesters, and that you have been assisting the DiMatteo's by advising them in these activities."

The parish priest was struggling to remain silent.

"According to the rumors, you're the new family consigliere!" he loudly accused the parish priest.

"THAT IS NOT TRUE!" Fr. Fitz stood up from his chair and screamed back at the Cardinal.

"I have created a very trustful friendship with Tony DiMatteo, and we both happen to enjoy each other's company. We have fascinating discussions regarding the current violence going on in our city and some of the sociological approaches with dealing with such violence."

"Sit down, Father! And cut the crap! I've known you and your far-right political opinions for a very long time. You were reprimanded and silenced for your capital punishment protests several years ago. Do you not remember?"

"Yes. And I threatened to leave the priesthood back then as well. Do you not remember that? Your Eminence?"

Markowitz started to chuckle at Father Colin Fitzgerald's reference to his potential exit from his vocation.

"Wait, are you telling me that you would leave the priesthood for your association with the DiMatteo Family?"

"No, Your Eminence. But I will not be accused of being a 'made-man priest' to an organized crime family."

Cardinal Markowitz laughed out loud.

"You wouldn't be the first, Father."

They both silently looked at each other for several seconds.

"Brush up on your history, Colin. There was a corrupt Cardinal in Rome many years ago named Cardinal Giovanni Masellis, a very prominent and powerful cardinal within the Vatican Curia," Markowitz began his papal lecture.

"He was considered one of the most powerful cardinals in Vatican City during the sixties and seventies. He was deeply involved in the Banco Ambrosiano scandal, where several cardinals and bishops were lining their pockets from the millions of dollars funded by the Vatican. There were rumors and allegations that he was affiliated with the corrupt Cesario Family in Italy and that he had a hand in Pope John Paul the First's death."

"Yes, I do recall."

"He was also a 'made-man,' Father. They said that he was an 'honorary member' of the Cesario Family."

The two of them were silent for several moments.

"Those were just rumors, Your Eminence. I knew Cardinal Masellis very well."

The Cardinal looked surprised.

"Really?"

"Yes. I was his understudy while I was doing my seminary studies at Loyola University in Rome back in 1982. I always admired him for his strength, power, steadfastness, and his fortitude. There was no doubt to anyone familiar with the Vatican Curia about who was really in control. Masellis was a very powerful, very formidable, very influential cardinal. Cardinal Giovanni Masellis was a great man."

Cardinal Markowitz glared at the parish priest for several long seconds. Familiar with Cardinal Masellis and his notorious, evil reputation, he became quickly aware of the kind of people Fr. Fitz considered as the role models that he so personally admired. It had become evident to him that Fr. Colin Fitzgerald was very much attracted to the 'dark side.'

"Again, I can assure you that this is not the case," Fr. Fitz reiterated.

"Colin? How is Little Tony treating you lately? Is he still coming around for your weekly chess matches?"

"Well, no, he hasn't shown up these last weeks."

"Doesn't that make you a little suspicious?"

Fr. Fitz looked at the Cardinal in silence, as his wheels were starting to turn.

"As you know, the authorities and especially the FBI have begun intense investigations regarding the DiMatteo Family and the summer violence that they are accused of being involved with. Do you honestly think that Little Tony is going to take any personal responsibility for that violence?"

A moment of silence.

"If anything, he going to blame you for lecturing him on the importance of capital punishment in society and how your radical viewpoints greatly influenced their crime family behavior. He's not going to take responsibility, neither to the authorities nor to God himself."

Fr. Fitz was now listening intently to the Cardinal.

"Little Tony is going to blame you, Father. He is going to say that you made him and his family directly shoot those looters on Jeweler's Row last summer, and all of the violence that has since erupted."

He loudly coughed while taking another sip of his ice water.

"DiMatteo is not a man who will take culpability for his actions."

Fr. Fitz was smiling and shaking his head.

"I think that Tony is a little more reasonable than that, Your Eminence."

"Don't flatter yourself, Father. And stop giving him more credit than he deserves. He's not that reasonable or that logical. And he certainly will pass the blame onto you rather than take responsibility for his actions."

He paused for a moment.

"He's a 'wise guy,' Father Fitzgerald."

There was another pause in their dialog.

"That's how 'wise guys' think."

Cardinal Markowitz took a long sip from the glass of ice water sitting on the other side of his lavish wooden desk.

"And when the time comes, when he no longer has any use for you and blames you for his problems, your life will be in danger."

Fr. Fitz only sat there silently, not saying a word. The two of them quietly reflected on the conversation that the two of them were having. His Eminence was using that silent moment to make the parish priest understand the dangerous relationship he was having with Chicago's most dangerous mobster.

"Fr. Fitzgerald, may I speak to you off of the record here, if you don't mind?"

"Please do."

"There was an instance several years ago in Mexico where a prominent Catholic priest named Father Alberto Martinez became involved with one of the heads of the drug cartels there in Puerto Vallarta," the Cardinal began to explain.

"It all started very innocently, with the priest becoming a personal counselor and confessor to the head of the drug cartel. He had intentions of trying to convert the dangerous drug lord into rediscovering his Catholic faith. When the authorities started raising the heat, several drug criminals were captured and killed. The drug cartel then began blaming Father Martinez. The drug lord accused him of being a government informant. The priest was badly beaten within an inch of his life. It was certain that his life was in danger, and finally, the local diocese and the Vatican interceded."

"Really? What happened?"

"Let's just say that, like the U.S. Government, the Vatican has its own 'witness protection program' of sorts. In that instance, the Vatican made him disappear when they realized that his life was in danger."

"So, what happened to Fr. Martinez?"

"Let's just say he is serving the Lord in another part of the world."

The Vatican and the Catholic Church have always dealt with its priests' problems on their own for centuries. They were not about to allow any diocese priest to remain in a dangerous situation without interceding. Like any sovereign state, its bishops and priests' malicious or personal affairs were beyond the reproach of any federal or state laws prohibiting such behavior. According to the Vatican, the laws of God were far higher than any insignificant criminal laws of any state, or the United States for that matter. This is how the pedophile priests were shuffled and relocated for decades. The church has always taken care of their own, and they would certainly never allow any vengeful act from an organized crime family to be brought against one of its priests.

Fr. Fitz only shook his head. "I don't believe that will ever be necessary, Your Eminence. My life is not in danger here, and I am certain that Tony DiMatteo would never take any retribution on me or our personal relationship. Tony is a stand-up guy, and he wouldn't do anything to hurt me personally."

"You're viewing this man through rose-colored glasses, Father. Little Tony DiMatteo is a dangerous, ruthless criminal whose unspeakable, murderous crimes are infamous. Just because he has dinner with you and plays chess with you once a week doesn't mean he won't gauge your eyes out if you anger him."

The Cardinal paused for a moment.

"Little Tony is a zebra whose stripes will never change."

At that moment, Fr. Fitz became impatient with the conversation, as he quickly stood up.

"Is there anything else? Your Eminence?"

The Cardinal looked at him, intently for a moment.

"I can't tell you who to play or not play chess with Father. But please be very careful. I don't like reading about my priests in the papers."

Fr. Fitz walked over to the Cardinal and kissed his ring, while Markowitz grasped both of his hands.

"You're a good priest, Fr. Fitz. Please watch your back. I certainly don't want to lose you."

They both shook hands again, and Fr. Fitz exited the Cardinal's lavish office. As he got into his Ford Escape, he started to think about what Cardinal Markowitz had said intensely. The parish priest had worked very hard to gain the Capo dei Capi's trust, and he and his parishioners have so far benefited from their very close, personal relationship. Tony DiMatteo has been very generous to the St. Simeon Parish. He has made several large donations, including new air conditioning units and a new furnace for the rectory. Tony had asked him several times 'if he needed anything,' and he has been nothing short of generous and gracious to him and his parishioners. He didn't believe for one moment that Little Tony would ever retaliate against him for any issues that his sociological lectures and personal advice may have caused.

As he drove southbound on State Street, he smiled and shook his head. Cardinal Markowitz was totally out of line and did not know the Capo of the DiMatteo Family in the same way that Fr. Fitz knew him.

Tony DiMatteo was not your typical wise guy, Fr. Fitz thought to himself. He firmly believed that Little Tony was extremely loyal to him and their friendship, and Tony's trust in him was solid. He knew that Little Tony completely trusted him and would never do anything that would endanger their personal relationship.

It was a dangerous assumption that would eventually cost him his life.

CHAPTER THIRTY-FOUR
LIVE FROM CNN -OCTOBER 16TH

It had been a very hectic day, and I had just walked into the house that evening at a little after eight o'clock. I was so tired and hungry that night that I immediately went into the bedroom, changed out of my clothes, and put my pajamas on.

I had some pasta leftovers that my mother had sent home with me over the weekend for dinner. I was standing in front of the microwave in my pajama bottoms when my cell phone loudly rang.

"McKay, turn the CNN news channel on."

It was my boss, Tom Olsen.

"Tom, I just got home from work. Can't it wait?"

"No, McKay...turn it on, NOW!" he demanded.

I put my cellphone on speaker and tuned my television onto Channel 302, the local CNN twenty-four-hour news channel.

There on my television was my new love interest, Talia Bowerman, doing a live news feed in front of St. Simeon Church on West 79th Street. In her live newsfeed, she had practically regurgitated my whole news article published the other day in the Chicago Tribune. She continued to use the 'Chicago Gambit' reference to the chess game conducted weekly at the St. Simeon rectory between Fr. Fitz and Little Tony. She assumed that Fr. Fitz was the DiMatteo Family's new 'made-man' and that the crime family had new connections into the local Catholic Church. At the bottom of the screen was a 'LIVE -BREAKING STORY' banner flashing at the television screen's bottom.

Throughout her report, she made no mention of either me or my already published article in the Chicago Tribune.

"What the fuck?" immediately came out of my mouth.

"Who is this bitch?" was Tom Olsen's urgent response.

"She's a CNN reporter whom I've been dating recently. We've been seeing each other casually over the last few weeks, and we discussed in detail the 'Chicago Gambit' story."

"Yeah, well...you've been played, my friend. She's on the air in front of the St. Simeon Church doing a 'Live Breaking Story' which she is obviously taking credit for."

I kept shaking my head, not believing anything that was going on.

"She had mentioned that she was going to reference my story that was published in the Chicago Tribune the other day," I tried to reason.

"Yeah, well, guess what, buddy boy? Whatever kind of pillow talk or agreement that you had with her just went out the fucking window."

"And she didn't make any mention of me or my published article in the paper the other day?" I innocently asked.

"Nope."

"What the fuck?" I said out loud again.

I felt like Talia Bowerman had played me, and Olsen laughed out loud over the phone.

"CNN is notorious for doing shit like this," Olsen explained.

"They will reference other news stories from other media sources and put them on their live news feeds as if they're the ones who are breaking the story. They do this dogshit all of the time. You can't trust any of these fucking reporters, especially the ones from CNN. They plagiarize other news stories and put them on the air as if those articles were investigated and researched by their own reporters," he said.

There was a moment of silence on the phone.

"They've done this shit before," Olsen repeated.

I shook my head in disbelief. I never figured Talia to be this kind of 'dirty' news reporter. I had only been dating Talia very briefly, and we had only gotten intimate at her place that one time the other evening. I was so surprised that she reported the story. I was more surprised that this was a 'breaking story' exclusively reported by CNN, not even mentioning my name or the name of my newspaper.

"So how are we going to handle it?"

"Usually, our paper will put out a call to CNN, letting them know that their 'breaking news story' was a story that was initially printed two days ago by our paper. In that case, they will apologize, like they always do."

"So they'll just say, 'I'm sorry'? Big fucking deal. The damage is already done. Now everyone in town that didn't see the article in the Tribune will think that it was a CNN breaking story."

"Yep. That's what they do. That's their M-O, buddy boy."

"What a bunch of fucking scum bags!" I cursed them out loud.

Tom Olsen only laughed again out loud.

"They're all ruthless bitches, Pallie," Olsen declared.

"I learned that the hard way. Start doing more thinking with the big head, not the little one, McKay. I'll see you tomorrow."

As my assistant editor hung up the phone, I sat there on my couch, staring at the CNN newscast blaring loudly on my TV set. I couldn't fucking believe it. I had never had a relationship with another news reporter before. I had never had the experience of another reporter stealing my news material that had already been published in the paper and calling it their own on live TV.

I had talked to Talia a few times since our date and sleep-over a few days ago, and she didn't mention anything about doing this story again other than what she had casually said to me that evening.

I walked back over to my microwave and warmed up the home-made gnocchi's that my mother had made over the weekend. After feeding Bruno, my yellow Labrador, I sat back on my couch while eating my dinner and continued to watch the CNN news broadcast.

Talia's news broadcast came back on three-more times that night, all 'Live Feeds' from St. Simeon Church on West 79th Street. Not in any one of her live newscasts did she mention the Chicago Tribune article or my name as the reporter who had initially broken the "Chicago Gambit' story.

I initially didn't know how I was going to play this. At first, I wanted to call Talia on her cell phone and leave her the nastiest message that I could think of. I wanted to call her every fucking rotten name in the book, starting with the letter 'A' and abruptly stopping off at the 'C' word.

But then I thought better of it. Being silent and playing very cool, calm, and collect was probably the best method of handling it. I decided to be non-responsive and not confront her. If she felt guilty and wanted to talk about it, she would call me and clear the air.

When it doubt, always play it cool, my father always used to tell me growing up.

Let them think there's cold water running through your veins.

With Bruno lying next to my feet, I fell asleep on the couch that night, as I could not keep my eyes open any longer. I had not shut off the television, and CNN was blaring all night long in my living room.

When I abruptly woke up on the couch at three-thirty in the morning, the TV was still on. The first thing I did was look at my cell phone to see if Talia might have texted or called me. We had talked several times previously, and it was not unusual for her to leave me a 'good-night' text these last few days.

But tonight, there was nothing.

I shut off the TV and the lights, and Bruno walked along the side of me into my bedroom. I then crawled under the covers of my king-size bed, trying desperately to forget Talia Bowerman and to put her out of my mind. My heart was hurting, and I felt as though I had been used.

Where I had initially thought that Talia was a beautiful, smart, classy lady who cared enough about my feelings not to do anything to hurt me, I had now realized that she had no such scruples. The cutthroat, competitive world of Chicago journalism was alive and well, and Talia had just used me as another throng to push herself up the corporate media ladder.

I cursed her name under my breath and closed my eyes, vowing to put her name and her face as far away from my memory as possible. I had now learned a new adage to insert into my personal playbook of life's worthwhile lessons:

All is fair in love and journalism.

CHAPTER THIRTY-FIVE
THE MAYOR'S OFFICE -OCTOBER 25

The early morning fall snow flurries were starting to accumulate in front of 121 North LaSalle Street, as Mayor Raymond Sanchez arrived early that morning, just after seven o'clock. It had been an unexpected early snowfall, as the temperatures were hovering around the freezing mark. The weather forecasters predicted that the snow would melt later as the temperatures were expected to rise above forty-five degrees.

Mayor Sanchez took off his overcoat and placed his Starbucks coffee on top of his wooden mahogany desk. He then opened up his top desk drawer and took a valium, as his daily migraine headache had arrived early on that day. He picked up a copy of the Chicago Tribune and read the front page.

"Fuck!" he exclaimed out loud.

Sanchez slammed the paper on his desk as if to magically hope for the headlines to disappear.

"Fuck! Fuck! Fuck!"

It had been a difficult three months for Chicago's new mayor.

There on the front page of the Chicago Tribune were the headlines that he had been dreading to read:

Federal Agents Begin Mayoral Investigation

The newspaper article went on to discuss the office raid that was conducted by the Federal Bureau of Investigation the day before.

The agency confiscated all of the computers, files, software, file servers, and other documents from the mayor's office, hauling away sixty-seven banker's boxes in all. They had been notified of some of Mayor Sanchez's various commission demands and exorbitant 'application fees' made upon the city's building and permits department for new city projects. Citywide developers were complaining about the increased costs of doing business with the city, and all of them knew that these fee demands were directly going into the mayor's pocket.

Having openly advertised his mayoral office as a new profit center of bribery and corruption, it didn't take long for the word to get out that Sanchez would do whatever was necessary to benefit from his office financially. The new mayor brazenly hustled and marketed his unique brand of corruption to various council members, city developers, and lobbyists to further progress the city's future plan.

This was a shock to everyone in the city except to Alderman Eddie Barrett, who knew all along that their new mayor was more than just a wolf in sheep's clothing. He was a political criminal out of control. There became open accusations of the city's first Latino mayor taking bribes and payouts to get various projects and city ordinances voted on and passed. The city's most potent alderman openly accused Sanchez in the media of being the city's 'most corrupt mayor since William Hale 'Big Bill' Thompson from the Roaring Twenties.'

Many scoffed at the media war that had now ensued between the Fourteenth Ward alderman and Mayor Sanchez over the last five months. Many council members had joked that Eddie Barrett was insulted to discover a Chicago politician who was more openly more corrupt and dishonest than he was.

Raymond Sanchez was indeed an opportunist, and he wasn't bashful about peddling his mayoral influences on anyone willing to compensate him for his efforts. He was openly called 'a liar,' and 'a thief,' and several of Barrett's 'Dirty Dozen' gang of aldermen had begun drafting a formal motion of impeachment. Almost all of the city council had branded him as a criminal, using the media as an open pulpit to voice their political frustrations against the mayor.

Unfortunately, Mayor Sanchez didn't take any of these city council threats very seriously. 'El Rey' as he was infamously called, had some dirty information against all of his political foes. He had made it a point to call in every one of his city council enemies and openly threaten them with any corrupt, dirty deals that he had covert knowledge of. He would broadcast to the media whatever sensitive information he had if their attempts to remove him from office continued.

But when the federal agents raided his office two days ago, Mayor Sanchez suddenly realized that he would possibly be spending the remainder of his mayoral term in federal prison.

As Sanchez tried to settle in and calm his nerves, his desk phone suddenly rang.

"Yes?"

"Mr. Mayor, your eight o'clock appointment is here to see you."

"My eight o'clock appointment?"

"Yes. You have an on-camera interview with Chaz Rizzo from Channel Eight News."

Mayor Sanchez had forgotten to cancel the scheduled interview that he had made with Chaz Rizzo last week before the federal raid. With the new media backlash that had been going on against him, Sanchez thought last week that having a one-on-one taped interview with Channel Eight's star reporter would allow him to clear his name and to openly deny all of the slanderous accusations that were mounting against him.

'El Rey' sat there for several long moments, not initially responding to his receptionist. With all that had recently happened, he initially wanted to cancel the interview. He knew that the recent federal raid of his office would be new fodder for the outspoken news reporter, and he wasn't in the mood to sit down with him.

He then took out his keys and unlocked the bottom drawer of his desk. Rolling up a crisp, one dollar bill, he pulled out his usual Eight-Ball of cocaine. He gently deposited a thin line of cocaine using a small teaspoon and then snorted it up immediately. He had now taken his regular morning fix.

"Mr. Mayor? Shall I send him in?"

There was more silence.

"Mr. Mayor?"

"Alright, send him in."

Sanchez knew that canceling his televised interview with Rizzo would be a public relations mistake, as a cancellation would be presented to the public as though he was blatantly guilty of all of the alleged allegations.

Within seconds, a Channel Eight news crew of several cameramen and engineers barged into his office, ready to set up the elaborate interview with the Chicago mayor. Two lighting specialists began bringing in equipment and setting up lights around his office, as Chaz Rizzo strolled into his office, making his usual grand entrance. Wearing a black, Brunello Cuccinelli three-piece suit and crisp white shirt with a striped tie, the news reporter looked as though he was auditioning as a prosecutor for a legal television show.

"Good morning, Mr. Mayor. Glad you could accommodate us this morning for our interview today," Rizzo said as he shook the Mayor's hand.

"Now, Rizzo, we did agree that this interview would be recorded and edited to my satisfaction, correct?"

"Of course, Mr. Mayor. We will email the final taped interview before we go on the air tonight," Rizzo promised.

"Good. I don't want to give any bad impressions to the public regarding these recent developments," Sanchez reiterated.

"Oh, of course, Mr. Mayor. We're here to help you clear the air and vocalize your position regarding these new political events."

It was as though Chaz Rizzo was crossing his fingers behind his back. Anyone aware of Rizzo's ruthless journalism tactics knew that the Channel Eight reporter was callous and couldn't be trusted. Rizzo was out to exploit any and every politician who had a story to tell, and he was not ashamed of presenting them in the worst light possible. The lighting and engineering crew took about thirty minutes to set up their lights and equipment. A make-up artist came to dab some makeup and blush on the mayor's face so that he wouldn't look so shiny on camera. As Mayor Sanchez sat down across from Chaz Rizzo, the reporter began their extensive interview:

"This is Chaz Rizzo from Channel Eight Eyewitness News, here with Chicago Mayor Raymond Sanchez," he began.

"Thank you for having me."

"Mr. Mayor, what are your comments regarding the recent FBI raid of your office two days ago, and what information are the federal agents going to find?"

"Let me start by saying that I am innocent of all of these absurd charges and false accusations being levied upon me by the newspapers and the media. I am more than happy to share my office and files with these governmental agents, as they will discover that none of these charges and allegations are true," Sanchez stated.

"So you are saying that there is absolutely no evidence of any bribes or 'pay-to-play' accusations that have allegedly occurred by you or your office staff?"

"Absolutely not."

Holding a set of notes in front of him, Chaz Rizzo began openly referencing some incidents that had occurred over the last five months.

"A developer named John Patrico from Utica Developers, a South Loop development group has accused you and your office of demanding bribes and commissions above $100,000 in return for construction permits to allow the rezoning of some vacant land on South Michigan Avenue. Is this true?"

"That is not true. Mr. Patrico was given the permits that he requested after several changes and proposals were made by our building department to his original building plans of a thirty-nine story office development on South Michigan Avenue. He paid the appropriate fees for our zoning department and inspectors to analyze his plans for that property properly," Sanchez answered.

"But Mr. Patrico has gone on record as saying that the building department demanded the permit fees to be paid in cash, expressly delivered to your office more than the normal permit and application fees," Rizzo said in an accusatory voice.

"That is absolutely not true," the Mayor vehemently denied.

The bright lights that were focused on the mayor were beginning to make him feel extremely warm and uncomfortable. Sweat was now starting to pour down Raymond Sanchez's face, as he was openly beginning to show his nervousness on camera.
"What are your thoughts regarding the new motions of impeachment that are going to be proposed by the city council this week?"
Sanchez began to adjust his tie, now feeling the dampness of his collar tightly around his neck.
"I am confident that the city council's attempts to begin this political coupe will be unsuccessful, as these motions have no merit."
Chaz Rizzo began to smile under his breath as he continued to ask more and more comprehensive questions regarding the bribe accusations, monetary kickbacks that were allegedly paid to the mayor's office, and several other defamatory accusations regarding

Raymond Sanchez's character. With each question, the Mayor became uncomfortable, adjusting, and loosening his tie several times. At one point, he withdrew his handkerchief from the breast pocket of his suit and wiped his forehead several times, as protruding sweat continued to drip across his forehead.

The fact that the mayor felt uneasy and uncomfortable in front of the lights and cameras were not a coincidence.

Rizzo purposely set the bright lights at the hottest, most brilliant position, hoping that the heat from those lights would make Sanchez look openly uncomfortable on camera.

The interview lasted for over thirty minutes on camera, as Chaz Rizzo ended the interview by blatantly asking the Mayor one final question:

"Mr. Mayor, are you a crook?"

Sanchez, now beginning to show his anger openly on camera. He suddenly stood up from his chair and demanded that the news crew stop rolling the cameras.

"This fucking interview is over, Rizzo," as Mayor Sanchez walked out of the intense, broadcasted conversation with Rizzo's microphone still on.

He had recorded the Mayor's loud expletive, which he fully intended to broadcast as part of the interview on that evening's six o'clock news. Sanchez spent the remainder of that day fielding questions and answering derogatory emails from various city council members, with his desk phone ringing off the hook. Several reporters tried to clamor their way into city hall, knowing that Sanchez's days on the fourth floor of City Hall were numbered with the federal investigation now going on.

Later on at the Channel Eight newsroom, Chaz Rizzo began reviewing the taped interview with Mayor Sanchez. He needed to condense the interview down to ten minutes, and he did so, keeping all of the highlighted Mayor's answers when he began showing nervousness, sweat, and fatigue. He made sure that 'El Rey' was presented in the worst possible light on the camera, including his storming of the interview after swearing on camera, which he conveniently 'bleeped' out.

Mayor's Chief of Staff, Pedro Alvarez entered his office at four-thirty that afternoon. He began debriefing him with some of the new issues that plagued him and how dire the mayor's situation was rapidly deteriorating.

"By the way, Mr. Mayor, I have a video of that interview that Channel Eight will be running at six o'clock," Alvarez said, holding his laptop in his hand.

As the Chief of Staff set up his laptop and began playing the interview, Sanchez looked on in horror.

"This mother-fucker!" he yelled out loud as he knocked Alvarez's laptop off of his desk, breaking into several pieces as it crashed onto the marble floor.

"Get out! Get the fuck out!" he yelled out to all of his office staff.

At that moment, 'El Rey' locked himself inside of his spacious mayoral office. He called his chauffeur, telling him that he would find his own way home. He shut off his computer, his television playing in the background, and all other electronic devices. Sanchez unplugged his desk phone. He wanted peace and quiet within his own inner sanctum, and he did not want to be disturbed.

He unlocked the bottom left-hand drawer of his desk again and rolled up a dollar bill. A little cocaine was left from the eight-ounce bag that he had purchased from Javier, his drug supplier, the night before. Using a small teaspoon, he deposited several coke lines, snorting all of it up quickly.

He had finished another eight-ball.

He then opened up his right-hand desk drawer and took out his Beretta 9MM handgun, with the silencer still attached.

At about eight o'clock, the cleaning lady arrived to clean and vacuum the offices on the Mayor's fourth floor. Looking at the mayor's office's closed doors, the Polish cleaning lady noticed that there was still a light on from inside of his office.

She knocked on the door several times, but there was no answer. Finally, she used her master key to open up the mayor's office.

The sight of what she had suddenly seen made her gasp with horror, and she began to scream uncontrollably. She ran out of the office and called the security guards downstairs, who then called the Chicago Police Department.

When they arrived, they saw the horrific sight of Mayor Raymond Sanchez. His head was slumped across his desk with a bullet lodged into the right side of his temple. Blood was spattered across his desk, with his brain matter scattered around his desktop and the floor. It had looked as though Sanchez had shot himself at close range. Near his disfigured head was his Beretta revolver, which was used to deliver the fatal gunshot.

Raymond Sanchez had taken his own life.

Several police units, along with the Chief of Police, Walter Byron, had arrived at the crime scene, questioning various staff members and assessing the circumstances which led to his suicide.

That evening, the Honorable Judge Augustino Chiaramonte was sitting at home, watching television and trying to enjoy a glass of wine. He suddenly went into shock when Channel Eight Eyewitness news interrupted their scheduled program and announced the mayor's sudden death.

"Oh dear God," he exclaimed out loud, as he immediately dialed Eddie Barrett's cell phone several times.

There was no answer.

Within the next forty-eight hours, a barrage of media news reports and articles began pouring in, speculating on why Mayor Sanchez had taken his own life. Many political analysts theorized that Sanchez probably didn't have the guts to face the music in their newsroom commentaries. There was a federal investigation in his office, and the Chicago City Council was about to propose new motions demanding his impeachment. With all of the open corruption, dishonesty, and criminal activities that were flagrantly going on, his sudden suicide was not a surprise.

Raymond 'El Rey' Sanchez was openly called a coward, and he was quickly and quietly put to rest with very little fanfare.

Within a few days after the mayor's tragic death, his autopsy results were written and disclosed to the Intelligence Unit of the Twenty-First District. That report was marked 'Top Secret' and was designated to be informed by those very few within the 'Top Brass' of the Chicago PD.

When Chief Byron received the mayor's autopsy report, he suddenly buried his face in his hands.

The toxicology reports indicated a sizable amount of cocaine in his bloodstream, which may have significantly altered his behavior in recent weeks.

His receptionist later stated that the mayor spent a significant amount of time with the door closed and locked in his office during the afternoons.

Pending investigations found traces of cocaine on his desktop, and the coroner discovered several needle marks on his left forearm on the day of his suicide.

Based on the coroner's best guess, Mayor Raymond Sanchez had been a closet drug addict for years, which would explain why he insisted on accumulated substantial amounts of cash during his short term as Mayor.

With significant drug use, hallucinations, extreme paranoia, and suicidal thoughts are quite common. With long term drug use, schizophrenia is also prevalent. The stresses of his new mayoral position, along with all of the pressure from all of the bad publicity from the media, had pushed him over the edge.

It became apparent to those few who knew about the Cook County Coroner's report that the late Mayor Raymond J. Sanchez was a serious drug addict.

Chapter Thirty-Six
All Soul's Day - November 2nd

That second day of November was a rainy, autumn day, with the red and yellow oak and maple leaves wet and scattered across the lawn of the church's rectory. It was All Soul's Day, and the parish priest at St. Simeon's had celebrated two masses in the morning and then once again in the afternoon.

A large, red book register was placed in the back of the church, near the vestibule, listing all of their parish members who had died during the last twelve months. There was another large binder next to the red register book, which had plastic leaf pages holding all of the mass cards for which their funerals were held.

There were three hundred and forty-two deceased souls to pray for.

All Soul's Day was always a very somber religious observation at St. Simeon's Parish. With all of the violent deaths that had been occurring in and around their community, that register book included a long list of children of parishioners within the neighborhood who have grown up to become dangerous gangbangers and drug dealers. Each entry represented an innocent child who had grown up on the streets, only to experience an early, vicious death.

Fr. Fitzgerald felt for the death of all of their young people in his parish. Having mostly African American and Latino families attending mass each week, he knew each and every parishioner in his small parish on West 79th Street. He personally officiated over every mass, every confession, every anointing of the sick, and every funeral mass. He tried to counsel those families who were experiencing hardships with all of the violence lingering around them.

The children of the St. Simeon community were not safe. Watching an eight-year-old boy walking the Auburn-Gresham neighborhood streets with a gang member jacket and a large gun stuffed in his baggy pants was not unusual. One was never protected walking the streets of that neighborhood. Even with the Chicago P.D., patrol cars perusing the side streets off of 79th Street could protect the local residents. After the darkness prevailed and the streetlights came on, all of the excessive shootings and the gang-related violence were always a nightly event.

All-Souls Day was a sad day indeed.

Fr. Fitzgerald had completed mass that afternoon and quickly walked over to the rectory. It was Wednesday evening, and he was looking forward to his weekly chess match with his close friend, Tony DiMatteo. The Chicago capo had called and canceled their meetings recently. DiMatteo hadn't shown up for their chess matches for the last three weeks, and the pastor was looking forward to hopefully meeting up and socializing with his close friend again.

It was almost six-thirty when the doorbell rang. Fr. Fitz looked outside and noticed the black, late-model Maserati parked in front of the rectory on West 79th Street, and he eagerly opened the front door.

"Hey Tony," the priest warmly greeted his usual weekly guest.

"Please come in."

He looked at Little Tony and immediately knew that there was something terribly wrong. There was anger in his eyes, and his expression was anything but pleasant.

"I won't be staying for dinner, Father. Is there somewhere we can go to talk?"

"Of course."

Little Tony followed the parish priest into the rectory living room, where they usually played chess. They sat down across from each other at the two velvet red chairs where they normally play chess, and Fr. Fitz could feel the coldness in his eyes.

"What's up, Tony?"

"Father, have you been reading the papers?"

"Yes, I saw the article that was in the Chicago Tribune two weeks ago."

"Did you bother to read it?"

Fr. Fitz looked at Tony, and he immediately knew that he had come over to confront him.

"Yes, Tony. I did read that article. None of that information was given to that reporter, Larry McKay, about the two of us playing chess together and..."

"Did you read the part about your advising me to start all of the new violence that was now going on in the city?"

"Yes, Tony, I did..."

"Did you read the part about your pushing me to start offering security services to all of these local jewelry stores?"

"Yes, Tony, I did read that."

"Did you read the part about your being my new consigliere?"

"Yes, Tony, I called the reporter who put that story together."

"Do you fucking realize what you have fucking started? Not only is everyone looking at you as some kind of violent, war-time monster, but the feds are now coming around and hanging around my parking lot."

"Tony, I'm sorry, but I didn't..."

"How the fuck did this reporter get all of this information? How the fuck did this reporter find out about what we discussed every week while we played chess on Wednesdays? Where the fuck did this reporter get all of this fucking information?"

"Tony, I didn't tell him anything. He came snooping over here during a chess game tournament, and he called the rectory a few times. I did not give him any information."

"Then how the fuck did he get it?" Little Tony started talking louder to the priest.

"I don't know, Tony. I did not tell him anything."

"Now I've got three CPD coppers and some FBI assholes sitting in my parking lot every fucking day, thanks to our little fucking chess matches. I've got a parade of fucking cars following me around wherever I go now, no thanks to you."

"Why are you blaming me, Tony? I didn't leak out any information to anyone?"

"He quoted you, Fitz. He mentioned you in the article, referring to the fact that you're my new war-time consigliere."

"Tony, you did mention that I was..."

"I was only making a friendly comment, Fitz. I never said you were a 'made-man' in my family. I never said that you were a part of our 'outfit.' How the fuck did this reporter get all of this information?"

There was a long silence.

"It had to come from you, Father. You're the one who started this shit. We were perfectly fine, running our business and staying out of the limelight until you pushed me into getting involved in all of the 'street security.'"

Another long moment of silence.

"This was all your idea, Father. You wanted this. Now everybody is killing everybody. All of the gangs are gunning after us and each other, and the fucking coppers are walking around with their thumbs up their asses!"

Little Tony paused for a moment.

"Tony, I never said this was going to be easy."

"You should have never said anything at all, asshole! With all of the news media publicity, everybody now thinks I'm the new Al Capone, and we're out shooting everybody who gets out of line. There is a new bloody street war going on right now, and everybody's lives are in danger."

"Tony, I know how you feel."

"No, Fitz, you don't know shit," Little Tony was starting to raise his voice.

"Our family is now under the microscope, and we didn't need to get into this shit. I should have thought twice before listening to you, Fitz."

Tony's voice was getting louder and louder.

"We should have just let those young punks keep looting and robbing those stores in the city. The heat that we're now fucking getting isn't fucking worth it. And all of this is your goddamn fault."

Another silent moment and Little Tony was trying to control his violent temper.

"It's bad enough that I let you hustle me for a few bucks to the church and beat me in chess. But I should have never let you lecture me on how to run my business. I should have stuffed those chess pieces into your mouth the minute you started getting me involved in this shit."

Another silent moment.

"You used me, Father. You used me to get involved in all of this city-wide political bullshit. You used me to take out your revenge on all of these fucking gangbangers," Tony's anger was now starting to boil over.

"You want these gangbangers dead? Why don't you fucking shoot them yourself, instead of getting me involved?"

"I'm sorry that this happened, Tony."

"Fuck you, Fitz. You're not sorry about shit. You knew this would happen. You knew the heat was going to come down hard on us. We're under fire and are being watched by the Feds, the FBI, and the CPD more than we ever have before, while you sit on your ass on your red velvet chair and move around fucking chess pieces."

Tony paused for a moment.

"And then you give an interview to the papers."

"NO, I DID NOT!" Fitz screamed back at the Capo dei Capi. "I SAID NOTHING!"

"Oh, so what are you trying to tell me? They've got bugs on the fucking walls here?

Where the fuck did this reporter get all of this information?" Tony asked.

The Capo was getting even angrier.

"It came from you, Fitz. You like being a wise-guy priest, don't you? You like being my consigliere and advising me on who to whack and who not to whack. You love this shit, don't you?"

"No, Tony, I do not. I only hoped that with your influence and your power, that you would be able to take control of all of the violence that has been happening in this city. I never wished for any of this to hit the papers."

"Well, guess what? Our family is under a lot of fucking heat right now. And when these bastards start coming around and watching our every move, somebody is going to end up getting indicted."

There was a moment of silence.

"These fucking Feds know everything, Father. Where there are flies, there's shit. And if they can't find any shit, they're going to make up some shit. Either way, we're going to fucking lose."

"Tony, I'm sorry."

"I didn't need this crap right now, Fitz. And you talking to the papers is the worst thing you could have done."

Fr. Fitzgerald continued to deny Tony's accusation to no avail. Little Tony was extremely angry with him, believing that all of the government pressure and police scrutiny he and his crime family were now under would have never happened. DiMatteo should have stayed clear of all of the city's unrest instead of being pulled into all of this with his exclusive 'security services.' He should have stayed far away from getting involved in any of this.

Little Tony DiMatteo rose from the red velvet chair that he usually played chess on and started walking away from the parish priest. Before leaving, he looked directly at Fr. Fitz.

"You fucking used me, Fitz. Now I hold you directly responsible for whatever fucking happens. Say the rosary and hope this fucking shit dies down," he said in a loud voice.

"Stay the fuck away from me, and watch your fucking back," he now threatened.

Fr. Fitzgerald only sat there, absorbing the brunt of Little Tony's ferocious temper.

"You better pray that all of this shit goes away, Fitz. And tell your reporter buddy to stop putting my name in the fucking papers."

Little Tony barged out of the rectory living room with that directive and abruptly pulled out of his parking space on West 79th Street. Fr. Fitz noticed several unmarked cars suddenly begin to follow Little Tony's Maserati. The priest suddenly realized that the Capo dei Capi was indeed under a tremendous amount of pressure.

"Will Tony be staying for dinner?" a timid Mrs. Valenti inquired, afraid to approach him after hearing DiMatteo loudly screaming at the pastor. She had overheard Little Tony screaming in the living room, and she was praying the Little Tony wouldn't become suddenly violent towards the priest.

"No, Mrs. Valenti. Tony won't be back."

The priest sullenly walked upstairs to his bedroom and closed the door. He was no longer hungry, and he didn't wish to speak to anyone.

He felt hurt and dejected. Fr. Fitzgerald was feeling terribly remorseful, knowing that he had taken advantage of a good friend.

He knelt down on his kneeler and began praying the rosary, which he often did regularly. He felt remorseful for using Tony DiMatteo to take advantage of his generosity and use his ego to take revenge against all the inner-city violence.

Fr. Fitz knew that he used him for his own selfish agenda, and Tony was now about to make him pay for it. Although he once believed that the two of them were close friends, he now realized that he had taken advantage of him, and Little Tony had every right to be angry.

He then recalled his conversation with the Cardinal a few weeks ago. Remembering some of his predictions regarding Little Tony, he realized that he was right.

Fr. Fitz prayed for Tony's forgiveness, hoping that all of this would one day pass. He also prayed for all of the additional victims that the DiMatteo Family had so ruthlessly killed for breaking and looting in the city.

But most of all, he prayed for his own safety.

Chapter Thirty-Seven
A Missing Priest – November 16th

It was three o'clock in the afternoon as Mrs. Valenti arrived at St. Simeon's Parish Rectory for work. As the pastor's cook and housekeeper, her duties were like any other regular house servant. She attended to Fr. Fitzgerald's needs, cleaning his house, doing his laundry, and cooking his meals. Fr. Fitz was always very attentive to her needs as well, as he allowed her to take random days off for doctor's appointments and time off to spend with her daughter and grandchildren who lived out of town. Besides her regular salary of six hundred dollars a week, he would give her some extra cash that he would receive from the collection box or candle donations, which she always appreciated.

On that autumn afternoon, Mrs. Valenti was surprised that Fr. Fitzgerald was not at his office in the rectory, taking calls, attending to the sick, and conducting various meetings regarding the management of St. Simeon's parish. As she began to clean and scrub the kitchen, she happened to notice that the garage door was open, but Fr. Fitz's Ford Escape was still in the garage. She had walked past his office when she came in but noticed that he wasn't in.

At first, she thought nothing of it, as Fr. Fitz liked to take his long morning walks daily, and thought that perhaps he had taken a long, afternoon walk instead. As usual, Mrs. Valenti prepared dinner, believing that Fr. Fitz would at least be home for dinner.

She had prepared chicken cacciatore and broccoli and baked cheese, one of Fr. Fitz's favorite dishes. At 6:30, their normal dinner time, Fr. Fitz was still not home, and she hadn't seen or heard from him that whole day.

Mrs. Valenti decided to put on her coat and look around the church, especially in the church sacristy, where Fr. Fitz sometimes spend some private time in prayer. She also went upstairs to the church choir balcony, where he was nowhere to be found. Several worshippers were praying in the church as well, and no one had seen him.

She hated to call him on his cell phone, which she didn't like to do. But now worried, she dialed his number. It was totally unlike Fr. Fitz to completely disappear during the day and not contact her, especially with his car still parked inside the garage.

Mrs. Valenti dialed his number several times but only got his voice mail, as there was no answer. She tried texting him several times from her cell phone, but there was still no response.

The rectory housekeeper, who was wracked with worry by now, waited until nine o'clock before finally calling the Chicago P.D.

"District Sixteen, Sergeant Walker speaking."

"Yes, I would like to report a missing person, please," Mrs. Valenti.

"Who is this regarding, Ma'am?"

"My boss, Fr. Colin Fitzgerald. He's the pastor here at St. Simeon's Church. I have not seen or heard from him all day today, and his car is still parked in the garage."

"When was the last time you saw him, Ma'am?"

"Yesterday, when I completed my shift."

The desk sergeant continued to ask her for more information, then finally telling her that they would be sending a squad car over to the church rectory to report and file a missing person's report.

Within twenty minutes, three squad cars showed up in front of the church rectory on West 78th Street. Because of whom Fr. Fitz was and his popularity within the city, several more squad cars showed up in front of the church. Several patrolmen began scouring the neighborhood, while others drove around the immediate vicinity looking for him and asking questions to those establishments and coffee shops where he usually frequents.

By ten o'clock, the news media trucks began to show up, reporting the Fr. Fitz had not been seen in the last twenty-four hours and starting the rumor that 'foul play' may be involved. Several detectives came over to the church rectory and interrogated Mrs. Valenti to the point where she began sobbing.

There was no sign of Fr. Fitzgerald. None of the neighbors had seen him since the night before, as Mrs. Valenti was the last one to see him alive.

The next morning, the Chicago Tribune reported the headlines:

St. Simeon Activist Priest Missing

No one had seen or heard from the parish priest, and within forty-eight hours, prayer vigils were being conducted in front of St.

Simeon Church. Several hundred people gathered in front of the church steps, singing songs of hope and joy, hoping that the popular, beloved priest of St. Simeon would turn up somewhere with the City of Chicago.

There were signs and banners everywhere around the city, especially within the southside of Chicago in the Auburn-Gresham neighborhood. Within a week of his vanishing, there was even a billboard dedicated to his disappearance.

The sign going alongside the Dan Ryan Expressway simply said, 'Have You Seen Our Missing Angel?' along with his picture below.

There wasn't a trace of Fr. Colin Fitzgerald anywhere.

Knowing that Fr. Fitz was still having chess matches and dinners on Wednesday's with Little Tony DiMatteo until the time of his vanishing and disappearance, several detectives attempted to go over to his warehouse to speak to him interrogate him regarding his being missing.

There was only one problem with that CPD interrogation: Little Tony DiMatteo had been under police surveillance since July, with a patrolman standing guard in his parking lot and watching his every move. The Chicago P.D. can account for Little Tony's complete whereabouts throughout that whole time. Besides going home or to work, Little Tony didn't go anywhere else or do anything unusual, other than his weekly chess matches.

"Get the fuck out of here," DiMatteo told one of the detectives who showed up in front of his warehouse.

"You guys know where I've been more than I even fucking know," he ridiculed the Chicago coppers.

"If I need to know how many times I went to the bathroom last week, all I have to do is call you fucking guys."

Detectives Dorian and Morton picked up Little Tony DiMatteo at his South Ashland warehouse. They had brought him into the Sixteenth District interrogation room to question his relationship with Fr. Fitzgerald. Upon Dorian's insistence, they respectfully allowed DiMatteo to remain uncuffed while taking him into custody.

"Why do you fucking guys have to disrupt my schedule and make me come down here to waste my time," Little Tony protested while sitting in the interrogation room with both detectives.

"I never took you for a chess player, Tony."

"There's a lot of fucking things you don't know about me, Dorian. I'm really a pretty intellectual guy."

Detective Dorian rolled his eyes in the air. "Yeah, sure, Tony. Whatever."

Detective Morton then began his inquiry.

"You were playing chess with him every week, Tony. You got to know him well, and you obviously had a problem with him," Morton stated.

"Yeah, I did have a problem with him. He was a chess master. I couldn't beat him at chess, and I let him hustle me for some money, which was really a donation," he pointed out with a slight smile.

"I felt like I was playing pool with a pool shark. He let me win a few games, and then he hustled me for some donations to his church," DiMatteo joked, his tongue in cheek.

"That doesn't mean I'm gonna take him out to Bum-Fuck Egypt and kill him. It's a cardinal sin to kill a priest," the Capo dei Capi reasoned.

"Murder has always been a sin, Tony," Dorian interjected.

"Yeah, right, Dorian. But I never had a beef with Fr. Fitz. He was a good man."

Dorian glared intently at the mob boss.

"The word was out that you were pissed off at the priest for giving you some bad advice. Some others got the impression that he was your new consigliere."

"That's ridiculous! Give me advice about what, Dorian? How to fucking play chess? He invited me over for dinner. We had some interesting discussions, and then we spent a few hours playing every week," Little Tony said.

"What the fuck do you expect two old men to do on a Wednesday night?"

"And you donated some money to his church, right?" Dorian asked.

DiMatteo then put a toothpick in his mouth and smiled.

"Sure, I did. He had some bum HVAC units that needed to be replaced, so I donated some money."

"Was it cash?"

"I wrote him a check, asshole. Talk to my controller. Sal Marrocco knows all the details."

He then smirked at both detectives.

"He kept trying to get me to go to mass and confession. I told him I was only gonna help him fix his units, not the broken rafters when I walk into his church."

"And you never had a problem with him? You never threatened him?" Morton asked.

"What are you, Morton? Fucking deaf? I already told you, Fitz and I were fine. I never had a beef with him."

Detective Dorian had taken the liberty to talk to Fr. Fitzgerald's housekeeper, Mrs. Valenti. On All Soul's Day, she stated that Little Tony DiMatteo came over to the rectory to have their usual dinner and play their regular chess match on that Wednesday. Apparently, she overheard the Chicago wise guy berate and yell at the parish priest about something that sounded like a betrayal of some sort. She didn't recall the whole conversation, but Little Tony walked out of the rectory somewhat angry with Fr. Fitz.

"Fr. Fitz's housekeeper overheard you threatening the priest during the last time you were at the rectory, stating something to the effect of 'you better watch your back.'"

"That's total bullshit. I was angry because he had beaten me in chess again and was trying to hustle me into another donation."

Dorian and Morton looked at each other. They both knew that the Chicago Capo was handing them a line of crap.

The two detectives held him for most of the day at the Sixteenth District. When his lawyer, Michael Prescott, finally showed up that afternoon, the two detectives had no other choice but to cut him loose.

The rumors started flying around the city by the holidays, claiming that Fr. Fitz, like perhaps Jimmy Hoffa, had met the same fate because of his recent underworld connections. Several bumper stickers were floating around the neighborhood, which simply said, "Where's Fr. Fitz?"

There wasn't a trace of him anywhere. The Intelligence Unit at the Twenty-First District ran Fr. Fitzgerald's credit cards, but there were no recent hits on any of them since his disappearance date. They ran his prints and DNA through the system, but there were no matches anywhere, and nothing turned up.

Father Colin J. Fitzgerald had vanished and disappeared off of the face of the earth.

Chapter Thirty-Eight
Final Payoff – November 27th

  The Bridgeport warehouse on West 33rd Street and Aberdeen was a well-lighted building leased by the S & V Cartage Company. The building was owned by the brother-in-law of Amatore 'Three-Chin' Steward, and they used it as a meeting place for various occasions. It was a dark, misty evening, near eleven o'clock that Friday night after Thanksgiving. This meeting between Three-Chin Steward and the actual shooter in the mayor's assassination had long been overdue.
  The payoff of the actual contract fees of one hundred thousand and sixteen dollars had been postponed several times, as the police investigation into the mayor's murder had been attracting media attention. The two parties wished to lay low for some time until the detective's investigation and the media became focused on other, more prevalent police matters.
  It was just after eleven o'clock, as Three-Chin arrived by himself in a black, late model Cadillac Escalade, with low-rider wheels and darkened glass windows. Although the building was equipped with surveillance cameras, he had asked his brother-in-law to temporarily make them 'out of order' for this final meeting.
  Three-Chin was more than happy to be rid of the contract fee that had been finally collected from the Black Cobras and be passed on to the actual assassin. He was carrying a briefcase filled with the tight bundles of one-hundred-dollar bills, stacked neatly on the top.

Steward smiled to himself, knowing that he and his Satan Disciple brothers were about to make the final handoff of their substantial score.

When Javier contacted the Black Cobras to use a trained sniper in their gang to accomplish the mayor's assassination, Two-Bit Harding realized afterward that no one in their brotherhood was a trained sharpshooter to accomplish this task. Two-Bit then contacted his cousin, Three-Chin, a Satan Disciple, to help him find an accomplished sniper.

They did.

They found a white, bust-out drug-dealer from the west side who bragged about being able to shoot an apple off a deer from one hundred and fifty yards away. That drug-dealer was an undercover detective with the Chicago P.D.

When the veteran detective met with Two-Bit and Three-Chin, he demonstrated that he could indeed shoot an object precisely from any target. It had never occurred to them that any specialized sharpshooter who had these shooting skills had to have been specially trained by the armed forces like the Army or Marines, or in this, the Chicago Police Academy.

At first, the detective continued to play the undercover cop to the assassination plot, hoping to bust the Black Cobras and Satan Disciples for the planned hit and the drug trafficking they were increasingly involved with.

When the detective approached Chief Byron, letting him know of the assassination plot ensuing, Chief Byron made a sudden change of plans.

His original plan called for one of the members of the Black Cobras gang to assassinate the mayor. With the lack of finding a competent sniper, the Black Cobras contacted Satan's Disciples to find an adequate candidate. Byron then told him to continue with the undercover ploy and *assassinate* the mayor. The veteran undercover detective would receive the actual cash proceeds from the murder contract and pay Byron a commission.

It was a lucrative, clandestine conspiracy.

The Chicago P.D. had their motives for displacing and getting rid of Mayor Kollar. The mayor's office had strongly criticized Chief Superintendent Byron for several instances in his lapse of judgment. The mayor had publicly and openly banned the city's police department from using the brutal force of any kind against any of the city's criminal element.

The Chief of Police had personally contacted the detective's superiors in terminating his undercover assignment, and this convoluted plan would be conducted covertly by the veteran detective. The house next door to the mayor's home was surreptitiously leased for several months by Chicago's Intelligence Unit, and the plan was set in motion.

After the assassination, the parking lot handoff proceeds were given to the Black Cobras. He had personally observed the handoff between 'Javier,' the bag man who worked for Eddie Barrett, and 'Terrell,' who worked for the Black Cobras. The detective sat in an unmarked squad car in the parking lot and personally witnessed the handoff, almost being shot at by Javier in the process.

In turn, they would pay a 'finder's fee' to Satan's Disciples for locating an appropriate sniper to do the job. But the Satan's Disciples, especially Three-Chin Steward, killed the four Black Cobras, including his cousin Two-Bit Harding, to acquire all of the cash proceeds.

The $150,000 contract fee, less the collection fees, and the Satan's Disciple cut would dilute down to $116,400. Of that $116,400, the actual assassin would receive $100,000 in cash, with a $16,400 'commission' paid out to Byron.

The undercover detective's only contact was with Chief Byron himself, and he had no idea that Alderman Eddie Barrett was also involved in this plot and had fronted the money.

This cash fee for this contract was posted by Alderman Eddie Barrett, who had his motives for getting rid of the mayor. Barrett maintained a large safe in his law office on North LaSalle Street. Over two million dollars in cash stashed inside of that hidden safe in his office at any one time, behind a large painting in his law firm wall. Barrett was more than happy to front the contract fees, with the return of Mayor Kollar's violent demise.

Three-Chin walked into the empty warehouse alone, holding a black briefcase, with all of the currency neatly stacked with one-hundred-dollar bills. He also had a Smith and Wesson .38 revolver shoved in the left side of his blue jeans, with its dark brown walnut handle sticking out of his shirt.

Three-Chin was ready for this late-night meeting.

The undercover police detective pulled into Aberdeen Street adjacent to the parking lot in his black, older model Ford Explorer. He parked his car behind the building on West 33rd Street. The detective temporarily shut off his ignition and sat there on Aberdeen Street for several long minutes.

The undercover copper then lit a cigarette, taking several long drags, then blowing the smoke out of his nostrils.

He was fearful, nervous, and scared, all at the same time, while being overly vigilant. He wanted to make sure that his contact, Three-Chin Steward, was the only person in the parking lot.

Being a veteran detective, he was well aware of a potential trap that could be waiting for him, and he wanted to make sure that he could safely receive his money and safely walk away.

He took his last drag and finished his smoke, flicking the Marlboro Light cigarette butt outside of his car window. At that moment, his cell phone rang.

It was Clara, his wife.

"Tommy, could you pick up a gallon of milk on your way home, please?"

"Certainly, dear. As soon as I am finished with this meeting," he quickly hung up his cell phone.

It would be the last time the detective would use talk to his wife.

Detective Tommy Morton knew of the inherent risks of his becoming a 'dirty cop.' But having been on the Chicago police force for over twenty-five years, he had little to show for all of his late-night risks, stakeouts, undercover assignments, and dangerous sacrifices that he had been involved with throughout his career. He had become increasingly despondent with his career choice to be a Chicago cop. He had just taken out a second mortgage to pay the over forty thousand dollars of credit card debt that both he and his wife had accumulated over the years. His bride of over twenty-five years, Clara, had their kitchen in their home in the Galewood neighborhood remodeled two years ago. He had paid for his two sons' college tuition and went on a lavish vacation with his wife to celebrate his fiftieth birthday.

 With all of the debt that the Morton's had accumulated, he briefly considered suicide, as his $500,000 life insurance policy would be more than enough to take care of his wife and pay off their rising debts.

 Detective Tommy Morton, with his home on Neva Street worth less than two hundred thousand fifty dollars and over three hundred thousand in debt, was figuratively now broke. He had looked into the possibility of bankruptcy but decided against it when he realized that his credit would be completely decimated for the next seven years. He had attempted to take on a few jobs as a security guard for a jewelry store on South Wabash, but that just didn't work out.

 As Tommy Morton needed to make a big score, this secret assignment became his ticket to financial security.

 The Superintendent Chief of Police Walter Byron of the Chicago Police Department was well aware of this secret 'hit.'

When the opportunity came for him to accept this contract and assassinate Mayor Kollar, he wanted to make sure that Chief Byron allowed him to do so under his approval. Byron had told him to accept and pursue this murder contract, with the caveat that if anything ever went wrong that he would have complete deniability. Morton was playing both sides of the street. Byron assisted him in getting set up for this assassination contract.

Morton was also assigned on the investigative team by Byron, along with Detectives Romanowski and Dorian, to investigate the assassination of the mayor that *he* had perpetrated. He would then collect a cash payoff of $116,400 that evening, which he would cut up at the agreed amounts and pay the commission to the city's 'Top-Cop.'

For many reasons, Tommy Morton was unusually nervous. He knew of the inherent risks to accomplishing this covert task. After the assassination, Morton had set up a dependable backup plan if anything ever happened to him.

Morton had written a note, dated August 21st that past summer, of his connection and involvement in Mayor Kollar's assassination. In it, he disclosed his role and partnership with Chief Byron in this murder. Tommy had written the note and taped it inside his gun case as a possible clue for his colleagues to find if anything ever happened to him. In Morton's bedroom closet, he had the folding stock, collapsible Ruger 10-22 rifle, with a detachable scope and silencer in a locked, steel gun case with the note inside. He had also mentioned to his wife several times last summer:

"If anything ever happens to me, honey, and I don't come home, you make sure that they know about that rifle."

Clara Morton had no idea what he was talking about. But because she always feared for her husband's life and his sometimes-dangerous job duties, she faithfully intended to honor her husband's request.

The word 'they' that he referred to meant the Chicago Police Department's detectives and, especially, his trusted partner, Detective Phillip Dorian.

Morton took out his burner phone and texted Chief Byron.

"I'm here."

Morton then started up his Ford Explorer's ignition and pulled his vehicle into the empty warehouse's parking lot. He immediately noticed the surveillance cameras attached at each corner of the building. Morton then got out of his truck, pulled a black polyester hat over his face, and knocked on the steel door three times in succession:

Knock, Knock, Knock.
Knock, Knock, Knock.
Knock, Knock, Knock.

At that moment, Three-Chin opened up the steel door and let him inside. He then led him within the warehouse, where there was a collapsible steel table. And on top of that table was the black briefcase containing the cash proceeds.

Three-Chin opened up the briefcase, not saying a single word to Morton. Morton pulled off his hat and inspected the contents, noting the bundles of one-hundred-dollar bills neatly stacked at one-thousand-dollar money bans spindled within each stack of currency. He counted out the piles, noting that there were one hundred and sixteen stacks of paper currency, with four one-hundred-dollar bills stuffed neatly on top.

"It's all there, man."

Morton nodded his head, his right hand still very close to the gun holster. He looked at Three-Chin, and the two shook hands. Morton then closed the briefcase and proceeded to walk out of the warehouse. Knowing the cameras were probably working, he had pulled down his black hat over his face as he left the warehouse.

Morton got into his truck and started the ignition. He then slowly pulled out of the trucking warehouse and onto Aberdeen Street. Morton made a right-hand turn onto 33rd Street from Aberdeen, as a black Cadillac Escalade pulled up next to his older model SUV.

Suddenly, both windows of the large model SUV truck's passenger side were rolled down, and two AK-47 rifles started rapidly firing into the vehicle. Morton had less than a second to react as he tried in vain to duck down on the front seat of his car. The killers continued to fire over fifty rounds of bullets into the driver's side of the vehicle. One of the killers then got out of the Ford Expedition and reached inside the Ford Explorer's front seat, grabbing the black briefcase that contained the cash.

With his body collapsing on the steering wheel, Detective Tommy Morton was instantly killed. He had absorbed over fifty rounds of bullets into his body. His car then slowly started to roll onto the middle of 33rd Street. The black Ford Expedition swiftly and immediately squealed its tires, driving quickly away from the murder scene and going westbound on 33rd Street.

Because it was past eleven-thirty at night, there was very little traffic on 33rd Street and the Bridgeport neighborhood. The older model Ford Explorer slowly rolled into the middle of the road, stopping when it hit the curb of Bridgeport's main street. Morton's body had fallen against the horn of the vehicle, and it was loudly going off.

A white Toyota Camry approached the vehicle as it was going eastbound on 33rd Street. The driver, a middle-aged man who lived in the Bridgeport neighborhood, immediately saw the bullet holes and a body laying up against the steering wheel. He got out of his car and observed the bloody crime scene. Morton's head was unrecognizable, as his face, body, and hands had absorbed over fifty rounds of machine-gun bullets. There was blood splattered everywhere. The cracked windshield and broken glass were sprayed onto the front seat of the SUV, and more blood was dripping onto the floor of the driver's side of the vehicle.

It was a gruesome crime scene. The Toyota driver immediately ran back to his car and dialed '9-1-1' on his cell phone.

He then got out of his white Toyota Camry and threw up on the side of the curb.

Chapter Thirty-Nine
A White Envelope-November 28th

"Hello?"

"Phil, it's me, Clara. Tommy hasn't come home yet. I'm worried sick."

It was approximately twelve-thirty in the morning when Detective Phillip Dorian's cell phone loudly went off. He began rubbing his eyes.

"Did you try calling his cell?"

"Several times. He's not answering."

Dorian continued to rub the sleep from his eyes as he looked at his illuminating clock on his nightstand.

It was 12:32 am.

"Ok, Clara. Let me make some phone calls, and I will call you back," as he quickly hung up the telephone.

He looked at his yellow Labrador, Ginger, who was still fast asleep on her doggy-bed, unfazed by the sound of his cell phone.

"You're a lucky dog, Ginger. You never have to get up in the middle of the night," he smiled as he rolled out of bed and walked into the kitchen of his West Loop loft.

Getting out of bed and wearing only his underwear, he started to make some phone calls, seeing if he could track Tommy Morton down using the police radio. Dorian called the dispatcher over at the Sixteenth District Area Five in Jefferson Park.

"Chicago P.D., District Sixteen, Officer Rubino speaking."

It was Sergeant James Rubino on duty that night, and he was obviously in charge of dispatch.

"Jimmy, it's Phil."

"Hey, Phil, what's up? You can't sleep?" he jokingly asked, already presuming he had been drinking too much espresso that night.

"No, unfortunately. Got a call from Clara Morton," he replied.

"Do me a favor? Could you contact Tommy Morton on his radio and see if you can get a hold of him? His wife just called me in a frenzy. She's all worried and shit."

"Did you try his cell phone?"

"Yeah, no answer. That isn't like him. He usually picks up his cell phone."

Sergeant Rubino shook his head for a moment, as he was silent for a few seconds on the phone.

"Let me check the scanners and the police radio. I'll call you back."

"Thanks, Jimmy."

Dorian got up from his kitchen table and walked into the bathroom. It couldn't have been more than sixty seconds before his cell began to ring again.

It was District Sixteen.

"Hello?"

"Phil, there is a report on the scanner about a drive-by shooting on 33rd Street in Bridgeport. It looks pretty messy."

"Yeah, so?" Dorian answered slowly.

There was a ten-second silence on the phone, as Rubino knew of the intensely close partnership between Dorian and Morton.

"Does Morton drive an older model Ford Explorer? 2005 perhaps?"

Dorian thought for a moment.

"Yes. Why?"

Another few moments of silence.

"There is a fatality in an older model Explorer...it's been shot up pretty bad. There are several patrol units there from the Twelfth. The SUV plates register to a Thomas Morton, residing on 2607 North Neva Street in Chicago."

At that moment, Phil Dorian turned three shades of white, almost dropping his cell phone. There was a long silence as he was trying to absorb this sudden, tragic information.

"Phil, CSI and Chicago Fire are already there at the crime scene. They've just blocked off 33rd Street."

"Radio back and tell them not to do anything until I get there."

Dorian raced to throw on his jeans and shirt and flew down to the parking lot of his condominium loft unit on North Peoria Street. Turning on his sirens, he raced towards 33rd Street in the Bridgeport neighborhood, blowing off every single traffic light going south on Halsted Street. As Dorian approached the crime scene, he could see the blocked-off street with a patrolman redirecting traffic. He parked his squad car and ran up to the location of the accident, showing the patrolman his badge.

"What happened," he frantically asked, looking at the shot-up, black Ford Explorer severely disabled in the middle of the street.

Several bullet holes were scattered along the driver's side of the vehicle, with radiator and brake fluid spilled all over the street. The patrolmen at the accident scene had taped a white sheet over the driver's side of the car and the victim, while several other patrol units had blocked off the roads on Aberdeen and 33rd Street.

"This was more than just a drive-by shooting. This looks like an assassination."

"Do we know the identity of the victim?"

At that moment, another Fireman Jim Swenor, who knew both Dorian and Morton, pulled the detective off to the side of the street.

"I'm sorry, Phil. It's Tommy."

At that moment, Dorian grabbed his stomach and became overly emotional. He then grasped his gold crucifix and said a quick prayer to himself. After a few minutes, Phil looked at the fireman.

"Can I go see him?"

"It's pretty gory, Phil. I wouldn't go there if I were you."

Ignoring his warning, Detective Dorian quickly walked up to the disabled Ford Explorer and looked behind the white sheet that was covering up the driver's side of the vehicle.

At that moment, Dorian turned white.

Detective Tommy Morton's face was completely unrecognizable and covered in blood. His face and his mouth were ridden with bullet holes, and his nose had been shot off, leaving a large cavity in the middle of his face. Both of his eyes had been shot out, and his head looked twisted while splattered in blood. It looked as though the force of all of the bullets had dislodged his head. There was broken glass strewed across his face from the windshield, and the steering wheel was still dripping with blood.

"Oh my God," Dorian said again, as another patrolman put his arm around the detective as if to catch him before falling.

He walked Detective Dorian over to the curb while he buried his face in his hands. The patrolman, who did not know Dorian, embraced him tightly while he loudly wept. At that moment, Commander Cahill of the Sixteenth District arrived at the crime scene. He had already been briefed and glanced at the shot-up vehicle, with Morton inside. He was wearing his 'blues' uniform, dressed as though he knew that he would have to go on air with the news media and explain what happened.

Cahill then approached Dorian.

"I'm so sorry, Phil. I know you guys were pretty close."

Dorian, now drying his eyes, nodded his head.

"Does anybody know what happened?" Cahill asked one of the patrolmen.

"There were no witnesses. The driver of that white Toyota Camry parked over there on the side was the first one to approach the disabled vehicle. He's the one who called it in," the patrolman answered. "His name is Henry Wysocki, and he's pretty shaken up."

"Nobody saw the shooters?" Dorian asked.

"No. Apparently, no one was driving on 33rd at the time of the shooting," the patrolman answered.

Dorian shook his head.

"Somebody must have seen something. Have some more patrolmen knock on some of these doors here in the neighborhood and see if there were any witnesses."

Several Chicago police officers started combing the neighborhood, with several police officers going door to door around the surrounding houses and buildings, asking if anyone had seen anything. There were security cameras in the front of the warehouse building adjacent to the crime scene, but no other surveillance at the closed hot-dog drive-in establishment next door. The investigating officers contacted the warehouse landlord, who sheepishly said that the security cameras had not been working recently.

At that moment, the Channel Eight News Truck pulled off to the side of 33rd Street, and Chaz Rizzo, who was impeccably dressed at one o'clock in the morning, got out of the news truck and approached Detective Dorian.

The two of them didn't say a word to each other. They only embraced in the middle of the road, crying and comforting one another at the same time.

"Don't run anything on the air, and don't announce the identity of the victim until I can call his wife," Dorian requested, still drying his eyes.

"Okay," Rizzo respectfully said.

After several more minutes, Rizzo went back to his news truck and began putting together the story with his cameraman.

Almost an hour had passed before another patrolman approached Commander Cahill and Detective Dorian about an eyewitness account that they had just discovered.

"The white, older woman who lives in that apartment behind the warehouse saw a black, late model Cadillac Escalade fire several shots into that Ford Explorer," the patrolman stated.

"Did she see anyone inside?" Cahill asked.

"She wasn't sure, but the car had chrome low-rider wheels, and it looked like some of those cars that the gangs normally drive around in," the patrolman answered.

"Get her name and a statement," Cahill directed.

As the coroner was taking Tommy Morton's body away from the crime scene, Detective Dorian made the dreaded phone call to Clara Morton.

"Clara, I'm so sorry," Dorian initially said over the phone.

At that moment, the detective tried to control his emotions while Tommy Morton's widow began crying uncontrollably over the telephone. He explained that they had no idea what the circumstances were and why her husband Tommy had gotten caught up in some kind of gangland-style shooting. He promised he would contact her when he knew more information.

By four o'clock in the morning, several other news trucks had shown up and began running the story of a "Sixteenth District Detective killed in a gangland-style shooting." Commander Cahill did an on-air interview with Chas Rizzo, disclosing Morton's identity, with the facts and circumstances of the detective's murder.

No one knew of any rhyme or reason why Tommy Morton, who lived in Galewood on the west side of Chicago, would be doing in the Bridgeport at that hour. No one had a clue what Morton was doing on the south side of Chicago, not far from the Chicago White Sox baseball park at eleven o'clock. No one could figure out who Morton was meeting or what he was doing in that dangerous gang-infested neighborhood at that time of night.

Philip Dorian was well aware of the undercover assignment that Detective Morton had been designated late last spring. During that undercover assignment, he didn't see much of Morton. When he did finally hook up with him last summer, Morton had only mentioned that he had been pulled from the assignment. He had said something to the effect that the violent gangs he was posing as a drug dealer were too dangerous and felt that his cover had been compromised. It wasn't unusual for different detectives from various districts to get placed in areas that they were unfamiliar with when going undercover.

Dorian was now sitting in his Crown Victoria squad car, trying to make sense of this senseless killing. Had Tommy gotten himself involved with something unusual?

Or worse, something illegal?

The coroner's van had placed Tommy Morton's body inside, and Commander Cahill planned for all of the police squad cars in the Sixteenth District to meet at the police station at five in the morning. There would be a long procession of over one hundred Chicago police squad cars that would follow Detective Morton's body to the Belmont Funeral Home on Belmont Avenue.

Afterward, Tommy decided to drive over to Neva and Grand Avenue to the Morton home and pay his respects to his wife. He rang the doorbell at six o'clock in the morning. Clara Morton immediately answered the door, embracing Dorian for several long minutes while crying on each other's shoulders.

"Would you like some coffee?" she asked while entering the door and taking off his coat.

"Would love some," he answered.

He then followed her into their small kitchen while she made a fresh pot of coffee.

"I was going to call you, Phil. I sort of figured that you were going to stop by."

"You know that I'm here for you."

"You've always been old school like that. Tommy loved you for that very reason."

Dorian whipped the tears away from his eyes. At that point, both of his brown eyes were utterly bloodshot from all of the excessive crying he had been doing all night.

Clara poured him a fresh cup of coffee into a ceramic mug, and they both sat down at the kitchen table.

"Any ideas what Tommy was doing in Bridgeport last night?"

"No idea, Philly. He said that he had an important meeting there. When I asked who, he only said it was police business."

There were several moments of silence as both drank their coffee. Clara got up and put out some pastries that she had in the refrigerator.

"Sorry, I don't have any Dunkin' Donuts," she smiled.

They both started laughing and reminiscing, recalling that her husband always saying how much Dorian enjoyed his Dunkin' Donuts pastries.

"Yes, and Tommy definitely enjoyed his cigarettes. To him, coffee and cigarettes were the breakfast of champions."

They both laughed and cried together, recalling stories about Detective Morton and how much he loved his wife and two sons.

"He was the love of my life, Phil," she tearfully said, trying not to break down again.

Several more silent minutes passed as Clara got up to pour Phil a coffee refill. She looked at the detective and made a directive.

"Phil, would you mind coming upstairs with me?"

Startled at her request, he dutifully followed her up to their Chicago bungalow's second level to the master bedroom.

"I just remembered that Tommy told me something last summer," she said.

Phil Dorian watched her go into her closet and pull out an encased, steel rifle gun case. She placed it on top of their king-size bed after presenting it to the detective.

"He told me last summer that if anything ever happened to him, that he wanted me to give you this rifle."

Confused and thinking that it was a gift, Dorian looked at the steel gun case and noticed that it was locked.

"Do you have a key?"

"No. I don't think he ever wanted me to open it."

Dorian looked at the steel gun case and studied the lock. He then took out his pocketknife and jammed the point of it several times, picking the lock open. As he opened it, he was surprised at what he had found. Enclosed was a folding stock, collapsible Ruger 10-22 rifle, with a detachable scope and silencer. And inside that gun case was an envelope with a letter inside, with the word

'DORIAN' in bold black letters written on top of it.

At first, Philip Dorian was going to open it up immediately but then thought better of it. He put the unopened letter back inside of the gun case along with the weapon.

At that moment, he had gotten a nauseous feeling in his stomach. He closed up the gun case and calmly explained to Clara that he would bring the rifle with him and open up the letter when he had more time.

They both went downstairs and finished their coffee, making more small talk and reminiscing about Tommy. He then promised her that he would help her with the funeral arrangements. He had already contacted the Belmont Funeral Home, where Tommy's body had been immediately taken after being examined by the coroner.

Dorian also told her that he would see about getting the paperwork started on Tommy's early pension distributions, death benefits, and life insurance claims.

"You were a wonderful partner to my hubby, Phil. You always had his back." Clara suddenly and unexpectedly kissed Dorian on the lips, then giving him a tight, emotional hug.

"I am always here for you, Clara."

They both embraced each other again.

"I'll call you later," Dorian said as he grabbed the gun case with the rifle inside and walked to his squad car, which was parked on Neva Street.

He started the ignition and decided to drive back to his loft in the West Loop, knowing that his dog. Ginger needed to be taken out and walked early that morning, which was her regular routine. Although the curiosity and anticipation were getting the best of him, he controlled his inquisitiveness until he got back home to his loft.

It was just past eight o'clock in the morning, and Dorian hadn't gotten much sleep the night before. After walking Ginger and making himself a cup of coffee, Dorian decided to reopen up the steel rifle gun case and examine the letter addressed to him inside.

Taking out his pocketknife again, he jammed the lock and opened up the gun case, carefully tearing open the white envelope.

As he sat down at his kitchen table, he read the contents of the letter. It was written neatly in Morton's handwriting. As Dorian read the letter, he buried his head in his hands.

"Oh my God," he said to himself loudly several times.

He read it several more times, making sure that he comprehended everything that his gunned-down, fallen partner had written.

Dorian then took a hot shower, got dressed like normal, and put his partner's letter into his coat pocket. He then put on his gun holster with his Glock 17 sidearm, this time making sure that it was cocked and loaded, with the gun clip filled with bullets. He put on his bulletproof vest zipped under his sport coat.

Dorian turned the safety off of his gun. He then made a telephone call, telling his desk sergeant that he would be late coming into work that day.

Phillip Dorian was furious. He was so angry that he was beside himself. His fury and wrath were beyond comprehension, as the only thing he wanted to do was dole out justice to all of the 'Top Brass' of Chicago who had hung his beloved partner out to dry.

At that moment, Detective Dorian only wanted revenge. He could taste it in his mouth.

Dorian had figured it out. He had solved Mayor Kollar's murder. In his mind, the mystery had been finally cracked. With that letter, Dorian had answered all the questions lingering about how and why the Mayor of Chicago was assassinated. He had realized what had tragically happened to his partner and who was truly responsible.

His beloved partner, Tommy Morton, had been hung out to dry by the 'Top Brass' of the Chicago Police Department. The veteran Chicago detective had put it all together. Detective Dorian decided to make that short little drive to 5701 West Madison Street, near Ashland Avenue.

On that morning, less than ten hours after his partner's violent death, Detective Phillip Dorian was going to pay an unannounced visit:

To the office of the City of Chicago Chief of Police Superintendent Walter M. Byron.

CHAPTER FORTY
OFFICE OF THE CHIEF OF POLICE-LATER THAT MORNING

On that November day, the rays of sunshine were brightly beaming down through the windows of the large waiting room of the Superintendent of Chicago's Police Department.

Dorian walked in and immediately demanded to see Chief Byron.

"I'm sorry, but the Chief is in conference right now."

"Let him know that Detective Dorian is here. It's important."

"Okay, Detective. Please have a seat."

The receptionist suddenly informed Chief Walter Bryon of his unexpected guest.

"What is it, Kelly?"

"Detective Phillip Dorian of the Sixteenth District is here to see you, sir."

Bryon had heard a few hours earlier of Detective Morton's gangland shooting and death in Bridgeport earlier that morning. He had not been given a chance to drive down to 33rd Street and Aberdeen where the violent shooting had taken place, as several of his lieutenants felt that the area was still unsecured and could not be safe.

He had heard that Morton was the victim in this violent homicide, and Byron suddenly became very nervous. He had received a text from Detective Morton at 11:05 that evening before the shooting on his burner cell phone, letting him know that he was about to make the cash pickup from Three-Chin Steward of Satan's Disciples.

Byron sat at his desk for almost ten minutes, his hands folded and in deep thought. Knowing a little about Detective Phil Dorian and his reputation, he grabbed his Glock 17 9MM pistol in the top drawer of his desk and cocked back the chamber. Byron then placed it on the corner of his desk within his reach.

He was very reluctant to let Dorian into his office.

"Chief, Detective Dorian is insisting on coming into your office," Kelly said.

Within several seconds, there were three knocks on his double door, and Detective Dorian walked in. Although he had only met Dorian a handful of times, he knew that he was outraged by the look on his face.

"Good morning, Detective Dorian, what a pleasant surprise," Byron was trying to be cordial.

"Cut the bullshit, Chief. My partner was gunned down in Bridgeport last night. What do you know about it?"

At that moment, Dorian noticed the Glock 17 9MM pistol lying on the corner of his desk. He pulled back his sport coat, showing that he, too, was armed.

"I'm sorry about your partner, Dorian. I just heard the news."

"You did, Chief? Really? Being that you are so sympathetic to the deaths of your detectives, it was very nice of you to show up at the crime scene on 33rd Street," Dorian sarcastically replied, his voice starting to get louder.

"My lieutenants advised me that the area wasn't safe, and they were afraid that there would be another..."

"More bullshit, Chief. There were several fire trucks, ambulances, and squad cars there last night. Bridgeport was the safest place to be last night after that shooting," the detective loudly pointed out.

"Look, Dorian, I know that you're upset, and I get it. You need to leave. When you're not as emotionally caught up in all of this, you can..."

"Who's Three-Chin Steward?"

"Who?"

"You fucking heard me, Chief. Who's Three Chin with Satan's Disciples?"

There were several seconds of silence.

"I don't know who you're talking about?"

"Who is Two-Bit Harding, Chief? Who is Javier, your bagman?"

Chief Walter Byron was now beginning to look very nervous, and sweat was starting to protrude from his forehead. His left hand was now within inches of his Glock 17 pistol.

"You need to leave, Dorian."

"Fuck you, Chief," as the detective pulled out the detailed note that was left behind by Morton in his rifle case.

He then unfolded it and walked closer to Chief Byron, who was now sweating profusely at his desk. Dorian held it up for Byron to see.

"Extra, extra, folks! Read all about it! Chief of Police Byron hires Chicago detective to assassinate Mayor Kollar!"

At that moment, Chief Byron grabbed his Glock 17 pistol with his left hand and pointed it at Dorian. Simultaneously, Dorian dropped Morton's letter on the floor and pulled out his gun, which was cocked, loaded, and ready to fire.

The two of them stood in the middle of Byron's office at a standoff, each pointing their guns at the other. There was a moment of silence, as they both knew that whoever fired the gun first would be on the hook for second-degree murder. There would be no self-defense. Byron warned Dorian to leave. The Chief of Police felt threatened by the detective, and they both drew their weapons simultaneously.

Dorian then smiled. "If you shoot that gun, Chief, you better not miss. You've got one shot, and I've got a feeling that I'm a much better shooter than you are."

At that moment, Byron noticed that Detective Dorian had his bulletproof vest on. Byron now realized that he had one headshot, and he knew that he couldn't miss it. At that moment, Kelly, his receptionist, who was now hearing all of the commotions, barged into Byron's office.

She covered her mouth and kept herself from screaming with fear as the two men stood there with their guns pointed at each other.

"Tommy Morton left a little love note in his rifle gun case, addressed for me in case anything happened to him," Dorian exclaimed.

"Apparently, Morton was on 33rd Street in Bridgeport last night to pick up his contract fees for acing Mayor Kollar on July 19th. You had originally hired one of the Black Cobra's to do the job. When they couldn't find anyone who was a competent sniper, they went to Satan's Disciples. They didn't have anyone either, so they found a bust-out drug dealer from the southside to do the job," Dorian recapped.

"It turned out that the bust-out drug dealer that they hired was an undercover detective named Tommy Morton, my partner," he continued.

"Morton, who was still undercover, approached you last May, letting you know what was going on. Because the gangs were already aware of your plot to assassinate Mayor Kollar, you convinced Morton to go through the murder. You promised him $100,000 in cash, and you would get your cut off the top of over $16,000. Some of the original $150,000 were supposed to get cut up between the Cobras and the Disciples."

Dorian was still pointing his gun at the Chief of Police.

"But the Disciples got greedy. So they gunned down the Cobras for all of the cash. And then last night, they gunned down poor Tommy for the cash he was supposed to receive for doing your fucking dirty work."

"Why didn't you just kill her yourself, Chief? Why involve somebody like Tommy Morton, who was in dire financial straits? A veteran detective whom you knew was desperate and needed some quick cash?"

A moment of silence as Dorian and Byron still had their guns pointed at each other, and the receptionist observed the whole incident. At that moment, Detective Romanowski appeared at the door of Chief Byron's office with a dozen or more patrolmen, all with their guns drawn and pointed at the Chief of Police.

Detective Dorian had called Detective Denny Romanowski of the Twenty-First Intelligence Unit that morning on his way to the Chief of Police's office on West Madison Street. He explained Morton's letter contents and the exact circumstance of how and why Morton had gotten ambushed and killed the night before.

"Good morning Chief," Detective Romanowski said, his gun pointed at Byron.

Byron then calmly put his gun down and smiled, his hands now in the air.

"That's quite a creative story, Dorian. How long did it take you to write that fucking letter?"

"Tommy was my partner and one of my best friends. As desperate as he was for money, he always had a habit of covering his ass. I'm sure the handwriting experts will verify that he wrote this letter. And CSI will probably authenticate the ballistics of that rifle as the Mayor's murder weapon," Dorian pointed out.

By now, there were two dozen or more people in Byron's office, some with their guns still drawn, ready to take the Chief of Police Walter Byron into custody.

"But I've got one question, Chief. Who fronted up the money? And where is that money now? You're not that stupid to let the Disciples kill Morton and keep all that money for themselves. The detectives found Morton's cell phone last night, and one of his last texts was to a burner phone, which I'm sure we're going to find somewhere here in your office," Dorian smiled.

A moment of silence.

"Along with a briefcase full of cash."

Apparently, the Chief of Police Byron was not at the murder scene of Tommy Morton because he had planned to meet Three-Chin Steward after the murder. Byron met up near

Cellular One Baseball Stadium in a desolate alley with the Disciples gang leader to split up the cash proceeds. They had cut out Detective Morton's sniper fees and split the money fifty-fifty.

Amatore 'Three-Chin' Steward had been working for Chief Walter Byron all along.

But Detective Dorian still had one nagging question that he still couldn't answer in this whole assassination plot:

Who originally fronted up the money, and where did it come from?

"Well, gentleman," Byron said, now smiling with his hands still raised.

"If I'm gonna go down, I ain't going down alone. When you boys find my cell phone here in the top drawer of my desk, you'll find some recordings of my recent breakfast meetings with Eddie Barrett," he stated.

"I think you may find them very interesting."

Dorian started smiling, then whispered '*son-of-a-bitch*' under his breath.

That rotten bastard, Eddie Barrett, was involved in this plot too. Barrett was the one with the deep pockets. He fronted up the cash contract fees.

At that moment, several Chicago patrol officer's walked over to the Chief of Police and handcuffed him, grasping his arms, and escorting him out of his office.

Dorian then looked at Romanowski, shaking his head.

"All of this fucking greed," Dorian said, as Detective Denny Romanowski gave him a brief hug.

"Morton didn't have to do this."

"I know. Tommy was desperate, and he was broke. And he trusted Byron, figuring that he had a good enough relationship with the Disciples to have them collect the money from the Cobras, and he would collect his cash. As sharp as Tommy was, he never figured that Chief Byron would double-cross him and cut him out."

Romanowski shook his head.

"I guess we have some work to do. We need immediately to get a warrant and tear up this office and his house in Lincoln Park."

The detectives and the other policemen filed out of Bryon's office, with one of them standing guard outside to make sure no one else entered his administrative offices until it was thoroughly searched. By that afternoon, Byron's home in Lincoln Park and his office on West Madison Street had been combed, searched, and rummaged. His cell phone was immediately found on his desk. And hidden in his closet, behind some boxes and files stacked there for storage, was a black briefcase, with $58,200 in unmarked bills. Dorian knew that the total sum of $116,400 was supposed to be collected that night by Morton. The detective immediately knew who had the other half.

It wasn't until three o'clock in the afternoon when Detective Denny Romanowski finally arrived back at his office at the Eighteenth District. He grabbed several stale donuts in the kitchen as he had not had any time to eat lunch that day. As he sat down at his desk, he decided to call up his buddy at the Chicago Tribune. He figured he better give him the correct, accurate information before he got it from somewhere else. Besides, maybe this was a good chance and the right opportunity to get his name spelled right in the papers.

"Lawrence McKay."

"Hey McKay, it's Denny."

"Hey, Denny. What's up? I was just going to call you on Detective Morton's murder in Bridgeport last night. I was sorry to hear about his death. He was a good cop."

"Thanks," the detective replied.

"Listen up, McKay. Why don't you pack up your laptop and come over here? And since it's gonna cost you some lunch anyway, bring me a Jimmy John's turkey sandwich with the works, extra mayo."

There was a silent moment on the phone, as Larry McKay was initially confused.

"Alright, but what's up?"

"Just come over here, and we'll finish your story on Kollar's murder."

McKay smiled. "You got it. I'll be there in thirty minutes. Anything else?"

Detective Romanowski smiled over the telephone.

"No. Just make sure you spell my fucking name right this time. You don't do well with long-ass, 'pollock' names."

McKay chuckled over the phone.

"See you in a few."

The veteran reporter ran out of his office with his laptop and backpack in tow. Finally, he was all excited to locate the missing pieces to this intricate, complex assassination plot that had been haunting him since last July.

For the price of a Jimmy John's sandwich, Larry McKay was about to find out how elaborate this plot really was.

Chapter Forty-One
A Contract With The Devil-December 13th

It was past eleven o'clock in the evening, as a black Maserati was speeding southbound on the Dan Ryan expressway on that Tuesday night. Little Tony DiMatteo had just finished attending a Christmas Party for a few of his vendors at the Morton Steakhouse and was driving home.

The late-night traffic was light in the expressway's left lane, as DiMatteo struggled to keep his eyes on the road. With his daily, 5:00 am workout routines, and after three of his 'Crown Royal on the Rocks' cocktails, DiMatteo was more than a little tired. He was drowsy and was struggling to keep his car under control. But he needed to get home quickly and in bed before his usual wake-up time of four o'clock in the morning.

While he was driving, he wasn't paying much attention to his speedometer. The needle was climbing past ninety-five miles an hour, as he was taking the expressway curve a little too fast past the South Archer Avenue exit. He didn't notice the Chicago Police squad car parked on the Dan Ryan expressway's far-left side, whom he had driven past. The patrolman clocked his speed, then put on his sirens and followed the speeding, black Maserati. His radar gun recorded the car's rate of speed, going faster than 97 miles an hour.

Little Tony was struggling to stay awake and loudly turned on his radio. There was an Andy Williams Christmas song, 'The Most Wonderful Time of the Year' playing on a Sirius XM oldies station as he was turning up the volume. As Tony started singing along, he didn't notice the police squad car that was chasing after him until the cop car pulled up right next to him on the I-94 expressway and, blowing his sirens loudly, ordered him to pull over.

"Good evening, Officer, Happy Holidays," Little Tony politely said as he rolled down his window.

"Driver's License, Registration and Proof of Insurance, please," the unamused patrolman answered, shining a flashlight on Little Tony's eyes and around the front and back seats of the sports car. Tony's eyes were dilated, and the distinct smell of alcohol was more than evident as he was fumbling with his wallet and the papers in his car's glovebox. He finally, after some delayed searching, retrieved the requested identification.

"Have you been drinking, sir?"

"I had a cocktail, but I'm fine. Why are you asking?"

"Sir, step out of the car, please."

"No, officer, I am not going to step out of my car," Tony loudly replied, always remembering his attorney's advice when getting pulled over after having too many drinks.

DiMatteo knew that he shouldn't cooperate with the officer, knowing he would get asked to blow into a breathalyzer machine. The patrolman angrily took the driver's identification and typed in the information into his squad car computer, along with the driver's license plate number. It was then that the Chicago police officer suddenly realized who he had just pulled over.

Tony DiMatteo was then forcibly arrested and brought to the Seventh District.

It was just past eight o'clock in the morning when Detective Phillip Dorian picked up his very loud ringing desk phone.

"Detective Dorian," he answered, still rubbing his forehead.

He had been out to a Christmas party the night before and was suffering from a mild headache, resulting from three Gentlemen Jack's on the rocks.

It had been a difficult two weeks for the veteran detective. He had to bury his partner and close friend, Tommy Morton, after his gruesome murder. He had to also read about the mayor's assassination plot in the newspapers and watch all of the Chaz Rizzo's newscasts, about how his financially desperate his partner was and how he got involved in the mayor's slaying, at the directive of Chief Byron.

Detective Phillip Dorian was physically and emotionally grieving, and he was mentally not in a good place. He had lost over fifteen pounds in the last few weeks and had no appetite.

He was also spending a lot of time with Tommy's widow, Clara, assisting her with all of the paperwork needed to collect his pension, life insurance, and death benefits. He had been to the Morton residence almost daily, comforting his widow and trying to help her put all of the pieces of Tommy's murder back together. She became his emotional crutch and spent several nights sleeping on her couch while trying to comfort her throughout this grieving process.

Dorian was also going to Ascension Church on West Hubbard Street, attending daily mass at 6:30 am whenever he could and praying for the repose of Tommy's soul.

"Phil, it's Sergeant Anderson over at the Seventh District."

"Hey Sergeant, Happy Holidays."

"Happy Holidays to you, Phil. I'm sorry again for the loss of your partner."

"Thanks."

"Do you remember that standing request you have with all of the desk sergeants for your special boy if he ever gets picked up?"

"My special boy? Who are we talking about?"

"Come on, Phil, you know, the one you have under surveillance. You know, the mobster, Tony DiMatteo. We're holding him here at the Seventh. It seems he was out drinking and driving on the Dan Ryan Expressway again last night."

"Little Tony DiMatteo? No kidding?" the detective acknowledged, trying to consume a much-needed sip of his Dunkin' Donuts coffee at the same time.

"Yep, that's the one. We have him here on a DUI. He's been in our holding room all night."

Dorian couldn't believe what he was hearing. "Has he 'lawyered up' yet?"

"No, not yet. He was so drunk last night; he's been sleeping with his head down at the table."

The detective started laughing to himself.

"He was pretending to be Mario Andretti and was racing his Maserati down the Dan Ryan when he got pulled over. We thought you might want to come down here and have a little 'chit-chat' with him."

"And his lawyer, Prescott? He hasn't shown up yet?"

"He hasn't called anyone. He was busy entertaining everyone in the district last night with his smart-ass comments until he finally passed out in the holding room. If he weren't who he was, we would have already thrown him in the shithouse by now," the Sergeant replied, tongue in cheek.

Dorian wasn't surprised that the 'Capo' of all the crime families in Chicagoland was getting the royal treatment at the Seventh District.

"Thanks, Commander, I'll be right down."

Phil Dorian was shocked, and he couldn't believe it. Little Tony's bad habit of drinking and driving after one too many cocktails was becoming a regular habit with him, as he had remembered arresting him two summers ago while he was investigating those 'Pedophile Priest Murders' that were going around.

Dorian took another sip of his black coffee.

He knew that the "Capo dei Capi" was way too smart to be speeding down the Dan Ryan 'all juiced up.' This would be DiMatteo's third DUI offense, and Dorian couldn't put his head around all this sudden stupidity. He jumped into his Crown Victoria squad car, turned on the sirens, and raced down to the Seventh District on West 63rd Street.

"Thanks for coming down, Detective," Sergeant Charles Anderson said, as he guided him to the holding room where they were keeping DiMatteo. He was an older, overweight police officer who had probably made more than his share of memorable visits to the donut shop. The detective could tell he was having a hard time walking and getting around, as the desk sergeant was in pain, escorting him around the district office.

"I keep forgetting about what a cocky bastard this son-of-a-bitch is," he commented. "I'm hoping this won't be a waste of time for you, Detective. Maybe you can get some information out of him on some of those murder investigations you have going on."

Dorian opened the door to the holding room with the desk sergeant behind him. Of course, there was no need for any formal introductions. Little Tony DiMatteo was now comfortably sitting on a chair at the table, and his face seemed to light up when the detective walked into the room.

His white, naturally perfect hair-sprayed hair was somewhat disheveled, and he looked like he had been up most of the night. The Chicago mobster was always in good shape, very fit and trim, and 'dressed to the nines.' He was wearing a grey sport coat and black collared shirt, sporting several diamond rings and an oversized gold Rolex watch. Except for that morning, DiMatteo always looked impeccable.

"Well, well…if it isn't Detective Philip 'Fucking' Dorian," he said, broadly smiling from ear to ear.

"It's a pleasure to see you again, Tony." he amusingly replied.

"I heard you were racing down the Dan Ryan again last night," he quickly said, hoping for a straight answer.

"Yeah, I was drag racing some little old lady down on the expressway in a '59 Edsel," he sarcastically replied.

"That was your excuse that last time you were picked up," Dorian smiled.

"What the fuck do you want from me, Dorian. I was racing the same fucking old lady."

Dorian walked over to the other side of the holding room table and made himself comfortable.

"We've gotta stop meeting like this, Tony. The other coppers are starting to think we've got this thing going on and that maybe we're becoming fast friends."

Along with his late partner Tommy Morton, Dorian had been to his warehouse office to visit with him several times over the last few years. With the recent city violence now going on, the detective had his suspicions about who was involved. He knew right away that Little Tony DiMatteo had his unique signature written all over them.

"Don't get too excited, Dorian. That will never happen. Besides, I love drinking and drag racing down the expressway so that we can sit down and have more of our enlightening little conversations."

"That's what I'm thinking, Tony. I think you're starting to like me."

"Fuck you, Dorian. That will never fucking happen."

Dorian smiled and took another long sip of his coffee.

"Can we get you anything, Tony? Some coffee, perhaps?"

Little Tony DiMatteo was taken aback by Detective Dorian's sudden friendliness.

"Fuck your coffee, Dorian. Every time I drink the coffee made by one of your coppers, I end up sitting on the fucking toilet all day."

"Maybe that's your secret to your slim and trim figure, Tony," Dorian joked. "More Chicago P.D. coffee."

They both smiled as they seemed to be getting comfortable with each other. Little Tony was starting to get suspicious, and he was noticing how nice Detective Dorian was acting early that morning.

"I was sorry to hear about your partner, Tommy Morton. He seemed like a likable guy. He was still kind of a prick like you, of course, but at least he was likable," Tony said, expressing his condolences.

"You, on the other hand…" he joked.

"Thanks, Tony."

The two of them sat there at the holding table for several moments in silence. Dorian then started looking around, noticing that there were two surveillance cameras in the holding room. There was also the one-way window where the other officers and detectives could observe the potential prisoner being held. He then got up and picked up the telephone that was hanging on the wall.

"Sergeant, is there a place where we can have some privacy?"

"Yeah, sure. We've got another holding room downstairs with no windows or cameras," Sergeant Anderson promptly responded.

"Okay, thanks."

At that moment, Detective Dorian asked DiMatteo to get up and follow him, along with two other officers, to the Seventh District's private holding room, which was in the old, dusty basement of the Seventh District's police station. As Tony was starting to get up, he became suspicious.

"Dorian, where are we going? You gonna take me downstairs and fuck me now, or do I need my damn lawyer?"

"Relax, Tony. Tell Michael Prescott to stay home. I just want to have a little chit-chat with you off the record."

The two of them took the elevator down to the Seventh District's police station's basement floor. The building was rather old, constructed during the Great Depression, as the basement walls and foundation were constructed out of bricks painted repeatedly. The dimly lit basement had rows of boxes stacked three and four at a time, and towards the back of the basement was a long, dilapidated wooden table with several steel folding chairs. The Chicago P.D. liked to use this police station's basement for meetings and sometimes confrontations that no one wanted to be recorded on their surveillance tapes upstairs. In the basement corner was a four-by-four cyclone fence cage, with a bench inside and secured by several locks. This was used for extreme criminals where coppers and detectives used excessive force to pull information from their perpetrators.

Little Tony followed Dorian over to the wooden table, as two policemen followed them downstairs.

"Do we need to cuff him?" one of the patrolmen asked.

"No. He's not going anywhere," the detective responded.

As they sat down, Dorian thanked the two police officers, and they were left alone down the basement.

Then Dorian pulled out one of his business cards, scribbled something on it with his black pen, then handed it over to DiMatteo.

Little Tony looked at the card and laughed out loud.

"'Get Out Of Jail Free,'? What the fuck is this, Dorian?"

"Exactly what it says, Tony. It's a 'Get Out Of Jail Free' card."

Little Tony started laughing again, totally amused by Dorian's visual aide.

"So what is this supposed to mean? That you're gonna cut me loose on a DUI charge? You crack me up, Dorian."

"No, Tony. Besides the fact that this is gonna be your third DUI conviction, the charges against you are much worse."

Little Tony looked at him again, puzzled at what he was about to disclose.

"You're gonna pinch me on another DUI? Is that all you got, Dorian? What the fuck, do you actually think I give a shit? I've got so many truck drivers who would be happy to chauffeur me around this fucking town in my parked Mercedes, collecting dust in my garage," Tony replied, totally amused.

"Do you really think I would go through all this trouble just to watch you get pinched on another DUI? No Tony, trust me, you're into some much deeper shit."

"Oh, really, Dorian. Now you've got my attention."

Dorian smiled, calmly taking another sip of his Dunkin' Donuts coffee.

"We've got the owner from that jewelry store on South Wabash, Albert Mancini, on the record. You remember that store, don't you? He's willing to testify that you extorted him for over $10,000 in cash to protect his store from looting that night. He is also willing to identify the shooters with the AK-47 rifles that shot up and killed those four gang members from Satan's Disciples."

At that moment, Little Tony was silent.

"That was a hired hit, Tony. You guys practically lured those kids to that jewelry store to rob and looted it, and when they went in, your boys were waiting for them with AK-47 rifles."

DiMatteo started to smile.

"You can't make that stick, Dorian. Those gang members were armed, and my security boys were protecting my client's property. Their lives were being threatened. Those kids were armed, and they were ready to do damage," Little Tony replied.

"That's not what Mancini is saying. He's saying that you used his store as a set up to lure those kids in and murder them." Dorian paused for a moment.

"You made a statement to the other gangs by luring them in and shooting the living shit out of them."

Little Tony started to laugh again.

"You amuse me, Dorian. You know all of this is a fucking stretch, and you know it."

"Not really, Tony. I already talked to the State's Attorney, Doug Janes. He thinks we can get four involuntary manslaughter charges at a minimum, especially with Mancini's testimony."

Detective Dorian was bluffing. He had no such conversation with Janes, as Little Tony continued to smile while shaking his head.

"My boy, Michael Prescott, will make fucking dog food out of your little fucking prosecutor, Doug Janes. He's done it before."

"Your boy is running out of lucky horseshoes, Tony. Doug Janes is willing to take the chance and hold you on four counts of manslaughter." More bullshit.

"We'll beat it, Dorian. Bet the fucking farm."

"And by the way, we're still looking into that disappearance of that priest, Father Fitz, your chess partner. I gotta hunch that you know something about that as well and how he suddenly disappeared."

Tony laughed.

"Fuck you, Dorian. That priest and I were tight. You haven't got shit on that one."

"Do you want to take that chance, Tony? Do you want to try your luck again at the poker table? Is that another gamble that you want to take?"

Little Tony glared at the detective, his temper starting to boil.

"You keep taking bets at the poker table, and you keep walking away on top. You know the odds, Tony. One of these times, you're going to lose."

They both sat there in silence for several long minutes.

"Sooner or later, the house is going to win."

"Fuck you, Dorian."

"You know, Tony, sometimes I think you're the luckiest wise-guy on the face of this earth. You make John Gotti; the 'Teflon Don' look like an amateur altar boy. I can only imagine how much more dangerous you would be with a few years of law school."

Tony smiled at the inference of the detective's compliment.

"My mother would have been proud," he smiled, still thinking about her loss over the summer.

They were both silent for a moment or two.

"Okay, Dorian. I'll bite. What is it that you fucking want now that I have your little fucking 'Get Out Of Jail Free' card?"

Dorian calmly finished his coffee and then got up to throw the empty cup into the wastebasket located near an abandoned wooden desk twenty feet away. He then turned around and, from a distance, named his price.

"I want Three-Chin Steward."

DiMatteo smiled and commented.

"Okay, Dorian. Go pick him up. What the fuck do you want from me?" Tony smiled.

Dorian leaned up against the empty desk with his arms crossed.

"No, Tony, you're not getting it. I want Three-Chin Steward...dead."

Tony looked at the Sixteenth District detective as if he had three-eyes. He shook his head and then chuckled.

"So what else do you what? John the Baptist's fucking head on a silver platter?"

"No, Tony. Just Three-Chin's."

Tony looked at Dorian, still trying to figure out if he was serious. Dorian walked back over to the wooden table and sat down again across from DiMatteo. They stared at each other for several long seconds in silence.

"He killed my partner, Tony."

"Your partner killed the Mayor."

"My partner was lured into killing her by Chief Byron, who happens to have Three-Chin and his boys on his goddamn payroll. He partnered up with Three-Chin, and his gang ambushed and decimated Tommy."

DiMatteo shook his head in disbelief.

"So you come to me for revenge?" Tony asked. "What the fuck, Dorian? I don't believe you. You've got a lot of fucking balls," he loudly replied.

"You've been breathing heavily down my neck for years, trying to clip me on anything you can find. You even keep a fucking cop car in my parking lot, watching my every move. Then when your partner gets fucking whacked by some gang members, you come to me crying with your little bullshit 'Get Out Of Jail Free' card, a DUI charge, and some trumped-up horseshit about us whacking some gang members last summer."

Detective Dorian only sat there, listening intently to the Capo dei Capi.

"You crack me up, Dorian!"

"Look, Tony. Do you really think I need you to take out Three-Chin? He knows who I am, and he knows I'm gunning for him. The problem is if I take him out, I'll be the first person they come to, especially since I busted Chief Byron on this whole assassination scheme. Byron has a lot of friends in this city, and they're all pissed off right now because Romanowski and I exposed their little plan."

DiMatteo listened intently to the detective.

"I can handle the heat, Tony. In a few more years, I can retire and get the hell away from this goddamn, rat-infested city."

They were both quiet as Tony sat there with his legs crossed.

"But I'm not going to let Tommy's killers walk away. We can't find any evidence to pick up any of Three-Chin's gang members on this murder, and nobody is talking."

Tony DiMatteo smiled.

"That's not true, Dorian. You could probably 'trump-up' enough evidence to pick up Three-Chin and get a murder conviction," he replied.

"The problem with you is," he paused, "a life sentence for this fucking gangbanger in Stateville isn't fucking good enough for you."

A silent moment.

"As I said, you want his head on a silver platter."

Detective Phillip Dorian studied his nemesis for several long moments. Tony DiMatteo was smart enough to know what it was that the detective wanted from him, and the gangster knew that Dorian wanted it bad enough to cross the line to make it happen.

"You're a very smart man, Tony."

Dorian then shook his head in defeat.

"You're right, Tony. This isn't a good idea. And my crossing the line and making a deal with you for the murder of this rotten son-of-a-bitch just isn't worth it."

At that moment, Dorian got up from the table.

"Let's go upstairs so you can call your lawyer, Tony."

Feeling defeated, he then turned his back and began walking towards the elevator to go back upstairs. Dorian then quickly turned around and looked at Little Tony DiMatteo, who was still sitting comfortably at the table.

"Aren't you coming upstairs, or would you rather I lock you up down here in the cage?"

The Capo looked at the detective. He then rose from the table and tendered Dorian's business card, as if he were turning it over and cashing it in during the middle of a high-stakes Monopoly game.

"I will see what I can do, Dorian."

Dorian, displaying a shadow of a smile, walked back to the table as Little Tony rose from his chair. He then extended his hand, and the two of them shook hands as if they were making a solemn pact.

Chicago P.D.'s Detective Phillip Dorian had just made a contract with the devil.

CHAPTER FORTY-TWO
SABOR LATINO RESTAURANT-DECEMBER 23RD

North Avenue's noisy holiday traffic on that winter day didn't seem to distract the four African Americans from enjoying their late-night dinner. The four gangbangers were well-known street hoodlums from the neighborhood, and they were popular to all the patrons who came into the Sabor Latino Restaurant.

Satan's Disciples were a smaller street gang on the west side of Chicago, with an enormous reputation. Within the last several months, the rebellious street hoods went from being virtually unknown within Chicago's streets to becoming infamously feared. They were approximately forty-five members, maintaining a house on Springfield Street, past Mozart Park that was well-entrenched into the Hermosa neighborhood.

Although they were a small group of renegade gang bangers, they were ruthless. Like their callous, brutal gang leader, Amatore 'Three-Chin' Steward, they didn't believe in following anyone's rules and could never be trusted, especially when it came to doing business.

The biggest mistake that Three-Chin's first cousin, Giovante 'Lil' Bro' Johnson, had made, was trusting the Satan's Disciple leader in believing that they could do business together without letting their gang affiliations get in the way.

But the Satan's Disciples were ruthless. Unlike the Black Cobras, they had no rules, no ethics, and no scruples to follow. They were considered by the Chicago P.D. investigative gang unit in the Fourteenth District as being the most dangerous and the most callous of all of the powerful street gangs in Chicago.

It was of no surprise to the Chicago Police Department and its detectives that the Satan's Disciples were responsible for Detective Tommy Morton's assassination death and that they were involved with the political factions and dangerous liaisons of Chicago's most powerful Fourteenth Ward alderman. At the time of Tommy Morton's murder, several gang members, including Three-Chin, were picked up and held on suspicion of murdering a Chicago police officer, detective, and a well-loved family man.

The only eyewitness to the shooting was an eighty-nine-year-old lady, who saw a black vehicle that looked like a large SUV fire multiple rounds into Tommy Morton's vehicle from her bedroom window. But when she was pressed for more specific information, she had difficulty distinguishing the car's make and model, as the shooting took place in the dead of night without streetlights or oncoming traffic. They were soon released, and Three-Chin was back on the street. He was now bragging to his friends that they had made a huge score, thanks to the Chicago Police Department.

Just two days before Christmas, Three-Chin Steward was now feeling invincible. He had played his cards right and killed off his first cousin. Steward acquired away the cash proceeds from the Mayor's assassination plot and aced off the Chicago detective responsible for her death. And he then successfully 'split the pot' of over $116,000 in cash proceeds with

Chicago's Chief of Police, his secret boss, and commander.

Three-Chin actually believed that he was now untouchable. He had the Chief of Police in his back pocket, even though he was now sitting in Cook County Jail. He believed that the Black Cobras street gang were essentially afraid of him, knowing that he was crazy enough to do anything. With Detective Morton's gruesome murder, Three-Chin's thirst for power and respect in the city's underground was now at hand. He had made a name for himself, knowing now that every gang member of every street gang in the City of Chicago ultimately feared him.

Three-Chin Stewart and three of his gang lieutenants had just finished their late-night dinner at the Sabor Latino Restaurant on West North Avenue. Their expansive Mexican cuisine included several spicy enchiladas, fish tacos, pollo fritos, and bistec encebollados, washing it all down afterward with several bottles of Dos Equis beers.

It was no secret that Three-Chin Steward enjoyed his large quantities of food. He enjoyed his breakfast, lunch, and dinner several times a day. When Three-Chin wasn't eating or having mindless sex with anyone one of his several girlfriends, he was doing a line of blow.

Three-Chin was an intense cocaine addict and went through an 'Eight-Ball' (an eighth of an ounce of 'coke') daily. He was amply named for his five-foot, six-inch, two-hundred-and-eighty-pound frame. And as always, he was wearing his three large 18-karat Italian chains around his neck, one of them bearing a medallion of a large gold pitchfork, the symbol of his very dangerous street gang.

It was almost eleven-thirty on that Tuesday evening in December, and the four of them had just exited the restaurant and got into their late-model Cadillac Escalade. They were about to go back home, which was a short distance away.

Darryl 'C-Note' Henderson was Three-Chin's trusted lieutenant and was the driver that evening. As two other gang members got into the car, Three-Chin got into the Cadillac Escalade's back seat. 'C-Note' started the vehicle, while Three-Chin pulled out a bag of cocaine. He was about to do one last hit for the evening before going home.

Suddenly, two black Ford Explorers pulled in front and alongside the Cadillac Escalade. Before C-Note could even take out his weapon, all the windows from both cars were blown out, and five AK-47's unleashed a barrage of bullets into the vehicle.

The multitude of bullets fired into the windshield was so extensive that all of the glass was shot out and splattered onto the vehicle's front seat. The Ford Explorer from the side of the car continued shooting into the driver's side and back window, while more glass and blood were splattered everywhere on the car's back seat.

When over two hundred rounds of bullets had finally finished being fired into the Cadillac Escalade, a large man with even a larger knife came out of the back seat of the Ford Explorer parked alongside the Cadillac. Besides a knife, 'Crazy Eight' Incandella had brought a large black plastic bag along with him.

Crazy Eight opened up the back door of the Cadillac. There sitting in the back seat, was Three-Chin Steward, all shot up and his body riddled with bullets. His eyes were bloodied and shot out, with more bullet holes pierced into his body, neck, and face.

Using a massive knife with the skills of a union butcher, Crazy Eight cut up Three-Chin and put something large inside of the black plastic bag. Within minutes, the killers in the black Ford quickly drove off, away from the front parking lot of the Sabor Latino Restaurant and onto North Avenue.

The restaurant employees were hiding in the backroom, afraid to come out, when they heard the bullets being fired in the front parking lot. Someone had dialed '911' from their cellular phone, but the two squad cars did not arrive at the crime scene for several minutes until the shooting had subsided.

When the patrolmen arrived, they were aghast to see the victims, violently shot up and unrecognizable inside the bullet-ridden Cadillac Escalade.

One female patrolperson, Officer Lori Munoz, opened the back door of the passenger side where Three-Chin Steward was sitting. She was a rookie cop, having recently graduated from the police academy and had not been with the Chicago P.D. for more than two weeks.

When she saw the bullet-ridden body of Three-Chin, she covered her mouth and loudly started screaming until another officer came to her aide.

A large part of Three-Chin Steward's anatomy had been removed.

Chapter Forty-Three
A Styrofoam Container - December 24

The drab, gray walls of the ten by twelve-foot prison cell were dreary and dilapidated, as former Chief of Police Walter Byron sat on the single mattress, situated within the middle of the room.

It was Christmas Eve, and he had been at Cook County Jail for more than a month. During his arraignment, he had been denied a monetary bond at his bail hearing. Knowing that Byron was a flight risk, Judge Lisa Mariano had denied bail to the former police chief. She had publicly made note that his violent plot to kill the Mayor of Chicago was so deplorable and so shocking that his betraying the trust of the people of Chicago should only allow him to 'rot in jail.'

On that cold afternoon, Byron had just arrived back to his jail cell from having lunch in the mess hall when one of the jail guards came into his cell.

"Byron, we have a large package being delivered here for you. We need to take you to the conference room."

"What is it?" he asked.

"It's Christmas, dude. Who knows? 'Tis the season," the jail guard replied.

Byron was then escorted in handcuffs and ankle chains out of his jail cell and into a conference room with only three filthy, high ceiling windows. The walls bore a drab, green paint color that was so old and dirty; it turned yellow.

As he sat down on that cold, steel chair, he overheard the voice of another prison guard knock on the entrance door. He then entered the room, bringing in a large cardboard box wrapped tightly around a styrofoam container. The box seemed to be refrigerated, with the contents sealed tightly into that box. There was no address from where the package was from, and the correctional officer had the shipment x-rayed. It looked as though there was refrigerated food inside. Being that it was Christmas Eve, it was not unusual that day for the inmates to receive food and other edible items in large, refrigerated containers.

Walter Byron, his hands still handcuffed and in shackles, did his best to open up the styrofoam container with his bare hands while one of the correctional officers looked on.

He then opened the container and removed the ice packs.

Suddenly, Walter Byron started screaming at the top of his lungs. His shrilly, loud voice reverberated and echoed against the drab, green walls of that prison conference room. The former chief's voice was drenched with the deafening eerie sounds of absolute horror.

Inside of that sealed, styrofoam container, wrapped up in dry ice, was the decapitated head of Three-Chin Steward.

CHAPTER FORTY-FOUR
A Gift From Santa – Christmas Eve

It was lightly snowing outside on South Ashland Avenue, just after one o'clock on Christmas Eve. The last truck deliveries were coming back from their usual daily stops, and everyone was preparing to close down the DiMatteo Tomato Distribution Company for the rest of the day. The truck drivers were excited that afternoon, receiving their holiday cash envelopes and preparing to go home and celebrate the Christmas holiday with their families.

Sal Marrocco was in his office, preparing to leave, when he received a package from an Amazon delivery truck, addressed to Anthony DiMatteo. The return address only said "835 North Rush Street, Chicago," on the label.

The Consigliere smiled as he opened up the package on behalf of his boss, which was the usual routine. He read the attached note and knew that Tony would be ecstatic to receive this package. Marrocco picked up the box and walked over to the other side of the warehouse building, knocking on Tony's office door.

"Tony, it's me. You have a gift from Santa."

Sal Marrocco brought the partially opened gift box over and set it on Tony's desk.

"Someone thinks you've been a good boy this year."

Looking puzzled, Little Tony gazed inside the box and finished unwrapping the delivered gift. When he realized what it was, he began laughing out loud.

"Well, I'll be goddamned."

He then finished unwrapping the gift. It was an expensive, ivory chess set, complete with an Italian marble chessboard and a mahogany hand-carved wooden case, with individual holders for each black and white chess piece. The gift was imported directly from Costa Rica and was probably worth over one thousand dollars.

Tony gazed at the expensive chess set and set it aside on his desk. He then read the attached card and smiled to himself one last time before destroying the religious Christmas Card.

It was a hand-written holiday card from the Archdiocese of Chicago that simply said:

Merry Christmas, Tony, and thanks for all of your help. May the Lord watch over and protect you and your family in the coming new year.

Yours In Christ,

Joseph Cardinal Markowitz

CHAPTER FORTY-FIVE
A NEW YEAR – JANUARY 2

It had been heavily snowing all evening, as the city crews with their snowplows had been clearing off the five inches of snow that had already accumulated overnight. That cold morning was hovering around fifteen degrees, with the wind chill factor and blowing winds pulling the temperature down to a minus ten below. The forecasters predicted an additional three to five more inches, as the early morning traffic in the Chicago Loop was practically at a standstill.

It was a miserable winter day for the first business day of the new year. But this didn't stop the veteran Alderman Eddie Barrett of the Fourteenth Ward from going into his office on that early Tuesday morning. He arrived at his law office early, as usual, catching up on oncoming events, emails, and voicemails.

On that morning, the veteran alderman had a copy of the morning edition of the Chicago Tribune in his hand, and he placed it on top of his desk while putting down his Starbucks coffee. The newspaper had been placed in his mail bin by his receptionist for him to read, a routine that he had done every morning for the last fifty years. But that morning, he tried not to glance at the headlines until he sat down at his desk.

The morning headlines of that day made the veteran alderman exceptionally nervous:
DOJ Vows To Clean Up Chicago Corruption

He had been tipped off by several of his Washington D.C. connections that the U.S.

Attorney General Robert Irsuto had been gunning for him and his cronies ever since his office at the Fourteenth Ward had been raided last March. They had confiscated all of his file cabinets, computers, and computer file servers, along with over fifty years of microfiche documents to sort out and search for any prosecutable evidence.

The FBI had been unusually silent over the summer, especially after Mayor Raymond Sanchez took office in August. With all of the blatant corruption and bribery that was going on at City Hall, it seems that the Attorney General's office was temporarily distracted.

On the advice of his best friend, the Honorable Judge Augustino Chiaramonte, Eddie Barrett met with several special agents over the summer, tipping them off on some of Mayor Sanchez's monetary kickbacks. Hoping that he could cut a deal with them, Barrett handed over what information he knew to the U.S. Attorney General's office last September, hoping that he could cut a deal and possibly get some leniency in their investigation.

When the word finally came back from Attorney General Robert Irsuto, it was only a very cool 'we'll wait and see' response. The U.S. Justice Department was well aware of the criminal offenses that Eddie Barrett had been committing in Chicago for the last fifty years, and it was going to take more than just turning over their corrupt, newly elected Chicago Mayor to cut a deal with them.

Moreover, Eddie Barrett knew that he was being implicated in Mayor Janice Kollar's assassination plot. Unbeknownst to him, Chief of Police Walter Byron had been secretly tap recording their covert meetings at Mister K's Restaurant since last May. The state prosecutor had proof of him with Chief Byron on tape plotting the Mayor's assassination, and he was expecting a visit from Chicago Police and the FBI at any day.

Eddie Barrett knew that he was on limited, borrowed time.

He expected the Intelligence Unit from the Twenty-First District to come in and arrest him when Chief Byron was indicted and charged last November. But because of the upcoming holidays, the Department of Justice decided to wait until after the new year to begin their investigation again into the Fourteenth Ward and his possible arrest.

Since Mayor Raymond Sanchez's sudden death, the Chicago City Council decided to have the Mayor Pro-tempore Waylon Smith act as mayor until a special run-off election could be held in March. Eddie Barrett and his Dirty Dozen had lost a significant amount of clout within the Chicago City Council, having been blamed for pushing such a corrupt, self-serving alderman to become Mayor of Chicago last August.

It was going to happen any day, Barrett thought to himself. He knew he would get arrested sometime soon, and there was nothing he could do about it. His passports were confiscated from him after Chief Byron's arrest, and he was told by the state prosecutor's office to 'enjoy the holidays with your family.'

Eddie Barrett was also 77 years old. He had spent his whole professional and political career serving the City of Chicago, both as a real estate attorney and Fourteenth Ward

Alderman. He was too old to do anything else, and he was certainly too old to do federal prison time.

At approximately one o'clock in the afternoon, Sandra Pawlowski, his legal and administrative assistant, called him on his desk phone.

"Mr. Barrett, you need to come out here, sir. There are some people here waiting to see you."

Eddie Barrett swallowed hard and turned a shade of pale white. He then walked over to his humidor, grabbed several Cohiba cigars, and put them in his pocket. Barrett cut and lit up one of the cigars, knowing it would be the very last time he could enjoy one of his imported Cubans in his law office alone.

The Chicago Alderman's faithful moment had finally come. He put on his suit coat, making sure that his vest was buttoned and that his hair was well combed. He knew that, including those others wishing to apprehend him, that the news channels and photographers were out there. The veteran alderman wanted to look his best for the cameras.

While puffing on his cigar, Eddie Barrett then opened his office door. Waiting for him outside were almost thirty people, crammed up against one another, taking pictures with the news media camera crews everywhere. Channel Eight Eyewitness News was there, along with Channel Three and CNN. The Chicago Media were all there to witness the final demise of Chicago's most powerful, most arrogant politicians. Eddie Barrett only stood there, erect and proud, as the Cook County

State's Attorney, Doug Janes, announced his arrest along with a search warrant for his Chicago Loop law office.

"Alderman Barrett, we have a warrant here for your arrest, on the charges of conspiracy, illegal tax fraud, twenty counts of bribery, and an accomplice to the murder of Mayor Janice Kollar," the district attorney announced.

Eddie Barrett only stood there in his well pressed, three-piece suit, with his arms extended forward and a lit-up Cohiba cigar in his mouth. One of the plainclothes detectives handcuffed him and read him his rights as he was escorted out of his LaSalle Street law office and taken to a holding cell at the Eighteenth District on North Larrabee Street.

Later that morning, eight detectives and patrol officers went through Eddie Barrett's law office with a fine-tooth comb, uncovering several pieces of valuable documents and evidence supporting the crimes he had been accused of. Behind one of his expensive Thomas Kinkade paintings was a large wall safe. Using a CPD locksmith, the wall safe was opened, and the contents were examined. There were approximately $1.8 million in cash and currency, over one million dollars in gold bars, various gold and silver coins, and an expensive foray of gold and diamond jewelry. Along with two Luger 9MM pistols and several boxes of ammunition, there was something else that was very interesting inside of Eddie Barrett's safe:

There were five kilos of pure, white cocaine.

CHAPTER FORTY-SIX
FALL OF A CHICAGO ALDERMAN-JANUARY 5TH

My phone had been ringing off the hook that day, as I was trying to keep up with all of the recent news of the Chicago City Council and Alderman Eddie Barrett's indictment. There was a Jimmy John's Turkey Sandwich sitting on the corner of my desk, with lettuce, tomato, and extra mayonnaise that I hadn't had time to touch. I was working on the story and putting the finishing touches on my news article regarding Chicago's most powerful politician.

He had been picked up and arrested at his office the day after New Year's and was being held without bail at the Cook County Correctional Center on Twenty-First and California. Knowing that Eddie Barrett was loaded with cash and would have no trouble posting bail, Judge James McCaskey knew he would be a flight risk.

Besides the conspiracy, tax fraud, bribery, and being an accomplice to a murder, they now found a significant amount of cocaine in his safe.

Why would there be cocaine in the alderman's personal safe? He was not known to be a drug user, and he had no cocaine or other illegal drugs in his system. According to the toxicology reports, the most extreme foreign substance in Barrett's bloodstream was all of the nicotine from his exotic, Cuban cigars.

I had pumped some information the other day from my buddy, Detective Romanowski, who said that Barrett had no idea how the cocaine ended up in his safe. His prints and

DNA were nowhere to be found in Mayor Sanchez's office on the day of his murder.

But according to the Cook County State's Attorney Douglas Janes, it just didn't matter. He was more than happy to add the illegal drug procession to his already extensive criminal resume. He was going to make sure that Alderman Edward J. Barrett spends the rest of his natural life in jail, and there wasn't going to be any plea bargain made.

According to the Illinois and Cook County Prosecutor's office, Chicago's streets were now a safer place without Eddie Barrett. The city's most powerful alderman was now locked up in prison, an accessory to the planning and murder of Mayor Janice Kollar, along with Police Chief Walter Byron.

The headline to my story the next day appeared on page one:

The Fall Of Chicago's Most Powerful Alderman

When I arrived at my office cubicle the next day, there was a yellow sticky note on my computer screen:

See Me – The Boss

Great.

I was either getting my ass chewed out for the way the article was investigated, written, and published, or I was being second-guessed by my assistant editor for some other stupid reason. Either way, I was not looking forward to starting my day with my assistant editor, J. Thomas Olsen.

I grabbed a cup of coffee from the newsroom cafeteria and braced myself for the worst.

"What's up, boss?" as I entered his office.

"McKay, sit down," Olsen demanded.

As I sat in front of his slovenly arranged desk, Olsen glared at me for several long seconds.

"Nice article, McKay. Glad you were able to put all the pieces together regarding Eddie Barrett."

"Thanks, boss."

A moment of silence.

"After reviewing your news article and reading it over several times, I still have one open question: Why were there five kilos of cocaine in Barrett's safe? Especially since he wasn't a drug user and had no habit of ever doing drugs?

"I don't know, Tom. And according to Prosecutor Janes, he doesn't care. He has enough on Barrett to get him life in prison, even without the drug possession charge."

"Yeah, I get that. But why were there drugs in his safe? Was he holding them for someone? If so, who?"

"I don't know, Chief."

The assistant editor sat back in his chair, took out one of his Lucky Strike cigarettes, and put one in his mouth.

"I think that's the bigger story here, McKay. Call up your detective buddies and see what you can find out."

After quietly eating my lunch that day, I called my go-to pallie over at the Eighteenth District.

"Detective Romanowski speaking."

"Denny, it's McKay."

"What's up? Saw your article in the papers today. Nice job."

"Thanks. But I have my assistant editor asking me some complicated questions that I don't have any answers for."

"Like?"

"Like why five kilos of cocaine was there inside of Eddie Barrett's safe?"

Dennis Romanowski started to chuckle as I asked the question.

"We all had the same question when we interrogated Barrett the night we opened his safe. We did a blood test on him, and there were no traces of any kind of drugs in his system."

"So, what was his explanation?"

"He said he was holding it for a friend."

I laughed out loud on that one.

"Really? What friend?"

I was shaking my head with amusement.

"He was holding five kilos of cocaine for a friend? Eddie Barrett makes it sound like he was holding a pair of gold cufflinks. Doesn't he realize that the cocaine drug possession is just going to push out his prison sentence even longer?"

"We've been trying to get more answers out of him. But Barrett is a tough cookie, and he's not cracking for anyone."

There were several moments of silence on the phone.

"You know, McKay, I did hear a rumor that you might want to pursue."

"Really? And what is that?"

"I heard that when they did Mayor Sanchez's autopsy, the toxicology reports indicated that there were significant amounts of cocaine and heroin in his bloodstream. It was listed in the coroner's report. The guys over at Intel might know more about it."

I was suddenly in shock. The fact that Mayor Sanchez was under a significant amount of drug influence would probably make a lot of sense as to why he was making so many irrational, desperate decisions.

"Who could I contact?"

"There is a detective there named Max Palanti. I could ask him to pull out his files and see if he can answer more of your questions."

"What time can I call him?"

"Give me an hour. I will let him know you're calling him."

"Thanks, Denny," I replied as I hung up the telephone.

It was just after three o'clock in the afternoon when I finally got hold of Detective Max Palanti of the Intelligence Unit of the Twenty-First District.

"Palanti speaking."

"Detective Palanti, this is Larry McKay of the Chicago Tribune. Denny Romanowski over at the Eighteenth asked me to give you a call."

"Oh yeah. Denny told me you would be calling. He's a great guy, that pollock."

'Yes, he is. He said you might have some information regarding the investigation into Eddie Barrett and those drugs that were found in his safe."

"Yes. We tried to interrogate him, but he refused to give us any real explanations."

A pause.

"I hear you need some information regarding that coroner's report on Sanchez."

"Yes, what can you tell me about it?"

"Apparently, Raymond Sanchez was a long time drug user, and there were significant traces of cocaine and heroin in his blood."

'Really?"

I thought about it for a moment. I had heard that there was no love lost between Eddie Barrett and Ray Sanchez, especially after he was appointed as the new mayor after Kollar's death. From what I had gathered from some of Barrett's Dirty Dozen, Sanchez refused to be the Fourteenth Ward's puppet and end up being controlled by his tight group of city hall cronies. There were several confrontations between the two of them during his short tenure as mayor.

"Did Eddie Barrett know that Sanchez was a drug addict?"

"I don't think he acknowledged it publicly, but I'm sure he knew. Eddie Barrett knows everything about everybody."

Suddenly, a light bulb went off in my head.

"Detective, did you run any tests on that cocaine found in Barrett's safe?"

The was a long pause.

"In fact, we did. It was the more potent Columbian kind of coke, the yellowish kind. It had a ninety-eight percent purity rate. This stuff is the more deadly kind that makes you trip out or hallucinate."

A pause for a long moment.

"Or potentially, commit suicide," I inserted.

There was a long silence on the phone.

"Max, could you send me a copy of those coroner reports? I would appreciate it."

"Sure thing, McKay. I will scan them and email them right over. What's your email?"

"Lmckay@chicagotrib.com"

"Got it. I will send them right over."

"Thank you, Max."

I now had another hunch that I decided I wanted to play. But it was going to take some help from Romanowski, and it wasn't going to be easy.

"Denny, it's Larry again."

"Hey, Larry."

"Denny, could you meet me over at Eddie Barrett's law office early tomorrow morning? We need to interview his administrative assistant."

"Okay, but what's up?"

"I've got a hunch. I've got a gut feeling that she may have some information about how those drugs got into his safe and why they were there."

There was a long pause.

"Bring some backup," I said as I hung up the phone.

Bright and early the next morning, Detective Dennis Romanowski and another detective from the Eighteenth District, Mike D'Aiello, met me at Edward J. Barrett's law office at 225 North LaSalle Street at eight o'clock.

Sandra Pawlowski was a tall, attractive middle-aged legal assistant, who worked as an administrative assistant and paralegal for over twenty-five years, and the alderman trusted her completely. She assisted him in all of his city and legal office transactions on a day-to-day basis. I was surprised that the Chicago P.D. hadn't made a better attempt at interviewing her immediately when Barrett was arrested.

There were many political and personal skeletons hidden in Barrett's office, and we all knew that she was mindful of where each of them was buried.

"May I help you," she eagerly asked before Romanowski and D'Aiello flashed their CPD stars.

"We would like to ask you some questions regarding the contents of your boss's safe," D'Aiello asked.

She initially didn't say a word. She only began dialing a number on her desk phone, which we assumed was probably her attorney's office.

D'Aiello immediately grabbed the telephone away from her hand.

"Why do you want to do that? Why do you need to talk to your attorney? Do you have something to hide, Sandra?" he interrogated.

"I'm not going to talk to you guys without my lawyer," she insisted.

We both looked at each other while letting Detective D'Aiello take charge of the situation. He then pulled out his cell phone and made a directive to another officer over at the Eighteenth District.

"Yes, Officer Johnson...go over to that drug perp over on North Homan Street we talked about.... yes, Michael Pawlowski...yes, that's him. Put out an arrest warrant for him."

"Wait! Why are you arresting my son?" Sandra loudly protested.

"Your eighteen-year-old kid is in violation of his parole. He's been busted several times for drug and cocaine possession, and those drugs in Barrett's safe were obviously for your fucking kid."

"No, they were not his!"

"Are they yours?"

"No, they are not. And they don't belong to my son either!"

"I don't want to hear it," D'Aiello exclaimed.

The administrative assistant started very getting emotional, almost pleading with the Chicago P.D. detective.

"Why are you arresting my son? He's been in drug rehab and has been clean for nearly a year," Sandra continued to protest loudly.

D'Aiello looked at her intently.

"Do you want to do all of this the 'nice and easy way,' or do you still want to call your lawyer and we pick up your son on a parole violation? It's quite obvious to all of us that those drugs in the safe are for your drug pusher kid."

"No!" she screamed.

Now Sandra Pawlowski started openly crying. I could tell by her reaction that the alderman's most trusted disciple was conflicted.

"Look, ma'am. We all know that the alderman is not a drug user, and for all intents and purposes, you aren't either. He was obviously holding five kilos of cocaine for someone close to him, and the next closest addict and drug supplier would be your kid."

"No!" she loudly yelled out again.

"They were for Javier."

The three of us looked at each other as Denny Romanowski's face turned pale and immediately changed. He was well aware of who Javier was.

I later realized that 'Javier' was the alias for a well-dressed gentleman named Anthony Maisano. He was a close associate of the alderman who was sometimes his chauffeur, bodyguard, street enforcer, and bag man. He was responsible for doing a lot of Eddie Barrett's 'dirty work.'

That dirty work included cash payouts and street collections, roughing up reluctant victims and associates who reneged on their street contracts with the alderman, and sometimes, I came to realize afterward, various drug deals.

It didn't take an Ivy League genius to figure out what was really going on. Eddie Barrett knew that Alderman Raymond Sanchez had a prolific drug problem. But if he was supplying his drugs through his enforcer, 'Javier,' it would be another way for Barrett to control the Mayor.

And every other Chicago politician who had a drug problem.

As Raymond Sanchez was pushing Eddie Barrett away, he still went back to Javier for his direct line of cocaine supply. Eddie Barrett was then able to acquire a stronger, more potent brand of coke, knowing that Sanchez would probably either overdose or eventually cause harm to himself. When Ray Sanchez put that Beretta 9MM handgun up against his temple last October, it was all according to plan. Eddie Barrett knew all along that Mayor Raymond 'El Rey' Sanchez would eventually, one way or the other, destroy himself.

Anthony Maisano was picked up that afternoon and put into a holding cell at the Eighteenth District. After two days of intense interrogation, he confessed that those drugs in Eddie Barrett's safe *really were* the alderman's drug supply, which the Barrett paid for and profited from. Maisano peddled that cocaine on behalf of Barrett exclusively, at a discounted price of course, to Sanchez and any other

Chicago politician who needed some pure, potent, upscale white powder.

Selling genuine, high-density cocaine was just another means for Fourteenth Ward Alderman Edward Barrett to continue to control City Hall.

CHAPTER FORTY-SEVEN
STARVED ROCK STATE PARK- FEBRUARY 20

There was an early spring thaw during February, and all of the ice from the rivers, lakes, and streams within Illinois were starting to melt. Several boats were on the water, taking advantage of the early spring defrost.

The Illinois River is a navigable stream that flows from northern to central Illinois. There are parts of the river between Dixon and Sterling where the depths are as deep as fifty feet. The bottom of the river is mostly bedrock, with extensive layers of gravel and silt.

Most fishermen head out to the Starved Rock Dam on the Illinois River to take advantage of the walleye and sauger fish available, especially when there is a very deep, early thaw. Many decided to start fishing for smelt, as the early Spring warm-up usually brings the smelt fishing season to an early beginning.

One Sunday morning in February, a fisherman with his fishing boat headed out to Starved Rock near the dam. He threw his fishing trowel out several times when he suddenly unattached something very large, down in the deepest part of the river. The fisherman had apparently unhinged some heavy, corroded chains tied with some weights while he was troweling the bottom of the river near the dam.

A large black bag suddenly floated to the top of the river. When the fisherman pulled the heavy object onto his boat, what was inside wholly shocked him.

He had unlatched a black body bag with the decomposed remains of a body matching Fr. Colin Fitzgerald's height and weight. The waterproof body bag had been filled with large lime bags, which enhanced the body's decay and decomposition. Mostly skeletal remains, there were remnants of his clergy uniform and several pieces of jewelry, which included a black onyx ring with a diamond that he always wore. His gold 18 karat crucifix was still attached to the body. Included with the remains of his garments was his wallet and driver's license, which still had twenty-three dollars inside.

Oglesby Police were called, and Detective John Wells arrived at the crime scene and several other patrol officers to begin the investigation.

When the LaSalle County Coroner's office was called, they could not locate any recent dental records or other identification to positively identify the severally decomposed remains. They observed a large hole in the back of the head, which the coroner attributed to an ax of some sort.

The Oglesby detective then theorized that Fr. Fitz had decided on that day to take a hiking trip to Starved Rock, which was ninety minutes away from Chicago. This was not unusual, as the pastor often made impromptu trips to the state park without mentioning anything to anyone. While he was hiking, someone must have assaulted him with an ax or ice pick of some sort. His body was then placed in a waterproof body bag filled with lime bags, then chained down with weights at the deepest part of the Illinois River.

But why was his car still in the rectory garage? And more importantly, what was the motive? It couldn't have been a robbery, as his jewelry and wallet were still intact. It was some kind of a 'contract hit,' as no other motive could be concluded.

Other than the recent threats he received from Little Tony, Fr. Fitz didn't have many enemies. But Tony DiMatteo, being under surveillance, had an airtight alibi. If he had ordered the hit, it had to be directed to one of his henchmen. But who? The DiMatteo Family utilized so many contract killers, and it could have been several suspects.

The Oglesby police had no other clues or information other than the decomposed victim's identification. So they immediately contacted the Archdiocese of Chicago, who swiftly ordered the body to be transported to the Michael Delaney & Sons Funeral Home on West 95th Street in Chicago.

For various other reasons, his Eminence Cardinal Markowitz strictly emphasized that there would be no other autopsy performed on Fr. Fitz's severally decomposed body. Because his remains were in the LaSalle County Coroner's possession, the detectives within the Twenty-First District of the Chicago P.D. had no jurisdiction over the body. The LaSalle County Coroner concluded that there was no reason or any additional evidence that could be obtained from a grossly decomposed corpse.

There was little time for the State's Attorney's office to obtain a court order demanding an examination of the body. Although it was still clearly a murder inquiry, no court order was made requesting that the

Cook County Examiner carefully examine the body. A determination was made by LaSalle County that there was no other significant evidence from the decomposed body, other than the blunt trauma wound to the head. He had probably been in the Illinois River for more than four months, and no additional important information could be determined regarding the killer.

No one had seen anything. No one had heard anything. No one wanted to know anything.

Fr. Fitz had no immediate relatives living in the area, so the Archdiocese of Chicago took charge of all of his funeral arrangements.

Fr. Fitz's body was going to be cremated.

Chapter Forty-Eight
A Priest's Discovery - February 22

It was a warm Monday in February as I walked from the train station to my office at the Chicago Tribune Building on 435 North Michigan Avenue. My BMW X5 SUV was in the shop that day and using the train to work was my only option from my townhouse in Sauganash. I had over 140,000 miles on the car, but I was hoping I could squeeze another 40,000 to 50,000 more miles without having to spend a fortune on repairs. This was my big plan for keeping my old car without having to pay a king's ransom for a new one. So far, my plan wasn't working.

My car left me stranded on Belmont Avenue yesterday. Between the towing company and the auto mechanic, I realized that I would probably have to rob a few Seven-Eleven convenience stores just to get my car out of hock.

Just I had arrived at my desk, a half-hour late, of course, there was a note taped on my computer screen to see my assistant editor, Tom Olsen.

I grabbed a cup of coffee and a stale bagel that was sitting on the kitchen table and walked into Olsen's office.

"What's up, boss?"

"They found him."

"Huh?"

"They found him," he repeated.

"They found who?" I had no clue what he was talking about.

"That missing priest, the activist, what the hell was his name?"

For a moment, my mind was drawing a blank. Since I did that 'Chicago Gambit' story on him and that small blurb on when he disappeared in November, I hadn't thought much about him.

"Do you mean, Father Fitzgerald?"

"Yeah, McKay. That's him."

"Where was he hiding?" I tried to joke, knowing that the odds of him still being alive were slim to none after four months.

"Starved Rock, over in Oglesby, Illinois, about ninety minutes away from here."

Oglesby is a small town in LaSalle County, Illinois. The population is almost 3,800 and is roughly seventy-five southwest of Chicago. The only attraction is the state park, a thirteen-mile hiking area alongside the Illinois River, and is considered one of Illinois's most beautiful natural attractions.

The park's eighteen geographical canyons feature vertical walls of moss-covered stone formed by glacial meltwater that slice dramatically through tree-covered sandstone bluffs. The thirteen miles of trails allow access to waterfalls, fed season runoff of natural springs, sandstone overhangs, and spectacular overlooks. The lush vegetation supports abundant wildlife; white oak, cedar, and pine grow on drier, sandy bluff tops, which have made it a popular tourist attraction for nearby residents year-round that are looking for the natural midwestern beauty of Illinois.

Not being a nature lover, I was forced to go hiking there a few times with my ex-wife, Mary Jo (who happened to love state parks) many years ago, and I really didn't enjoy it.

After seeing illusions of Ned Beatty and Burt Reynolds canoeing along the river, with echoes of 'Squeal like a pig' reverberating off of the canyon walls, I thought I was doing a scene from the fucking movie 'Deliverance.'

"Really?" I replied.

"Some fisherman dredged him up from the mouth of the Illinois River. According to the local police, he was weighted down in a body bag, still had his wallet and crucifix," Olsen mentioned.

I thought about it for a few seconds, and I didn't need a law degree to figure out who probably put him there.

"They were able to identify the body?"

"Barely. I guess the body bag was covered in lime, and the body was pretty decomposed. The priest's body was probably fish food there in the bottom of the Illinois River."

I shook my head for several moments and tried to get my head around all of this. I found it interesting that it had taken so long for Fr. Fitz's body to turn up after all these months. Having had experience investigating homicides before, I realized that the ones with the heavyweights, steel chains, and body bags were usually professional hits.

And those professional hits weren't usually done by the Hadassah Jewish Ladies Club.

"Why don't you see if you can put a story together here?"

"You got it, boss," as I finished my coffee and stale bagel and went back to my desk.

I sat down and did some digging, probing and investigating any information from the internet, and making some phone calls. The first one I made was to the Archdiocese of

Chicago. I talked to the Cardinal's media spokesperson, Vince Marino. He had put out a media statement stating that the popular activist priest was found in Oglesby after being missing for four months. They asked the members of the St. Simeon's Parish and the rest of Chicago to pray for the soul of the murdered priest.

I then called my friend, Detective Dennis Romanowski. We had gotten to be pretty good friends over these last several months, and he was usually civil with me over the telephone.

"What's up, McKay?"

"Not much, Denny. Just heard about Fr. Fitz."

"Yes, what a shame. He was a good man and quite an activist for his church and community. He's going to be sorely missed."

"Yes...so, what else did you hear?"

"Only that his body was over ninety percent decomposed, and had it not been for his wallet and jewelry, the coroner down there would have had a hard time identifying him," Romanowski mentioned.

"His body has been turned over to the Archdiocese, who is currently handling the arrangements."

He was talking with his mouth full. I could hear him munching, probably on one of his sandwiches while he was talking.

"What's for lunch at 9:30 in the morning?" I asked.

"Do I tell you what time you can fucking eat?"

"It's a meatball sandwich. I can smell the marinara sauce over the phone."

Being half Italian, I had a sharp nose for food, even when it was only over the telephone.

"It's an eggplant parmesan sandwich. It's last night's dinner, and my wife packed it for lunch. Nice guess, though, McKay."

"Did you guys talk to the usual suspects?"

"You mean his chess game buddy, Little Tony? We were going to pick him up again, but Dorian decided against it."

"Really? How come?"

Romanowski laughed.

"It's hard to pick up a wise-guy on suspicion of murder when you've had him under surveillance since the beginning of the summer."

I laughed out loud.

"Little Tony played you guys again, I see."

We continued to discuss the case over the phone, including the Oglesby Detective John Wells' details and what he had uncovered in the investigation.

"Ya, know, McKay, this Detective Wells mentioned something that I thought was a little unusual."

"And what was that?"

A moment of silence.

"There was a hiker who was reported missing last November at Starved Rock, who still hadn't been found. When the fisherman pulled that body out of the water, the police had thought for sure that it was the missing hiker."

I raised my eyebrows for a moment.

"Really? Well, didn't they test for any DNA to see if it was the hiker?"

"Detective Wells said they didn't have to. This dead body came with a wallet, pieces of his religious garments, and his identification. So they knew right away that it was Fitzgerald."

"Are they still looking for that missing hiker?"

"Guess so, McKay. In the meantime, they say that they helped us solve our missing person's case here in Chicago."

A few more silent moments as I was taking notes.

"Aren't you guys going to get the body back for a second autopsy?"

"We can't. The Oglesby coroner already did that. We would have to get a court order to perform another one, and the Archdiocese of Chicago already has custody of the body."

I shook my head over the phone, almost not believing what I was hearing.

"So, what a minute, Denny. Let me get this straight. Since this decomposed body conveniently came with a wallet, some religious jewelry, and a driver's license, the 'kitty coppers' over at 'Mayberry' figured they had the dead body already ID'd?"

Romanowski started chuckling over the phone.

"I reckon' so, Andy," referring to Sheriff Andy Taylor from the 'The Andy Griffith Show,' a comedy that was on television years before all of us were born.

Alarms were immediately going off in my head. What law enforcement agency pulls a dead body out of the water without doing a DNA test, matching it to any others who may be reported missing?

I then decided to make a phone call, seeing if I could get a statement from the detective handling the discovery and this investigation.

"Oglesby Police, Detective Wells," the voice answered the telephone.

I could tell I was calling a small-town police department because I wasn't put on hold by a dispatcher, as the detective answered his own direct phone.

"I'm Lawrence McKay with the Chicago Tribune. I was wondering if you can answer a few questions for me about that recent dead body that was pulled up from the Illinois River at Starved Rock."

"Oh, sure."

"Could you tell me what kind of condition the body was in when it was recovered?"

"Oh, it was pretty decomposed," Detective Wells replied. He had a bit of a downstate, good-ole-boy accent.

"And you did a positive ID on him?"

"Oh, we didn't have to. His ID was still in the body bag when we found him."

"Wow, that's pretty convenient, huh, Detective? You didn't even have to bother to make sure that you had the right body or have to do a DNA test there, right Detective?"

"Oh, we don't do those here. We send those out to the lab in Springfield. We matched his identification to the body, and it looked correct."

I started biting the side of my mouth to keep myself from laughing.

This *really was* Sheriff Andy Taylor. The face of this severely decomposed body must have matched the picture on his driver's license pretty well.

"Any information on the killer, Detective?"

"No, not really," he answered slowly.

"Nobody saw nuttin', and it was in the remote part of the state park, so it must have been done where there wasn't anyone 'round."

"Musta' killed him in 'da dark," he added.

"Where is the priest's body now, Detective?"

"Oh, we called the Archdiocese of Chicago, and they sent a funeral hearse right over to pick him up. He's gone already."

I continued to shake my head.

"Okay, Detective, thank you," as I tried to hang up the telephone politely.

"Does this mean I'm gonna have my name in your paper?"

"Yes, Detective."

"Okay, you make sure that you spell it right. It's W-E-L-L-S."

"Why, thank you, Detective. We'll make sure your name in the news article is spelled correctly," I kindly replied.

Un-fucking real.

A dead body magically appears out of the Illinois River, complete with jewelry and a driver's license, and the coppers downstate are okay with it. It's a positive match, they assume.

I started to write the story from my desk, noting the facts that I had uncovered regarding the decomposed body's positive identification, attached wallet, and driver's license. I made another call to the Chicago Archdiocese, who stated that Michael Delaney and Sons Funeral Home had the body and were preparing it for the memorial service that Saturday.

I then called the funeral home. When I inquired, I just presumed that Fr. Fitzgerald's memorial service would be a closed casket.

"No," the undertaker stated.

"It will be a closed urn."

"So the body is being cremated?"

"Already has. About an hour ago."

I was shocked.

"Since when is the deceased rushed to be cremated?"

The undertaker quickly corrected me.

"It wasn't rushed. We like to cremate them immediately when the deceased body is in that bad of shape. There are sanitary issues that we need to consider when accepting a decomposed body in that condition. We do that, so they're not lingering around here. Besides, the Archdiocese insisted that the body be cremated to cut down on the funeral costs and expenses in preparing the body for burial."

Because of the lack of money that was available for his burial, his body was immediately cremated, and his remains were placed in a large decorative urn for the memorial service at St. Simeon Catholic Church.

This cremation was also unusual, as the Catholic Church had frowned upon the deceased's cremations for many years. I thought that explanation was extraordinary. Being raised a Catholic, I knew that the church had only recently started looking the other way on cremations. Years ago, the Catholic Church took the position that a cremation did not show 'dignity for the human body.'

According to the Vatican, cremations many years ago were strictly prohibited. But now, they seem to be the preferred choice, according to many funeral homes. Families would rather pay the low cost of depositing their loved ones in a fancy urn and tossing their ashes off some exotic destination somewhere than in a cemetery plot or a marble condominium. I found it rather odd that the Archdiocese had advocated Fr. Colin Fitzgerald's body being cremated.

Just for the hell of it, I decided to scour the internet for some information regarding the missing hiker that hadn't been found since he went out at Starved Rock State Park back in November.

The missing person's name was Jeffrey Jakeway, of Ottawa, Illinois. According to the information posted, he was forty-two years old, Caucasian, dark brown hair, blue eyes, and average build, five feet, eleven inches tall. He had been last seen entering the state park and had checked in the Starved Rock Lodge last November 15th.

Father Fitzgerald was around six feet tall, with salt and pepper hair, clean-shaven, wore horned rimmed glasses, and was physically fit for a man in his mid-sixties. It was uncanny that the missing man closely matched the description of Fr. Fitz.

Knowing that Fr. Fitz was closely affiliated with Little Tony DiMatteo and their intimate weekly chess games, I seriously wondered if the Chicago mobster had a hand in the activist priest's demise.

But it surprised me that Cardinal Markowitz and the Chicago Archdiocese had so easily and so quickly gone along with the cremation process before the memorial service.

Very unusual. With all the recent current events in this city, it was just another piece of the puzzle that I couldn't put together.

That following Friday, Fr. Colin John Fitzgerald was eulogized as an 'amazing disciple of the Lord.' He was an activist who 'saw the wrongs of society and tried to fix them' while caring for his endless flock of worshippers. There were several hundred mourners who paid their respects to the charismatic, well-loved pastor. The church was packed, with many clergy, Chicago politicians, various Catholic clergy, and several Chicago P.D. detectives were in attendance. Three of those detectives were Philip Dorian, Denny Romanowski, and Mike D'Aiello. They were sitting in the back of the church and were both completely surprised and dumbfounded. The detectives were shocked at how swiftly the Chicago Archdiocese had taken control of Fr. Fitz's body and cremating it before the funeral.

"This isn't adding up," Dorian kept saying.

"How did Fr. Fitz end up in LaSalle County, in a waterproof body bag?"

"This was a professional hit," D'Aiello concluded, "and there is only one person in the world who knows what happened to him."

It was apparent to the three of them that this investigation had been rushed by the Oglesby Police Department and the Archdiocese of Chicago. Other than interrogating Little Tony, the Chicago P.D. had no participation in determining who the killer was. Father Fitzgerald's murder case was immediately closed.

His suddenly disappearing, and then his lifeless body found in the Illinois River four months later was the final closure that Chicago's Catholic community truly needed.

Privately, it was no secret to anyone within the Archdiocese of Chicago that Fr. Colin Fitzgerald was a massive thorn in the side of Cardinal Markowitz. He believed that this was a fitting end to a radical, activist pastor who thrived on media publicity, cast judgment over violent gang members. He favored capital punishment and street violence over the sanctity of life.

But to the parishioners of St. Simeon, he was a local hero and activist priest who had dedicated his whole life to trying to fix society's wrongs.

His bronze urn was placed within the dark corridors of the greystone mausoleum of Resurrection Cemetery in Chicago.

And almost as quickly as he was cremated, Fr. Fitz's murder was classified as unsolved.

A plaque dedicating his life's work to the parish and the community was erected on the back wall near the sacristy. A new pastor was then immediately assigned.

And just like that, Fr. Colin J. Fitzgerald, age 65, was gone.

CHAPTER FORTY-NINE
A SLICE OF BANANA CREAM PIE – MARCH 4TH

It was just after three o'clock that Friday afternoon, and I had a severe case of spring fever. It was a bright sunny day, almost sixty degrees, and the last thing I wanted to do was sit in my cubicle in the newsroom and work on a news story. I decided to walk over from the Tribune Building to the Franklin Street Café, where I continued to maintain 'an office' in my favorite corner booth.

The mayoral primaries were coming up, and I was in charge of doing factual, sleepy, uninteresting biographies on every irrelevant, insignificant candidate running for mayor that spring. Besides Waylon Smith, the Mayor Pro-Tempore who had been appointed to take over Sanchez's position until the election, several other candidates had submitted petitions to run for office, a total of twelve candidates in all. Their names and backgrounds ranged from various city council members and officeholders from the Cook County Board to LGBTQ candidates from Boys Town and the South Loop.

Gloria, my favorite coffee shop waitress, gave me a freshly brewed cup of coffee when I arrived, along with a huge, delicious piece of banana cream pie, my favorite.

"I know you really need this," she said with a smile.

Her pink waitress uniform looked like it had been newly pressed and cleaned, with three of her uniform fasteners unbuttoned. It only took me three seconds to figure out that she was wearing a red, Victoria Secret sheer lace bra.

"Thanks, honey," I gratefully answered.

I unpacked my computer and took out some manilla folders, beginning to type away at the article deadline that I needed to get in before eleven o'clock that evening.

It certainly was a beautiful afternoon, and my mind began drifting onto the subject that it always drifted off to whenever I was in the Franklin Street Café since last autumn.

I started daydreaming about Talia.

Since she had done that 'Live Broadcast' from St. Simeon Church on that 'Chicago Gambit' article that she took credit for, I had not heard from her. I had deleted her number from my cell phone, and it didn't take me long to forget her number completely. I didn't contact her, and she certainly didn't call me. She never contacted me with an explanation, let alone an apology, of why she so brazenly took credit for a news story that I had worked so hard to put together.

No call. No text. No apology. No Christmas card.

It was like she had disappeared from my life, and the brief romantic fling that we had shared and enjoyed meant absolutely nothing, other than an opportunity for her to steal my 'Chicago Gambit' story.

Fuck her, I said to myself.

It was a phrase that I frequently used every time the thought of her crossed my mind.

I had been working on my news story that afternoon, banging away at my laptop while Gloria was busy filling up my coffee cup and anxiously waiting for me to ask her out. After about an hour or so, a familiar woman walked into the Franklin Street Café, and I suddenly froze. She was wearing a black blouse, tanned skirt, and black Zanotti high heels that matched her gorgeous, curly brown hair.

I had forgotten how beautiful she was. My fingers were suddenly unable to type, and I felt my heart rate jump up to two hundred and twenty beats per minute.

She pushed open the front door and bee-lined it over the front counter, ordering a cup of cappuccino and a croissant sandwich to go. The beautiful woman then locked her eyes with mine, and I felt myself melt right there in the corner of the coffee shop.

It was Talia.

At first, we didn't say anything to each other, as her eyes could not look anywhere else while I studied her standing in front of the cashier's counter. The CNN news reporter looked as though she had been frozen in time and was unable to move. She was probably wondering whether or not she should even greet me, let alone walk over to my booth and say anything.

Gloria handed Talia her coffee and sandwich while she simultaneously gave her some cash, telling her to keep the change.

And then, she suddenly walked towards me, and I felt my hands sweating.

"I'm sorry," she loudly said, standing in front of me, waiting for me to greet her and probably make some small talk.

I nodded my head as if to acknowledge her apology.

"My news producer wanted me to take credit for your story, and I had no choice. When I initially mentioned you in my original news transcript, he made me take it out. It wasn't my decision."

I only snickered at her excuse.

"My assistant editor says that you guys over at CNN are famous for that shit."

There was a long pause, and she looked very uncomfortable standing in front of me, holding her cappuccino and her brown paper bag with her dinner inside.

I then noticed her eyes starting to well up.

"I know I hurt you."

"You could have at least called," I angrily responded.

"I wanted to. But I was afraid. I was afraid that you would be upset."

"You're right. I was upset."

She stood there nervously, trying to find more words to say that would comfort me and give her the forgiveness she was suddenly seeking.

"I've been scared to come back in here because I was frightened that I would find you here working."

I smiled. "I pay rent here, remember?" I joked.

She stood there quietly for several long seconds, not knowing what else to say. I then noticed tears starting to stream down her cheeks as she struggled to calm her emotions.

"Well, McKay, for whatever it's worth, I missed you. And I'm sorry that I hurt you."

And as if she didn't want to hear my response, she quickly turned and walked out the door without saying good-bye.

I sat there for a moment, completely stunned. The woman who had managed to make love to me and take my breath away over four months ago had apologized. All I managed to do was to sit there, speechless, looking as though I was still angry with her.

    I had suddenly realized that it had taken a lot of guts for her to approach me and apologize after these past four months. I could have at least been friendlier to her and made her feel more comfortable, I thought to myself. But the angry, 'prick' side of my personality came out, and I only managed to glare at her, totally unforgiving.

    Talia stood there with tears in her eyes, apologizing. But I only managed to sit there and do nothing.

    I then said, "Fuck it," out loud, as my raw emotions suddenly took control of my actions.

    I jumped up from my corner booth and ran out of the coffee shop, chasing after her while walking on the sidewalk towards Union Station.

    "TALIA! TALIA!" I yelled out her name several times, chasing after her until she turned around and saw me running towards her like some kind of possessed madman.

    When I caught up with her, she suddenly dropped her coffee and bags and put her arms around me. We then started kissing each other profusely in the middle of the sidewalk with several bystanders watching.

    "I'm so sorry I didn't call you. I'm so sorry that I hurt you. I've missed you so much," she exclaimed, and I continued to kiss her cheeks, which were still drenched in tears.

    "I missed you too," I said to her as we continued to kiss and embrace each other out in the open.

    "I promise, Larry, it won't ever happen again."

"I don't give a shit about the story. Just don't walk out of my life again. I need you," I said, as I could feel my eyes welling up with tears.

We must have stood there on that sidewalk embracing and kissing each other for close to ten minutes, as several bystanders were looking on. I even heard one of them laughing and yelling out, 'Get a room!'

I smiled at her.

"That may not be such a bad idea!"

She only smiled as we put our arms around each other as we walked back toward the Franklin Street Café.

I felt so exhilarated, as I now had the most beautiful reporter in the city, holding my hand and kissing me again.

I had blown my deadline that night, but I didn't care. I called my editor and told him he would get it in the morning, like it or not.

On that day, I had finally discovered the pure joy of being in love again. We went out for dinner at Mancuso's Italian Steakhouse that evening, then went back to her place in the West Loop. We then made passionate love the whole night long.

On that day, I had finally realized that finding the one true love of my life was far more important than any newspaper deadline. For the first time in many years, I felt some deep, inner peace come over me, and I hadn't felt this happy in years.

On that day, at the ripe old age of fifty-eight years old, I had finally found true love.

And after that spring afternoon, we both paid rent for our cozy little corner booth at the Franklin Street Café.

CHAPTER FIFTY
NEW ROSS, IRELAND – FEAST OF ST. JOSEPH – MARCH 19TH

The small Catholic Church of St. Mary's in New Ross, Wexford County, Ireland, had just finished mass on that bright Sunday morning in March. It was the final week of the Lenten season before Palm Sunday, and the parishioners of that quaint, small church were preparing for the upcoming Easter holiday.

The newly arrived priest, Fr. Damen MacMurray, had preached the homily that morning about the reconciliation of every Christian's sins.

MacMurray was an older man of average height, probably in his mid-sixties, thinning white hair with a long, bushy white bread and silver wire spectacles. He arrived four months earlier to the small parish in New Ross and felt comfortable with his new surroundings and parishioners.

He had a bubbly, upbeat personality and became well known in town for his humorous, entertaining sermons. The Christmas Club in the parish had plans for him that year, as they asked him to try to gain some additional weight so he could play Santa Claus for the children at their annual Christmas play.

On that morning, Father MacMurray reminded his flock of worshippers of how important it was to make peace with the Lord before entering the Holy Week. The older priest strongly encouraged his parishioners to embark on the Holy Sacrament of Reconciliation that week before Easter.

The Irish Catholics of that small little town faithfully attended mass each Sunday in their tiny little church in New Ross. They were looking forward to the upcoming Holy Week observances and the Easter holiday.

It was also the Feast Day of St. Joseph on that Sunday, and all of the parishioners were preparing for their St. Joseph Table celebrations around their little town. This memorable holiday included a spread of endless food, including pasta and macaroni dishes, Irish bread, and various fish specialties. But never any meat, which was the tradition of that holy celebration. The town had just celebrated St. Patrick's Day a few days earlier and was now preparing for the religious feast day of the Patron Saint of Fathers and the Roman Catholic Church.

New Ross is a small quaint town in southwest County Wexford, Ireland. It is located on the River Barrow, near the border of Kilkenny County, about twenty kilometers northeast of Waterford. With a population of over eight thousand people, most of the Catholics there were either members of St. Mary's Church or attended the larger St. Michael's Church on the other side of town.

The town of New Ross is famous for the American political dynasty that originated from that region. Patrick Kennedy, the great grandfather of the thirty-fifth U.S. president, emigrated to Boston in 1846 from New Ross, Ireland. He and his family escaped the Great Potato Famine that was rampant in Ireland during that turbulent time.

Fr. MacMurray also had distinctive roots from that area, as his great grandfather had sailed over to New York's Ellis Island from Wexford County in 1906.

As the parishioners had greeted the new priest and filed out of St. Mary's Church, he quickly changed out of his mass celebrant's garments and swiftly walked over to the town square in the middle of New Ross, where a spring celebration was about to take place. About twenty tables with chess boards and time clocks were set up for those who enjoyed playing the game in the middle of the town square. Besides the local St. Joseph Table celebrations that were being sponsored around that quaint little town, there was also another special event going on that day:

It was the New Ross Twentieth Annual Chess Tournament.

The excited priest sat down at one of the tables, expecting his chess opponent to finally arrive after celebrating his Catholic service at St. Michael's Church on the other side of town.

His new friend and frequent chess opponent, Fr. Thomas Keegan, had been appointed pastor of St. Michael's Catholic Church six years ago. He was in his early forties and had been born and raised in Wexford County. The two of them had met a few months ago and became fast friends.

Fr. Keegan wanted to make the new priest in town feel welcome, and they had been out to dinner together several times in weeks past. He had befriended the newly arrived older priest of St. Mary's, having lengthy discussions regarding religion, sociology, and American politics. Besides the two of them having their religious vocations in common, they both had many other common interests as well.

They also had a shared love for the game of chess.

"Hello, Fr. Tom," the older priest greeted his newly arrived chess opponent while carrying two cups of black Irish coffee for the two of them to enjoy.

"Top of the mornin', Father Damen," in a thick, Irish accent.

The two Catholic priests made small talk about their mass services that they had just celebrated, as they were both looking forward to Palm Sunday, the Easter holiday, and the end of the Lenten season.

As they started the timeclock, Fr. Keegan, who was playing white, made the first move.

White – Nf3.
Black – d4.
White – Nc3.
Black – c6.

Keegan had begun the chess game moving both of his white knights, while his opponent moved his pawns and advanced his bishops across the board.

Father MacMurray, a lifelong chess player, was very familiar with the Sicilian Defense method that Fr. Thomas Keegan was implementing on the chessboard. He knew of several strategies he could implement in stopping this very popular chess tactic.

After twelve moves, Father MacMurray, playing black, had captured both of his opponent's knights, both rooks, a bishop, and several of his pawns.

"You brought along you're A-game today, Father," Father Keegan stated in a very distinctive Irish accent as he moved his queen in retreat.

He then hit the time clock. Both chess players were now deep in thought. A few minutes went by as the older clergyman contemplated his next turn.

Patiently waiting, Father Keegan tried to nudge his opponent.

"It's your move, Father."

Father Damen noticed that his opponent's king was cornered, and that Father Keegan had moved his queen to a position on the chessboard to where he was now vulnerable.

He then moved his black rook across the board, taking the queen and cornering his opponent's king.

"*Rook takes Queen,*" the older priest declared.

Surprised, Father Keegan grinned at his opponent, knowing that he had again fallen victim to his Chicago rival. Shaking his head and laughing to himself, Father Keegan immediately tipped over his king, quietly acknowledging his defeat.

Fr. Colin J. Fitzgerald, alias 'Father Damen MacMurray' was now gloating as he took a sip of his black Irish coffee.

He then winked his eye and softly whispered to his opponent:

"Checkmate."

MORE GREAT BOOKS

BY CRIME NOVELIST EDWARD IZZI:

Of Bread & Wine (2018)

A Rose from The Executioner (2019)

Demons of Divine Wrath (2019)

Quando Dormo (When I Sleep) (2020)

El Camino Drive (2020)

When A Rook Takes the Queen (2021)

New Book Releases Coming Soon:

The Buzz Boys (Spring, 2021)

They Only Wear Black Hats (Fall, 2021)

His novels and writings are available at www.edwardizzi.com, Amazon, Barnes & Noble, and other fine bookstores.